The Stalker

THE STALKER

Marina Martindale

Good Oak Press, LLC

Good Oak Press, LLC
www.goodoakpress.com

Editor: Cynthia Roedig
Proofreader: Gloria Gray
Cover Illustration: Wes Lowe
Cover Design: Good Oak Press, LLC
Typesetting: Good Oak Press, LLC

Acknowledgments

Thank you to the team who helped me create *The Stalker*, my editor, Cynthia Roedig, and my proofreader, Gloria Gray. Thanks also to Wes Lowe for another outstanding cover illustration. It's one of your best ones ever. I also wanted to thank a few real life friends, who wish to remain anonymous, who shared their stories with me. You were the inspiration for *The Stalker*.

To Ingrid

❧ONE❧

RACHEL BENNETT TURNED onto a quiet side street and drove up a steep hill. Desert landscaping lined both sides of the roadway, and a sign with an arrow pointing to the right soon appeared. She pressed down on the brake pedal, making a sharp turn onto another road. The hotel, with its three signature arches, stood at the top of the hill. Moments later she pulled underneath one of the archways. Rolling down her window, a muscular young man walked up to her car and greeted her with a warm smile.

"Welcome to the La Paloma," he said. "Are you here for the Desert Sunrise High School reunion?"

"Yes, I am."

He opened the car door and Rachel stepped out. The warm breeze felt soothing. As she reached for her purse the man handed her a claim ticket.

"Go in through the main door and veer to your right. Head down the hallway, and it'll be in the third room on your right."

"Thanks," said Rachel as she dropped the ticket into her purse and slug it over her shoulder.

"Is there anything else I can do for you?" he asked as Rachel turned and looked behind her.

"No, I'm fine. Thanks." She took a deep breath and stepped inside. Walking down the hallway she saw a number of people milling around. Some looked vaguely familiar. A few smiled and nodded as she walked past. She smiled in return as she tried to ignore the butterflies roiling in her stomach. Two women sat at a table in front an open pair of double doors. One looked up and gave her a friendly greeting.

"Rachel? Rachel Bennett?"

"Yes." Her voice sounded anxious. Hopefully, the women hadn't noticed. "And it's still Bennett, by the way."

"I understand." She nodded toward the other woman sitting next to her. "Shannon and I haven't gotten married yet either, but it's only our ten-year reunion. Now, if it was our twenty-fifth or thirtieth…" As they exchanged knowing smiles, Shannon handed Rachel a nametag and the other woman extended her hand.

"I'm Carly Rios. We took a couple of English lit classes together, and we were also in Mrs. Tanner's world history class."

"That's right." Rachel smiled at the memory as she pinned her nametag on her blouse. "I always liked Mrs. Tanner. She was one of my favorites."

"You and a lot of others," said Carly, "and we did invite her, but she couldn't make it. She's retired now, and she and her husband are taking a cruise to Europe."

"Really? Well, good for her, and how wonderful that she gets to see all the places she taught us about."

Carly handed Rachel a program, and as Rachel stepped into the large ballroom, her mind flashed back to her first day of high school. It, too, had been nerve wracking, but by the time graduation rolled around she was sad to see that chapter of her life come to an end. She looked around the room, hoping to spot some of her old friends, but so far none had caught her eye. Her circle of friends had been small, and, like her, they had been quiet and reserved. It was entirely possible that none would be attending the reunion. She glanced at her watch. It was still early. Perhaps they might show up later.

As she looked around the room a second time a smile broke out across her face. On the opposite wall stood a table with their yearbooks on display. She quickly crossed the room, and as she flipped through the pages, happy memories filled her mind. Other classmates soon joined her, but none were people she had known. She checked her watch again and a profound sense of disappointment came over her. It was now twenty-five minutes past seven, and dinner would be served at seven-thirty. It appeared that none of her old friends would be attending. She went to look for Carly. Rachel may not have known her well, but at least they had remembered one another. Then, once dessert was served, she would find a convenient excuse to leave before the slideshows and games started. A moment later the former class president walked up to the podium to make a welcoming announcement and ask everyone to please be seated.

Rachel looked around the room one last time, but she didn't see Carly. Perhaps she was still outside taking care of last-minute arrivals.

She turned her attention back to the tables. Several had empty seats, and as she approached the one closest to her someone called her name. A man seated at another table appeared to be waving at her. He had wavy red hair and well-chiseled features. He also seemed familiar, although she couldn't quite place him. She pointed to her chest and gave him a quizzical look.

"Yes, you," he mouthed back. He pulled out the empty chair next to his and extended his hand she approached him. "It is Rachel, isn't it?" he asked.

"Yes." She extended her hand in return and he gave her a mischievous smile.

"But you don't remember me, do you?"

"No, I'm afraid not. I'm so sorry."

He reached into his pocket for a sheet of paper, grinning as he slowly unfolded it and handed it to her. "Maybe this will help."

It was a printout of a page from their senior yearbook. At the top was a photo of three young men seated in front of a whiteboard covered with a long mathematical formula. The one in the middle had long red hair, swept back in a ponytail, and he wore a pair of black, horned-rimmed glasses. The caption over the photo read, "The Math Club."

"Okay," said Rachel as she studied it closely. "It's one of the photos I took. I'm just trying to remember the math club."

"It really wasn't much of a club." They took their seats and looked at the photo together.

"We didn't have a president or a secretary or anything like that. It was just us three geeks, hanging out at lunchtime and seeing which one of us could stump the other two. And you're Rachel, from the yearbook committee."

"That would be me." She studied his face for a moment and then looked at the photo a little closer. "And you certainly look different now."

"I know. It's amazing what a haircut, a new suit, and a pair of contact lenses will do. You, however, look much the same, although your hair looks a little lighter."

"Yes. I added the highlights about a year ago."

"And they certainly look lovely on you," he said as he gave her another smile. "The name is Shane, by the way. Shane MacLeod."

Rachel smiled in return. "Nice to meet you again, Shane."

Shane and Rachel introduced themselves to the others at their table as the waitstaff delivered their salads. One man had been in Rachel's biology class, but aside from him, neither knew any of their tablemates. Desert Sunrise was a big school, with many different groups and cliques. By the time the main course was served, Rachel and Shane were busy getting reacquainted with one another. Both had attended the University of Arizona. It, too, was a big school, and they had never crossed paths. Rachel studied art and marketing, while Shane got his degree in engineering. He then went to graduate school at the University of Texas at Austin. Before long the servers returned to pick up their empty plates and deliver their chocolate mousse desserts. Rachel eagerly dipped in her spoon but was soon disappointed.

"I love chocolate," she said, "but this is way too rich."

Shane tasted a sample as well, his nose wrinkling as his set his spoon down. "It is a bit overpowering. Tell you what, they'll probably take a short break before they start up the slide shows, so why don't we step outside for a few minutes and I'll buy you a drink?"

"Thanks. I'd like that."

They excused themselves from their table, and Shane led the way to a lounge on a lower mezzanine level. A man playing a guitar sat off to the side while a few hotel guests were seated around the tables. Shane led her to a long sofa and a waitress soon arrived.

"Would you like a glass of chardonnay?" he asked.

"Yes. It's my favorite. Thanks."

He turned to the waitress. "Make it two."

Their server stepped away and Shane turned his attention back to Rachel. "So, now that we know all about what we did in college, what happened after that?"

"I ended up in Reno, Nevada," said Rachel. "I accepted a position with a regional magazine called *Sierra Life*. It was a lifestyle publication with features on local history, architecture, home decorating ideas, places to visit, that sort of thing."

"I see. So, what did you do there?"

"I worked in the art department. I did most of the ad layouts, and I helped the art director put each issue together. It was challenging but fun at the same time, sort of like putting a puzzle together." She stopped for a moment and a frown came over her face.

"What's wrong? All of a sudden, you don't look so happy."

"While I was there, I had some, unexpected, challenges."

"Really? Like what?"

"Well, I'll spare you all the boring details. Let's just say I had a co-worker who turned out to be, well, rather difficult."

"You mean you had a co-worker from hell."

"That, my friend, would be an understatement," she said. "Hell wouldn't have wanted him, because he would have taken the place over."

"Wow. So who was he?"

"One of the staff writers. We never dated, or anything like that, but he got into the habit of joining me in the break room for coffee, and we'd talk. Nothing serious, just, you know, everyday chitchat. I guess you could say he was an office buddy, although I did look up to him. Then, later on, the art director left, so I applied for her position. By then I'd been with the magazine for about eighteen months, so I knew the formula, inside and out. I figured it would be a good career move. However, what I didn't know at the time was that, Craig, my break-room friend, didn't exactly agree."

"How so?"

"I didn't want word getting out that I'd applied for the job, so I didn't mention it to anyone, not even Craig. Therefore, I had no way of knowing his girlfriend's niece had also applied for the job. Fast-forward a few weeks. They offered me the job, which I accepted. Then, the next thing I know, Craig is unleashing his wrath on me and he's accusing me of sleeping with the boss."

Shane's expression turned serious. "Good grief. What is wrong with people these days? So what did you do then?"

"The usual. I told my supervisor about it. Craig was reprimanded, but not fired. I was told it was because he was the best staff writer they had. My supervisor also showed me a copy of an email his girlfriend's niece had sent the magazine. She was thanking them for the interview, but was happy with her current job and didn't want to leave."

"I see," said Shane.

"Unfortunately for me, the damage had been done, and it soon became a hostile work environment, so I'd started sending out resumes. About six months later we were told the magazine would be folding. Everything's going online these days, and they just couldn't complete, so I stayed until the final issue went to print. After that I went to work for an advertising agency in Phoenix."

The waitress arrived with their wine. As she stepped away, they raised their glasses and toasted to new beginnings.

"So tell me the rest of your story," said Shane as he set his glass down. "You were saying the magazine folded and you moved to Phoenix."

"Yes, I did." Rachel swirled her wineglass as she spoke. "I went to work for an advertising agency. I loved my job and I would have stayed until I retired, but then they decided to downsize and outsource. So, I came back to Tucson about six months ago, and, since everyone seems to be outsourcing these days, I'm now a freelance graphic designer." She took a sip of her wine. "So, how 'bout you, Shane?"

"Well, nothing quite so dramatic for me. After I got my master's degree, I worked for a high-tech firm in Houston. Then, about a year and a half ago, I came back to Tucson as well. I got a job at Raytheon, but I can't tell you what it was. It's classified."

Rachel chuckled. "Which means if you told me, you'd have to kill me."

"Something like that." He gave her a wink. "But then I left that too. I got tired of working for big corporations. Sure, the pay is great, and they have all kinds of wonderful perks and benefits, but after a while all the office politics starts getting old."

"Tell me about it."

"Indeed. So I now work for a small Internet security company. It's just me, my boss, and the office manager. It's not quite as much money as I was making before, but they still pay me a fair salary, and it's a lot less stressful without all the brown nosing and game playing. I also get to be a real person instead of a number." He stopped and raised his glass. "So, here's to us, and our future endeavors."

They sipped their wine and spent the next few minutes listening to the music.

"He's quite good," Shane finally said. "Sort of a jazzy, Spanish style. It has a nice, romantic feel to it." He looked her in the eye. "So, I was wondering, are you by chance seeing anyone these days?"

"No, not at the moment."

He gave her a grin. "I see. Well, in that case, would you mind giving your phone number? I'd really like for us to stay in touch."

"Me too." Rachel reached into her purse and handed him a business card. "I work out of my home, so my business number is also my cellphone, but don't tell anyone, okay?"

"Your secret's safe with me."

Their waitress returned a short time later and Shane took care of their tab. As Rachel made her way toward the stairs, a sheriff's deputy came into the mezzanine and blocked her path. He noticed her nametag.

"Ms. Bennett, I'm afraid I'm going to have to ask you to leave, and I'm here to escort you off the premises."

Rachel was stunned. "What?"

Shane came up to join them. "What seems to be the problem?"

"Do you know this woman?"

Shane bristled. "Yes. She's with me."

The deputy nodded toward the bar. "Unfortunately, we've had a complaint about your friend. She's been harassing one of the hotel guests, so I have to ask her leave."

Rachel still looked stunned. "I have no idea what you're talking about. I'm here for my high school reunion. As soon as I arrived, I went straight down that hallway to the room where it's being held, and it's a private party. None of the other hotel guests would have been allowed in, and I haven't bothered anyone. I also have a room full of witnesses to back me up. This gentleman, who's also here for the reunion, invited me out here for a drink, and I've been with him the entire time. I haven't been anywhere else in the hotel."

"And, I can assure you that other than a waitress, no one else has approached while we've been here," said Shane.

"I understand, sir," said the deputy as turned his attention back to Rachel. "However, I just finished speaking to the man who made the complaint. He tells me, Ms. Bennett, that you approached while he was seated at the bar, and that you yelled at him and caused a scene."

"That's impossible," said Rachel. "I haven't been anywhere near the bar."

"And again, we have a room full of witnesses who can tell you it never happened." Shane motioned toward the sofa. "We were sitting right over there, the whole time, and we were just getting ready to go back and rejoin our group when you came in." He pointed out their waitress, delivering drinks to a table near the bar. "She was our server. Why don't you go talk to her? She'll tell you we've been here the entire time, and that Rachel was never anywhere near the bar. I think you've mistaken Ms. Bennett for someone else."

The deputy shook his head. "The person who made the complaint mentioned Ms. Bennett by name, and he was able to point her out to me, but if you two will wait here, I'll go have a talk with the waitress."

Rachel felt a sick feeling in the pit of her stomach as the deputy approached their waitress. He pointed to them as they talked, and she shook her head. He returned a minute later.

"Well, Ms. Bennett, your story checks out. She said she's been here since the middle of the afternoon, and she says nothing unusual has happened. She also said you two have only been out here for about twenty minutes or so, and neither of you came into the bar area."

As the deputy talked, Rachel looked back toward the bar and spotted a man seated on one of the barstools. The sight of him chilled her to the bone.

"What the hell? What's he doing here, and how did he find me?"

"What's going on?" asked the deputy.

Rachel nodded toward the bar. "The man seated at the bar. With the brown hair and mustache, wearing the light-blue shirt. He's been stalking me for years." She looked at the deputy. "I need to talk to you someplace private."

"Who is this person?" asked Shane.

"I'll fill you in later, Shane. Right now, I have to talk to the deputy."

Shane glanced toward the hallway. "Will you be coming back in when you're done?"

"No. As soon as I'm done, I want to go home."

"Are you sure you're going to be okay?"

She gave him a reassuring smile. "I'll be fine. I'll ask the deputy to walk me out, and I'll see if he can wait with me while the valet brings me my car. I'll be okay. I promise."

Shane hesitated before he extended his hand. "It was good seeing you again, Rachel, and I'll call you soon. Goodnight."

"You too, Shane. And I look forward to hearing from you."

❧TWO❧

RACHEL WAITED UNTIL Shane was gone before turning her attention back to the deputy. His nametag identified him as Joseph Gonzalez.

"And so another wonderful evening gets ruined, thanks to Craig Walker," she said with a disappointed sigh. "I first met Shane, the man who just left, back in high school, but I never really talked to him until tonight, and I could tell something wonderful was about to happen. Then you showed up."

"I'm sorry, ma'am. I'm just doing my job."

Her toned softened. "I know you are, and forgive me for being rude. This really isn't your fault. You got duped by Craig Walker, just like I did."

The deputy motioned for her to take a seat in the corner of the lounge. As she settled into her chair, he took a small notepad from his pocket and sat down across from her.

"Okay, Ms. Bennett, can you please tell how you know Mr. Walker?"

"Craig Walker is an ex co-worker who I first met in Reno, Nevada, where we both worked for a magazine."

"Were you ever romantically involved with him?"

"No," said Rachel, firmly, as she shook her head. "Mr. Walker and I have never been romantically involved. It was strictly a business relationship." She went on to describe their talks in the break room, and how he had turned on her after she was hired as the new art director.

"So," said Gonzalez, "you said he was reprimanded after this incident. Did the harassment stop after that?"

"He never actually spoke to me after that, but he still gave me the evil eye whenever he saw me, and he always made a point of contradicting me at staff meetings, even when everyone else agreed with me. I probably could have said the sky was blue, and he would have said no, it was green. And then things started getting really scary."

"What do you mean by scary?"

"I started getting some really nasty emails in my personal account. They came from different senders, but they all had pretty much the same verbiage. I was a hack who didn't know how to do my job, and the only reason I got my job was because I'd slept with the boss. Changing my password, and blocking the senders, didn't seem to help. So, I finally went back to my supervisor, but I was told that unless I could prove Craig was the sender, they couldn't do anything about it. They suggested I open a new email account."

"Did you?"

"Yes, and after that I made a point of not checking my personal email from my work computer. Later on, I found out someone was using the contact form on the magazine website to complain about me, but management simply ignored it. They knew what was going on. They just didn't want to get involved. It was about the same time we learned the magazine would be going out of business."

The deputy went over his notes. "You mentioned something about this not being the first time you had an evening ruined by Mr. Walker. Could you please explain what you meant by that?"

"Back in Reno, it seemed like every time I went out with friends, Craig would be there. If we went to a bar or restaurant, he'd be at another table. If we went to a movie or show, he'd be seated in the auditorium; always giving me a cold, hard stare. It was as if he knew my every move, even though I'd made a point of keeping my private life private. I never discussed any of my plans with co-workers. Then there was Eric."

"Who was Eric?"

"Eric Hawthorne was someone I was seeing while I was in Reno. It wasn't anything overly serious, but we enjoyed each other's company. So one night while we were out having dinner, Craig was brazen enough to approach Eric in the men's room. He told him what a lying, two-faced bitch I was, and that I was sleeping with the boss, and why was wasting his time with someone like me when there were so many other women out there who were better? The confrontation apparently didn't last long, maybe a minute or so at best, but it really made Eric mad, not to mention how embarrassing it was for me." Rachel sighed. "Eric sent me an email a few days later. He said he was sorry about the problems I was having with Craig, but he wanted to end the relationship. He wished me luck and hoped there'd be no hard feelings. After that, I never heard from him again. So, once again, I went to my supervisor. She said she was sorry, but since it happened after hours and away from the office, they weren't going to get involved."

"I see." Gonzalez scribbled down more notes. "Is there anything else?"

"Other than the fact that he harassed me via the company email account at my next job, and through social media, I can't think of a thing."

"How did he do that?"

"I was working for an advertising agency which, for a time, had the company email directory posted on its website. They eventually took it down, but by then it was too late. Craig had my email address. The harassment started once again, so I had to set up a new email account. He'd also set up social media accounts under different names and send me friendship requests, as well as friendship requests to some of my other online friends. Then, after I'd unknowingly accept the request, he'd post some pretty inflammatory rants about me. I'd report it, but they never seem to do much about it. They just tell you to block them if you find them offensive, as if I hadn't done so already. I even tried going to the police, but they just don't seem to take these things too seriously either."

"Well, Ms. Bennett, I'm sorry you're going through this. Unfortunately, what you've told me would be considered a civil matter, so unless he were to actually harm you, or damage your property, there really isn't much we can do either, other than take a report. You may want to consider going to court and filing an injunction against harassment."

Rachel rolled her eyes. "I know. I've heard it all before, but I'm afraid taking him to court is much easier said than done. All l can tell you is I'm really losing faith in the system."

* * *

Deputy Gonzalez waited with Rachel until the valet brought her car. Once she left, he went back inside the hotel, only to discover Craig Walker had left the bar. He questioned some of the hotel staff. Mr. Walker was indeed a guest, but when they called his room no one answered. He looked around the lobby and mezzanine before heading downstairs to the restaurant in the lower lobby. Craig Walker was seated at one of the tables, enjoying a shrimp cocktail. He looked up and greeted him with a smile.

"So, did you ask her to leave?"

"She left, but not because I asked her to." The deputy gave him a stern look. "We have a serious problem here, Mr. Walker. Ms. Bennett and her companion tell me no such altercation occurred between the *t*wo of you, and I've talked to a waitress who verified their story. Filing a false police report is a crime. It can get you up to six months in jail, along with a hefty fine."

Craig gave the deputy a hard look in return. "Well then, I guess I didn't make myself clear the first time. Ms. Bennett was alone when she approached me, and it was before she and whoever was with her showed up in the lounge upstairs. It happened well over an hour ago, and, unfortunately, I was alone at the bar when it happened. I guess all of the wait staff must have been in the kitchen. Ms. Bennett isn't a stupid woman. She would never do anything so outrageous in front of other people." He took a sip of his drink, setting the glass down with a loud thump.

"It's like I told you before. I'd just returned to the hotel and thought I'd enjoy a drink at the bar before dinner. I'd barely sat down and was waiting for someone to come take my order when she suddenly appeared out of nowhere. She wanted to know why I was there, and she insisted that I leave. I could tell she was getting really agitated, but before things got out of hand I saw the bartender coming back toward the bar. She saw it too, so she left in a hurry. She was only there for about a minute or so at the most, so I decided I wasn't going to say anything." He picked up a piece of shrimp, toying with it as he spoke.

"Then, about forty-five minutes later, she shows up again, only this time she has someone with her, and they take a seat in the lounge. I didn't want any more trouble, so that's when I called you. I've already told you I don't want to press charges. I simply wanted her to leave, and now she's left. Thank you for taking care of this for me. As far as I'm concerned, the matter is settled. So, if you wouldn't mind, I'd like to enjoy the rest of my meal in peace."

Craig gloatingly popped the shrimp into his mouth. Gonzalez knew he was lying, but he couldn't prove it. There was nothing left for him to do but file a report.

❧THREE❧

THE LIGHTS DIMMED as Shane returned to his table. The PowerPoint show was about to start. Ten minutes later the lights came back up, but before he could excuse himself someone at his table volunteered him to be a contestant in the *Jeopardy* game. Another thirty minutes would pass. Upon returning to his table he grabbed his coat and quickly said goodnight, saying he had an early morning commitment the following day.

Once he reached the lobby, he looked for Rachel and the deputy, but saw no sign of either one. No doubt both had already left. He searched his pockets for her phone number and sent her a text message, asking if she'd arrived home safely. As he waited for a response he looked around and noticed Craig Walker had left the bar. Playing a hunch, he went to the bar and ordered a beer. A basketball game was playing on the television set, and he made small talk with the bartender. Twenty minutes later his patience paid off. Craig Walker stepped up to the bar and took a nearby seat.

"I'll have a Bailey's and coffee," he told the bartender, "and make it decaf."

Shane casually sipped his beer, wondering if Walker would try to strike up a conversation. He wouldn't have to wait long.

"Hey, I know you," said Craig. "You were over in the lounge area, about an hour or so ago, listening to the guy with the guitar, weren't you?"

"Yep." Shane remained nonplussed as he took another sip of beer.

"And you were sitting next to a blonde woman."

"Yep." Shane looked Craig in the eye. "I was here for my high school reunion, and she just happened to be sitting at my table. I thought she looked kind of hot, so I introduced myself. After dinner, I brought her out here, thinking if I played my cards right, I just might get lucky tonight, but then some cop showed up, and it put a damper on things real quick."

"Sorry buddy, but if it's any consolation to you, I feel your pain."

"Really? How so?"

"I've been wanting a piece of her for years, but she never gave me a chance."

Shane made a mental note. "I see. So, I take it you know her."

"Yeah, I know her alright. I used to work with her, back when I lived in Reno. We both worked for a magazine." He extended his hand. "By the way, the name's Craig Walker."

Shane gritted his teeth as they shook hands. "William. William Hollister, but my friends call me Bill."

"Nice to meet you, Bill. As I was saying, I worked with her back in Reno a few years ago. I'd watch her go into the break room, and then I'd go in and join her. She was single, apparently unattached, with a body to die for, and she seemed to be completely unaware of her sexuality, which made her even more appealing. But being co-workers and all, the timing just wasn't right, so I decided to just be friends with her, at least for the time, and perhaps mentor her. That way she'd learn to trust me. Then, when the time was right, I'd make my move."

Shane clinched his jaw as he took another sip of beer. "I see."

"But then fate dealt me a hand I wasn't expecting."

"Really?"

"Yep." Craig's face turned hard. "I had another girlfriend at the time. Her name was Diane. She had a niece who worked for an advertising agency down in Las Vegas. She'd mentioned several times that her sister, her niece's mother, had wanted her daughter to move closer to home, so, when word got out that the magazine's art director was leaving, I told Diane about it. She contacted her niece and told her to apply for the job, but then they gave the job to Rachel. Not only did she not tell me she'd applied for it, she wasn't even qualified. Obviously, she went into the boss' office and got down on her knees, if you know what I mean."

Shane swallowed hard. "Rachel mentioned something about working for a magazine in Reno, but she said it folded."

The bartender delivered Craig's coffee. He stopped to take a sip. "It did, but by then the damage was done. All I said to her was that I didn't think she had the experience for the job, but then she complained to management about me, and I got reprimanded. Can you believe that? Then, to add even more insult to injury, I found out Diane's niece had emailed the magazine, thanking them for the interview, but turning them down. They gave me a copy, along with the reprimand, so when I got home that night I showed it to Diane. I wanted her to know just how ungrateful her niece was, but then Diane, being a typical woman, turned on the tears. I come home the following day, and she's packed up her stuff and left. Stupid bitch. Of course, I was going to dump Diane once I had my way with Rachel, and I was going to have my way with Rachel, whether she wanted it or not. Let's face it. A young pussy tastes a whole lot nicer than an older one, don't you think?"

An icy shiver ran down Shane's spine. "Hmm, I haven't really thought about it." He drained his bottle and set it back on the bar. "Well, Craig, it's been nice talking to you, but I gotta hit the road. I have to be somewhere early tomorrow morning."

"Aren't you coming back for more of your class reunion? I hear they're having a big picnic tomorrow afternoon."

Shane concealed his surprise. "How do you know about that?"

"I overheard someone talking about it."

"I see." He dropped some money on the bar to cover his tab. "Have a good evening."

"You too."

Shane hurried out of the hotel, checking his messages while he waited for the valet to bring his car. To his relief, Rachel had responded. She was home safe. He sent her another message to let her know he would call her first thing the following morning.

🙖 FOUR 🙔

ACHEL PULLED AWAY from the hotel entrance and drove into the parking lot. After finding an empty parking space, she reached for her phone and pulled up a number. To her relief, her call was answered on the second ring.

"Mom?"

"Rachel? Is everything okay? You don't sound right."

"He showed up. Again."

"Who?"

"Craig Walker. I just found out he's staying at the hotel where my class reunion is being held. As soon as he saw me, he called the cops, claiming I'd been harassing him when I had no idea he was there. So what the hell is he doing here?"

"I don't know, but what I do know is this isn't a coincidence, and I'm sure as hell going to get to the bottom of it. I've been saying for some time now that he's been hacking into your computer, and I think this finally proves it. How else could he have possibly known about it?"

"I don't know," said Rachel. "I've been so careful. I only go on Facebook to post on my business page, and it seems like I'm constantly changing my email passwords."

"What about your website?"

"I already told you, Mom, I only use my business name only on my website. So what does he want from me? It's been years since *Sierra Life* folded, and he knows his girlfriend's niece never wanted the job. Why can't he just move on?"

"Because he's a sick, obsessed man." She paused for a moment. "Rachel, where are you?"

"I'm in the parking lot at the La Paloma Hotel. The sheriff's deputy who responded to Craig's call was kind enough to walk me out and wait for the valet with me."

"So, I take it you told him your side of the story."

Rachel felt her anger subsiding. "Yes, I did. I also had some eyewitnesses to back me up."

"I'm glad. Look, why don't you head on home and try to get some *rest?* Would you like for me, or your sister, to come stay with you?"

"No, Mom. I'm fine, really. I'm just a little ticked off right now. You need to spend some quality time with Bruce, and if Alice isn't working tonight then she's probably with Donny. I'll be fine. I wasn't planning on going to the picnic tomorrow anyway." She let out a long sigh.

"You sound like you're disappointed about something."

"Yeah, I am. I was just starting to get reacquainted with someone I barely knew back then, and things were going really well. Then the deputy showed up."

Rachel heard a smile in her mother's voice. "I take it this person was a man."

"Yes, Mom, it was a man. He was someone I met, just briefly, my senior year. I took the photo of his club for the yearbook, and he remembered me."

"I see. So, is he by chance single?"

Rachel finally smiled. "Yes, Mom, he's single. I know where you're going, and yes, I gave him my phone number." Her voice suddenly turned sad. "Then, right after that, Craig Walker threw a damper on things."

"Maybe, or maybe not. Let's see what happens, okay?"

* * *

Rachel's mother sighed in frustration as she disconnected her phone and looked at her husband.

"Let me guess," he said. "Craig Walker has reared his ugly head once again."

"He showed up at the hotel where her class reunion is being held. Then he staked himself out somewhere where he could see her, and as soon as he spotted her, he called the cops on her. I've been saying all along, Bruce, that he's somehow hacking into her computer."

"I've thought the same thing myself. Tell you what, Monday morning I'll have a talk with the school's IT guy and find out who he thinks is the best computer geek in town for this sort of thing."

"I'll do the same. Between the two of us, we're bound to find Someone who can get to the bottom of this, once and for all." She stopped to think for a moment. "So what happens if we're able to prove he's hacked into her computer?"

"We call the authorities, and then we take him to court and go after him for damages. He needs to pay for all the hell he's put Rachel through."

"Can we afford to do something like that on two teachers' salaries?"

"Don't worry, Julie. We'll figure out something, when the time comes. In the meantime, is she okay?"

"I think so. She's understandably upset, but otherwise she's fine. She said she's heading straight home. She also said she'd met someone there who caught her fancy, then Craig showed up, and now she's worried he won't call her. I guess we'll have to wait and see what happens next."

* * *

Rachel looked around before turning into her carport. No one had followed her home, and no suspicious vehicle was parked nearby. Shutting down the engine, she grabbed her purse and unlocked her front door as quickly as she could. Once inside, she securely locked the door behind her before turning on the lights and heading off to the bathroom for a long, hot soak in the tub. She checked her messages when she finally came out. Much to her surprise, she found a text message from Shane, wanting to know if she'd arrived home all right. Her face beamed as she posted her reply.

"Home safe and sound. Thanks." She set the phone on the nightstand and stepped away to get something to drink. When she returned, she found another message. Shane was asking if she wanted to get together the following day. She quickly sent another replay, saying yes.

❦ FIVE ❧

RACHEL'S PHONE RANG as she switched on her coffeemaker. Not recognizing the number, she hesitated until she remembered Shane's message from the night before. She took a deep breath and accepted the call.

"Hey, Rachel, it's Shane."

A big smile broke out across her face. "Shane. I'm so glad you called, and I hope you'll accept my apology for what happened last night."

"Stop right there." His voice was firm. "What happened last night wasn't your fault, and you have nothing to apologize for."

"I know, but it's still embarrassing."

"It's not your fault, Rachel." His voice remained firm. "Anyway, it's not the reason why I'm calling. I was wondering if you were planning on going to the picnic this afternoon?"

"No. When they sent me the information about the reunion I decided to only do the Friday night dinner. The picnic sounded like something for those with kids, which wouldn't be me. Were you planning on going?"

"I wasn't sure. I figured if I ran into any of my old friends, and if they were going, then perhaps I would, but now I think we'll do something else instead." He paused for a moment. "You know, there's a movie theater not too far from where I live that serves meals."

"I think I know the place. It's on the east side. I live about a mile or so away from it."

"You do?" He chuckled. "Well then, I guess we must be neighbors. I live close to it as well. So, I take it this would be a yes."

"It all depends on what's playing," she said, coyly.

"Well, then, let me read you the list."

Within minutes both had agreed on an action adventure film. They would meet in front of the theater and catch the early afternoon show. After it was over, they went to a nearby coffeehouse and ordered lattes.

"I really shouldn't be doing this on top of such a big lunch," said Rachel as she settled in her chair. "I have to watch my girlish figure, you know, and after today I'll have to put in some extra time at the gym."

"You look just fine to me. You women worry too much about your weight. I prefer a woman who looks healthy, and not too skinny."

"You're very kind."

"No, I really mean it," he said. "Back in high school I got into the habit of going jogging after I got home. It was a good stress reliever, so I kept it up during and after college. Unfortunately, as the years have gone by, it's become too hard on the knees, so I finally gave it up."

"I see. So, what do you do now?"

"I have a dog."

Rachel's face lit up. "Really? I love dogs. What kind?"

"She's a mixed breed of some sort. I got her from an animal shelter. She looks sort of like a small, Irish setter. I call her Lucy, because of her red coat, and every morning she and I take a nice long walk before I head off to work. We do the same thing in the evenings, as soon as I get home." He paused for a moment. "I originally got her as a pet for Fiona, who I was living with at the time."

Rachel felt a sudden twinge of jealousy. "I see."

"It was a few years ago. We'd been seeing each other for a while, and at the time I was renting a nice house in the suburbs of Houston, so I asked her to move in with me. She did, and for a time things were good, but then, later on, we started drifting apart. I was ready to settle down, but she still wanted to go out and party. One day we finally sat down and had a long talk, and we both realized it wasn't going to work. She packed up her things and left, but she didn't want the dog. Later on, Lucy and I came to Tucson, so now it's just her and me."

"Were you in love with her?"

"Who? Fiona? Or the dog?" he asked with a grin.

"Fiona."

"For a time, yes, but once I realized she wasn't the person I thought she was, I let her go and moved on. At least it wasn't a total loss. I ended up getting a good dog out of the deal."

* * *

It took some time for Craig to find his way around Reid Park, but he eventually found the Desert Sunrise alumni picnic. He casually strolled around, pretending to be just another park visitor on a balmy Saturday morning. Before long, a bench near the playground opened up. He took a seat and watched the people go by. The picnic had a good turnout, but so far he hadn't spotted Rachel among the crowd. He checked his watch. It was half past eleven. The picnic was supposed to last until two, so perhaps she hadn't arrived yet. He reached for his phone and checked his messages as he watched the caterers set up.

The scent of grilling hamburgers and hot dogs soon filled the air. His mouth watered and he made a mental note to grab a burger on his way back to the hotel. Leaning back on the bench, he kept a close watch on the crowd, but there was still no sign of Rachel or Bill, her companion from the night before. People soon lined up for lunch, and he waited patiently as the crowd worked its way through. He checked his watch once the last person was served. It was nearly one o'clock and the games were starting, although a few late arrivals were still showing up. He remained on the bench until the caterers started breaking down. A few people were starting to leave as he slowly rose to his feet and brushed himself off. Part of him was disappointed she hadn't shown up, but the rest of him felt elated. He had succeeded in scaring her off. He smiled to himself as he strolled back to his car.

❧SIX❧

CRAIG TOOK IN his surroundings as the car turned off the main road and into another quiet residential neighborhood.

"This is the last one on the list," said the woman behind the wheel. "It's still occupied, but the tenants will be out by the end of the month. The landlord will be doing some repairs once they're gone, so it won't be ready for move in until the fifteenth, but she's being very generous with the rent."

"Anything I should know about the place?"

"It was built in the mid-fifties, just like the second house we saw, only this one is quite a bit smaller, just two bedrooms and one bath. It had been the landlord's mother's house, before she went into a nursing home, so there's a good possibility it may go on the market in the near future. If so, the landlord says she'll offer it to the tenant first. In the meantime, she's willing to rent it out on a six-month lease."

They pulled into the driveway stepped out of the car. Other than a tricycle and a few children's toys littering the front yard, the house looked clean and it appeared to be well cared for. It also had a single car garage instead of a carport.

"Watch your step," she said as she held the front door open. "I know it's a little cluttered in here, but it looks like the tenants are packing up, and I don't see any major damage." She led him into a small kitchen next to the living room. "It's small, but compact, and the appliances are still fairly new."

"It's okay. I'm not much of a cook. All I need is a coffee pot and a microwave."

"Gotcha."

A door off the kitchen opened into the backyard. Other than a number of toys, it too appeared to have been well maintained. A small breakfast nook sat across the kitchen, with another door leading into the garage. Craig inspected the garage and gave the agent a smile as he stepped back inside and followed her down the hallway. The two bedrooms were fairly small, but both had plenty of closet space and the bathroom had recently been upgraded. She led him back to the living room and made her final pitch.

"She's replacing the carpets with ceramic tile and repainting the interior. As I mentioned before, she may decide to sell it. So, what do you think?"

He gave the room a final glance. "Well, it's like I said earlier. I'm an investigative journalist and I'm here to do a story on human smuggling, so a six-month lease would suit my needs perfectly, especially for what she's asking."

A big smile broke out across the agent's face. "Well, in that case, let's head back to my office and I'll have you fill out a rental application. But keep in mind that with today being Sunday, I may not be able to get in touch with the owner today."

"It's okay," he said, reassuringly. "I have to catch a plane tonight anyway. You'll let me know as soon as everything goes through, right?"

"Of course."

He extended his hand. "Well then, I think we've got a deal."

❧SEVEN☙

RACHEL SMILED AS she checked the caller ID and took the call. "Hey, sis. What's up?"

"I'm good, but I just got off the phone with Mom. So what happened Friday night?"

"An unwelcome guest crashed my class reunion."

"I hear he called the cops on you."

"Yeah, Alice, he did. Fortunately, I had a witness with me when the deputy showed up, who sent him over to talk to another witness. After that he was on my side. Then, as I was leaving, the deputy told me he was going to go have a serious talk with Mr. Walker, and I've not heard anything about it since. Still, it ruined what was turning into a very nice evening."

"Yeah, Mom said something about you meeting up with an old friend."

"Well, sort of. I ended up sitting next to someone I met briefly back in high school, but hadn't really known."

"Well don't keep me hanging. Tell me more."

"There, really isn't much to tell. We were just getting reacquainted when the deputy showed up."

"Hey, I'm your sister, not your mother. You can talk to me."

"Okay, but jeez, you're almost as bad as she is." Rachel heard her sister giggling through the phone. "His name is Shane. He was in the school math club, and I'm the one who took their photo for the yearbook."

"A nerd?" A disapproving sound resonated in Alice's voice as Rachel laughed.

"Well, not really. He had a slightly nerdy look back in high school, but now that he's all grown up, he's actually quite good looking."

"Really?"

"Yes, really." Rachel looked at the kitchen clock. "Hey, can I call you back later? I'm right in the middle of making Sunday brunch for Pilar. You remember her? My friend from my networking group?"

"Of course."

Well, I've got something that's about ready to come out of the oven."

"So of course you have to hang up on me, just as things are getting interesting. Anyway, the reason I'm calling is because Donny has to work today while I'm off, and I just got looped into having to have dinner with the folks tonight. Expect a call from Mom, real soon."

"Thanks for the warning."

The kitchen timer buzzed as they ended the call. Rachel took the coffee cake out of the oven, and as she savored the cinnamon smell the doorbell rang. Pilar had arrived, right on time. Rachel greeted her friend with a smile and a warm hug as she invited her inside.

"So where's Jacob?" asked Rachel.

"He's spending a little quality time with his grandmother today, so it'll just be us girls." Pilar took her seat at the bistro table in the breakfast nook and started rummaging through her purse.

"I wanted to give you this before we get started. A couple came into my office Friday morning wanting a quote for a business policy. They're florists getting ready to open their own shop. So, I asked them a few questions while I worked on their quote. They need a logo, business cards, and a website. You know, the works. So I told them about you, and gave them one of your cards. I also told them you'd be giving them a call this week." She handed Rachel a slip of paper, with the information neatly printed out.

"Thanks. I'll call them first thing tomorrow morning. In the meantime, would you like some coffee?"

"Yes. I can get it. You go put that some place safe."

Rachel hurried down the hall to her office, and returned to find Pilar pouring some coffee into a mug.

"I'll have some of that too."

"Of course." Pilar quickly filled another mug. "So, how was the class reunion?"

"It was interesting," said Rachel as she took a package of bacon and an egg carton from the refrigerator. "None of my old friends showed up, which really didn't surprise me. We weren't the cool kids, and we pretty much kept to ourselves."

"Well, for what it's worth, they say the cool kids oftentimes don't fare so well in real life. So, what'd you do?"

"I mostly went for the dinner, and I did meet up with someone I'd met, briefly, back then."

Pilar perked up. "Really? Was it by chance a man?"

"Yes, it was a man." Rachel's eyes rolled as she peeled off some bacon and dropped it into a skillet. "What is it with all of you? Yes, I met a man, who just happens to be single, nice looking, and quite charming to boot, and now everyone's acting as if this was some sort of major event. Just because I'm single and unattached, and have a younger sister who's living with a drop-dead gorgeous fireman who she'll probably end up marrying, doesn't automatically make me an old maid, you know."

"I know it doesn't, but at least you're not a single mother like I am. It's hard to find a guy when you have a kid. A lot of them just don't want the extra baggage."

"I know. My mom was a single mother when she had me. Bruce came along a couple of years later."

"Really? I just assumed he was your dad."

Rachel shook her head as she popped the remaining bacon back into the refrigerator. "Bruce is actually my stepdad. My real dad was never in love with my mother, and she wasn't in love with him either, which is why they never married. Bruce is the one who actually raised me. My birth father is more like an uncle."

"Well, then I'm happy for both you and your mom that Bruce came along. Hopefully someday I'll find someone just like him, who'll be a father to Jacob."

"I hope so too, but for now I'm perfectly content with things as they are. If I meet a man, great. If I don't, I don't. Either way, the sun will still come up in the morning."

"Yeah, right." Pilar's voice was firm. "Granted, I may not have known you for very long, but I can still tell when you're lying. Of course you want to find a man. Who doesn't? So, tell me more about him. We know he's single and nice looking, so what else can you tell me about him?"

"Well, let's see…he's a software engineer who used to work for Raytheon, but now he works for a small Internet security company."

"Then it sounds to me like he's got a good job. So, what's his name?"

"Shane. Shane MacLeod."

"Nice name. Sounds Scottish."

"He is," said Rachel. "He told me his grandfather was a teenager when his family came here from Scotland. Then the World War Two started, and it was still going on when he turned eighteen, so he enlisted in the army. Fortunately, the war ended a few months later."

"I'd say that was a good thing."

"Indeed. Afterwards his grandfather went to college, and then to medical school, and he eventually became a professor at the u of a medical school. That's how the family ended up in Tucson.

"Well then, it sounds like he comes from a good background."

The bacon had a good sizzle going. Rachel stopped to turn it over. "So, how do you like your eggs?"

"Over easy. So, are you going to see Shane again?"

"I already have. Yesterday afternoon we decided to skip the alumni picnic and go to the movies instead. Then, after the show, we went out for coffee."

"Wow. So you've already had your first date. Are you going out again?"

"Who knows?" said Rachel with a shrug. "He says he'd like to see me again, but it's too soon to tell if he'll call again or not."

"I understand. Maybe what I should have asked is do you want to see him again?"

"Of course I would, but I'm not getting my hopes up. At least, not yet."

* * *

After Pilar left, Rachel caught up on her housecleaning and went grocery shopping. Her phone rang shortly after she returned home. She perked up, hoping it might be Shane, but her excitement faded once she saw the caller ID. As expected, her mother wanted her to join the family for dinner. Alice was there by the time she arrived, and it didn't take long for Craig's name to come up in the conversation. Rachel thought his being at the same hotel as her class reunion had been a fluke, and she reassured everyone that he had no way of knowing where she lived or how to contact her, but upon arriving home her curiosity got the better of her. She called the La Paloma and asked for Craig Walker's room, only to be told he had checked out. A sense of relief came over her as she ended the call. Craig Walker was gone.

❧EIGHT❧

CRAIG SIGHED AS HE straightened up the front desk. His shift was about to end, and the night auditor would arrive soon. Times had changed, and not for the better. The Internet had created an army of bloggers, and as a result, he was no longer able to support himself working full time as a writer. Hopefully things would change once his three-part exposé on human trafficking was published. If all went according to plan, he might even win a Pulitzer Prize, but for the time being he had to take a job as a desk clerk at run down motel off the Interstate. The motel, however, also employed a number of undocumented workers. Craig planned on getting to know them well enough so they would share their stories with him. He was reaching for the broom when the phone rang.

"Front desk."

An irritated voice waited on the other end of the line. "I'm in room one twelve, and they're making way too much noise next door. Lots of yelling and screaming."

"Okay, I'll see what I can do."

The motel catered to the kind of people who didn't like the cops coming around, so Craig would have to address the problem himself. As he stepped out to the parking lot, a first-floor guestroom door flung open and a young woman in a tight-fitting, short skirt raced out. Two men stepped into the doorway and screamed obscenities at her. One tried to follow her into the parking lot, but upon seeing Craig he ran back into the room, slamming the door behind him. As the woman came closer Craig noticed her face was bleeding.

"Are you okay?" he asked.

"I don't know." She suddenly burst into tears. "He didn't tell me he had a friend waiting in his room when he brought me here. And they wanted me to—" She stopped short of completing her sentence and tried to pull herself back together. "Hey, I'm leaving. You don't need to call the cops, or anything like that."

She spoke with a Spanish accent. Craig decided to play a hunch.

"Your cheek is swollen, and your face is bleeding. Why don't you come into the office and we'll get you bandaged up."

"No, I'm fine, really."

"I promise I won't call the cops, but right now you're in no condition to go back out on the street. I just want to make sure you're okay."

Fresh tears streamed down her cheeks. "Thank you."

He took her into the office and led her into a small room in the back. Once inside, he pointed out a chair and handed her a box of tissues before he grabbed the first aid kit.

"Looks like he hit you pretty hard."

She looked down at the floor and nodded.

Craig crouched down in front of her and studied her face for a moment. "I see you've got a small cut on your lip, and your left cheek is pretty swollen." He stepped away and returned a moment later with an ice pack.

"This should help with the swelling, but you're probably going to get a really nasty black eye."

"Thank you," she said as she placed the ice pack on her cheek. "You're very kind. Are you a doctor?"

"No, I'm not a doctor. I'm just working here until something better comes along. How about you? How did you end up becoming a… working girl?"

"I used to be a maid, at another motel, just down the road, but then it closed down. I tried to find other work, but…"

"You don't have a green card, do you?"

Her gaze returned to the floor and she shook her head.

"So, you have a name?" asked Craig.

"Marta."

"Just Marta?"

"Yeah. Just Marta."

"Okay, Just Marta." He poured some peroxide onto a cotton ball and dabbed it on her lip. "So, how long have you been in the country?"

"Almost eight years. I came here with my mother and little sister. I was fourteen at the time, and for a while things were good, you know, but then my mother decided to go back to Mexico, and she took my sister with her, but I wanted to stay. I thought I'd have a better life here. *So* are you about done?"

Craig nodded. "Yep, I'm done, but you'll need to keep that ice pack on your face for a little while longer." He put the first aid kit away and reached into his pocket for his wallet. Marta gave him a strong look.

"Well, can I at least have some aspirin first? I'm starting to get a really bad headache."

"This isn't what you think. I'm also a writer, and I'm working on a story about human trafficking. If you wouldn't mind, I'd like to include your story. The money is so you can take a cab home once we're done."

<h1 align="center">✎ NINE ✎</h1>

RACHEL HOPPED UP from her seat and greeted her sister with a warm hug. "So how've you been, Alice?"

"Good," said Alice as she sat down across the table from Rachel. "I'm so glad you invited me to come join you. I hate it when I have a night off, but Donny has to work."

Alice looked around and took in her surroundings. The restaurant was hardly fancy. The bar and dining room had a well-worn vinyl floor, and the flat, tan-colored walls were covered with vintage movie posters. The vinyl upholstery in the booths matched the walls, but several of the benches were also worn and cracked.

"You know, I've driven past this place dozens of times, but I've never been inside before."

"Don't let the décor fool you," said Rachel. "It may look dated, but the food's delicious and it's cheap. Shane and I've been here a few times for the Friday night fish fry, and it's great."

Alice's ears perked up. "Shane, huh? Sounds like you two have been seeing a lot of each other lately."

"No, not really. It's only been a few weeks since our class reunion, and besides, we're just friends."

"Uh-huh. It's what you always say." Alice gave her a knowing grin. "So, would he, by chance, be another friend with benefits?"

Rachel groaned and rolled her eyes. "That would have been Eric, back in Reno, thank you very much."

"And Shawn, up in Phoenix, and, let me see, Brian, back at the U of A."

"That's enough out of you, sissy. They were all great guys and I enjoyed their company. I just wasn't in love with any of them."

"So what about Shane? Will he be your next conquest?"

Rachel chuckled. "Well, I guess we'll have to wait and see, won't we? But I will admit that the more I get to know him, the more I like him."

Their server came to take their drink orders. As soon as he left, Alice continued with her questions.

"So, when do I get to meet him?"

"Soon."

Alice looked intrigued. "Really? How soon?"

"Really, really soon. As a matter of fact, he'll be joining us tonight."

Alice grinned as she picked up her menu. "Well, now, that certainly gives me something to look forward to."

Shane arrived a short time later. Once again Rachel hopped up from her seat, greeting him with a warm embrace as he kissed her on the cheek. As she made the introductions, Shane and Alice exchanged smiles and shook hands.

"Well, I can see a family resemblance through your eyes," he said as he sat down next to Rachel.

"We both have our mother's eyes, but Alice gets her dark hair and those gorgeous high cheekbones from her dad, Bruce."

"Oh boy. Here we go again," said Alice as she rolled her eyes. "My sister always saw herself as a plain Jane, when, in reality, she happens to be gorgeous. So what about you, Shane? Any brothers or sisters?"

"Just one sister, who's quite a bit older than me. She's married and has two boys, and she's been living up in Idaho for years." He stopped and thought it over for a moment. "You know, I can't recall the last time I actually saw her. We're ten years apart, so we just weren't that close. It's like my parents raised two only children."

"Lucky you." Rachel gave her sister a smirk as she picked up her menu. "So are we all doing the all-you-can-eat fish fry?"

"Of course," said Shane.

"Might as well," said Alice.

Their server soon arrived to take their orders, and over the meal Alice talked about working at the Old Tucson movie studios when she was a teenager.

"I really wasn't into acting," she said, "but Amanda, my best friend in high school, loved the theater. So one day she decided to apply for a job there, and I came along, just for laughs. But then, wouldn't you know, they ended up hiring me instead of her. I'd walk around in a saloon girl outfit, and sometimes I'd have a bit part in the stunt shows. They even used a photo of me for some of their advertising, but that was about it. Acting and show biz just wasn't my thing. I was more into science. I was only there to make money for college."

"I hear you," said Shane. "So, what about Amanda?"

A sad look came over Alice's face. "It put a real crimp in the friendship. She found a job with another local theater group a few months later, but she never really forgave me, so we went our separate ways. Then I was on my own for a while. Sometimes I'd get bored during lunch break, so I'd go mess around in the chemistry lab."

"She used to horrify our mother when we were kids," said Rachel. "Instead of playing with her dolls, she'd dissect them."

"Because I wanted to see how they worked," said Alice, "and when I was done, I'd put them back together. Sort of."

"Sounds a bit like my childhood," said Shane, "only I wasn't into dissecting dolls. I was into taking apart old electronic gadgets and playing with the circuit boards."

"You both sound a little twisted to me," said Rachel with grin.

"My sister was the quite art student," said Alice, "but she really is talented. I'm hoping that maybe one day she'll find her Prince Charming. Then she can quit her day job and be a full-time fine artist."

Rachel's fork slipped out of her hand. It clattered loudly on her plate.

"You okay?" asked Shane.

"I'm fine. Sometimes I'm a little clumsy." She steered the conversation to a safer topic. "Anyway, my baby sister grew up to be a nurse. She now works in the emergency room at Catalina Community Health Center, which is where she met Donald, her fiancée."

"We call him Donny," said Alice. "He's a firefighter paramedic. We got to know one another saving people's lives."

"Sounds interesting," said Shane.

"It certainly is." The pride resonated in Alice's voice. "Granted, working in the ER can be pretty stressful as each day brings its own set of challenges. But when all is said and done, there's nothing quite like the feeling of knowing you've helped save a life. It's the most rewarding thing you could possibly imagine, and I wouldn't have any other job in the world."

"Sounds like you've found your true calling."

"Indeed, she has." Rachel's face beamed as she spoke. "And we're all very proud of her."

Alice turned her attention back to her plate. "So, what about you, Shane?"

"Well, I'm sure Rachel's probably told you that my father, and my grandfather, were both medical doctors."

"As a matter of fact, she didn't."

Rachel cringed as Shane turned his mock anger toward her. "What? Do you mean to tell me that I'm not your number one topic of conversation?"

Rachel shook her head and stared at her plate as Alice laughed.

"I see," he said, teasingly. "Well then, I guess I can forgive you this one time, but don't ever let it happen again." He turned his attention back to Alice. "I'm a software and Internet engineer, and I'm currently working for a small Internet security firm. It's fascinating work. Sometimes we track down hackers, but our main job is helping our clients have more secure websites. It's sort of like an extension of what your sister does. She designs sharp looking websites to help companies sell their products and services, while we work behind the scenes to help keep their data secure."

Alice gave him a grin. "Sounds like a match made in Heaven. At least, from a business standpoint."

Their server stopped by their table. Shane ordered another helping of fish, and the conversation steered toward Alice's wedding plans.

"It's not official just yet," she said, "although we've set the date for the end of September. Here in Tucson it's simply too hot for a June wedding. We've also picked out my engagement ring, and we plan on making our announcement next Friday night. We're just trying to decide on the restaurant."

"How 'bout this place?" said Rachel with a smirk. "The fish is delicious, and with it being June, everyone's on vacation, so you'll practically have the whole place to yourselves."

"Very funny." Alice looked at Shane. "Hopefully, you can come too. We need someone to keep her in line."

"I'd like that," he said. "Although I'm not making any promises regarding your sister."

"Just keep it up you two," said Rachel.

The conversation steered to some of their childhood memories, and the next time their server stopped by Shane was too full to order more fish. Their waiter picked up their plates and delivered their check. Alice wanted to pay her share of their tab, but Shane wouldn't hear of it.

"This is my treat," he said. "You can make it up to me at your engagement party."

"Deal," said Alice. "But for now, it's getting late, so I'm heading home."

"We'll walk out with you," said Rachel.

The three made their way out to the parking lot. Once Alice drove away, Rachel turned her attention to Shane.

"So, what'd you think?" she asked.

"I like her. She's like you, in a lot of ways."

"You think so? I always thought that with our only being half-sisters, we weren't very much alike."

"Well, in that case, you're each other's better half. Seriously, you two have a great relationship. I wish I could have been closer to my own sister, but there's such a big difference in our ages. By the time I was old enough to really get to know her, she'd gone off to California for college. After that she only came home for short visits."

"It's never too late, you know," said Rachel. "Maybe you should call her sometime, just to say hello."

"Well, maybe. We'll see. Meantime, I'll walk you to your car."

Rachel's car was parked a few spaces away. "Thank you again, Shane, for such as wonderful evening," she said as she reached inside her purse for her keys. "I'm glad you liked my sister."

"You're welcome." He gazed into her eyes and slowly leaned down to kiss her. It was a gentle, yet passionate kiss. When it was over, he wrapped his arms around her and pulled her in close as he kissed the top of her head. A sense of calmness came over her as she basked in the warmth of his embrace, but her mood quickly shattered when pair of glaring headlights shined in her face. A red pickup truck slowly drove past. She watched it closely as it turned out of the parking lot and drove away.

"Are you all right?" asked Shane.

She nodded toward the street. "That truck. I've seen it a lot lately. Over the past few weeks it's been going up and down my street."

"Are you sure? There are plenty of red pickup trucks in Tucson."

"Yes, I'm sure. It's a red Dodge Ram, with California plates."

"Which is a popular model. Maybe someone from California recently moved into your neighborhood."

"Maybe," she said, "but that particular truck has a small dent, right above the left rear wheel, and I recognized the same exact dent on the truck that just drove by."

"It's okay, Rachel. I know what you're thinking, but it's been weeks since we bumped into Craig Walker, and you've heard nothing of him since. I'm beginning to think his being at the same hotel where we had our reunion was one of those weird coincidences. In the meantime, we're only a few blocks away from your place, so it's entirely possible that someone from California has recently moved into your neighborhood."

Rachel remained unconvinced, but she didn't want to start an argument. "Well, hopefully, you're right. Maybe it is just a coincidence."

She unlocked her car door and Shane gave her a final hug and another quick kiss before she slipped behind the wheel. He stood by as she fired up the engine, waving goodbye as she slowly drove out of the parking lot.

❧TEN❧

ONCE RACHEL'S CAR drove out of sight Shane reached for his phone. He had gotten a good look at the license plate on the red pickup truck, and as he entered it into his phone, he prayed he was right; someone from California really had recently moved into Rachel's neighborhood, and all the truck sightings were simply a coincidence. When he arrived home, he put Lucy out and placed a call. To his relief, it didn't go to voicemail.

"Northrup Investigations."

"Lamar. It's Shane."

"Hey, Shane, how you doing? I sure hope you're not calling to give me a hard time about not coming to the class reunion. I really was in the middle of a case."

Shane was intrigued. "So what was it? Some sort of cybercrime?"

"Well, sort of. Someone thought one of their employees might be embezzling funds, but he didn't know who."

"Well, at least it had something to do with numbers. I still can't believe you ended up becoming a cop and then a private investigator. I always figured you'd be the next Steve Jobs."

"Nah." There was a chuckle in Lamar's voice. "One Steve Jobs was enough, and there'll never be another one like him. Besides, I love this job. It's much better than being a cop. Better pay, and a hell of a lot less stress."

"I'll bet."

"I've also started working with a community outreach program for African-American youth." Lamar's voice pitched with excitement as he spoke. "And let me tell you, those kids can really keep you on your toes, but it's great to be a positive role model, and that's what it's all about." His tone changed. "But something tells me that's not the reason why you're calling."

"No, I'm afraid it isn't."

"I see. So what's up?"

"It has to do with Rachel. Rachel Bennett. I saw her at the class reunion, and since that time we've become good friends. You may remember her. She took our math club photo for the senior yearbook."

"She did? Sorry, but it doesn't ring a bell. I know the photo you're speaking of. I just can't recall who took it. So, what's going on?"

Shane quickly got to the point. "A few years ago, Rachel was working in Reno, and she befriended a co-worker who, unbeknownst to her, wanted to be more than just friends. Then she got a promotion he felt she didn't deserve, so he turned on her and started stalking her. Later on, she took another job in Arizona, so he cyberstalked her, at least for a time. Then he turned up at the same hotel where we were having our class reunion, and as soon as he saw her, he called the cops. He made up some story about her harassing him."

"I have to ask. Did she know he'd be staying at the same hotel?"

"No." Shane's voice was firm. "I saw her reaction when the sheriff's deputy showed up. She was genuinely scared, although she tried her best to hide it. Then, after she left, I went into the bar and struck up a conversation with him. The guy is creepy as hell, Lamar. I can certainly understand why she'd be afraid of him."

"So what exactly did you say to him?"

"I gave him a phony name and told him I'd only met her that night, but it was obvious, by the things he said, that he's a total control freak who has to have it his way or else." A chill ran down Shane's spine as he spoke. "Then he asked me if I was going to the alumni picnic the following day. Fortunately, Rachel and I had exchanged phone numbers, so I called her the next morning and took her to a movie instead. After that, we thought the guy was gone, but now I'm not so sure."

"So what happened?"

"Earlier this evening, as we were leaving a restaurant, a red pickup truck drove past us in the parking lot, and Rachel got upset as soon as she saw it. Apparently, she's been seeing it around her neighborhood for the past few weeks. It has California plates, and since you're in San Diego, I was wondering if you could find out if the truck is registered to a man named Craig Walker."

"Do you have the license number?"

"I sure do." He quickly read it to Lamar.

"I'm at my computer, so let me see what I can do. You said Craig Walker, correct?"

"Yes."

Shane waited anxiously for Lamar to come back on the line.

"It's a red Dodge Ram pickup, registered to a Craig Thomas Walker with a Sacramento address."

Shane's blood turned to ice. "Damn. You're sure about that?"

"Positive. It's on the screen right in front of me."

"So why is he in Tucson if he lives in Sacramento? And how the hell did he get her address?"

"Those are very good questions, and I'd be happy to do some digging for you. Hopefully, I can find out what he's up to."

"I'd appreciate it, Lamar, and please, send me a bill when you're done."

"Will do. In the meantime, please tell her to be careful. I'm not familiar with Arizona law, but she might want to go have a talk with the local cops."

"She already has, apparently more than once, and she keeps getting the run around. They keep telling her it's a civil matter and to get a restraining order."

"I understand, so let's see what I can find out. Maybe it'll help her case."

"Thanks, Lamar. At least we know where the red pickup truck came from."

Shane sighed as he ended the call. Rachel would have to be warned, and he wanted to do it in person. He checked the time. It was getting late and he already knew he wouldn't sleep well that night. He picked up the phone and called her. Her voice sounded cheerful as she answered.

"I just wanted to make sure you got home okay."

"I'm fine, Shane, and I'm sorry if I got carried away over that pickup truck. You're right. It's probably someone who's just moved into my neighborhood. I'm being way too jumpy."

He grimaced at her words and tried to not alarm her. "I know, but it never hurts to make sure your doors and windows are locked."

"Of course. I always lock the door behind me as soon as I get in, and I don't open the door to strangers either."

"Good to know." He paused for a moment as he searched for the right words. "And speaking of which, I keep meaning to ask you, do you have any kind of security software on your computer?"

"I have a Mac, and it has a pretty good firewall."

"I know, but it still wouldn't hurt to have your friendly neighborhood computer nerd stop by and take a look at it."

"I see. Well, since you've so generously treated me to dinner the last few times we've gotten together, I suppose I could return the favor and invite you over for a nice, home-cooked meal. And I just happen to have a pork tenderloin in my freezer."

"Sounds wonderful. I love pork roast. So, when is good for you?"

"I don't know." Her voice sounded coy. "What's your schedule like?"

"Well, let's see…tomorrow's Saturday. I need to stop by the office for a little while, but then I'm free for the rest of the day."

"And I'm getting together with Pilar tomorrow afternoon."

Shane didn't want to sound too anxious. "I see. So are you free tomorrow night?"

"Yes. Pilar and I are going to the mall, but I should be back in plenty of time to get the roast in the oven. How does seven o'clock sound?"

Her voice still sounded cheerful. He hated the idea of having to tell her about Craig, knowing it could ruin their evening, but she also needed to know he would do everything in his power to protect her.

"Seven o'clock would be perfect. I'll see you then."

❧ELEVEN❧

Rachel greeted Pilar with a smile as she stepped outside. "Well, you certainly look chipper today," said Pilar. "In fact, you're positively glowing. Anything I should know about?"

"Life is good." Rachel turned her attention to Jacob, who held tightly to his mother's hand. "So how's my favorite little man today?"

The child smiled and stepped behind his mother. Pilar looked down and stroked his head.

"I guess he's being shy today. He gets in his little moods sometimes. So, are you ready to go, Jacob?"

Pilar placed him back in his car seat as Rachel hopped into the passenger seat. Once Jacob was secure, Pilar slipped behind the wheel and fired up the engine. "You really do look happy today, Rachel. So, what's up?"

"Just, you know, the usual."

"Sure," said Pilar as she put the car in gear. "So, I take it you're still seeing Shane."

"Yes, I'm still seeing Shane. We've become good friends. In fact, I'm having him over for dinner tonight. The last few times we've gotten together he's picked up the tab, so now it's time for me to return the favor."

"Really? Well, in that case, let's see if we can find you a sexy new outfit at the mall."

"Pilar, please." Rachel's eyes rolled as she spoke. "We're just good friends. Really, really good friends."

"Sure you are."

Rachel changed the subject. "So, is there anything new and interesting in your life?"

"Same stuff, different day." Pilar turned on the car radio and the two women chatted as they made their way to the mall. Upon arrival Jacob was secured in his stroller and they entered through one of the big department stores.

"Shall we start here?" asked Rachel.

"Jacob needs new shoes, but I think I might find a better deal at one of the shoe stores in the mall." She nodded toward one of the displays as they walked past the lingerie department. "But perhaps we should stop here and get something for you."

"Pilar, please."

Pilar shot her a look. "Whatever. The point is, you're cooking dinner for him at your place, so you need to be prepared, just in case."

Rachel groaned and shook her head as they strolled into the mall. The food court was nearby, and the scent of cooking food made her mouth water.

"I don't know about you, but I'm starting to feel a little hungry. Why don't we grab some lunch now, before it gets too busy."

Pilar checked her watch. "You're right. It's eleven-fifteen, and it might not be a bad idea to feed his nibs now, before he starts getting cranky. I have a peanut butter and jelly sandwich packed away in the back of his stroller."

Minutes later they had their lunches, but Jacob started fussing as they took their seats. Pilar quickly reached behind the stroller for his sandwich.

"I don't know how you do it," said Rachel. "If it were me, I'd probably lose my patience."

"It's not easy, and believe me, I have my moments." Her voice took a more serious tone. "Don't get me wrong. I love being a mother, and I wouldn't trade him for the world, but you know this was totally unplanned."

"Weren't you on the pill?"

Pilar shook her head. "No, I wasn't. His dad and I had only gone out a few times, so it wasn't that serious of a relationship, but then we went dancing one night. We had a few drinks, then one thing led to another, and we ended up at his place."

Rachel nodded toward Jacob. "So I take it that was the night?"

"No, not that night. We kept seeing one another for the next few weeks, but every date ended at his place. Then one morning he woke up and told me he was ready to move on. By then my period was already a few days late. We'd been using condoms, but they're not totally goofproof, so when my period didn't come the second month, I bought a home pregnancy test. It came out positive." Pilar stopped to wipe the peanut butter off the child's face and hands and give him some water.

"So, I went to a clinic. They told me I was two months pregnant. As soon as I got home, I called my old boyfriend."

"So how'd he take it?"

"Not very well. He vehemently denied being the father, but then he offered to pay for an abortion."

"Nice guy." Rachel's voice had a sarcastic tone. "So what happened after that?"

"I told him I didn't think I could go through with an abortion, and he kept denying he was the father. The conversation finally ended with him telling me that if I ever called him again, he'd call the cops on me."

"Wow," said a stunned Rachel. "He sounds like a total creep. So where'd you meet this guy anyway?"

"Would you believe I met him through a church singles group?"

"No way."

"It's true. I guess it goes to show that just because someone goes to church, it doesn't necessarily make them a good person."

"I suppose not," said Rachel with a shrug. "So, did you file a paternity suit?"

"No, I didn't, but I sure thought about it. By then I'd joined some online mom's forums, so I asked them for advice. The consensus of opinion was that a guy like him would be a lousy father, and sometimes it was better to not have a relationship with the father at all, because a bad relationship with someone who'd already rejected the child could do more harm than good. So, I decided to leave him be. Once Jacob's an adult, I'll give him his dad's name. Then it'll be up to him if he wants to pursue it or not."

Rachel's expression turned sad. "I understand. As you know, my parents were never married either."

"I remember you telling me about that, and my wish is to find someone like Bruce, who'd be willing to be a real father to Jacob."

"They're out there, Pilar, although they may not always be easy to find."

"I know. So, at the risk of barging in, I have to ask you if you're on the pill. I'm not trying to be nosy. I just don't want you ending up like me."

"I've always had an irregular cycle, so I've been on the pill for some time. In fact, I'm not sure if I want kids. I've even thought about having my tubes tied."

Pilar picked up a napkin and wiped more peanut butter smudges off Jacob's face. "Let's wait and see how things develop with Mr. Shane first. You may just change your mind."

They soon finished their lunch and Pilar took Jacob to a small play area next to the food court. He joined in with some of the other children and eagerly ran back and forth between the play equipment, but he soon tired. Pilar scooped him up and put him back into his stroller.

"It's almost nap time," she said, "so let's go find him some new shoes before he passes out."

They headed down the mall and Pilar soon spotted a shoe store, but Jacob started crying once she started trying shoes on him. She quickly found the right pair, and as she paid for the shoes Jacob fell asleep in his stroller.

"It's amazing how little kids can do that," said Rachel.

"Yep, and he'll be out for a while, so let's go find you something sexy."

Once again Rachel rolled her eyes as she followed Pilar back into the mall. They found a lingerie store few doors down, and Pilar quickly steered the stroller through the door.

"Wait a minute," said Rachel as she rushed in behind her friend. "Shane and I are just—"

"Well, he doesn't actually need to see it," Pilar said firmly. "But the fact that you have it on will make you feel sexy and you'll give off a good vibe. Now, let's see what we can find." Pilar soon spotted a matching red lace bra and panties. "Here you go. These would be perfect."

"Wow," said Rachel as she looked them over closely. "These really are sheer. You'd be able to see everything right through them."

"Which is the whole point. As I just said, even if nothing happens, you'll still know you're wearing them, and it'll make you feel incredibly sexy. So, what else are you wearing?"

"I'm not sure. It's summertime you know, so I was thinking of wearing a short skirt."

"Perfect. You've got great legs, so you should show them off. What color is the skirt?"

"It's black, and it's faux leather."

"Awesome. So, what are you wearing with it?"

"Just a short sleeve top, and a pair of sandals."

"What color is the top? And do the sandals have heels?"

"Yes, the sandals have heels." There was an exasperated tone in Rachel's voice. "They're black, with three-inch stiletto heels. The top is a gauzy red tunic. It's loose fitting so I'll tie a blue scarf around my middle like a belt. And if I leave the top button unbuttoned it'll be low cut."

"Good, then leave the top button unbuttoned. So, do you like these in red? If not, we'll find another color."

"No, red is fine. In fact, it's about the same shade as my top. So, are we done now?"

"Not yet. Let's see what else they've got."

Rachel groaned again as they looked around the store. Pilar soon found a light yellow three-piece, baby-doll nightgown ensemble. Once again, Rachel shook her head.

"We're not sleeping together, at least not yet, and I prefer to sleep in an old cotton t-shirt."

"I know you're not sleeping together, but it's the perfect color for you and it's on sale. I think you should get it and save it for later on."

"All right, all right." Rachel took the items to the register and handed over her credit card, waiting patiently as each item was carefully wrapped in tissue paper and placed in a bag. She sighed in relief as they stepped back into the mall.

"I think we ought to head back home," said Rachel, "I want to give the bra and panties a quick wash before I wear them, and I need to make sure they have enough time to dry."

"Good idea," said Pilar. "You've got a special evening to get ready for."

❧TWELVE❧

SHANE TRIED TO shake off his gnawing sense of dread as he parked Rachel's driveway. She needed to know about the red pickup truck, but he hated being the messenger. Rachel looked sexy and radiant when she came to the door, greeting him with a warm hug and taking him directly to the kitchen.

"Nice place you have," he said

"Thanks," she said as her face beamed. "I really like it here."

He reached into his bag and presented her a bottle of chardonnay. "See, I remembered."

She gave him a broad smile. "You certainly did. So would you like to open it now?"

"Let's wait until dinner." His toned turned serious. "Rachel, can I ask you something?"

"Sure."

"Have you ever checked your computer for spyware?"

"No. It's like I said before. It already has a good firewall, and it hasn't been running unusually slow."

"I know it has a good firewall, but humor me. I've brought something with me from the office, and I'd like to take a look at it, if you don't mind."

"What is it?"

"A flash drive," he said as he reached into his pocket and presented it to her. "We use our own proprietary software, and I promise it won't damage any of your files."

A troubled look came over her face. "Okay. So what exactly are you looking for?"

"Let's just say I'm a curious computer geek."

"All right. Follow me." She led him down the hallway to a bedroom which had been converted into an office. Her laptop sat on top of the desk.

"Thanks, Rachel. I'll only be a few minutes, I promise."

Rachel looked troubled as she stepped away. Hopefully, his hunch would be wrong, and Craig Walker cruising through her neighborhood was nothing more than a fluke. Shane plugged in his drive and went to work, and soon found what he feared the most. Taking a deep breath, he rose from his chair. Rachel was in the kitchen, stirring something on the stove. Once again, she had a concerned look on her face as she turned the burner off.

"Is there a problem, Shane?"

"I'm afraid so," he said, searching for the right words. "Rachel, are you in the habit of clicking links to strange websites? For instance, if one of your friends had emailed you a link, with a message saying, 'check this out,' would you have clicked on the link?"

"Well, yes and no. No, I don't click on links coming to me in the manner you've described. However, website design is a big part of my business, and oftentimes a prospective client wants me to look at their current website so I can see what they want redone."

"Do you know any of these prospects?"

"Sometimes, but not always. Why?"

"Because I found a problem. Someone has planted some spyware on your computer. It probably came from a website you visited, and it downloaded without you knowing it."

Rachel looked startled. "What kind of spyware?"

"I haven't determined what kind yet. Most likely it came from unscrupulous marketers monitoring your buying habits so they can pitch products to you."

"I see, so can't you just delete it?"

"I could, but I'd like to have my boss take a look at it first. He does Internet forensics, so he might be able to find out exactly who put it there, and why."

The color drained from Rachel's face. "Are you saying Craig Walker could be behind this?"

"Let's not jump to conclusions, okay? I'm just saying that under the circumstances, we should be cautious and try to find out what's really going on."

Her tone turned sober. "Now you sound just like my mother. She's been on me for months to get my computer looked at. She even gave me a referral to a Jonathan somebody."

"Jonathan Fields?"

"I think that may have been the name. I wrote it down somewhere."

"Don't worry about looking for it," he said with a reassuring grin. "I already know who Jonathan Fields is. He's my boss."

"Really?"

"Yes, really." He touched her hand as he talked. "I'll email Jonathan and ask him if he can take a look at it first thing Monday morning. The sooner we can find out who's behind this, the better."

Rachel looked puzzled. "I understand, but how would Craig have had access to my computer? I've never included my name on my business website, and I've been very cautious on social media."

"You said it yourself. He got your work email address from your last employer. Did you ever answer any email from your old work account from your personal computer?"

"Sometimes."

"Then that's all it would have taken, and I wouldn't be at all surprised if the same spyware is on your old work computer as well."

The kitchen timer went off. Rachel took the pork roast from the oven and placed it on a trivet. "Sorry, Shane," she said after inserting a meat thermometer, "but it isn't quite done yet. It needs to cook a little while longer."

"No problem."

Rachel put the roast back in the oven and turned up the thermostat. "So, what do we do now?"

"You let Jonathan take a look at your computer. Once he tracks down the source of the spyware, he'll get rid of it, and we'll do our best to undo the damage."

A troubled look came over her face. "So why do I have the feeling there's more?"

"Because there is." Shane motioned to the bistro table. "Let's sit down for a few minutes."

"So what's going on?" she asked as she took her seat.

"I got the license number off that red pickup truck, and as soon as I got home, I called Lamar Northrup. He was one of the other guys in the math club, and he's now an ex-cop working as a private investigator in San Diego, so I asked him to run the plates."

"Did he?"

"Yes, he did." Shane looked her in the eye. "The truck is registered to a Craig Thomas Walker in Sacramento."

Rachel's face turned ashen. "You're joking."

"I wish I were."

"This can't be happening."

He reached across the table and squeezed her hand. "It's okay, Rachel. I'm going to help you. The first thing I need to do is find out how he found you. That's why I want Jonathan to go over your computer with a fine-tooth comb. He has a real knack for tracking down bad guys, and if Craig Walker has anything to do with the malware on your computer, we'll turn the information over to the authorities and let them take it from there."

"I appreciate the thought, Shane, I really do, but I already know what they'll say. It'll be the same old song and dance I've heard before. It's a civil matter, and you have no idea how tired I am of hearing that."

"So, what would you like for me to do?"

Rachel thought it over for a moment. "Let's go ahead and have Jonathan take a look at it. That way I can at least document it, and yes, please clean up the mess as best you can, and do whatever you can to make it more secure. I guess it's all we can do."

She hopped off her chair and opened the bottle of wine, returning a moment later with a glass of wine in each hand.

"Are you okay, Rachel?"

She set the glasses on the table and took her seat. "I'm fine, all things considered."

"It's like I told you before. You're not alone in this. I'm going to help you. Lamar will do more investigating. We'll try to find out why Craig is in Tucson, and if we find anything incriminating, we'll go to the cops. Stalking is a still a crime."

"I know, but trying to get anyone to do anything about it is nearly impossible."

"Have you thought about moving?"

She looked surprised. "What?"

"Have you thought about moving? I know you like this place, but now that Craig knows where you live, you might want to think about moving. I know it'll be a hassle, but it could be worth it if it'll give you some peace of mind. It would ease my mind as well. I do worry about you, you know."

"Thank you for saying that, and I appreciate the thought, but I can't."

"I understand. I know it's hard to break a lease, but—"

"I'm not on a lease. My aunt owns the place, and she's renting it to me at cost. Unfortunately, at the moment, I'm not in a position to afford anything else. At least not anything in a decent neighborhood."

"I understand, but here's what I have in mind. I have—"

Rachel suddenly sat up straight. "What's burning?"

"What?"

"Something's burning. Can't you smell it?"

Shane caught a whiff. "Yes, I can. It smells like burning meat."

A horrified look came over her face. "Oh no! I forgot about the pork roast."

Rachel jumped off her seat and raced to the stove. Smoke poured out of the oven as she opened the door. Shane was right behind her. He turned on the exhaust fan as she grabbed an oven mitt and pulled out the smoldering roast.

"It's okay, Rachel. Pork is supposed to be cooked well done."

"Well done, yes. Cremated, no."

She put a hand to her eyes. Shane wrapped his arms around her and held her close.

"It's okay, Rachel." He stroked her hair as he spoke. "We may be able to salvage it."

He held her until she excused herself and stepped away. Once she was gone, he reached for a carving knife, giving her a broad grin when she returned.

"It's a little crisp around the edges, but not too much. I tried a sample and it's actually quite good. The pan drippings are what really burned. Now, if you'll hand me some plates, we'll get this served up."

* * *

A scowl came over Craig's face as he eased up on the gas pedal and let the truck slowly crawl past Rachel's house. A blue sedan sat in her driveway. Obviously, she had company. Perhaps it was the same man he saw with her in the parking lot the night before. He seemed familiar, but the parking lot was dimly lit so he couldn't see the man's face. He pulled over, but when he put the truck into park his stomach growled. As he watched and waited, the gnawing in his stomach grew more intense. He made a mental note to stash a jar of nuts in the glove box as he fired up the engine and slowly drove away.

❧THIRTEEN❧

SHANE PUT HIS SPOON Ådown and pushed his empty dessert dish aside. "Now that was a good chocolate mousse. Not too sweet, and just the right texture."

"Thanks," said a smiling Rachel, "although I have a confession to make."

"What's that?"

"I used a mix."

"Really? Well, I would have never guessed."

She gave him a sheepish look. "My cooking skills are okay, but not great, as you discovered with the pork roast."

"The pork roast was fine."

"Well, the sauce I put on top of it helped, and that part I made from scratch, but it's a fairly simple recipe. Everything else was either frozen, or it came from a mix. Most nights I have a frozen entrée, with canned fruit or a bagged salad." She stopped for a moment and chuckled. "But at least my lack of cooking skills is good for one thing."

"What's that?"

"I don't have very many dishes to wash."

"Ah, mademoiselle, not to worry about the dishes." He spoke with a flirtatious tone as he hopped off his chair and began clearing off the table. "I will help with the cleanup."

"No, Shane, you really don't have to do this. I'll take—"

"Don't argue with me, young lady. You worked hard to prepare a wonderful meal, so now it's my turn."

Rachel picked up her plate and followed him to the sink. Shane stood by with a dishtowel as she filled it with dishwater.

"I can take it from here," she said. "Why don't you go have a seat?"

"I'm fine."

She loaded the plates in the dishwasher as Shane wiped down the stove and countertops. Within minutes their task was complete.

"I think that's all for now." Rachel spotted something on the table. "Whoops, we forgot the wine glasses."

"No, we didn't. I left them there on purpose. I thought we might enjoy a little nightcap." He grabbed the bottle and refilled their glasses before taking them to the coffee table. Rachel was hanging up the dishtowel when he returned, and he escorted her back into the living room. She turned on the stereo, and as they took their seats on the sofa, he wrapped his arm around her shoulder. She leaned against him and sighed.

"You okay, Rachel?" he asked.

"Yeah."

"Sorry I had to bring up Craig, but you needed to know."

"I know I did."

He gave her a reassuring squeeze. "It'll be okay. We're going to beat this guy."

"How?"

"We'll figure out something."

"I've tried everything I can think of, and so far nothing's worked. He's like a big, giant cockroach."

"Well then, I guess I have to get a big, giant can of bug spray, won't I?"

Rachel laughed in spite of herself. Shane pulled her in close and swept a lock of her hair away from her eyes.

"See, I knew if I kept at it long enough, I'd manage to get a smile out of you."

He leaned forward and kissed her passionately, his fingers running through her hair as his other hand rubbed her back. She wrapped her arms around him and squeezed him in return. When it finally ended, he looked into her eyes.

"Maybe I should go now."

"It's okay. I'd like for you to stay."

"Are you sure?"

Rachel nodded and they kissed again. This time he brushed her cheek and the side of her neck. She moaned softly as he worked his way down her chest and gently caressed her breast. She was breathing hard once the kiss was over. He untied the scarf around her waist and dropped it on the floor. He kissed her again, this time even more passionately, as he slowly unbuttoned her blouse, revealing her sheer, lacy red bra underneath. Rachel gave him a demure smile.

"Wow, Rachel. You're absolutely beautiful." He gently eased her down on the sofa. She ran her fingers through his hair as he laid his head on top of her chest and listened to her beating heart. His finger circled around her nipple. He smiled as he felt it turn hard.

"You like that, huh?"

She softly moaned and licked her lips. He kissed her again as his hand went inside her bra. Her breast felt soft and warm. As they came up for air, he ran hand down her thigh, slipping it underneath her skirt and brushing his fingers across her lacy panties. She moaned softly as he gently caressed her.

"I see you like that too."

She moaned with pleasure as he unzipped her skirt, pulling it down and tossing it aside.

"Well, I see you're wearing a matching set, and it's incredibly sexy. And did I tell you red's my favorite color?"

She smiled and shook her head. "No, you didn't."

"Well, it is. Red reminds me of Christmas presents, and there's nothing more fun and exciting than unwrapping a Christmas present."

Rachel lay still and watched him as he kicked off his shoes and took off his shirt and jeans. Tossing them aside, he stood and gathered up the crocheted afghan draped over the back of the sofa, giving it a firm shake and letting it settle on the floor. Smoothing it out, he helped her out of her blouse and sat her down on the afghan. He reached for his wineglass and sat down next to her.

"You know, I almost didn't go to our class reunion. It really was a last-minute decision."

"Me too. I argued with myself the entire way there."

He set his glass down and gave her hand a firm squeeze. "But I'm so glad I went. I've always been drawn to you, Rachel. I felt something special about you the day you took the photo for the yearbook. From that day on I watched you from afar, but I was too damn scared to approach you."

She put her finger to his lips. "It's okay. We were both very young. It was too soon for us to be together."

Shane licked her finger as he gently swept her hair away from her face. "Maybe so, but that was then, and this is now. So, if it's okay with you, I'd like to open my present now."

He kissed her lips and chin. She giggled as he kissed his way down her throat. As he kissed down her chest he reached back and unhooked her bra, smiling with delight as he pulled it away and tossed it aside. She giggled and wrapped her arms around the back of his head, holding him tight as he licked and kissed her breasts.

"You like that, don't you?"

"Well, it's okay, I guess," she said, flirtatiously.

"Okay, you guess?" he said with mock anger. "Well then, I suppose I'll have to do that again, so you can decide if you really like it or not."

She ran her fingers ran through his hair as he swirled his tongue around her nipples. They turned erect in his mouth. When he came up for air, he gently eased her down to the floor. His body burned with desire as he gazed down at her. He kissed her breasts and slowly kissed his way down, stopping once he reached her panties. She moaned softly and arched her back.

"And now, for the rest of my present."

He slowly pulled her panties down and gazed at her fully naked body. She looked a little nervous. He stroked her face and gave her a reassuring smile.

"I know, you probably feel a little vulnerable right now, but Rachel, I promise you, right here and now, that I will never, ever do anything to hurt you. You know that, don't you?"

"I know, Shane, and I trust you. I really do."

He lightly caressed her sweet spot. Her moans grew louder and more intense.

"You know, I really do love my present. You're more beautiful than I could have possibly imagined."

He removed his shorts, stroking her and pushing his fingers inside. She groaned louder as her pleasure grew. "That's it," he said. "Just relax so I can open the rest of my present."

Watching her body writhe in pleasure made him feel like he was about to burst. He entered her, his mouth covering hers as she wrapped her legs around him, squeezing him hard as he too moaned with pleasure. As their bodies swayed together, his passion grew. She wrapped her arms around him, and as she cried out, he let himself go. He pushed his body into hers, squeezing her with all his might and moaning in his own pleasure until he too cried out in total ecstasy. As he relaxed and slowly came back down, she snuggled next to him and he softly stroked her hair.

❧FOURTEEN❧

CRAIG GRABBED A burger at the nearest fast-food drive-thru and hurried home. Once he arrived, he went straight to his study and logged into Rachel's email account, munching on his fries as he casually browsed through her inbox. Among the announcements about the latest sales at her favorite stores was a message from her sister. He unwrapped his burger and read the message. Alice and Donny's wedding and reception would be held at the La Corona Hotel in the nearby town of Oro Valley. Alice was confirming the day and time, along with all the other details. He plopped down his burger and printed out a copy of the email. Once it came out of the printer, he marked the message unread and resumed browsing through her inbox. He found a message from Pilar, wishing her luck with her dinner plans and she hoped Shane would like the lacy red underwear. Her words jolted him, so he tossed the remains of his burger aside. As he reread the message, his stomach twisted and his jaw clenched. So, Rachel had found herself another boyfriend. He leaned back in his chair, silently fuming as he recalled the scene in the parking lot the night before. He reread the email several more times more before finally marking it unread and logging out of her account. It was getting late, and he had to get ready for work.

The motel was in between night auditors, so Craig was filling in until they found a permanent replacement. Working the night shift gave him plenty of time to work on his human smuggling story, but being a day sleeper also meant less opportunity to keep watch on Rachel. Hopefully it wouldn't be much longer. He tossed what was left of his dinner into the trash and headed off to shower. Ten minutes later he was out the door, once again slowing his truck as he drove past Rachel's house.

The blue sedan was still there. He hesitated for a moment, but he knew if he lingered too long he might be late for work. He clinched his teeth and drove away.

Twenty minutes later the motel came into view and his jaw dropped. Four police cruisers, with lights flashing, had gathered in the parking lot, and yellow crime-scene tape barricaded one of the ground-floor guestrooms. As he turned into the entrance one of the officers stopped him while another walked up to the driver's side door. Craig quickly rolled the window down.

"The motel is closed," said the officer, bluntly "You'll have to leave."

"I work here. I'm the night auditor."

The officer looked him up and down. "I need to see some ID."

Craig reached into his back pocket and pulled out his wallet, carefully handing over his driver's license. The officer put it in front of his flashlight.

"So why do you have a California driver's license?"

"Because it's a temporary job," said Craig. "I'm staying with friends until I can find something permanent, but if it doesn't work out, I'm going back to Sacramento."

A pot-bellied man with a gray, stubbly beard approached the officer. "This man is one of my employees," he said, firmly.

The officer returned Craig's license and gave him a stern warning. "I don't care what your story is. You'd better get your driver's license and vehicle registration changed first thing Monday morning, because if I catch you with those out-of-state plates again, I'm pulling you over and giving you a ticket."

"Yes, sir."

The officer hurried away and the other man leaned into the truck window.

"So, what did you say to him?"

"Not much," said Craig. "He wanted to know why I didn't have an Arizona driver's license, so I told him I was only working a temporary job here, and that I might be going back to California."

"Really?" The man folded his arms across his chest and gave Craig a strong look. "So, is there anything I need to know about?"

"No, Eddie, there isn't. I simply have better things to do with my time than hanging out at the motor vehicle department."

"And I don't need any more unwanted attention from the cops, so I suggest you make the time if you want to continue working here. Anything else?"

"No, that was pretty much it. So what the hell happened?"

Eddie nodded toward the crime scene. "About an hour or so ago some guy got into it with his girlfriend, and she settled the argument with a forty-five."

"Really? So did she kill the guy?"

"He apparently died in route to the hospital, and she's been taken downtown. Then, just so my night would be complete, they found drugs inside the room, so now I've got the cops breathing down my neck. Meantime, I've shut the place down and refunded all of the other guests. At least it was a slow night. Most of them have already left, but as you can see, there're still one or two loading up their cars. We'll be closed until they complete their investigation, so you'll have to take tonight off. If all goes according to plan, we'll reopen at seven o'clock tomorrow morning, although room one-seventeen will be out of commission for a while, so I'll— Oh son of a bitch!"

A pair of headlights briefly illuminated the inside of Craig's truck. Seconds later a news van pulled up next to him. His boss stepped away and shouted at them to leave. Craig put his truck into gear and made a quick exit. He felt gleeful as he drove back across town. The opportunity for him to stake out Rachel's home would more than make up for the loss of a night's pay. He shut off the radio when he turned onto her street, but as he slowed down his joy turned into searing anger. Not only was the blue sedan still there, the house had gone completely dark. Obviously, Shane, this new boyfriend, was spending the night with her. The thought of him seeing her in the lacy red underwear and then having sex with her made his stomach turn. He shut down the engine and settled in for a long vigil. The sun came up a few hours later. It wouldn't be long before the summertime temperatures would rise to an uncomfortable level, and he didn't want to risk Rachel seeing him from her window and calling the cops. He fired up the engine and slowly drove away.

❧FIFTEEN❧

SHANE ENTERED THE office with his usual cheerful greeting. "Morning, Marissa. How was your weekend?

"Fantastic. The kids will be spending the next two weeks with their grandparents, so I'm enjoying my morning coffee in peace." She looked him up and down and smiled. "You seem different today."

"Really? How so?"

"I don't know. You just seem…different, but in a good way. It's almost like you're glowing."

He gave her a smile. "I see. Well, then, I guess it means my life is going well too." His mood turned more serious. "Is Jonathan in?"

"He's in his office."

Shane gave her a nod and headed down the hallway. Jonathan sat behind his desk. He looked up and motioned for Shane to come in.

"Did you bring your girlfriend's laptop?"

"It's right here." Shane unzipped his case and set Rachel's computer on top of the desk. "As I mentioned in my email, I've found some sort of malware, and I'd like for you to take a closer look."

Jonathan booted up Rachel's computer and popped in a flash drive. After a few clicks on the mouse, Shane pointed to something on the screen.

"See that?"

Jonathan squinted his eyes as he took a closer look. "I sure do."

"What do you think?"

"Wow. Whoever put it there really tried to hide it. We'll have to run some diagnostics in order to find out more, which may take a while. You said she uses her computer for her business, and she doesn't have a backup."

"Correct. However, we're in luck. Her sister just got engaged, so she's playing hooky from the office today, because they're out shopping for a wedding dress."

A gentle smile came over Jonathan's face. "Seems like it wasn't so long ago when we were planning my daughter's wedding, and if there's one piece of advice I can give you it's this; stay the hell out of their way."

"But it's her sister's wedding, not ours." Shane suddenly felt a strange surge of emotions. He stopped to clear his throat.

"It doesn't matter," said Jonathan. "Just step back and let them have at it. In the meantime, let's get this mystery solved."

The two men turned their attention back to the screen. Once all of their tests were complete Jonathan leaned back into chair and folded his arms across his chest.

"This is the work of a real pro."

Shane shook his head in disbelief. "I knew this guy had issues with her, but I had no idea he was this obsessed." He gave his boss a troubled look. "So, I guess the next step would be to link him to offending IP addresses."

"That, and writing a report. I'll send a report to the feds as well, but you know how it goes."

"Yeah, I know," said Shane. "Anyway, thanks for your help, Jonathan. At least we now know who's behind it."

"My pleasure." Jonathan took a more sober tone. "Keep a close watch on her, Shane. I've worked a few cases involving stalkers and they can be very dangerous, so don't underestimate this guy. If you need help building your case, I have a good friend up in Phoenix who's a top-notch private investigator."

"Thanks, but I already have someone working on it." He nodded toward Rachel's laptop. "Once you're done, I'll clean up her hard drive, and then I'm putting in a firewall so strong it'll be nearly impossible to hack." Shane stopped for a moment. "You know, there's nothing quite like locking the barn door after all of the horses have escaped."

* * *

Rachel smiled and nodded with approval. "Now this one I like."

Alice turned and looked at her reflection from a different angle. The floor length gown she wore was made of white satin, with short sleeves a beaded, lace bodice.

"It's simple, yet very elegant," said Julie.

Rachel pinched off some of the fabric on each side of the bodice and showed it to their mother. "It'll have to be taken in, but not too much." She turned her attention back to Alice. "And the neckline is just low enough to make you look sexy, but not too sexy."

"And we want it just a little sexy." Julie's eyes twinkled as she spoke.

"What about a veil?" asked Alice.

"I don't think you really need one," said Rachel. "Since the wedding is in late September, the weather will still be pretty warm. Something like a pearled headband, with a silk flower or some lace trim, is all you need."

"I agree," said Julie. "A veil would make it look too hot, and I don't mean sexy hot. It would be like a winter hat on a summer day kind of hot."

Alice took another look in the mirror. "I like this one best as well." She turned back to her mother and sister and smiled. "So, I take it we're all in agreement here?"

"We certainly are," said Julie.

They turned to the salesclerk, who stood off to the side. "This particular gown has been discontinued," she said, "so if you don't mind having one that's been tried on, I can let you have it for half off."

Alice's face lit up as she took another look in the mirror. "I don't see any stains or tears. Do you?"

"None that I can see," said Rachel as she took a closer look, "and it certainly looks brand new to me."

"You go change and I'll take care of it," said Julie.

"That's okay, Mom. I was planning on paying for my gown myself."

Julie stood her ground. "No, Alice. Your dad and I are paying for your gown. I didn't get to have the dream wedding I always wanted, so please, let me do this for you."

Alice gave her mother a long embrace. "Thanks, Mom."

A sense of guilt mixed with sadness came over Rachel. Her grandparents had never fully accepted the fact that their daughter had a child out of wedlock, so when Bruce came along, they refused to pay for the wedding. Her mother and Bruce were married in a small ceremony at his parents' home. As Alice headed back to the dressing room, Julie turned her attention to her other daughter.

"You okay?" she asked.

"Yeah, Mom, I'm fine."

"You sure? Because all of a sudden, you don't seem to be okay. Are you bothered by the fact that your younger sister is getting married ahead of you?"

"Not at all. I'm happy for Alice. Donny's a terrific guy and they're perfect for each other. I was just thinking about Grandma and Grandpa, and you not having your dream wedding because of me."

"Stop right there." Julie's voice was stern. "That was their problem, not yours, and I've never blamed any of this on you. Both of your grandparents had very strict upbringings. In their day, no one had sex until after they were married, and back then people got married at a much younger age than they do today. Look at you. You're almost thirty, and you're still single. In your grandparents' day, you would have been written off as an old maid, but nowadays a lot of women your age are still single, because you're busy establishing your careers and enjoying your lives, and no one expects any of you to still be virgins."

Rachel blushed. "Mom, please."

"I'm your mother, Rachel. I've loved you since the day I found out I was pregnant with you, and I've never once regretted having you." She wrapped her arms around her daughter and held her close. "I don't ever want to hear you say you feel guilty over anything your grandparents said or did. None of this was ever your fault."

"Is everything okay?" Alice returned from the fitting room with her wedding gown neatly draped over her arm.

"We're good," said Julie. "We were just having a moment."

"I'm fine," said Rachel, "so let's head on over to the mall."

"Not so fast." There was a determined tone in Julie's voice. "We need to find a bridesmaid's dress for you, since you're going to be the maid of honor."

"What?" Rachel gave her sister a puzzled look. "I thought Sara would be your maid of honor."

Alice shook her head as she handed off her gown to the salesclerk. "Donny and I decided to limit the wedding party to just a best man and a maid of honor. His twin brother will be the best man, and you're the maid of honor."

"But I thought Sara was your best friend."

"She is, but you're my sister."

Rachel remained unconvinced. "Is Sara okay with this? I don't want to create a rift between you two."

"We're good. Donny and I had decided this before we told her we were getting married."

Rachel groaned.

"Better suck it up, big sister," said Alice as she wrapped her arm around Rachel's shoulder. "And I promise we'll do our best to avoid you having to wear an ugly dress."

Rachel moaned again as her mother and sister started going through the bridesmaid's dresses. She shook her head at their first two choices. One was dusty pink and covered with sequins. The other had a nicer style, but it only came in peach, which didn't go well with her skin tone. As Julie put it back on the rack another dress caught Rachel's eye.

"Let me have a look at that one." Rachel took it from the rack and held it in front of her. The floor length taffeta gown was royal blue with lace trim. "Now this has some possibilities. It's similar to Alice's gown, and it's pretty enough that I could even wear it on New Year's Eve."

Alice looked at the gown and smiled. "I like it. What about you, Mom?"

Julie nodded her head in approval. "As long as you two are happy with it then I'm happy with it. Why don't you go try it on?"

Rachel headed off to the dressing room. Upon her return, the others gave their approval, and their mother announced she would pay for Rachel's dress as well.

"C'mon, Mom," said Rachel, "you really can't afford this."

"It's okay. We set up a rainy-day fund when you girls were little, and I can't think of a better rainy day then helping you out with your weddings."

Alice shot her sister a look. "Did she say 'weddings?' As in plural?"

"Don't look at me," said Rachel. "I'm perfectly happy and I'm not sure if I ever want to get married."

Finding the right shoes would be a bigger challenge than finding the right wedding dress. Each time Alice found a pair she liked the store would inevitably be sold out of her size. After searching in vain at two bridal shops and the mall, they went to a big-box shoe store where her luck finally changed. She found the perfect pair of wedding shoes in her size; white, open-toed pumps with tiny silver studs. Rachel also found a pair of sling-back pumps with silver-studded bows which met with her sister's approval and could even be special ordered in blue. After an exhausting day of shopping, the three women went out for a late lunch. Rachel received a text message as their server cleared away their plates.

"Anything interesting?" asked Alice.

"It's Shane, letting me know they've finished working on my computer and it's ready to be picked up."

Julie immediately perked up. "I see. So, what was wrong with it?"

"It's been running a little slow lately," said Rachel, not wanting to reveal too much, "and since I was taking the day off today, Shane offered to take a look at it. It probably just needed a tune up."

"I've been saying for months that you needed to get it checked. So, were there any problems?"

"Apparently nothing worth mentioning. He just said it's ready to be picked up." Rachel took a sip of her iced tea, hoping they would drop the subject.

"Must be nice dating a computer nerd," Alice said, teasingly. "At least you've got someone to fix it for you."

"Indeed." Rachel changed the subject herself. "So, you've got the dress and the shoes. What about all the other things you need?"

"I think I'll look for the rest of my accessories online. It'll be less exhausting, and I'll probably find much better deals on Amazon or eBay."

Rachel let out a long, silent exhale as Alice went over her list. Their server soon delivered their check and it was time to head home. To her relief, Alice dropped her off first.

❧SIXTEEN❧

RACHEL TOOK A deep breath before stepping through the door and introducing herself to the office manager. Shane soon appeared, but he looked troubled. Her stomach twisted as she followed him to Jonathan's office. He pointed to a chair and offered her a soft drink.

"No thanks." Her voice sounded anxious. "So, what'd you find out?"

Shane looked at Jonathan before he spoke. "I wish we had better news for you, Rachel, and I'm sorry to be the one to tell you this, but you've had a serious security breach."

A shockwave jolted through her body. "A security breach? What kind of a security breach?"

Shane looked her in the eye. "The spyware I found didn't come from an unscrupulous marketer. It was planted by a sophisticated hacker, whose identity is still unknown, and it has given someone access to all of your passwords."

"What?"

"Someone was able to get ahold of your passwords," said Jonathan, "and this individual has been using them to log into your email accounts. Both your business account, and your personal account."

Rachel's worst fears were now realized. "Who? No, wait. What am I thinking? We all know who it is, don't we?"

"Yes and no," said Jonathan. "It appears that only one computer and one mobile device have been used to access your personal information, but I need more time to find out who the computer and smart phone belong to."

"I'm afraid this is where it all gets really complicated," said Shane, "so I'm going to let Jonathan explain it to you."

"First of all, Rachel," said Jonathan, "Shane and I both believe as you do. Craig Walker is the person who's been hacking into your accounts. The good news, if we can call it that, is he's never logged into any of your bank or credit card accounts, even though he would've had your passwords. Nor has he ever logged in to any of your online shopping accounts. He's never so much as clicked on a link in an email from Amazon or eBay to find out more about the products you were buying. This means he had no intention of defrauding you for financial gain. His intent was to find out where you live, where you work, who your friends and associates are, and your general whereabouts. Please understand, what he did is still against the law. It's called, unauthorized access, and it's a federal crime."

Rachel perked up. "So does this mean he'll go to jail?"

"Possibly. Once we're done here, and after Shane helps you change your passwords, I'll send you a link to the Justice Department website so you can report it. However, there's no guarantee they'll pursue it, but if they do, we'll fully cooperate and do whatever we can to make sure he's convicted."

"So in other words, what you're saying is even though he broke the law, they may not go after him, which means he could still get away with it."

Jonathan shook his head. "No, not necessarily. I'm simply saying they don't have the resources to go after each and every violation, and even if they decide not to, it'll still be on the record. This means if he were to do this to someone else later on, they could still go after him."

"Great," said Rachel, sarcastically.

"I understand your frustration," said Jonathan. "We sometimes have to deal with it ourselves. However, you can certainly file a civil case against him, even if you've suffered no financial loss, because you still have a serious invasion of your privacy. And you do, then we'll do everything we possibly can to provide you with the evidence you need to prove your case."

Rachel remained in a state of stunned disbelief. "I can't believe this is happening. How long has this been going on? And what does he know about me?"

"I'm afraid it's been going on for some time now," said Shane. "The spyware was planted before Sierra Life folded."

"What? How can that be? That was a few years ago, and I've only had this computer for about eight months."

"I know. It snuck in when you imported your data from your old computer."

Rachel shook her head in disbelief. "So how much does he know?"

"Too much, I'm afraid. As Jonathan just said, he knows where you live, who your friends are, including me, and he knows all about your family. Anything mentioned in an email, he knows."

Rachel's voice was shaking. "My god. I feel like I've been violated. So when was the last time he looked at my email?"

"About eight o'clock this morning," said Shane. "Your computer is in my office and we're going to change all your passwords. I've already created a new one for you that's both secure and easy for you to remember. I've also removed the spyware and put in a protective firewall. It's now nearly impossible for anyone to hack their way back in."

Beads of sweat popped out on Rachel's forehead as a strong wave of nausea swept over her. "Where's your restroom?"

Shane looked concerned. "Are you alright? You look pale all of a sudden."

"I need to get to the restroom. Now. I'm about to be sick."

Rachel jumped from her chair. Shane grabbed her by the hand and raced her down the hallway to a small door. She rushed inside, and he offered her a damp cloth when she came back out.

"Are you okay?"

"I'm fine." The cloth felt cool and soothing as she patted her face. "I'm just, you know, pretty shocked, and not really myself right now."

"I understand. Is there anything I can do?"

Rachel shook her head. "No. I'm okay, Shane. At least physically. Emotionally, not so much."

"I understand, and I'm just as horrified by this as you are. As soon as you're ready, I'll take you to my office."

Rachel followed him down the hallway and Shane closed the door behind her. Her laptop sat on a small table across from his desk. He pulled up two chairs and as she settled into her seat, he sat down next to her and handed her a small slip of scrap paper.

"Here's the new password that I recommend you use." He gave her a pen and a pad of paper so she could take notes. "I'm also suggesting you make some variations of it as we go along. Now it may look like a jumble of random letters and numbers, but they'll actually make sense once I explain them to you. Are you ready?"

"Sure. Go ahead."

"Okay, the first two letters are for our old high school, Desert Sunrise, and the next two letters are for math club."

"Got it."

"I knew you'd catch on quickly. The number sequence is the month and year of our graduation, but as you can see, they're backwards."

Rachel finally smiled. "What a clever idea."

"Thanks. And because it means something to us, you'll remember it, but to anyone else it's just a bunch of letters and numbers. So, why don't you log into your email account and we'll change your password."

Jonathan tapped on the door a short time later. "Here's your purse, Rachel. You left it in my office."

She looked a little embarrassed as she thanked him.

"Are you alright?" he asked.

"I'm fine. I sort of went into shock for a little while, but I'm okay now."

"I know you did, and we're all just as shocked as you are." Jonathan paused for a moment. "My daughter once had a similar experience. The woman who stalked her is now in prison, but for a time she put us all through hell, so please, be careful, and don't underestimate this guy. I know you're pretty shook up, and I don't mean to frighten you any more than you've already been frightened, but you need to understand that he won't be happy once he realizes he's been locked out of your accounts, and he may try to retaliate. So, if you notice anything suspicious, or if for any reason you feel that you're in danger, you need call the police. Better safe than sorry."

A chill ran down Rachel's spine and she struggled to mask her fear. "I understand, and I'll be careful. I take it your daughter's okay now."

Jonathan smiled and nodded. "She's fine." He turned his attention to Shane. "Are you about done?"

"We're getting there," said Shane. "We've changed the passwords on her email accounts, and we've just finished changing it on Amazon. We still have a few left to do, but we shouldn't be too much longer."

"Then why don't you take her home when you're done? I really don't think she should be left alone right now."

"I agree. Thanks, Jonathan."

Rachel spoke up. "Before you go, how much do I owe you?"

Jonathan gave her another smile. "It's on the house."

"Are you sure?" she asked

"I'm sure. Take care, and if you need anything, please let us know. We'll do whatever we can to help you."

Rachel shook his hand. "Thank you, for everything, and I'm sorry I had to run out like that."

"You're welcome, and you have nothing to be sorry for."

Jonathan gave her a final nod and after he left, she and Shane went back to work. Fifteen minutes later their task was complete.

"Is that all?" Shane asked.

"I think so, and if I've missed anything, I can take care of it myself, but I'm still totally blown away by this."

"Me too." Shane turned his chair so he could see her face-to-face. "I know all about what happened with Jonathan's daughter, and trust me, he's speaking from experience when he says not to underestimate Craig.

He knows where you live, and he knows you're alone much of the time. And now that we've locked him out of your email accounts, I really think you should find another place to stay. The sooner, the better."

"I can't. I already told you. My aunt is renting me the place at cost, and I'll never find anything affordable in as good of a neighborhood."

"I understand, so here's what I'm suggesting. My house came with a small guesthouse. It's nothing fancy, but it has a decent sized room with a small kitchenette and bath. I was renting it out to a college student, but she left at the end of the semester, so it's now empty. It has a full-size bed with a nearly new mattress, a dresser, a writing desk and a small table and chairs. I think we should move you in, as soon as possible."

"What about all my stuff?"

"We can put your furniture in storage, if it comes to that."

Rachel thought it over for a moment. "I appreciate the offer, Shane, I honestly do, but I don't think it's a good idea. What if something were to happen, and we decided to go our separate ways? It would be too awkward."

Shane gave her a look. "Let's not go there, okay? I'm not asking you to move in with me. I'm fully aware we're not ready for that level of commitment. The guest house is detached from the main house, and it sits at the back of the property, so you'll have your privacy."

"I understand, and like I told you before, I really appreciate the offer, but I'm not sure about giving up the place I'm renting."

"It's okay. It wouldn't have to be a permanent arrangement. You'd only be there until Craig leaves town."

Rachel sighed in frustration. "And who knows when that might be. Let me think about it, okay?"

"All right, and just so you know, I'm considering you a guest, so I'm not going to charge you rent. Perhaps you could just bring your essentials, you know, your computer and your clothes, and leave the rest of your things at your place. With any luck, you'll only be there a short time."

"I don't know, Shane. Let me think about it, okay?" She stopped for a moment. "So, how often did he go snooping through my email?"

"Daily. Sometimes more than once a day. There wasn't any set pattern." Shane looked her in the eye. "So you can rest assured that sometime within the next twenty-four hours he'll know you've changed your passwords."

"But I've changed them before," she said. "I've had my personal email account for years, and I've changed the passwords many times since *Sierra Life* folded."

"And each time he was able to get your new passwords, but now that I've removed the spyware, he can't do it anymore, and I'm worried about how he'll react. We now know his being at the hotel where our class reunion was being held was no coincidence. He not only knew you'd be there, he was able to anticipate when you'd be arriving, which was how he was able to concoct the story of you harassing him at the bar. Then, after you left, I sat down at the bar and talked to him face-to-face. He's totally obsessed with you."

"What do you mean?" asked Rachel.

"He wanted to be more than friends with you. He said he planned on dumping girlfriend so he could pursue you, but then you got that promotion behind his back, so—"

"So he sees himself as some sort of jilted lover? Is that what you're saying?"

"Pretty much. So, until we can find some way to trip him up permanently, you're in danger, and I'll be damned if I'm going to let anything happen to you. If you don't want to stay at the guest house that's fine, but I don't want you staying on your own right now. You'll either need to stay with your mom, or your sister, or Pilar, until this blows over."

"I haven't told my mom or Alice about Craig being back in town. Alice just got engaged. She and Donny will make their official announcement Friday night. This is a big deal for them, and I don't want to spoil it by putting a damper on things. Pilar has a small child, and I don't want to do anything that could possibly endanger him."

"Then I think you've just answered you own question." There was a no-nonsense tone in his voice. "We'll stop by your place so you can pack a bag."

⋙SEVENTEEN⋘

JULIE RETURNED HOME to find Bruce busy with a minor repair to the kitchen faucet. He greeted her with a warm smile and a kiss.

"So, how'd it go? he asked. "I take you all survived your wedding dress adventure?"

"We did indeed." Julie's face was beaming. "Alice found the perfect gown, and she got a smoking deal to go with it."

He nodded his head with approval as he popped in a new washer. "Which is certainly good news for the father of the bride. Maybe now we'll be able to afford a better champagne."

Both started laughing. Then Julie's mood turned serious.

"It took a while for her to find the right shoes, and then, over lunch Rachel got a text message from Shane. Apparently, he worked on her computer today."

"Didn't she call the computer expert we referred her to?"

"Apparently not."

Bruce tightened the faucet handle and turned on the water to inspect his work. "But Shane also works with computers, doesn't he?"

"Yes, he does. So I asked her if there was any problem, and she said no, he didn't mention anything. She just said her computer had been running a little slow lately, so he offered to take a look at it."

He gave the knob a final twist. "Which he apparently did. So what's the problem?"

"I'm her mother. I know when she's holding something back, and there's something she's not telling me."

"Which could be anything. Maybe her business has been slow, and she doesn't want to worry you. Or maybe she's working with a difficult client. Or she and Shane could be having problems. I know you're anxious to get her married off too, but Rachel is her own woman. She always has been. Maybe she's just not ready to settle down."

"No, that's not it. There's something else going on."

"And there could very well be, but even if there is, it still might be none of our business." Julie started say something, but Bruce quickly cut her off. "She's an adult, Julie. You can't keep hovering over her like she's a child."

"I know that." Julie's voice sounded snappy. "But I also know my daughter. Something's bothering her. I could see it in her eyes. I'm wondering if she's still having problems with Craig Walker."

"Has she mentioned anything about Craig lately?"

"No, she hasn't."

"And it's been a few months since she saw him at that hotel, so if she hasn't mentioned anything about him recently, then I think it's a safe bet her running into him was a weird coincidence. He's a journalist. More than likely he was here working on a story, and now he's gone back to wherever he came from."

Julie thought it over for a moment. "I hope you're right, I really do, but I've had this nagging feeling for some time now that we haven't seen the last of Craig Walker."

Bruce wrapped his arms around her. "You know what I think? I think you're under a lot of stress right now, which is perfectly understandable. Our daughter is getting married. You want everything to be perfect, but there's a lot that has to be done in a very short period of time. And on top of that, summer break is nearly over, and we'll both have to report back to work soon so we can get ready for the next school year. So tell you what. Alice and Donny's engagement dinner is Friday night, and it shouldn't be that late. So what would you think of heading up to Flagstaff afterwards for a little weekend getaway? Alice and Donny can celebrate their upcoming nuptials while we celebrate being empty nesters. We finally get do what we want, when we want, and not have to worry about the kids."

"Just grandkids."

An astonished look came over his face. "What? Alice isn't pregnant, is she?"

"No," said Julie as she ran her fingers through his hair. "At least not yet. But it's a safe bet she and Donny will be starting a family someday."

"Someday, but certainly not today," he said as he gave her a gentle kiss. "So, now would be the perfect time for us to go have ourselves a little second honeymoon, and don't worry about Rachel. I'm sure she and Shane are fine, but even if it doesn't work out for them, she's still young. She'll find someone else."

❦EIGHTEEN❧

I T WAS MORE OR less back to business as usual at the motel. The news reporters had left, but the room where the shooting took place needed new carpeting, and some of the drywall needed to be replaced. A new night auditor would start the following week. Once he came on board, Craig would start the day shift. His job at the motel had paid off. It had given him plenty of opportunity to build up a good rapport with several undocumented co-workers, and, once he gained their trust, they opened up and shared their stories with him. Those stories would be included in a series of articles to be published in *The American Chronicle,* a well-respected national news magazine.

Craig smiled to himself as he stepped into the kitchen to pour himself another cup of coffee. Along with the *Chronicle* series, he had been doing freelance work for other clients, and, if all went according to plan, he would at long last achieve his goal of becoming a nationally syndicated columnist. He glanced around the modest little Tucson house was renting and imagined the New York apartment he hoped to someday live in. He took a sip of coffee and headed back to the small bedroom he had converted into an office.

Setting his cup down, he tried to log into Rachel's email account, but the password no longer worked. He leaned back in his chair and took another sip of coffee. Rachel changed her passwords from time to time, but with a few clicks of the mouse he would have the new one. He set his coffee down and went to work, but an error message appeared on his screen. He frowned and tried again, only to see the same error message reappear. After two more attempts he gave up and searched for an old, achieved file. Once he opened it, he grabbed his phone and dialed a number. Moments later a man with a foreign accent answered.

"Boris, it's Craig Walker."

"Who?"

"Craig Walker. I bought a special piece of software from you a few years ago."

"Did you?"

"Yes, I did. At the time I was doing a story on Internet spying, and you created a very special program for me. Among other things, it allowed me to get someone else's passwords."

"It did? Well, I can't say I recall. However, I'm no longer in that line of work. You'll have to find someone else. Goodbye."

"Wait! Boris, don't hang up. Just give me a minute to—."

Boris responded with a growl. "I told you I'm no longer in that line of work. Your feds shut me down. I'm lucky I didn't get shipped back to Moscow. You'll need to find someone else. I can't help you."

"Boris, it's okay. I think you've misunderstood something. I'm a reporter. Remember? The computer you hacked into belonged to a fellow reporter who was working with me on a story about Internet spying. She knew the malware you planted was there. It was all part of the project we were working on. Now we're doing a follow up story, but when I tested the software to see if it still worked I got an error message. That's why I need you to go back and plant a new program on her computer. Don't worry. It's all legit. She knows what you're doing, and you're not going to get into any trouble. And we're most certainly not going to mention your name in the story. Nor will we say anything about you that could make it easy for anyone to identify you. You'll just be an anonymous hacker."

After a long moment of silence Boris finally spoke up. "I think I'm starting to remember you now. You were with some magazine. I think it was somewhere in Nevada."

"That's right."

Boris' tone changed. "And as I recall, that article never ran."

"Yes, I know." Craig cleared his throat. "Unfortunately, the magazine went out of business before we'd finished the story, which is why it didn't run. However, we've recently found another publication that's expressed an interest, so we're reviving it. It'll be published at the end of the year."

"I see. So, who's publishing it?"

"What was that?"

"I asked which magazine will be publishing the story?"

Craig's patience was wearing thin. "Sorry, Boris, it's privileged information. I can't reveal it at this time."

Boris became hostile. "Really? So how do I know you're not trying to set me up? Nice try, Walker, but like I already told you, I'm no longer in the business. You'll have to find someone else."

Craig realized he had slipped up and he would have to think fast. "Look, Boris, I'm sorry if I upset you, but the contract I signed with the magazine included a nondisclosure agreement. I have to keep their name under wraps until the story runs. However, you can rest assured that I won't reveal my sources to anyone, not even the Federal Government. My credibility as a journalist depends on it."

"So you say."

Craig was becoming even more impatient. "And what does that mean?"

"It means I know all about your so-called shield laws, and they're not one hundred percent guaranteed. The feds could still force you to give me up."

"Look, Boris, no one will know who you are. Not the editor, or the publisher, or even the other reporter. I'm currently working on another story about undocumented immigrants, most of whom wish to remain anonymous, and I most certainly won't reveal their real identities either. That's what pseudonyms are for. As a matter of fact, I don't know your surname, or even if Boris is your real name. Nor do I need to know. All I know is you're some guy living somewhere in California, but I don't know exactly where."

After another long pause, Boris spoke up, but he had a condescending undertone in his voice.

"You couldn't spell my real name, much less pronounce it, but I admire your spunk, as you Americans call it. So, tell you what. I'll create some new spyware for you, and you can call me Roberto in your article. I've always liked the name Roberto. As soon as it's ready, I'll mail it to you on a flash drive. You just clink on a link to follow the instructions and it'll do the rest. But be forewarned, it's going to cost you, and I have to be paid in full, upfront, before I do anything."

"I understand. So, what's your fee?"

"An even thousand."

Craig felt a jolt. "What? Are you kidding me? You only charged me a fraction of that the last time."

"Times have changed, my friend. I already told you. I got caught and I now have a hefty fine to pay. So, I help you, and you help me. Take it or leave it."

Craig thought it over for a moment. Boris was one of the best hackers in the business. It would take some time for him to find someone else as good, and he didn't want to lose track of Rachel in the interim. He took a deep breath and hoped for the best.

"I really do need your help for this story, Boris. The magazine is counting on it, but we don't have that kind of money in the budget. Would you take five hundred?"

"Seven fifty." Boris' voice was firm.

Craig sighed loudly into the phone. "I don't think the magazine will go that high. I know for certain that I can get them to agree to six hundred, but that's pushing it. They won't go any higher. That I do know."

Boris hesitated for a moment. "All right, we have a deal. Six hundred. All payable in advance."

"I understand, and I'll have the money for you soon."

"Call me back when you have it, and I'll give you instructions on where to send it."

Boris disconnected the call while Craig pondered his computer screen. He had just billed a client six hundred dollars for a freelance job, and while he hated the idea of having to hand over his entire fee to Boris, he had to do whatever was necessary to keep tabs on Rachel. He glanced at his watch. It was time to get ready for work.

◈NINETEEN◈

RACHEL FELT CALMER once she arrived home. Stepping out of her car, she waited as Shane pulled into her driveway and exited his car.

"You know, I'm feeling much better now," she said, "and while I really appreciate your offer, I'm okay, and I prefer to stay home."

"No," he said, firmly. "I don't want you here alone. I'd stay overnight, but I have to be up early tomorrow morning for work."

"It's okay, Shane. Now I finally know how Craig was able to show up everywhere I went. And while he's made some pretty crass remarks about me to some of the men I've dated, he only accosted me to my face one time. It was back in Reno, when he first found out I'd been hired as the new art director. He told me I wasn't qualified for the job, called me a few derogatory names, and said I shouldn't have been hired, and that was it. After that, it was just dirty looks, or the occasional nasty email or Facebook rant. I'm not saying it didn't upset me, because it did, and yeah, he's creepy and he's a voyeur, but he's also a coward. So, now that we've taken care of my computer, I finally feel like I'm free again. I honestly don't think he has to guts to come knocking at my door, but if he does, I'll call the cops and have him arrested."

"I understand, Rachel, and, hopefully, you're right that he won't show up and it's really over." He gave her a stern look. "However, I'm not taking any chances. Up to now you've ignored him as best you could, but it hasn't stopped him. Now you're pushing back, and we don't know how he'll react. I don't want you here by yourself until this all blows over, so let's get you packed."

It was useless to argue with him. Rachel unlocked her front door with a sigh. Shane waited in the living room while she packed, and he loaded her bags while she packed up her laptop.

"Do you have everything?" he asked.

"For now, but it's going to be a hassle being away from my desk. What if I need something from the file cabinet?"

"Then you'll have to come back for it, but try not to stay too long."

She grumbled under her breath as they went out the door, but once they arrived at his place she felt more relaxed. Rachel had been to Shane's home a few times before, but never in the guesthouse. Once inside, she found it surprisingly comfortable. The pale green walls created a calm, serene feeling. Shane told her the antique maple furniture, including the four-poster bed, had once belonged to his grandmother.

"After she passed away neither my sister, nor my cousins, wanted it, but my mother just couldn't bring herself to sell it, so she put it in storage, just in case any of us changed our minds later on. Then, when I bought this place, she mentioned she still had it, so I grabbed it. I figure someday, if I'm ever lucky enough to have a daughter, I could repaint it and put it in her room." He ran his hand up and down one of the bedposts. "I'd even see if this could be made into a canopy bed."

Rachel perked up. "You want to have kids someday?"

"Of course I do. Don't you?"

She laid her suitcase across the bed and unzipped it. "I honestly don't know. I guess I haven't really thought about it that much. I've been so busy with my career and all. Anyway, I need to start unpacking."

"Of course."

Shane stepped out, telling her he would be in the house and to come get him if she needed anything. Before long both of her bags were empty, and her laptop was set up on the small desk next to the dresser. Shane knocked as she turned it on, and Lucy leapt inside when she opened the door. Rachel's face lit up when she saw the two big boxes he carried.

"You bought pizza?"

"Of course." He gave her a smile as he stepped through the doorway. "We didn't stop at the store so you have nothing to cook, and I didn't want you to starve, so I had them delivered. One has pepperoni and sausage, and the other is bacon and mushrooms." He set the boxes on the table and stepped back out. Lucy was right behind him. Rachel went to the little kitchen to look for some plates. Shane returned with a bottle of wine as she finished setting the table.

"Nice dishes," she said as she set the plates down. "Were these your grandmother's as well?"

"I'm afraid not. Everything in the kitchen either came from a thrift store, a yard sale, or the dollar store. I figured since I'd be renting the place out, it'd be best not to spend too much on the breakable stuff."

"Makes sense." Rachel opened another cupboard and found some wineglasses. "So where's Lucy?"

"We don't need a party crasher, so she's in the house, feeling very sorry for herself."

Rachel made a mock pouty face. "Aw, poor doggie."

"Poor doggie my Aunt Fanny. She's a spoiled brat and I left her with a heaping dish of fresh dog food. She'll be fine."

Rachel set the wine glasses on the table. Shane poured the wine and they dove into the pizzas. His phone beeped as they finished their meal. He popped his last bite of crust into his mouth and pressed a few buttons. A serious expression quickly came over his face.

"Is something wrong?" Rachel sounded concerned

Shane took his last gulp of wine and set his empty glass down. "It's an email from Lamar. He says he hopes to have his report on Craig Walker finished by Thursday afternoon."

"Sounds like there must be a lot to it."

"Lamar is nothing if not thorough. He was that way in high school too. I sent him an email earlier today about the spyware. He too finds it troubling, so, as my grandmother used to say, he's leaving no stone is unturned. He said if there's any evidence out there that could help you win your case, he'll find it."

She sighed and took a big gulp of her wine.

"Are you okay, Rachel?"

She shook her head and set her glass down. "No, I'm not. Lawsuits are ugly and unpleasant, and they can last for years. I once knew someone who filed a wrongful death claim. A drunk driver ran a red light and killed her brother, who was in the crosswalk and had the right of way. It was a slam-dunk case, but even so, the other side put her and her family through so much grief they wondered if it was even worth it."

"I'm sorry to hear it."

"Then there's the expense. Even with such a good deal on my rent, I'm barely squeaking by, so how can I afford a lawyer? I simply don't have the means to do this. As soon as I have Lamar's report, I'll take it, along with Jonathan's report, and file yet another restraining order against him. Then, if the judge grants it, I can have him arrested if he ever shows up around my house again. I want him out of my life, the sooner, the better. The last thing I need is to spend years fighting a nasty legal battle which, even if I won, would mean nothing because there's no guarantee I'd ever collect a dime."

"I understand," said Shane, "but I also want to see justice served. He's a bully who needs to be held accountable for his actions. Otherwise, he'll do what he's done to you to someone else. But on the other hand,

I certainly don't blame you for feeling the way you do. I'd probably feel the same if it were me. So, tell you what. Let's not talk about it anymore tonight. We'll wait for Lamar to finish up his report. Then we'll decide where to go from there."

Rachel felt her body relax. "Thank you, Shane, for being so understanding. I honestly do appreciate everything you've done for me. A lot of other guys would have simply said well that's too bad and moved on."

He reached across the table and squeezed her hand. "I'm not like other guys."

"I know you're not."

"So, would you like for me to stay overnight with you?"

She smiled and patted his hand in return. "No, not tonight, but thanks. I really do need to be alone for a while. Can we do it tomorrow night?"

He leaned over and kissed her. "Tomorrow night it is." He rose from his chair and headed for the door. "I'm going to take Lucy for a walk, but I'll have my phone with me, so if you need anything, and I mean anything, call me. I don't care if it's three o'clock in the morning. Call me. I'm only a few yards away."

"I know." She gave him a parting smile. "Goodnight, Shane. I'll see you tomorrow night, and it'll be my turn to cook, as long as you don't mind having a frozen skillet entree."

"Sounds great," he said as he kissed her goodnight. "See you tomorrow."

✣TWENTY✣

JULIE CLOSED THE dishwasher and was about to turn out the kitchen light when she heard her phone ringing in the living room. Thankfully, Bruce answered before the call went to voicemail.

"It's Rachel," he said, handing her the phone.

"Thanks." She sat down in her favorite chair. "Hey, honey, what's up?"

"Well, Mom, you were right. My computer got hacked." Rachel sounded despondent.

"How?"

"Craig Walker planted some malware on it."

Julie felt a sudden surge of seething anger. She took a deep breath and forced herself to remain calm. "All right, so what happened? From the beginning."

"Shane worked on my computer today."

"Yes, I know. You got his text message while we were having lunch, but you said there wasn't anything wrong with it, other than it had been running a little slow."

"It was never running slow, Mom. I just said it because I didn't want to worry you in case he didn't find anything. However, Shane thought as you did, that maybe Craig had somehow hacked into my computer. So, he took a look at it and found some spyware which was enabling someone to get my passwords. Whoever it was has been reading my email for some time now."

"I knew it!" Julie's rage boiled over and Bruce gave her a startled look. "I just knew the son of a bitch was hacking into your computer. Now we can nail the bastard, once and for all."

79

"What's going on?" asked Bruce.

"I'll tell you in a minute." She turned her attention back to Rachel. "So, how did he do this, and how long has it been going on?"

"Right now we can't be one hundred percent certain it's Craig," said Rachel, "although all of us, you, me, Shane, and Jonathan, Shane's boss, all believe it's him. We're just not sure exactly how he did it. We think he may have posed as a prospective client who emailed me a link to his so-called website so I could look it over and see if I'd be interested in redesigning it. The malware would have been downloaded when I clicked on the link."

"And when did this happen?"

"A few weeks before Sierra Life folded. I was doing a little freelance work on the side back then, and I very well could have mentioned something about it to Craig before we had our falling out."

Julie was calming down. "I remember. So did Shane take care of it?"

"He sure did." Finally, Rachel sounded more upbeat. "The malware is gone, he beefed up my firewall, and we've changed all my passwords. Craig can no longer hack into my email. Shane made sure of it. It's all over, Mom. His days of stalking me are through."

"Well, hopefully, you're right, but now he has to pay for what he's done. You need take his sorry ass to court and sue the crap out of him."

The anxiety returned to Rachel's voice. "How? How am I going to do that? It'll cost a lot of money, which I don't have, and, as I just explained to Shane, I want this to be over and done with. I don't want to spend the next few years of my life embroiled in a big, ugly legal battle with him."

"I see. So what did Shane say about it?"

"He understands my feelings, but he also said Craig's a bully, and if I don't make him accountable for what he's done, he'll turn around and do this to someone else."

"He's absolutely right," said Julie. "If you don't stand up to Craig, he will make someone else's life a living hell, just like he made yours."

"I know, Mom, but even if I wanted to take him to court, I don't have that kind of money."

Julie looked at Bruce and gave him a knowing smile. "You leave that to your father and me. We've already had a discussion about this, and we're prepared to help you."

"I can't do that, Mom. You guys aren't exactly rich, and you need to hang onto your money for your retirement."

"Rachel, I appreciate your concern, we both do, but you're our daughter, and we're here to help you. You've suffered a great deal because of what this man has done to you, and we've suffered right along with you. We want to see justice served as much as you do. Don't worry. We'll find the right lawyer, and if we can't find someone willing to work on a contingency then we'll find someone who'll work out a payment plan, but let's get this done."

"Mom, I really don't want to do this." Rachel was pleading, but Julie's response was swift and stern.

"Rachel, there comes a time in our lives when we have to do things we don't want to do. This man has wronged you. He's gone out of his way to harass you and to make your life as miserable as he possibly can. He's also made a concerted effort to ruin you professionally, so you can add libel, slander, and defamation of character to the stalking and harassment. He has to pay for what he's done. Your dad and I are going to Flagstaff for a few days after Alice's engagement dinner, but we'll be back before the Fourth. We'll start looking for an attorney as soon as we return. I want to get going on this before your father and I report back to work."

"Mom, I love you, and I appreciate what you're doing, I really do, but I'm getting a really bad feeling about this. It's like there's a voice inside my head screaming no, don't do this."

Julie wanted to reassure her. "Rachel, I think you're just scared. I would be too if it were me. Craig Walker is a pretty nasty guy, and you're right; this isn't going to be pleasant, but you won't be fighting him alone. Your father and I will be there with you every step of the way. We're going to nail this son of a bitch once and for all, and he's going to pay for everything he's done to you."

"But Mom—"

"No buts, Rachel. We'll talk more about it later." Julie changed the subject to remind her of Alice's upcoming engagement party.

"Shane's invited too, you know, so be sure and bring him along."

"I know, Mom. Don't worry. Shane and I will be there."

They finished up their conversation and as Julie disconnected the phone Bruce began questioning her.

"So what's going on? I take it there's more trouble with Craig Walker."

Julie looked him in the eye. "There sure is, and my worst nightmare just came true." She filled him in about Craig hacking into Rachel's computer.

"Son of a bitch! You're absolutely right. We have to file that lawsuit."

"No kidding," said Julie. "Rachel's a little hesitant. She says she's got a bad feeling about it, but it's just nerves. She's afraid of him, and who can blame her? But this has to be done."

"I agree, and like you told her, the three of us will have to sit down and have a little family conference. You're doing the right thing by not letting her drop it."

* * *

Julie awoke with a start as images from a nightmare replayed in her mind. Her heart pounded as recalled the dream. Rachel was trapped inside a moving vehicle and was crying out for help. Julie raised herself up on her elbow to check the clock on the nightstand. It was a few minutes past three. The witching hour, she thought to herself. She climbed out of bed, being careful to not disturb Bruce, and went to the kitchen for a glass of water. She couldn't shake the nagging feeling that something horrible was about to happen and she tried to shrug it off. Her overwrought imagination, coupled with her interrupted sleep, was playing tricks on her. Bruce still was sleeping soundly when she returned to their bedroom. She slipped back into bed, and as he snored, she tossed and turned until she finally fell into a fitful sleep.

✌TWENTY-ONE✍

LUCY RUSHED INTO the guesthouse and made herself comfortable on the bed. Shane was pleased to see Rachel bonding with the dog. Lucy would protect her if Craig were to somehow find out she was there. Over dinner he told her to keep the dog with her during the day, and to take Lucy with her when she went back to her place to pick up the food she'd left in her refrigerator. Once the dishes were done, Shane took Lucy back to the main house. He and Rachel made love in the antique maple bed and spent the night wrapped in each other's arms.

Lamar's report arrived late Thursday afternoon. Shane printed it out before he left the office. Once he arrived home, he went straight to the guesthouse. Lucy wagged her tail with excitement while Rachel greeted him with a kiss.

"Is everything okay?" she asked. "You look so serious."

"Can we talk?"

"Sure, just let me save something on the computer," she said as she walked over to the desk. "I've been working on a website all day, and about the time I think I've got it done, the clients decide to add something else, but at least they're okay with me billing them for the extra hours."

"Been there a time or two myself." He set his briefcase on the table and asked her to take a seat. As Rachel settled in her chair, Shane pulled out his stack of papers and sat down next to her.

"I have Lamar's report, and there's quite a bit in it."

"Really?" Rachel sounded anxious.

"Yes. As I told you before, Lamar is very thorough, so let's get started." He showed her the first page. "Craig Walker is forty-two years old. He was born in Sacramento, California to a single mother named Lisa Walker."

"Which I already knew," said Rachel as she skimmed over the page. "He told me a little about her, back when we were still office buddies, and you know, I was born to a single mother as well."

"I know you were. However, your mother later married Bruce, while Craig's mother never married. Did he ever tell you what she did for a living?"

"Not really. He said she had a job, but he didn't elaborate. I figured she was probably an office worker, or perhaps a waitress."

Shane shook his head. "Not even close. She was a teacher's aide at the time Craig was born. Unfortunately, she later got into drugs and became a working girl, if you know what I mean."

"You mean she was a prostitute?"

"Yes. She had a long history of arrests for drug use and prostitution, so Craig went in and out of foster care. She went into rehab twice, but it obviously failed, because she died of an overdose at the age of thirty-two. Craig would have been eleven at the time."

"Wow." Rachel sat quietly for a moment. "You know, in a way, I feel sorry for him. No kid deserves that kind of home life. Was there any other family?"

"According to the report, at the time of her death, Lisa's mother and older brother were living in Ohio, but they must not have been very close because neither of them wanted Craig."

"What about his father?"

Shane glanced at the bottom of the page. "It says his father was unknown. Apparently, Lisa quit her job and moved to California about six months before Craig was born, which suggests his father was probably married. Craig was placed in yet another foster home after his mother's death, and he remained there until he finished high school. After that, he got a job at a fast-food place and worked his way through college."

"Yeah, he once mentioned something about that as well. Only he said his mother died of cancer, and afterwards he lived with his uncle and aunt." Rachel stopped and thought it over. "Well, we all know he's been a first-class pain in the butt, but it doesn't sound like there's anything indicating that he could become violent."

Shane looked her in the eye. "We're not done yet," he said as he went to the next page. "Like his mother, Craig has never married. However, two former girlfriends put out orders of protection against him. The most recent was a woman named Diane Ingalls, who he lived with in Reno."

"I remember them living together when he was with the magazine. In fact, it was her niece who also applied for the art director position."

"Yes, I know. Craig told me the story that night at the hotel as well. He also admitted that after he found out about the niece not wanting the job, he vented his anger on Diane. Lamar has included a copy of a police report. I believe it's on the next page." He turned the page, pointing out the details as he talked.

"According to this report, they argued and he slapped her around. She called the cops, he was charged with aggravated assault and battery, and spent the night in jail." He turned back to Lamar's report. "She took out the order of protection the following day. His attorney managed to plea-bargain the charges down to simple assault, and he ended up with a fine but no jail time. The court also ordered no further contact with Ms. Ingalls."

Rachel shook her head in disbelief. "I remember hearing about him taking an unscheduled day off. Then later on I heard something about it being an unexpected family emergency, but it would've all been hearsay and office gossip."

"This is why I want you to stay here, at least for now. He really does have a history of violent behavior, and I don't want anything to happen to you."

"Neither do I. So, what about the other ex-girlfriend?"

Shane went to the next page. "Her order of protection came from a court in Sacramento, about five years before the incident with Diane Ingalls. She simply stated that the relationship had ended, but he kept harassing her and making verbal threats against her. There were no allegations of any physical abuse, nor were any arrests made. Then there's the order of protection that you filed for just before the magazine folded."

"I remember it well. The court wouldn't grant it, because they said I didn't have enough evidence. If only I'd known about Diane. If I had, they may have granted it, and he may have even gotten some jail time for what he did to her."

"Maybe, but who's to say? Other than that one incident, he has no criminal record, and oftentimes judges are lenient with first time offenders."

"Is there anything else in there I should know about?"

"Let's take a look." Shane thumbed through the rest of the pages. "He went back to Sacramento after the magazine folded, and has apparently been working as a freelance writer ever since. There's also a list of other places where he's worked. Mostly retail sales."

"Makes sense," said Rachel. "The sad fact is many of us have to work a day job in order to make ends meet. I may be soon be looking for one myself."

"Maybe not," he said with a wink. "Jonathan is getting ready to send some business your way."

Her face lit up. "Really?"

"Yes, really. You'll be hearing from him sometime next week. In the meantime, we need to get back to business." Shane turned to the next page. What he found nearly jolted him out of his chair. "What the hell?"

"What is it?"

He took a closer look. "According to this, he moved to Tucson, shortly after our class reunion. Here's his current address. Damn!"

"What?" Rachel looked stunned.

Shane scowled. "He lives within a quarter mile of your home. That's why you've been seeing his truck around your neighborhood. The son of a bitch has been doing drive-bys past your house. He also has a day job at a motel, just off the freeway. So what the hell is he doing here?"

"It could be anything. He's a journalist. He might be working on a story."

Shane shook his head. "Maybe, but why come here? Aren't there things to write about in other parts of the country? This is way too coincidental. He's up to something, and I don't like it."

Rachel shuddered. "It's been years since the magazine folded. Why can't he just move on and leave me alone? Even if they'd hired his ex-girlfriend's niece, the magazine would have still gone out of business, and she would have been out of a job, just like the rest of us. You'd think by now he would have figured out it was for the best when she turned it down and stayed in Las Vegas. So why isn't he getting this?"

"It's because you're thinking like a rational person."

A puzzled look came over her face. "And what do you mean by that?"

He looked into her eyes. "It means you're a normal, rational person, who expects others to be reasonable as well. Unfortunately, our friend Craig is hardly reasonable. I learned that when I had that little chat with him at the hotel bar. At the time I thought he was just an arrogant control freak with an overblown ego, but now that I've read this, I'm seeing something far more sinister."

Rachel looked frightened. "What do you mean, more sinister?"

"He thinks you got that promotion because you did some, shall we say, sexual favors, for the higher ups at the magazine."

"Which I already knew. He said it, in so many words, the day he confronted me. I've also seen his Facebook and email rants. They were full of all kinds of nasty little innuendos, like, 'all she has to do is wear a pushup bra, and they'll roll over and give her anything she wants.'" Her nose wrinkled as she spoke. "It's too disgusting to even think about, much less talk about."

"I know, but he also admitted to me that the reason why he befriended you in the first place was because he was sexually attracted to you. He even made some remark about your naiveté over your sexuality being a real turn on to him." Shane's stomach twisted as he recalled the conversation, but he stopped short of repeating Craig's comments about wanting to force himself on her.

"Shane, I was never, ever attracted to him in that way," said Rachel, firmly. "I saw him as a co-worker, perhaps even a mentor, but he wasn't someone I would have ever considered dating. I also knew he had a girlfriend. Sometimes I'd even ask him how she was doing."

"I know you were never attracted to him in that way. He knew it too, which was one of the reasons why he wanted you so badly. He doesn't look at women in a normal, healthy way. He grew up with a drug-addicted prostitute for a mother, so who knows what kind of debauchery he may have been exposed to as a youngster. All I can tell you is he sees sex as a means to dominate and control women."

Rachel stood from the table and went into the kitchen.

"You okay?" he asked.

"No, not really." She offered him a glass of wine, but he declined. She poured one for herself while he shuffled through the papers once again.

"I think that's about it," he said. "The rest is all backup documentation."

Rachel set her wine glass on the table and took her seat. "I've seen his Facebook posts, as well as his rants on Twitter. I finally had to give up and close out all of my social media accounts. It just wasn't worth the headache, especially when I wasn't getting any business from them. I've been getting most of my referrals from Pilar."

"And me."

A big smile broke out across her face. "And you."

She took another sip of her wine as he reached over and rubbed her back.

"We're going to beat this guy." He leaned over and kissed her on the cheek.

"Yeah, that's what everyone keeps telling me, but so far it hasn't happened." She took another swig of her wine, setting her glass down with a loud sigh.

"It doesn't matter what I do, or how hard I try, because it always ends up the same. Craig Walker gets to do what he wants, when he wants, while my world keeps getting turned upside down. I appreciate everything you're doing, Shane, I really do, but I'm afraid you're fighting a losing battle. At the end of the day, no matter what anyone does, Craig Walker always wins."

"No, not always." Shane's voice was firm. "As you've already pointed out, we've taken care of your computer, so he can't spy on you like he did before. I'll see if Lamar can monitor him more closely. Perhaps he can find out why he's in Tucson, and maybe he'll have some suggestions as to what we could do to convince him to leave."

Rachel picked her glass back up and swirled the wine around. "I called my mother the other night, right after we'd found out about my computer. She wants me to file a lawsuit against him. She and Bruce have even offered to pay for it."

His fingers worked on her neck and shoulders. "Wow. All of a sudden your muscles are really tight. I take it you don't want to do this."

She shook her head. "No, I don't. Tomorrow morning I'll go downtown and file another restraining order." She tapped the stack of papers as she spoke. "Hopefully this time around the judge will see it my way instead of telling me I need more evidence. Then, once I get it, you'd better believe I'll call the cops if he comes anywhere near me. However, I don't want to go through a lawsuit. It's like I said before. It would be a big, ugly battle and it would last for years. I just want him to go away, but my mother insists I file it, and she's not taking no for an answer, even though I've told her I have a very bad feeling about this." She took another sip of wine. "So tell me, Shane. What do you think? Should I file this lawsuit? And I want your honest opinion."

He wrapped his arm around her shoulder and pulled her body close to his. "I want him to go away as much as you do. I think a restraining order is a good place to start, and you most certainly have the right to take him to court. If it were me, I'd file the lawsuit, especially if your folks are willing to help with the cost. However, I'm not going to force you to do anything you don't feel comfortable doing, so let's wait and see what happens next. With any luck, now that he can no longer spy on you, he'll give up and move on. But if he doesn't, then your mother is right. You'll have to take him to court." It was time to steer the conversation to something more pleasant.

"So, have you had your dinner yet?"

"Nope."

"I didn't think so. So, why don't you go freshen up while I feed Lucy? I'll take you out for a nice dinner, and afterwards we might find a place with some live music. That should take you mind off things for a while."

She smiled and kissed him. "Sounds wonderful. I've been cooped up for days now."

He kissed her back. It was a long, passionate kiss. "I know you have, so why not have a change of scenery and sleep with me in the house tonight?"

Her faced beamed. "I'd love it. Just let me grab my nightgown."

He shook his head as a mischievous grin came over his face. "Sorry, but nightgowns aren't allowed in my bed."

"Shame on you, Shane MacLeod. In that case, at least let me change into my bathrobe before I come over. That way I won't have to walk across the backyard naked after you leave for work in the morning."

* * *

Shane took Rachel to a bar and grill which featured live music, and once they finished dinner, he took her out on the dance floor. Rachel was a good dancer, and during the slow dances he took in the sweet smell of her perfume as he held her body close to his. She seemed to be more at ease and even talked about how wonderful it felt to no longer have to look over her shoulder. The second set ended shortly after nine o'clock, and as the band stepped away to take their break, he told her it was time to leave. Once they returned home, she stepped away to the guesthouse while he put Lucy out in the backyard. She returned a few minutes later, clad only in her bathrobe. He led her to his bedroom, and within minutes her bathrobe was on the floor. Afterwards she looked him in the eye.

"Shane, why do you put up with me? I have so much baggage. Most guys would have simply said they were sorry and moved on."

He brushed the hair away from her face. "I'm not like most guys, because I happen to love you."

❧ TWENTY-TWO ❧

RACHEL ROLLED OVER and reached across the bed for Shane, but he wasn't there. Her eyes popped open and she heard the shower running. Of course Shane would be getting ready for work. She scooped her rumpled bathrobe off the floor, and as she stepped inside the kitchen the scent of freshly brewed coffee filled the air. She filled her mug and sat down at the table. Shane joined her as she poured her second cup.

"I'll have one of those as well."

"Coming right up." She handed him his mug with a smile. He took a sip and opened the refrigerator.

"Hope you like blueberry bagels," he said, "but I'm sorry to say I'm out of cream cheese."

"No problem. I'll just butter mine and pop it into the toaster oven."

He wrapped his arms around her and gave her a kiss. "Sounds delicious. I'll do the same."

He popped them into the toaster while she stepped away to freshen up. The bagels were on the table when she returned. She reached for the butter as he set a glass of orange juice next to her.

"So, what are your plans for today?" he asked.

"I have to take the morning off and go downtown. I need to get that restraining order taken care of as soon as possible, and I'm praying this time around the judge will grant it."

"Between Lamar's report, and Jonathan's report, I can't see why he wouldn't."

"I can't either, but stranger things have happened, and if he grants it, I'm going home. I honestly appreciate everything you've done for me, but having to run back and forth to get things from my file cabinet has been inconvenient, to say the least."

"Then we'll have to bring it over here. Tomorrow's Saturday, so we can take care of it then."

"I appreciate the thought," she said, firmly, "but no."

"What's the matter, Rachel?"

"Nothing's the matter. At least, not yet."

"So what are you saying?"

"I'm enjoying our time, together, Shane, I truly am. We've got a really good thing going here, and I want it to last. But I'm afraid our being in such close proximity to one another is just too big of a temptation for both of us, and we're moving way too fast. I want us to take things slow. I also have to catch Craig in the act, and the only way I can do it is by going home and calling the cops the next time I find him loitering around my house."

Shane suddenly looked sad. "I understand, and you're right. We won't catch him as long as you're here, but I still don't want you there by yourself. He's unstable. Who knows what he'll do next? So when you go home, I'd like to stay at your place, just in case he tries to do anything rash. I can always sleep on the sofa."

"And how tempting would that be? We're moving too fast, Shane. We need to step back and take a little breather. I promise I'll keep my doors and windows locked, but I want you to stay here."

"And what happens if you decide to go out some night? Yes, I know. Your front door is only a few feet from your carport, but it's not as secure as having—"

"It's okay," she said with a flirtatious grin. "The only time I go out at night is when I'm with you, and you always see me safely to my door."

He put on his sad puppy face. "Yeah, but then you'll slam it in my face and leave me out there to pine all night long."

"Maybe. Maybe not." She leaned forward and kissed him. "But for now, it's time for you to go to work, so off you go."

"Trying to get rid of me, are you?"

She tried to suppress a giggle but snickered in spite of herself. Her mood turned more serious after she swallowed the last of her juice. "I don't know how long it'll take to get this all done, so the sooner I get moving, the better. I still have a project to finish, and I hate to keep a client waiting. I'll see you this evening, and remember, Alice's dinner is tonight."

* * *

The downtown traffic was surprisingly light. The Fourth of July holiday was a week away, and it appeared as if many people had already left town. Rachel found plenty of empty spaces in the parking garage, and once her car was secure, she hurried to the court building. Passing through security, one of the guards directed her to where she needed to go to start her paperwork. To her relief, only one person stood in line ahead of her. She carefully filled out the form, but when she brought it back to the clerk, she was told she would have to come back after lunch to talk to the judge.

"Are you sure? I have to get back to the office."

"I understand," said the clerk, "but it's the soonest I can get you in. You need to be back here by one o'clock."

Rachel glanced at the clock on the wall. It was only a few minutes past ten. Even if she went straight home, she would only have an hour at most to get any work done before she would have to return downtown. If she were to run into unexpected traffic, or have trouble finding parking, she might miss her hearing altogether. It was too great of a risk, but with any luck, hers would be one of the first cases called, and she would still be able get home in time to complete all the changes her client wanted by five o'clock. She thanked the clerk and stepped away from the window.

The midmorning sun felt unseasonably hot as she exited the court building. She soon found refuge in a gourmet coffee shop a couple blocks away. After ordering herself an iced latte she sat down at a table by the window. Downtown Tucson was vibrant with its unique shops, restaurants, and theaters. Shane had mentioned wanting to take her downtown some night. She would have to remind him about it when he got home that night. Perhaps they could check out one of the trendy eateries over the weekend. Her latte was soon delivered, and she ordered a sandwich.

As she watched the people walking by, she took her iPad from her satchel and checked her email. A nervous Alice was fretting about what to wear that night. Several emails later her sister had the perfect outfit picked out. She exited her email app once her sandwich arrived, and afterwards went back online to catch up on other correspondence. Finally, she checked the time. It was nearly twelve thirty. She took care of her check and walked back to the court building.

Once again, she had to go through security, and the butterflies roiled in her stomach once she stepped into the elevator. They grew more intense as she entered the courtroom and took her seat in the gallery. A few other people were also waiting, but the judge hadn't yet arrived. She checked her watch. It was seven minutes to one. She nervously went through her satchel, once again making sure she had all her paperwork in order. The clock hardly moved, and as the minutes dragged on more people took their seats in the gallery. Finally, at three minutes past one, the judge, along with her clerk, entered the courtroom. Everyone was ordered to rise and be sworn in. As they took their seats the judge greeted everyone and quickly got down to business. The first three cases were called. All seemed to be routine matters, with most being granted continuances on whatever business they had with the court. The clerk then handed the judge the next folder.

"Bennett," she called. "Rachel Bennett."

Rachel's heart skipped a beat as she raised her hand. "Here, Your Honor."

The judge ordered her to come forward and take her seat at the plaintiff's table. She grabbed her satchel and cautiously approached. As she took her seat, the judge read her case out loud so it could be entered into the record.

"You're seeking an injunction against harassment from Craig Thomas Walker, is that correct?"

"Yes, Your Honor, it is."

"And why do you feel that Mr. Walker is harassing you?"

She reached into her satchel and pulled out her stack of papers. The judge's eyes popped with surprise.

"Mr. Walker is a former co-worker who's been stalking and harassing me for a number of years now. It all began when I got a promotion that he felt I didn't deserve." As she recounted the events, the judge interrupted her.

"Ms. Bennett, this all happened in Nevada, so why are you bringing it here?"

"Because we just found out that Mr. Walker has recently relocated to Tucson, and I've seen his truck driving past my house. I have the documentation right here. We also discovered that he hacked into my computer. I have that report with me as well." She went over the key points, handing the necessary documents to the clerk, who in turn handed them to the judge. She quickly looked them over, and then turned her gaze back to Rachel.

"Okay, I get the picture." She handed the documents back to her clerk, who motioned to Rachel to come up to the bench to pick them up. Her hands were shaking as she struggled to get them back in their proper places before putting them back in the satchel.

"I'm going to grant your injunction against harassment," said the judge. "You'll need to go downstairs and have the clerk finish the paperwork, and they'll give you instructions on how to have him served. Keep in mind, however, that Mr. Walker has the right to contest it, and should he decide he wants to contest it, we'll have to schedule a hearing and notify you by mail."

"I understand, and thank you, Your Honor." Rachel's body went limp with relief.

"You're welcome, and good luck." She called her next case and Rachel hurried to the elevator. Once the final paperwork was ready, she was given a list of process servers.

"Yes, I know the routine, thanks." She snatched up her copy of the paperwork and rushed out of the building.

The hot summer sun bore down on her as she made her way back to her car. It was nearly three o'clock by the time she arrived at Shane's guesthouse. After an enthusiastic greeting from Lucy, she made some phone calls. Fifteen minutes later she had a process server, and once she gave him her credit card number everything was ready to go. Craig would soon be served, and she'd be well on the way to ending an ugly chapter of her life. As she turned her attention to back to her computer, she felt as if a huge weight had finally been lifted off her shoulders. She took care of her client's changes with a newfound enthusiasm, sighing with relief as she completed his invoice and hit the send button. Once again she checked the time. It was a few minutes past five. She gave Lucy a quick hug and headed off the bathroom to get ready for her sister's engagement dinner. She and Shane had to be at the restaurant by six-thirty

∿TWENTY-THREE∿

LUCK APPEARED TO be on Craig's side. He had printed out a copy of the last message in Rachel's inbox before the software had quit working. It had come from her sister, confirming the time, date, and location of her engagement dinner.

He arrived at the restaurant an hour early, giving himself plenty of time to enjoy a meal before Rachel and her family arrived. He looked into the dining room as he stepped up to the hostess station. Once again, luck was on his side. A group of tables near the windows had been put together to accommodate a party of ten, and, for the moment, no other diners were seated nearby. He checked his watch. It was five-thirty-five. A young woman came up to greet him. He asked for a table for two, saying a friend would be joining him. She led him to a table in another part of the dining room, away from the large table.

"Actually, I prefer to sit by the window, near the back corner, if you don't mind." He pointed to an empty table near the larger one.

"Of course."

She led him to the other table. Taking his seat, she said his server would be there shortly. He had picked the perfect table. Not only was it close to where Rachel's party would be sitting, he also had an unobstructed view of the hostess station. When his server arrived, he ordered a beer and a chicken quesadilla appetizer.

The hostess returned as his beer was being delivered. Two black women followed her. One had a large, giftwrapped box, while the other carried a balloon bouquet with, "Happy Birthday," printed on the largest one. They set their items in the center of the big table and a third woman, also carrying a gift-wrapped box, arrived a minute later. As they took their seats, he overheard them discussing the guest of honor, a woman named Jada. Craig's heart sank. He had obviously spotted the wrong table and asking to be moved would be too awkward. For the time being, he would have to make the best of it. At least he still had a good view of the hostess station, and he would still be able to make his move once Rachel arrived. His server soon appeared with his appetizer, while two more women carrying gifts joined the group at Jada's table.

Craig dove into his quesadillas as the dining room quickly filled up. Jada soon arrived, along with the rest of her entourage, and the birthday party began in earnest. Craig quickly polished off his quesadillas, washing the last bite down with what was left of his beer. He checked his watch. It was a few minutes past six. The next time his server stopped by, he would ask for his check and then move to the bar. It would be the only place where Rachel and her family could be gathering. He glanced around the room, but his server was busy taking an order at another table. Several more minutes passed before he finally made his way over to check on Craig.

"Is there anything else I can get for you?"

"Just a check, please."

A puzzled look came over his face. "Is your friend still coming?"

"No, I'm afraid not. She just sent me a text message about an unexpected family emergency, so she had to cancel. I figure as long as I'm here, I may as well head over to the bar and see if there's a ballgame on TV."

"I understand, and I think the Diamondbacks are playing tonight. I'll bring you your check."

"Thank you, and can you tell me where the men's room is?"

The server pointed across the room, explaining that the restrooms were off to the side of a short hallway, just past the hostess station. Craig headed to the hostess station, and as he turned down the hallway toward the restrooms he saw a small, private dining room right next to the bar. He peeked inside, and once again, his heart sank. Two large tables had been set, each for about a dozen people, and some of the guests had already arrived. So this was where Rachel's sister would be having her party. His mind raced as he came out of the men's room. He needed to come up with another plan, and he had to do it quickly.

The check folder waited on his table when he returned to his seat. As he dropped his credit card inside a party of five entered the restaurant and approached the hostess. It included Rachel and Bill, the man he'd chatted with at the La Paloma bar a few months before. So much for Shane, she and Bill had obviously reconnected. A middle-aged couple and an elderly woman stood with them. The middle-aged woman was the same height and build as Rachel, but with chestnut colored hair. As they waited for the hostess, she glanced around the dining room. Craig's heart skipped a beat as she locked eyes with him, giving him a cold, hard look as she stepped between him and Rachel, blocking his view of her. No doubt she was Rachel's mother, and she seemed to know who he was. The hostess ushered the group down the hallway toward the private dining room. Rachel's mother maintained her position as they walked away.

* * *

Rachel greeted her sister with a warm hug as she stepped inside the dining room. "See Alice, I told you your little black dress would make you look like a knockout tonight. And those black stiletto sandals go with it perfectly."

"I know. It's just that Mom always used to say you're not supposed to start wearing black until August."

Rachel put her hands on her hips. "And while I mean no disrespect towards our mother, she isn't always right."

"What was that?" asked Julie.

"Nothing, Mom." Alice's face turned slightly pink as she tried to suppress a smile.

"We were just talking about Alice's outfit," said Rachel.

"It's perfect." Julie took her two daughters aside and spoke to them in a hushed voice.

"I don't want to create a scene, but we may have a problem."

"What's wrong?" asked a worried looking Alice.

"Craig Walker is here."

"What?" Rachel's startled voice carried across the room. Shane immediately snapped to attention. Julie reminded her to keep her voice down as Shane came over to join them.

"What's wrong?" He too looked worried.

"Craig Walker is here, in the restaurant." Julie kept her voice low. "I saw him as we came in. He's seated near a corner in the main dining room. Don't worry, I gave him a very strong look."

Rachel looked at Shane. "I thought you fixed my computer so he couldn't hack back into it anymore."

"I did." He sounded defensive. "And there's no way he could have. At least, there shouldn't have been."

"What do you mean?" asked Alice.

"Last Monday, while we were out shopping, Shane took a look at my computer," said Rachel.

"I know. I remember you saying something about that."

"Unfortunately, he discovered that someone had planted some spyware, and whoever it was has been reading my email. Of course, we all know who it was, and Shane took care of it, but now it looks like he's somehow found a way to hack back in."

"Wait a minute," said Alice. "I'm trying to remember when I sent everyone the email about where and when we'd be meeting tonight. Let me think…"

As her voice trailed off, a young blonde standing nearby grabbed her phone and pulled up her email. "I've got it," she said. "You sent it late Sunday night."

"That's right." Alice looked visibly relieved. "It was Sunday night. Thanks, Sara."

"Which means he would have read it either Sunday night or early Monday morning." Shane suddenly lit up. "Of course. The last time he'd gone into your email account was early Monday morning, before I'd started working on it."

"Then this should be the last time he shows up anywhere to harass her." Julie's voice sounded definitive. "So if he tries to pull anything tonight, we have plenty of witnesses." She looked at Rachel. "I don't want you to leave this room unless you have someone with you. And if you need to use the ladies room come get me and I'll go with you."

"Thanks, Mom."

"Have you found an attorney yet?"

"Not yet, but I went downtown today and got a restraining order. I've also made arrangements to have him served."

"How long will that take?"

"I don't know, Mom." Rachel suddenly felt pressured. "The process server told me he'd be going back to courthouse before the end of business today, so, with any luck, he's already picked up my paperwork. He said that once he has it, he'd serve Craig within the next few days. I've done all I can do for now. The rest is out of my hands."

"Which is all well and good," said Julie, "but you still need to sue the son of a bitch and make him pay for all the misery he's put you through."

Shane quickly came to Rachel's defense. "I understand how you feel, Mrs. Bennett. I feel the same way myself, but Rachel and I have already discussed this in length. She's concerned, and rightly so, about the time and expense of a lawsuit, so she wants to wait and see if the restraining order will be enough to convince him to move on."

"And what if it doesn't work and he continues harassing her? Her father and I have also offered to help with her legal expenses."

"I know you have, and we both appreciate it, but for now I have to agree with Rachel's decision. If Craig is wise, he'll disappear once he's served, and she'll never have to deal with him again. But if he doesn't, then yes; her next move would be to file the lawsuit."

"Sorry to interrupt." Alice motioned to the two men standing next to her. "I wanted to introduce you all to Matt."

"So, which one is which?" asked Sara. "I can't tell the two of you apart."

The two men were identical twins, although one was clean-shaven. His brother had a mustache and slightly longer hair. The mustached twin spoke up.

"I'm Matt."

"No, you're not," said his brother. "I'm Matt." He extended his hand to Sara. "Don't pay any attention to him. He always was a troublemaker. I'm the best man, and I'm told you're the maid of honor."

"Actually, that would be Rachel, Alice's sister." She tilted her head toward Rachel and Shane. "I'm Sara, and I'm a close friend of Alice's."

The two smiled and shook hands. Matt then introduced Emma, his wife, and Alice introduced everyone to her grandmother, also named Alice. More guests arrived, including Donny's parents and grandparents. Finally, Bruce walked up to one of the tables, tapping on the side of a glass with a spoon to get everyone's attention. Once the room quieted down, he announced it was time for everyone to take their seats. As the others found their places, he sat down between his wife and his mother, while Alice took her seat between her mother and Donny. Matt and Emma sat across the table from Donny and Alice, and Julie immediately turned her attention to Matt.

"So, Matt, are you a paramedic like your brother?"

"No, ma'am, I'm not. I'm an attorney."

"Really." Julie's face lit up. "So, what kind of law do you practice?"

"Mostly family law, but I also handle wills and trusts, and inheritance issues." He grinned at Donny and Alice. "And I do prenuptial agreements."

"I see," said Julie, "and while I normally don't mix business with pleasure, we may be in need of your services."

"Yes, Alice and Donny have told me about her sister having to deal with a stalker, and I also overheard your conversation when I came in. I have to agree with Rachel and Shane. He may very well cease and desist once he's served with the injunction. However, this type of case really isn't my specialty. My partner might be able to represent her, as she specializes in civil litigation, but it's up to Rachel to decide what she wants to do."

"Thank you." Rachel sat directly across the table from her mother. Her eyes fixated on Julie as she spoke.

"No doubt my mother will want one of your cards before you leave, but for now, if you all don't mind, I'd like to talk about something more pleasant, such as how the wedding plans are coming along."

The conversation steered to Alice and Donny's upcoming nuptials and two servers soon arrived with champagne. Once everyone's glass was filled, Donny stood from his chair.

"Well, we all know the reason why we're here tonight, and that's to make everything official, as if it wasn't official enough when Alice and I booked the La Corona for our wedding and reception." Everyone laughed as Donny reached into his pocket and took out a small, black velvet box. "However, she hasn't seen her ring yet, so, to make everything officially official, I have to ask this lady a very important question." He dropped down to one knee and looked up at Alice.

"Alice Nadine Bennett, will you do me the honor of being my wife?"

Alice nodded and replied with a heartfelt, "Yes."

Donny slipped the ring on her finger, and as he rose to his feet, Alice admired the ring and showed it off to her family. Rachel felt conflicting emotions as she looked at the ring. While she was genuinely happy for her sister, she also felt a twinge of envy she didn't quite understand.

"Penny for your thoughts," said Shane.

"I'm just happy for my baby sister."

"I know you are. I am too, but I can also tell when something's bothering you." He squeezed her hand. "I'm going to take a trip to the men's room, and while I'm out I'll take a quick look in the dining room. Hopefully, he's left by now. Then, when we get home tonight, I'm going to check your computer, just to be sure."

"Thanks, Shane. I don't know what I'd do without you. Sorry if I sounded huffy earlier."

He gave her a quick kiss and returned a short time later with a triumphant look on his face.

"Our unwanted guest has left the building," he said. "I didn't see him anywhere in the dining room or in the bar."

"Thank you for letting us know," said Julie. "Hopefully this will be the last we see of him until we go to court."

Rachel started to protest, but then backed down. It was neither the time nor the place for a family argument, but she would have to make a point of calling her mother and having a serious talk with her.

❧TWENTY-FOUR❧

CRAIG SEETHED IN quiet frustration as he signed his tab and put his credit card back in his wallet. So far as he knew, Rachel never had a photograph of him, but her mother certainly knew who he was. He clinched his teeth as he headed toward the door. Glancing over his shoulder, he took a quick glimpse inside the private dining room as he passed the hostess station. Rachel stood between her mother and Bill. All three had their backs to the door and were talking to several other people. No doubt the entire room would be soon alerted to his presence. All he could do now was make a hasty exit. He stomped his way across the parking lot and jumped into his truck, slamming the door so hard the window rattled. His teeth remained clenched as he fired up the engine and flipped on the air conditioning. Why did the stupid bitch have to tell her mother what he looked like?

As he waited for the inside of the truck to cool down, he realized he needed to cool down himself. He took a few deep breaths, and as his body relaxed he remembered; the magazine always printed his photo next to his byline. No doubt Rachel would have sent copies home to her mother, who, no doubt, would have told anyone who would listen to her about what a fabulous art director her daughter was. The thought turned his stomach, and he once again reminded himself to stay calm. He would have to wait for his client to pay him the six hundred dollars and fuming about it wouldn't make it come any faster. What mattered was that once he had the funds, he would contact Boris, and he would soon be back to hacking into her email accounts while she'd be none the wiser. He took a deep, relaxing breath and put the truck into gear. Driving out of the parking lot he remembered something else. He still had a printed copy of an earlier email with the date and location of Alice's wedding. He yawned as he turned onto the main road and headed home. He needed a nap before heading off to work. Tonight would be his final night working the graveyard shift. He looked forward to working regular hours again.

* * *

Craig punched his timecard and went into the lobby. Tom, who worked the evening shift, stood behind the counter.

"How's it going, Craig?"

"It's actually going pretty good."

"I hear you're starting the day shift on Monday."

"That's right. No more vampire hours for me."

"Good for you." Tom reached underneath the counter for his backpack and motorcycle helmet. "Well, I guess I'll see you then." He nodded toward a man sitting on a sofa in front of the lobby. "By the way, there's someone here who wants to talk to you."

Craig furrowed his brow. "Really?"

"Yeah. He must have a tip on a story or something. Anyway, I'm heading out, so you guys can talk. Have a good night."

"Thanks, Tom."

Tom left and Craig stepped up to the counter. He didn't recognize the man. Could word of his human smuggling story been leaked to the Border Patrol? He took a deep breath and hoped for the best.

"Can I help you?"

"Are you Craig Walker?"

"Yes, I'm Craig. What can I do for you?"

The man stepped up to the counter and handed Craig a sheet of paper. "You've been served."

Craig gave the paper a quick glance. It was a legal document. He looked up, but the man was already halfway out the door. He studied the paper more closely. It was an injunction against harassment, filed by Rachel Bennett and signed by a judge. As he read through it, a smile broke out across his face.

"So, you think you've won? Well, we'll just have to see about that, won't we?"

* * *

Shane kept a watchful eye out for a red pickup truck as Bruce, Julie, and Grandma Alice strolled across the parking lot with him and

Rachel. To his relief, he didn't see one, and as they stepped up to his car it was time to say goodnight.

"I mean it, Rachel." Her mother's voice was firm. "You need to get going on that lawsuit. The sooner, the better."

"We'll discuss it later, Mom." She turned to Bruce and her grandmother, giving both a hug and a kiss before slipping into the passenger seat. Shane closed the car door and she waved goodbye. As the others stepped away Shane got behind the wheel and fired up the engine.

"You okay?" he asked.

"I'm fine." A huge smile broke out across her face. "In fact, I'm more than fine. We foiled whatever he was up to. Mother even mentioned him sitting by a big table full of women. How much do you want to bet he got here before they did, thinking it would be our table? Thank goodness they put us in a private room. There was no way he could get to me in there." She paused for a moment as Shane drove toward the exit.

"I am, however, going to have to have a serious talk with my mother. You heard her. She won't let up about me filing that lawsuit, and I still have a bad feeling about it."

Shane turned onto the main road. "I know you keep saying that. What kind of a bad feeling are you getting? Are you worried about the cost? Or are you afraid you won't win?"

She shook her head. "Neither one. It's hard to explain. I just have this deep, foreboding fear that if I file this thing, it won't end well."

"So you're afraid you'll lose."

"I'm not sure. Maybe." She thought it over for a minute. "No, that's not it. I just have a very bad feeling that I'll be opening some sort of Pandora's box. I know it probably doesn't make sense."

"Actually, it does. Getting up in front of a judge is scary enough. Plus, you'd be going up against a bully who's not all there. The whole idea scares me as well, but for now, as you've been saying, we'll wait and see what happens with the restraining order. Maybe we'll get lucky and he'll decide it's not worth going to jail for and back off. He already had one night in jail, back in Reno, so he probably won't want to have another one."

"I hope so, Shane. I really hope so."

They remained quiet for the rest of the drive home. Once they arrived, Shane put Lucy in the backyard and changed into a t-shirt and a pair of shorts. A few minutes later he knocked on the guesthouse door. Rachel opened it and Lucy rushed inside, making herself at home on the bed.

"I'm beginning to think my dog loves you more than she loves me," he said with a grin.

"We are becoming gal pals."

"I thought so."

He reached into his pocket for his flash drive. Rachel nodded before she excused herself and stepped into the bathroom. He heard the shower running as he worked. The bathroom door opened a few minutes later, but he was still busy running a diagnostic. The bed creaked as she sat down on it.

"How's it going?" she asked.

"So far so good." His eyes remained on the screen as he talked. "Everything appears to be normal, and so far I'm not seeing any sign of any kind of malware."

"How long before you're done?"

"Not much longer. I just need a few more minutes."

She remained quiet as he continued working. Finally, he removed the flash drive and turned his chair to face her. She sat at the foot of her bed. Her bathrobe was loosely wrapped around her, and he could see her cleavage as she gave the dog a belly rub. He felt himself becoming aroused.

"Your computer is safe and secure. There's no sign of any malware."

"Thank goodness," she said as she smiled in relief. And Shane, once again, I'm so sorry for getting a little uptight with you at the restaurant. When Mother told me Craig was there, I got scared and angry."

"I see," he said as he kept his eyes on her chest. The dog rolled over, and as Rachel leaned over to pet her, he could see more of her breast. He suddenly felt like a hungry dog himself. He walked up to the bed, his eyes staring down at her chest.

"So, how sorry are you?"

She followed his gaze and looked down at her chest, giving him a coy grin. "I'm really, really sorry, Shane. More than I can possibly say."

"Really?"

"Yes, really." Her voice had a playful tone.

"Well, in that case, you'll have to apologize to me, again. And while you're thinking of what to say, I'll put Lucy outside." He opened the door and called the dog. Lucy leaped off the bed and ran out the door. Shane closed it behind her and sat down next to Rachel. Her robe remained loose.

"So, you'd better apologize to me again." He laid his head on her shoulder and patted her thigh.

"I'm so sorry, Shane, I truly am."

"Are you now?"

"Yes, I am. I'm really, truly sorry."

"So, how sorry are you?"

She chuckled. "More than I could possibly say."

He leaned over and kissed her. "That's kind of a vague answer. I think you need to apologize to me again."

Rachel tried to suppress her laugher. "I'm sorry Shane. I truly am."

"Keep talking." He kissed her again. "I can't hear you. Keep talking."

"I said I'm sorry, Shane, I'm really, really sorry."

He too tried to suppress his laughter as he shook his head. "I don't know. It didn't sound very sincere to me. I think you need to say it again."

She laughed as she spoke. "I'm sorry, Shane, and I mean it. I really do." She doubled up with laughter and lay back onto the bed.

"Now that's what I wanted to hear." He reached down and untied her robe. "Now say it again, only louder this time." He kissed her and she moaned.

"Louder. I want to hear it louder."

Once again, she tried to suppress her laughter. "Shane McLeod, I would like to sincerely apologize, and I deeply regret any inconvenience my actions may have caused you. However, it appears that a verbal apology simply may not be enough to satisfy you, so I'll apparently to have to show you just how deeply and sincerely sorry I am."

"Indeed, you will."

She giggled as he lay down next to her. After they made love, he held her in the afterglow.

"Apology accepted, Ms. Bennett, but don't let it happen again."

"I'll try not to, but I'm not making any promises."

"I see. Well, if you mess up again then I guess you'll just have to apologize to me again. And again and again and again and again." He kissed and squeezed her breasts.

"Stop that."

"What was that? How rude. Now you owe me another apology."

"Shane MacLeod, what am I going to do with you?"

He gave her a puppy dog look. "You're going to apologize to me."

"Later. Right now, I'm going to take another shower."

Shane sprang off the bed. "Good idea. I'm coming with you. We have to conserve water you know."

She sat up and reached for her bathrobe, but before she could grab it he kicked it away.

"You don't need that." He helped her off the bed, patting her bare fanny as she walked toward the bathroom.

"Something tells me I won't be getting much sleep tonight."

Shane shook his head in mock anger. "See, there you go being rude to me again. Tomorrow's Saturday, so we can both sleep in. Now you owe me two apologies."

Rachel let out an exaggerated groan as she stepped into the bathroom. Shane followed her inside and closed the door behind him.

❧TWENTY-FIVE❧

SOMETHING COLD KEPT poking against Rachel's arm, rousing her from her sleep. Opening her eyes, she found herself face-to-face with a dog, eagerly wagging her tail. She reached over and stroked Lucy's head.

"What's the matter?" She whispered softly, not wanting to disturb Shane. "Do you need to go outside?"

Lucy's tail thumped the bedpost as Rachel scooped her crumpled bathrobe from the floor. She tiptoed to the front door, opening it as quietly as she could while the dog rushed outside.

"I still say my dog loves you more than she loves me."

"Shane?"

His eyes were open, and he was smiling.

"I'm so sorry," said Rachel. "I didn't mean for her to wake you."

"It's okay. Lucy wakes me up most mornings. She's my four-legged alarm clock. I just wish she'd get the concept of weekends."

He patted on the mattress. Rachel came back to bed, dozing off as he cuddled next to her. The aroma of freshly brewed coffee woke her a second time. She opened her eyes and heard Shane scurrying around the kitchen. He stepped out with a steaming mug in his hand.

"Morning sleepy head."

"Morning." She sat up and yawned as he handed the mug to her. "What time is it anyway?"

"It's going on ten-thirty."

She instantly snapped to. "What? You're kidding. So why didn't you wake me?"

He stepped back into the kitchen to fill his own mug. "You were exhausted, and you needed your rest. Besides, I haven't been up too long either. Your phone beeped a few minutes ago, which is what woke me. I think you may have had a text message coming in."

He handed her phone to her and sat down next to her on the bed. A big smile broke out across her face as she looked through her messages.

"Craig Walker has been officially served."

"Really?"

"Yep." Rachel's face glowed as she spoke. "The process server sent me a message late last night. Craig was served around eleven o'clock. It must have come while we were in the shower."

Shane wrapped his arm around her shoulder and kissed her on the cheek. "Well, in that case, I think we should go out tonight and celebrate."

Her mood turned more serious as she looked him in the eye. "I'd like that, but first things first. I'm going home today."

Shane started to say something but stopped himself. "Yes, I know, and you're right. We have been moving too fast, and, as you keep saying, you need to be there to catch him in the act. However, I still worry about you, and I'll miss you."

"I'll miss you too, but it's not like I'm moving across the country. I'll only be only five minutes away." As Rachel turned her attention back to her phone a puzzled look came over her face. "Well, now, that's interesting."

"What's that?"

"The message that woke you came from Pilar. She wants me to call her, as soon as possible. She says she's just heard from Jacob's dad."

"She's the friend who's the single mother, right?"

"Yep. That's her. I'll send her a text to let her know I'll call her around noon, which will give me time to get my stuff packed and head back to my place."

"What about breakfast?"

She stopped for a moment. "Good question. All I have is a half a loaf of bread, and some peanut butter and strawberry jam."

Shane shook his head. "Nah, I don't want peanut butter and jelly. Tell you what. Why don't you get dressed? Then I'll help you load your stuff and we'll grab something to eat on the way to your place."

* * *

Pilar came over to Rachel's place that afternoon, arriving as Rachel finished folding a load of laundry. She greeted her friend with a hug and invited her to the kitchen.

"Can I fix you something to drink, Pilar?"

"Some iced tea would be great."

"I would if I could," said Rachel as she shook her head. "However, I've been away all week, so I haven't had the chance to make any sun tea."

Pilar perked up. "Really? So where have you been?"

"I was staying at Shane's?"

"Really."

Rachel gave her friend a look. "It's not what you think, girlfriend. I was actually staying in his guesthouse." She offered Pilar a glass of cranberry juice and brought her up to date.

"So yesterday I took the morning off to go downtown to get the restraining order, and this time the judge granted it."

"Sounds like you had more than enough evidence this time around."

"Between Lamar's report and Jonathan's report I certainly did. Craig was served late last night, which means it's now enforceable, which is why I'm back home. From here on out if I see him hanging around my street, I can call the cops, and he goes off to jail."

"Hopefully it won't come to that."

"Which is what we're all hoping too." Rachel noticed Pilar's glass was getting empty.

"Can I get you more cranberry juice?"

"Just a little, thanks, but not too much."

Rachel hopped off her stool and grabbed Pilar's glass.

"So, are you happy to be home?"

"You bet," said Rachel as she refilled the glass and set it back on the table. "I enjoyed my stay, but I had to keep running back and forth to get things from my file cabinet, and being in such close proximity to Shane had its challenges as well. We have a good thing going, but I don't want us moving too fast."

"I hear you."

"So, enough about me. What about you? You said you've heard from Jacob's dad. Is that right?"

Pilar nodded, but she didn't look happy.

"Well, don't keep me in suspense," said Rachel. "What happened?"

Pilar's eyes turned misty. "It happened out of the blue. Thursday night, the night before last, he sent me a friendship request on Facebook. At first, I was shocked, but then I realized I really should keep in contact with him, for Jacob's sake. So, I accepted his request, but I didn't stay on Facebook very long. Then, this morning, when I logged back in, I had a private message from Luis, Jacob's dad."

"So what did he have to say?'

Pilar took a deep breath. Her hands were trembling. "He said he'd looked through my photos and saw my pictures of Jacob, so he now knows Jacob is my son. He also said Jacob looks exactly like his youngest brother did when he was that age."

"Yeah, I've noticed he didn't bear much of a resemblance to you, so I assumed he took after his dad's side of the family."

Pilar nodded her head. "He does. He looks a lot like his dad."

"So, what did you tell him?"

"I've not responded yet. I'm not sure what to do."

Rachel looked her in the eye. "You tell him the truth. Yes, Jacob is his son, but you're doing just fine raising him on your own."

"I know."

"So did he offer you any kind of explanation as to why he acted the way he did when you learned you were pregnant?"

Pilar circled the rim of her glass with her finger. "Yes, he did. He admitted he'd started going out with me right after his girlfriend dumped him. Later on, she contacted him, wanting a second chance, and, unfortunately for me, it was about the same time I found out I was pregnant. He didn't want her knowing about the baby, which is why he wouldn't acknowledge being the father."

"Wow." Rachel was taken aback. "So, is he still with the old girlfriend?"

"Not anymore. He said they ended it for good about a year ago, and he's been wondering if I'd had the baby, so he finally looked me up on Facebook." Pilar let out a long sigh. "So, what do I tell him?"

"The truth, just like I said before. Yes, Jacob is his son, and he's doing fine."

"Which was my thinking as well. I'm just not sure if I'm ready to let him see Jacob."

"Unfortunately, he has rights, but let's not go there just yet. Maybe you might want to meet him somewhere for coffee, just the two of you, so you can find out what he wants."

Pilar nodded, and she seemed less tense and anxious. "Yeah, I was having the same thought. And if he wants to see Jacob, I want it to be a supervised visit. I was thinking that perhaps my mother could bring him."

"Good idea, and what about your sister-in-law? Might not hurt to have a backup, just in case something comes up and your mother can't do it."

"Gina? Hmm…I hadn't thought of her, but you're right. It's a good idea too. I guess I should ask her." She ran her fingers over her juice glass again. "Rachel, can I ask you a personal question?"

Rachel grinned. "Well, I suppose it depends on the question."

"How do you feel about your father? Not Bruce, but your real father? I mean, do you think he's an okay guy? Or do you resent him?"

"Well, to be honest, he's an okay guy. I didn't fully understand it all when I was younger, but once I became an adult, I got it." Rachel smiled at the memory. "Al is what you'd call a non-conformist. My mother started seeing him right after she'd broken up with a guy her parents were dead set on her marrying. Unfortunately, she just wasn't in love with him, and Al was everything the other guy wasn't. He rode motorcycles. He had tattoos and long hair and a beard. He didn't go to college and he worked in an auto body repair shop. Mom met him at a disco one night while she and her friends were having a girl's night out. She was on the rebound, Al has his charms, and one thing led to another, but their relationship didn't last long."

Pilar gave her a grin. "I'd say it lasted long enough."

Rachel chuckled and nodded in return. "It did indeed. Getting married wasn't an option for either of them, but to Al's credit, he never tried to pressure my mother into having an abortion. He loved kids and he was willing to go along with whatever she wanted. He also promised to help her out as best he could, and he was true to his word. Each month he sent her whatever he could, and he was in the delivery room when I was born. Mom also says he came to see me just about every weekend. Of course I was too young to remember, but once Bruce came on the scene things changed. They all agreed that Bruce would be a better dad for me, so after he and my mom got married, Al signed the papers allowing Bruce to legally adopt me. Even so, Al still came to see me from time to time, and he still sent me money for Christmas and my birthday, and he contributed whatever he could to my college fund. But then he moved to New Mexico, and he married a woman with a son from a prior marriage, who he ended up raising."

"Any half-siblings?"

"Just Alice. I've never met Michael, my stepbrother, in person, but I've always considered him a kindred spirit as our stepfathers raised us both. When we were kids, I used to write him letters and send him presents for his birthday and at Christmas. More recently, we were Facebook friends. He and Al are really close. He'd be about twenty-one by now, and Al thinks of him as his real son. He even adopted him, which just goes to show that sometimes life goes full circle."

Rachel stopped to think for a moment. "So if what you're asking me, is should you allow Luis to be a part of Jacob's life, then my answer would be yes, if it's at all possible. Jacob has the right to know his real father, and while I consider Bruce to be my father, I still love Al and I'm happy he's been a part of my life. And yes, he and I still keep in touch."

"So do you get your artistic talent from Al?"

"As a matter of fact, I do. He makes a good living painting custom graphics on hot rods and motorcycles, and he's had his own shop for years. My goal is to someday be just as successful as he is."

Pilar finished her cranberry juice and looked at her watch. Her mother was watching Jacob, and it was time for her to pick him up. Rachel walked her to the door and gave her a long, lingering hug before she stepped out.

"Thank you, Rachel, for your insight. I guess I'll have to just take it one step at a time and see what happens."

Pilar gave Rachel a final squeeze and stepped outside. Once she drove away, Rachel closed the door and went to her office. Taking her seat at her computer, she composed an email to Al, bringing him up to date on Craig, and letting him know she had taken out a restraining order. To her surprise, he responded an hour later. He too was emphatic that she file the lawsuit. He was also willing to help her with the costs.

❧TWENTY-SIX❧

CRAIG SPENT THE weekend adjusting to sleeping nights again, but he still felt out of sorts when he reported to work Monday morning. Working the day shift would, however, have its advantages. He would have the opportunity to meet other co-workers, some of whom were undocumented. It would also be easier for him spend his off time doing photography. While not a photographer by profession, Craig was, nonetheless, highly skilled with a camera, and he occasionally submitted his own photos with his stories. His series for the magazine was coming along nicely, and he included a number of unrecognizable photos of the people he had interviewed. The first article was now complete and would appear in the October issue.

The other item on his agenda was Rachel. He was still waiting to collect his six hundred dollars. While the client was good for the money, the purchase order had to be signed off by a number of people before a check could be issued. In the meantime, her injunction against harassment would have to be addressed. Craig's new work hours conflicted with the court's business hours, and he wouldn't have the opportunity to go to the courthouse until after the Fourth of July holiday. Then again, he liked the idea of Rachel being lulled into a false sense of security. However, for the time being, he would have to avoid her neighborhood.

* * *

The Fourth of July was always a quiet event in Tucson, and this year would be no exception. While there were plenty of fireworks shows around town, it was also the hottest time of the year, with many people fleeing the desert heat to spend their holiday in the cool, northern Arizona mountains or on a southern California beach. Shane, too, had wanted to spend the holiday in the mountains, but Rachel still worried they were moving too fast. She suggested postponing it until late September, right after Alice's wedding. Realizing she was right, Shane made reservations for a week's stay at a lodge in the picturesque town of Sedona. They would leave the morning after the wedding, and both looked forward to the trip.

They spent the holiday relaxing around Bruce and Julie's pool. Their annual Fourth of July bar-be-cue had become a family tradition. The new school year would start soon after, so the bar-be-cue was always their last big event of the summer. This year, however, Craig Walker would be the main topic of their poolside conversation.

"I've already told you, three times now, that Craig has been served." Everyone could hear the edginess in Rachel's voice.

"I know that," said an equally frustrated Julie, "but he's a bully, and right now you're letting him get away with it."

"No, I'm not."

"Yes, you are. That injunction, restraining order, whatever you want to call it, isn't much more than a piece of paper. You still need to file a lawsuit."

As Rachel and her mother argued back and forth, Alice looked at Donny and Shane and rolled her eyes.

"Trust me, Mother, I've been keeping an eye out, and I haven't seen his truck anywhere since he's been served. It's as if he's beamed back up to the mother ship."

"But an injunction doesn't last forever," her mother reminded her. "Who's to say he won't show up the day it expires."

Rachel wasn't giving in. "Then I'll have to file another one. Look, I know you mean well, and I love you for it, but I've been saying all along that I have a really bad feeling about filing this lawsuit, so let's just leave well enough alone, shall we? We've locked him out of my computer. Shane and Alice are monitoring his Facebook and Twitter pages, and he's not said a word about me on social media for some time now. I think we've finally turned a corner, so let's move on to some other equally stressful topics of conversation." She turned her attention to her sister.

"I got a letter in the mail a couple of days ago. The blue shoes I ordered for the wedding are on back order, but they assure me I'll have them no later than September fifteenth. I know we're cutting it close. So, just in case, I have a really nice pair of basic black pumps and I've only worn them a couple of times. Granted, it won't be quite the same look as it would with the blue shoes, but they'll still work as a backup pair.

And, with the exception of you, me, and Mom, no one will know the difference. So, what do you think?"

Alice thought it over. "Well, if you don't mind, I'd like to stop by, maybe tomorrow evening, after I get off work, and take a look."

"Of course."

"And if I'm not really thrilled with them, would you be okay with getting a pair of black ones in the same style as the blue?"

"Of course, assuming they still have a pair in my size."

* * *

Alice shook her head once she saw the shoes. "Don't get me wrong. They're perfect for a business meeting or a corporate event, but not for a maid of honor. You'll need something dressier. You're not upset with me, are you?"

Rachel shook her head and gave her sister a smile. "Are you kidding? Of course not. It's your wedding, and I want it to be perfect just as much as you do. Besides, I wasn't sure either, which is why I asked."

"Good to know. I just wanted to be sure you weren't just making conversation to steer Mom away from her 'you need to go file that lawsuit' tangent."

"I know. She means well, but it's my problem, and I'm the one who has to decide how to handle it."

Alice touched Rachel's forearm. "Actually, it is our problem too, because it affects the rest of us. We're all worried about you. I'm an emergency room nurse. I've had to treat real crime victims, up close and personal, and it's horrific. Oftentimes the person who harmed them started out by stalking them, and we don't want it happening to you."

A cold shiver ran down Rachel's spine. "Which is exactly why I have a bad feeling about going after him in court."

"You mentioned something about that yesterday. So what exactly do you mean?"

"It's hard to explain, but I'll try. It's one thing for me to take steps to protect myself, such as filing the injunction against him, but I also have this really bad feeling that if I push back too hard, he'll snap and take out his wrath on me. I've known for some time that he's not all there. Then, when Shane showed me Lamar's report and I learned about his upbringing; with his mother being a prostitute, and him spending his childhood in and out of foster care, it really scared me. No wonder he's the way he is."

"I understand, and I won't push you, but I really think you should at least consider it." Alice glanced at her watch. "Meantime, why don't we head back to the shoe store and see if they still have a pair of your shoes in black? Then we'll grab something to eat. I noticed there's an Italian place right across the parking lot."

"I know. Shane and I have gone there a few times, and their pizza is awesome."

Rachel and Alice headed out, only to find the black shoes were indeed sold out in Rachel's size. Fortunately, Alice found another pair in a similar style.

"Hang on to your receipt," said Alice as they left the store. "Then you can bring them back if the blue ones arrive in time."

"I know that, silly." Rachel rolled her eyes in mock exacerbation as they walked up to the car. "But they are really cute shoes, so I may decide to keep them after all. In the meantime, you're buying dinner to make up for my having to put up with you."

They soon arrived at the restaurant and Alice ordered a half-liter of wine. Once their server stepped away, she raised her glass. "Here's to my big sister finding the man of her dreams so we can start planning her wedding."

Rachel hesitated before clanging her glass on Alice's and taking a sip.

"You okay?" asked Alice.

"I'm fine."

"You know I meant it in a positive way."

Rachel gave her sister a reassuring look. "I know you did. I've just never thought of myself as the marrying kind."

"Why not?"

"I don't know," said Rachel with a shrug. "Maybe it's because I've been so wrapped up in my career."

"Maybe. Or is it because Mom didn't marry your father?"

"Mom and Al? Living happily ever after?" Rachel gave her sister a look. "I think not. It was just a rebound fling."

"I know. Mom told me. Many times. So do the circumstances of your birth make you feel less worthy? Because if they do, you need to get over it. You're here because you were meant to be here, and we all love you."

"I know you do. So does Al for that matter, and no, I'm not harboring any guilt because I'm the product of two people sharing a bottle of wine on a fateful Saturday night. It's because I'm more of a free spirit, like Al. I have nothing against anyone getting married and having a family. In fact, I'm all for marriage and kids. I just never imagined it for myself."

"But Al got married later on," said Alice.

"Yes, he did, but he was well into his thirties by then, and he was never out looking for a wife. As I recall the story, he met her when she brought her motorcycle to his shop, and from what Mom has told me about her, she's something of a free spirit herself."

"So, what about Shane?"

"Shane is an amazing guy all right." Rachel's face beamed with pride as she spoke. "And he's certainly a lot more than just another friend with benefits."

"Judging by your happy glow, I would say so."

"But just because he's the kind of guy I could have never imagined myself getting involved with, it doesn't mean I'll marry him."

"I understand, but it doesn't it mean you won't marry him either. I've seen the way he looks at you. He absolutely adores you."

"I know he does, but I also worry that we're moving too fast." Rachel picked up her wine and took a sip.

"A legitimate concern," said Alice, "but I don't really see it as being much of an issue. It looks to me like you're taking your time and enjoying the here and now. No one says you have to rush into marriage."

"I know, but he's already told me he wants to have kids someday."

"A lot of guys our age want to have a family someday. So what's the problem?"

Rachel shrugged again. "I'm not sure if I want kids nor not, so it could be a major obstacle down the road. Like I said, I'm a free spirit, just like Al."

Alice's phone beeped. She grabbed it from her purse and a smile came over her face. "Donny says to tell you hello, and he wants to know if you've called Matt's office yet."

"Well hello, Donny, and no, I haven't called anyone to discuss any lawsuit." The irritation grew in her voice. "You all need to give it a rest. If I decide to pursue it, Matt and Mom will be the first to know."

"Calm down." Alice's voice was firm. "He was simply asking, and I'll relay your message. In the meantime, we won't discuss it anymore."

"Sorry, Alice. I didn't mean to snap."

"It's okay. I understand. It's your decision, and you're right. We've been putting too much pressure on you. Especially Mom. So, for now, let's see how well the restraining order works. If we're lucky, he'll get the message and leave town, and then you can get on with your life."

❧TWENTY-SEVEN❧

ONE OF CRAIG'S foster parents used to warn him about being careful what you wished for, because it might come true. Lately, Craig had been wishing he had more time to take care of other matters, and, after the Fourth of July, the motel owner sent out a memo to the staff stating that due to slower than normal business, their hours would be cut. Craig would now be working one less day a week. Fortunately, he had picked up a few more freelance writing projects, including an article for a British travel magazine about ghost towns in western New Mexico. He planned on stopping by a used sporting goods store on his way home from work to see if he could find a good deal on camping equipment. He would have three consecutive days off the following week, and he planned to spend them camping in the New Mexico wilderness to take photographs and research his story. He would also stop by the courthouse on the way out of town and file the paperwork to contest Rachel's injunction against harassment. Once again, things seemed to be going his way. Hopefully, by the time he returned, he would have his six hundred dollars.

* * *

Rachel studied her reflection in the bedroom mirror after changing into yet another top. Shane would soon arrive to take her to his parent's house, but she still wasn't ready, and she couldn't understand why she felt so nervous. Perhaps it was because it would be the first time since high school when she would be meeting someone's parents.

Focusing on her refection, she let out another sigh. This time she had on the gauzy red blouse she wore the night she and Shane had made love for the first time, but instead of her short black leather skirt, she wore white pants and had no scarf tied around her waist. Overall her look was summery and not too suggestive, but she wondered if bright red would be too risqué for his folks. As she pondered about what to try on next the doorbell rang. As usual, Shane had arrived right on time.

"Nice outfit," he said as she opened the door.

"Are you sure it's okay? I don't want to wear something that's too—"

"It's fine." He stopped and gave her a quick kiss. "Truth be known, my parents lived together for about a year before they got married, and it was during a time when living together wasn't as acceptable as it is today, which means they're hardly prudes, so you can stop worrying."

"I know, but I still want to make a good first impression."

He gave her a reassuring smile. "Just be yourself and you'll be fine."

She quickly gathered up her purse, along with a shopping bag, and followed him out to his car. His parents lived close by, in a large bungalow near the country club.

"Nice house," she said as she stepped out of the car.

"Thanks. I was in junior high when they bought it. They keep saying they want to sell it and get a smaller place, but now that Dad's semiretired he's spending more time on the golf course, and it's practically within walking distance."

Rachel's stomach turned flip-flops as they walked up the driveway. An attractive blonde answered the door. She wore shorts with a tank top underneath a shear blouse. Rachel thought she might be Shane's sister, or perhaps a family friend. Her jaw dropped when Shane introduced her to his mother.

"Nice to meet you, Mrs. MacLeod."

"Likewise." She extended her hand gave Rachel a warm smile in return. "Shane's told us so much about you, so please, come on in."

Rachel cautiously stepped over the threshold as Shane followed close behind.

"Cute blouse," she said once Rachel came inside. "Red's my favorite color."

"Mine too," said Rachel as she handed her the bag. "I wanted to bring dessert, but as Shane may have already told you, I'm afraid I'm not much of a cook. I did, however, get some bakery cupcakes. They're yellow, with chocolate icing."

"Thank you, and don't worry. When I was your age, I wasn't much of a cook either." She led them to the kitchen and offered them some iced tea. As she handed them their glasses, Shane opened the sliding glass door and Rachel followed him outside. The backyard included a swimming pool and built-in grill, where his dad was busy cooking burgers. He and his son had the same red hair, although his was streaked with gray.

"Nice to meet you, Dr. MacLeod," said Rachel as Shane made the introductions.

"You too," he said with a warm smile. "Shane's told us a lot about you."

"Has he now?"

"Indeed he has," said another voice. Shane's mother had come out to join them, and she invited them to sit with her at the patio table. "Now that the sun's going down it's starting to cool off, so I thought it might be nice to dine out here, if it's okay with you kids."

"We'd love to." Shane turned on the outdoor lights and he and Rachel took their seats. Flames leapt into the air as Dr. MacLeod flipped the burgers.

"We did this all the time during the summer when I was a kid," said Shane. "Dad would grill burgers, and we'd eat by the pool."

"Assuming he didn't get called away on an unexpected emergency," said his mother. "It happened more often than you can imagine, but it goes with the territory of being a doctor's wife. Fortunately, my cooking skills improved greatly over time, and I got pretty good at taking over on the grill. Shane's a good griller as well."

Rachel immediately perked up. "He is?" She gave him a playful look. "So, what other hidden talents do you have that I don't know about?"

"You'll just have to wait and find out, won't you?"

Rachel had finally started to relax, and the conversation soon turned to stories of Shane's childhood. Before long the burgers were ready, so she offered to set table while Shane helped his mother bring out the side dishes. Shane's parents, Colin and Kelly, continued reminiscing over dinner.

"After I finished my residency in New Jersey, I accepted an invitation to join a practice here in Tucson," said Colin. "My specialty was sports medicine, so I jumped at the chance to return home, and this lovely lady sitting next to me was one of their nurses."

"Do you two still work together?" asked Rachel.

"Oh heavens no," said Kelly. "I took a job at another medical office once Colin and I started dating. Then when we had Katy, Shane's older sister, I quit nursing to become a full-time wife and mom. When Shane started high school, I thought about going back into nursing, but it's so different now, so I decided not to go back. I'd taken up yoga to get back in shape after Shane was born, and I was still doing it, so I ended up becoming a yoga instructor instead. It's a fun job, and I still teach it, but only part time now." She patted her husband's arm as she spoke. "Colin's cutting back on his hours as well as he plans to retire in about another year or so. After that, we plan on buying an rv and traveling around the country."

"Right after you sell the place, right, Mom?"

Kelly looked at Rachel. "See, no respect from my offspring. Typical, huh?" She turned back to Shane. "Actually, your dad and I have decided to sell the place to you. It's the perfect place for you to raise your own kids."

A jolt went through Rachel's body. She turned her attention back to her plate, wondering why everyone so fixated with the idea of her marrying Shane.

"One step at a time, Mom," said Shane. "Let's get Dad retired first. Then we'll see if you two really end up buying that RV."

As Rachel took a few sips of her iced tea, Kelly brought up something else.

"So, Rachel, Shane's been telling me that you've been having some sort of issue with an old boyfriend."

Rachel heard a slight tone of disapproval in Kelly's voice. She swallowed hard and carefully set her glass down. "He was never a boyfriend. He was a co-worker I once had, and, at the time, I considered him something of a mentor."

"I see. So, tell me about him."

"He had a live-in girlfriend, and we never saw one another outside the office." Rachel's voice was firm. "We simply took our coffee breaks together, and, as I said, I considered him a mentor. Then I got a promotion he felt I didn't deserve. That's when he turned on me."

"And why would he have done that?"

Rachel was quick with her response. "His girlfriend's niece had also applied for the job, and he thought she was more qualified than I was. And maybe she was, but she turned it down, so they offered it to me. Unfortunately, Craig, my former co-worker, didn't see it that way, and, for reasons I don't understand myself, he's been unable to let it go and move on."

Shane spoke up. "One of my old high school buddies, Lamar Northup, is now a private investigator in San Diego, so I had him look into it. It turns out Craig has some serious problems, stemming from his childhood, which Rachel was unaware of when she worked with him. Had she known then what we know now, she would have never befriended him in the first place. Unfortunately, people don't come with warning labels."

"I know that." Kelly sounded irritated. "I just don't want to see anyone getting hurt, that's all."

"It's okay, Mom. Rachel has it under control. She's taken out a restraining order against him, and her parents are willing to back her should she decide to take legal action. Hopefully, he'll move on, and it won't come to that."

Colin changed the subject and asked if anyone was ready for dessert. Kelly excused herself to go back to the kitchen, politely turning down Rachel's offer to help. She returned a few minutes later with fresh, strawberry shortcakes made from the cupcakes Rachel had brought. As they lingered over dessert, the conversation shifted back and forth between memories of Shane's childhood and discussions about his parent's future plans. Rachel remained quiet over the rest of the meal but offered to help with the cleanup.

"If you want to help clear the table, that's fine," said Kelly. "I can load the dishwasher later."

Once the table was cleared and the leftovers were put away, Shane took Rachel down the hall to show her his old bedroom. It still contained the furniture he grew up with, but a laptop sat at his desk, and a small file cabinet had been placed in the closet.

"Nowadays my folks use this room mostly as a home office," he said, "but, on occasion, it's also used as a guest room. Katy's kids stayed here the last time she came for a visit, but it's been a few years."

"So why are they keeping your old furniture?"

"Because if I ever have a son, it'll go in his room."

Rachel remained silent as they headed to the living room to join his parents. Shane had certainly put in a lot of thought about becoming a parent someday, and while she was becoming more attached to him, she still wasn't sure she if she wanted marriage and a family. She kept to herself as Shane and his parents chatted. When he finally looked in her direction, he gave her a concerned look.

"You okay? You've been awfully quiet."

"I'm just tired." She glanced at his parents as she stifled a yawn. "I've put in a long week. Shane's boss has been sending work my way, and it's kept me pretty busy."

Colin checked the time. "You know, it really is getting late, so why don't we call it a night?"

Rachel gathered up her purse and Shane's parents walked them out to their car, where all the goodnights were said. As they pulled away from the curb, Shane noticed the change in Rachel's mood.

"You okay?" he asked.

"I'm fine. I'm just a little tired. I really did put in a long week this week."

"I know you did, but you also seem a little upset."

She took a deep breach let out a long sigh. "I guess I got a little thrown when your mother referred to Craig as an old boyfriend. Trust me, I never, ever dated the man. I never so much as went out to lunch with him."

"I know you didn't, and I'm sorry it happened. Sometimes Mom gets wrapped up in her own stuff and she gets things mixed up. She also gets a little too overprotective at times, but believe me, she never meant any harm."

"I know she didn't, but you have no idea of how much people don't understand what I've been going through. They always assume it's somehow my fault because I somehow encouraged him, when I never did."

"I know you didn't, Rachel."

"And I'm glad you understand, because a lot of people don't. You wouldn't believe some of the stupid remarks people have said, such as, 'Well he obviously likes you, so why not give him a chance? You might even like him.' Uh, no, I don't think so. The thought of going out with him actually turns my stomach. Another time some woman said to me, 'Gee, I wish I had your problem. I can never get a man to give me a second look.' To which I wanted to respond by saying that perhaps she was too stupid to get anyone to notice her, but I was polite. I simply told her anytime she wanted to trade places it would be okay by me. Then there's the old standby, 'Boys will be boys,' excuse. Really? So does it mean that because he's a man, it's okay for him to stalk like me a predator and make my life a living hell? Give me a break."

"I know, Rachel, and I'm sorry. Believe me, I've been trying to help you as much as I can."

"I know you have, and I'm truly grateful for everything you've done for me. I'm just tired and stressed. I wanted so much to make a good impression on your folks, but once again, thanks to Craig Walker, I failed. Miserably."

"No, you didn't fail miserably. In fact, I could tell they liked you, Dad, especially. Trust me, I know the signs."

"Well, that's certainly a relief."

Rachel remained quiet for the rest of the ride. Shane pulled into her driveway a short time later.

"I'd like to stay overnight."

"I know, and normally, I'd say yes, but tonight I really am tired. Can we take a rain check?"

He gave her a disappointed look and she suddenly felt pangs of guilt.

"Are you sure you don't want me to stay?" he asked. "We don't have to do anything, you know."

"I know, but to be honest, Shane, sometimes the Craig stuff really does get to me, and right now I need a little time alone to sort through it." She gave his hand a squeeze. "But I still want you to know I had a good time, and I really did enjoy meeting your folks."

Shane still looked disappointed. "I understand, and they enjoyed meeting you too."

"Tell you what," said Rachel. "Let me sleep on it tonight, and by tomorrow morning I should be myself again. Why don't you stop by tomorrow evening? I'll fix dinner, and it'll be just the two of us. I really am trying to improve my cooking skills, and I have a new recipe I want to try, as long as you don't mind being a guinea pig."

"I'd love to, but I already have a prior commitment for tomorrow."

His comment caught her off guard. "Really?"

"Yeah," he said as he nodded. "Remember my old buddies, Rick and Marco?"

"Sure, I do."

"Well, as you and I have been getting closer, I haven't been spending as much time with them as I used to, so tomorrow we're doing a guy's night out and going to a sports bar for a pitcher of beer and a Diamondbacks game."

"I see." Now it was Rachel's turn to feel disappointed. "Well, that's okay. You need to spend some quality time with your other friends, and, now that I think about it, I really should call Pilar and find out the latest with Jacob's dad." She gave him a quick goodnight kiss and hopped out of the car. Shane stepped out as well, insisting on walking her to her door.

"Goodnight, Rachel." He gave her a final goodnight kiss and waited until she stepped inside. He still looked disappointed as she closed the door. She thought it over for a moment, realizing it would be okay for him to stay over it he wanted, but by the time she opened her door again Shane had already left. Rachel sighed as she closed the door and turned the lock.

❦TWENTY-EIGHT❦

RACHEL SCANNED THE room and spotted Pilar, who waved and motioned for her to come join her. "That's my friend over there, thanks," she said to the hostess. She walked up to the booth and Pilar hopped up to greet her with a hug.

"I've heard about this place," said Rachel, "but I haven't had a chance to try it yet."

"It's fabulous." Pilar returned to her seat and Rachel sat down across from her. "This is my third time here and I love it. Their burritos are out of this world, and their chimichangas are to die for."

"I think I'll pass on the deep fried." She looked the menu over. "Bad enough to be eating the Mexican food, but I think I can probably manage a green chili burrito, enchilada style."

"Oh come on, Rachel. You could stand to put a little meat on those bones. Most men don't like overly skinny women, you know. They actually prefer fuller figures."

Their chips and salsa arrived, and Pilar ordered margaritas. "I'm buying, because we're celebrating."

Rachel was intrigued. "Really? So, what are we celebrating?"

"I met Luis for coffee a few nights ago."

Rachel dipped her chip in the salsa. "You did? I've been wondering how it went."

"It went well. In fact, it went better than I could have hoped for. First, he apologized for the way he treated me before, and I could tell he really meant it. Then, once everything was out on the table, we had really a long talk. He honestly wants to be a part of Jacob's life, so I told him he could meet Jacob, and I'd have either my mother or my sister-in-law bring him, but he said no. He wanted me to bring him."

"Well, that's certainly encouraging. So, when will this be taking place?"

"It happened yesterday. Since it was Saturday, we decided to meet at the little park, the one with the playground, right around the corner from my house. Luis was already waiting on one of the benches when we arrived, and as soon as he saw Jacob, I could tell it was love at first sight. He picked him up and held him tight in his lap, and Rachel, he was crying."

"Wow."

Pilar's eyes were misty. "It was quite a moment all right."

"So what about Jacob? I know he can be a little shy around strangers."

"You know, that's the interesting part." Pilar stopped to dab her eyes with her napkin. "Jacob wasn't at all shy with Luis. It's like he somehow knew Luis was his daddy. He opened right up and started talking to him. Next thing I knew, Luis was pushing him on one of swings, and Jacob was laughing and having a really good time."

"I'm glad, Pilar, I really am, but at the risk of being a wet blanket, I have to ask. Will Luis take his responsibility as a parent? Is he willing to help you support your son?"

Pilar looked her in the eye. "You'd better believe he is. He has a good job, but I still have to consider his history and not take things at face value. This means I'll have to find a lawyer to draw up an agreement regarding visitation and child support and run it through the court."

"I know just the lawyer for you."

"Who?"

"My sister's soon to be brother-in-law."

"What was that?" Pilar chuckled and gave her a confused look.

"You're right, it did come out a little funny, didn't it?" Rachel reached into her bag for a pen and wrote the name down on the back of a business card.

"Alice's fiancé, Donny, has a brother, an identical twin, who's a family law attorney. His name is Matthew Wheeler. I don't know the number, but I can call Alice and get it for you."

"Thanks, but Alice probably has enough on her plate right now. I can Google it." Pilar gave Rachel a coy smile as she looked the card over. "Identical twin, huh?"

"I know where you're going, and no, I'm not interested in dating Donny's twin. Besides, Matt's already married to a lovely woman named Emma, and I've got a guy of my own."

"I know you do. I was thinking about myself."

Rachel immediately perked up. "What was that? Did I just hear you say you're interested in dating again?"

Pilar leaned back in her seat and gave her a smug grin. "You heard right. Now that Luis is finally going to take some parental responsibility, I think it's time for me to think about dating again, without the worry of anyone thinking I'm only interested in finding someone to play daddy to my son. Of course, it goes without saying that anyone I get serious with will have to love Jacob too, but for now, whenever Jacob is having quality time with his dad, it would be nice to go out and meet some new people."

Their margaritas arrived, and they placed their lunch orders. Once their server left, Pilar raised her glass. "So, here's to my son finally having his dad."

"Here, here. And here's to the new man who'll soon be coming into your life."

Pilar gave her a big smile. "I'll drink to that." Both took a sip, and once they set their glasses down she changed the subject.

"So, enough about me. What about you? How are things going with you and Shane?"

"They're good."

"So, you've been dating him for what, about four months now?"

Rachel nodded. "Our class reunion was last March, so you're right. It has been about four months."

"So, how is everything? I take it your seeing each other exclusively."

"As far as I know. I'm certainly not seeing anyone else, and somehow, I doubt Shane is either, although he and his buddies will be doing a guys' night out tonight, starting around five o'clock or so. They're all meeting at a bar to watch a Diamondbacks game."

"And you're okay with that?"

"Yeah." Rachel nodded again. "As long as we're having a girls' afternoon out, I really can't tell him no, can I?"

"No, you certainly can't, and later on, down the road, if you two end up living together or getting married, he'll still need to spend time with his buddies."

A slight frown came across Rachel's face as her body tensed up.

"Whoops," said Pilar. "Did I just say something wrong?"

"No, you didn't say anything wrong. At least, not intentionally. It's just that while I enjoy Shane's company, everyone seems to be going on the assumption that we'll get married someday, and I'm not sure I'm the marrying kind."

"Really? So why would you think that?"

Rachel sighed. "I'm not sure I even understand it myself. It's not that I don't enjoy male companionship, because I do. I've had a few boyfriends, if you want to call them that, over the years. I liked them as people and I genuinely enjoyed their company. I'll even admit the sex was great with them too. However, I was never in love with any of them. It's like I said. I honestly liked them, and we'd have a good time together, but then sooner or later one of us would decide it was time to move on, and that was that. Sure, I'd miss them for a while, but I was never really heartbroken."

Pilar looked surprised. "I see."

Rachel went on to explain. "Perhaps I'm a little different from most women. I'll admit I'm a free spirit, because I've never thought there was anything wrong with having sex with someone who I genuinely liked but wasn't in love with." Her voice was firm. "Granted, I've never believed in having one-night stands, but if I've taken the time to get to know someone, and I enjoy his company, then why not? If a man is having casual sex with a female friend no one gives it a second thought, so why should it be any different for a woman?"

Pilar didn't respond so Rachel continued her thought.

"Now, just so you know, I don't get sexually involved with every male friend I have. In fact, most of the time I don't. It's only with the ones whose company I really enjoy, and only after I've gotten to know them."

Pilar seemed unconvinced. "Well, maybe this is what you did in the past, but it certainly isn't the case this time around. You, of course, remember a day, not too long ago, when I had to all but drag you into that lingerie store because I wanted you to be ready, just in case something happened with Shane that night, but you were pretty hesitant."

Rachel shrugged. "Well, if I was, it was because I was self-conscious about having someone else pick out my naughty underwear for me."

Pilar chuckled and shook her head. "Nice try, but I'm not buying it. You were nervous about taking the next step with Shane."

"No, I wasn't." Rachel glanced around the room to make sure no one was in earshot. "If you must know, I did wear the red lace underwear that night, and Shane was most appreciative of it."

Once again, Pilar gave her a smug look. "Yeah, I figured he would be, but if Shane was just another guy, you wouldn't have been so nervous about it. Admit it Rachel, he's not like the others."

Rachel turned her attention to the nearly empty chip bowl. "I wonder if we can get them to bring us some more chips."

"Forget the chips." Pilar spoke in a firm voice as she pushed the bowl off to the side. "Our lunches will be out soon, and you're avoiding the subject. I'm nothing if not a good observer, and I've noticed a change in you. You're happy. In fact, you're glowing."

"It's because I've finally gotten Craig Walker out of my life for good. Who wouldn't be happy about that?"

Pilar nodded her head as she looked at Rachel more closely. "That's part of it, but there's more. I've also noticed the way you light up whenever you talk about Shane. Sure, you two started out as friends. Good friends. Which is a really good way to start a relationship, but he's become a whole lot more than just another, shall we say, convenient, friend."

"Okay, so what if he is," Rachel said grudgingly. "It still doesn't mean I'll marry the guy. Like I said, I'm not the marrying kind."

"I understand, and not everyone gets married these days, but mark my words, you two are destined to be together."

Rachel sighed in relief as their server interrupted them with fresh chips and salsa. When he left, she tried to change the subject, but she wasn't quick enough.

"C'mon, Rachel," said Pilar, firmly. "Stop lying to yourself. You're in love with the man. You just won't admit it."

Rachel became defensive. "So what if I am? It still doesn't mean I'm going to marry him, and I wish everyone would get off my case about it. As I said, I'm just not the marrying kind."

"And why is that?"

Rachel shrugged. "I don't know. I'm just not, and I never have been. I have nothing against marriage, but it's just not for me."

"Really? How interesting." Pilar leaned back in her seat once again. "You know, I've always had a knack for reading people, so here's what I think. I think you have issues with the fact that your parents, your biological parents, never married, and you feel abandoned by your real father."

Rachel tensed up once again. "No, I've never felt that way. Mom and Al were a mismatch. It would have never worked out between them."

"I understand, but Al didn't raise you, Bruce did. I know you love Bruce just like a real dad. You've told me that, many times, but it still doesn't change the fact that he's not your biological father. You've also told me that Al helped out whenever he could, but even so, you two have never had much of a relationship."

"No, we haven't," said Rachel. "It's because the three of them, Al, Bruce, and my mother, all agreed it would be best if Al kept his distance once Bruce adopted me. They didn't want me feeling confused about who my father was."

"Noble thoughts, and perhaps at the time they all thought it would be in your best interest, but it actually wasn't. It's left you feeling as though your father abandoned you, and you've carried this fear of abandonment into adulthood, which is why you see yourself as not being the marrying kind. It's also the reason why you have a long history of only getting involved with men you wouldn't or couldn't fall in love with." Pilar's words were making Rachel squirm.

"Really, Pilar, this is all psychobabble," said Rachel. "I know you mean well, and I appreciate your concern, but I've never thought of myself as being abandoned. I love Bruce, and I really do consider him to be my father. I'm just a free spirit. It's who I am."

"Rachel, it's okay," said Pilar as she looked her in the eye. "I know I'm not a shrink. I am, however, a single mother who's spent many a sleepless night worrying about how the impact of not having a father would affect my son. Jacob may only be two, but he'd already started asking questions about where his daddy was. Now my prayers have finally been answered, and I'm already seeing a change in Jacob. He's a little less shy and a little more sure of himself. He also wants to know when he can see his dad again. Rachel, you're human. There's no way you're not having Al around you when you were growing up didn't affect you, because it did. It's why you can't make a commitment, and Shane's the kind of guy who, sooner or later, is going to want a commitment."

"I know."

"So, what will you do when that time comes?"

Rachel shook her head. "I don't know. I honestly don't know."

"You don't want to lose him, do you?"

"Of course not."

Their lunches arrived. Rachel kept to herself until their server stepped away. Once he was gone, Pilar picked up her fork, but Rachel didn't feel like eating.

"Look, I didn't mean to get so heavy," said Pilar, "but you need to sort this thing out. You know what you could do, don't you?"

"What's that?"

"You could start reaching out to Al. I'll bet that once you build more of a bond with him, you won't be so worried about making a commitment to Shane."

Rachel sighed as she felt her body relax. She picked up her fork and sampled her food. "Wow, this really is good."

"Told you."

"I have to admit, though, that it's interesting how you brought Al up," said Rachel. "The other day, out of the blue, I sent Al an email to let him know what's been happening with Craig. Now he's jumped on the, 'you need to sue Craig Walker,' bandwagon. In fact, he sounded just like my mother. He's even offered to pay for it."

"See? This means he really does love you after all. So please, do him, and Shane, and especially yourself, a favor, and stay in touch with him."

❧TWENTY-NINE❧

CRAIG PARKED HIS truck in the garage and ran out to his mailbox. Sifting through the junk mail, he came across two important envelopes. The first was his long-anticipated, six-hundred-dollar check. The other came from the Pima County Justice Court. He grabbed his camera off the passenger seat, but the camping gear, along with his long overdue shower, would have to wait. He closed the garage door and hurried down the hall to his office. Switching on his laptop, he tore into the envelope from the court. His hearing to contest Rachel's injunction had been scheduled. He sat down at his desk, drumming his fingers as he waited for his computer finish booting up. Once it was ready, he entered the date and time on his calendar and placed a call to Boris. He didn't answer, so Craig left a message, stating that the magazine had finally approved the six-hundred-dollar expenditure and to please let him know where to send the payment. He whistled a happy tune as he unloaded his camping gear. Things were still going his way.

* * *

Rachel waved at the mailman as he drove away. Shuffling through the envelopes, she came across a letter from the Pima County Justice Court. Her heart skipped a beat. She rushed back inside, dropping the rest of the mail on the kitchen counter and opening the envelope. Her hands trembled as she unfolded the letter inside.

"Oh, crap," she said out loud. Her worst fear had come true. Craig Walker had contested her injunction against harassment, and a hearing had been scheduled for the first week in August.

"You stupid son of a bitch. You're just begging me to sue you, aren't you? Well, guess what? I'm more than happy to oblige." She flew down the hallway to her office and Googled Matt Wheeler. Clicking the link to his website, she took a deep breath and waited for the page to load. Once his phone number appeared on her screen, she placed her call. A minute later she was connected to his secretary.

"I know who you are," she said. "You're Alice's sister."

"Yes, I am."

"Matt said you might be calling, so I'm sending you over to Debra Armstrong. Matt may have told you about her. She's our senior partner, and she'll be more than happy to work with you. I'll connect you to Terri, her secretary, but before I go, is there anything else I can do for you?"

"Yes. Please thank Matt for me." Rachel waited for the call to transfer, and Terri soon came on the line.

"Matt told us a little about your case," she said, "but I'm afraid Ms. Armstrong isn't available at the moment. She's on another line and probably will be for some time. Can she call you back?"

"Of course." Rachel gave her the number and ended the call. Staring at the phone, she mulled over whom to call next, so she sent Shane a text message.

"Craig is contesting the injunction. Call me when you can."

Rachel took a deep breath and placed the next call. As she waited for it to connect, she prayed she wouldn't hear an, "I told you so." It was answered on the third ring.

"Hi, Mom. I hope I'm not interrupting anything important."

"No, not really. I'm just doing the usual stuff that has to be done before the next school year begins. So, what's up?"

"I just got a letter from the court. Craig Walker has contested my injunction, and a hearing has been set for the first week of August."

"Damn. I was afraid of that. Well, I know you tried your best to avoid it, but I'm afraid you don't have any choice now. You'll have to file that lawsuit."

"I know. I already called Matt's office and left a message with Debra, the partner he told us about. I'm waiting for her to call back."

"Well, in that case, I won't stay on the line too long. Do you need some money?"

"I might. Shane's boss has been sending work my way, but I doubt if I have enough to pay for more than a few hours of her time. And just so you know, the other day I emailed Al and told him about what's been going on. He's offered to pay as well."

"Really?" Julie sounded surprised. "Well then, I guess his business must be doing well."

"That's what he tells me." Rachel's phone beeped. "Okay, I have another call coming in."

"Call me later?"

"I will, and thanks, Mom." Rachel quickly disconnected and answered the incoming call.

"I just got your text," said Shane. "So what the hell happened?"

"I got a letter from the court today. Craig's contesting the injunction, and they've scheduled a hearing." She quickly filled him in on the details.

"I'll have to let Jonathan know I'm taking that afternoon off."

"You're coming with me?"

"Of course I'm coming with you. When I told you you're not in this alone, I meant it."

She sighed in relief. "Thank you, Shane. It means a lot."

"Did you call your mother yet?"

"Yes. She wasn't too pleased, as you can imagine."

"No doubt. So, does this mean you're going to file the lawsuit?"

"I'm afraid I have to. He's forced my hand." A shudder went through her as she spoke. She tried to shrug it off as stress, along with uncertainty, but was having a hard time convincing herself.

"I have to agree," said Shane. "You're making the right decision, but how do you feel about it?"

"Honestly? I'm scared, Shane. I still have a really bad feeling about it."

"I know you do, but it'll be okay. We're going to beat this guy, I promise, although he'll probably put up one hell of a fight along the way."

"No doubt he will."

"Why don't I stop by tonight on my way home from work?"

"I'd like that." Her phone beeped. "Shane, I have to go. I have another call. It might be the attorney."

"Okay, see you tonight."

They disconnected and Rachel answered the other call. Debra introduced herself and Rachel quickly got down to business, trying to sum things up as best she could. "But there's a whole lot more to it," she said. "In fact, it's pretty complicated."

"These things usually are," said Debra, "but it sounds like you've got a well-documented case, particularly over the past few months. Even if he's here for a legitimate reason, such as working on a story, he's still gone out of his way to harass you, and hacking into your email accounts is outrageous, not to mention illegal. I'd be happy to help you, Rachel, so let's set up a meeting at my office so we can get going on this thing. I'm sending you back to Terri. She handles all of my scheduling."

"Thanks, Ms. Armstrong. You don't know how grateful I am to finally find someone willing to help me."

"It'll be my pleasure, and please, call me Debra."

Rachel waited for the call to be transferred once they said their goodbyes and Terri picked up a minute later. Debra's first available appointment would be the following Monday.

"That's getting kind of close to the hearing for my injunction," said Rachel.

Terri made note of the date and time. "You'll be fine," she said. "Ms. Armstrong should have plenty of time to go over your file by then, and I'll be sure to schedule her to go with you to your hearing."

"She can do that?"

"She sure can. She's your attorney. That's her job." Terri asked Rachel a few questions as she finished setting up the file. Rachel held her breath as Terri told her what the retainer would be.

"Wow," she said. "I was expecting it to be a lot higher."

"You're in luck. Since you're one of Matt's in-laws, she's giving you a discount."

"Then please, tell her thank you. I can send part of it now, and I should have the balance in a few days."

They finished up their business and Rachel called her mother back. Thankfully, she and Bruce had the funds to pay off the remaining balance. As she thanked her mother, she made a mental note to call Al if any additional funds would be needed later. She would also make a point of paying them back. Her parents would refuse the money, but Rachel had something else in mind. Her mother loved sapphires. The next time she was out she'd stop by a jewelry store, pick out a nice sapphire bracelet or pendant, along with a gold watch for Bruce, and put both items on layaway. Her business really was picking up. With any luck she'd have them paid off in plenty of time for Christmas.

* * *

Boris replied to Craig's message two days later. He was to send the money through Western Union. Then, once the software was ready, he would mail him a flash drive. He ended his message with a reminder to send him a link to the magazine article, once it was published.

☙THIRTY☙

RACHEL FLUNG HER satchel over her shoulder and entered the building. Inside, she found a nicely furnished lobby with a clearly marked sign pointing to the elevators. Debra's office was on the sixteenth floor.

The suite for Armstrong, Redding and Wheeler was only a few yards from the elevators. A cheerful receptionist greeted her as she came through the door, offering her something to drink before ringing Debra's office. As she stepped away to get a bottle of water, another woman came into the reception area. She introduced herself as Terri, Debra's secretary.

"Did you have any trouble finding the place?"

"Not at all," said Rachel. "I know I'm a little early. I didn't want to take a chance on anything going wrong, you know, like being late because I got stuck in traffic."

"I understand, and don't worry about it. Ms. Armstrong will be more than happy to put these few extra minutes to good use."

The receptionist delivered Rachel's water and she followed Terri down the hall to a small conference room. A mature blonde, in a dark-gray, tailored dress, sat in one of the chairs. She looked up from her folder and extended her hand as she greeted Rachel with a warm smile. Once the introductions were made, Terri took her leave while Debra told her to take a seat.

"I've been going over Jonathan Fields' report. Outrageous doesn't even begin to describe it. He's an arrogant bully who needs to be dealt with."

A sense of relief came over Rachel. "You don't know how happy I am to hear this. I've been fighting this battle alone for a long time."

"I understand, but now you're in the right place, so let's see what we can do. For starters, Jonathan has done an excellent job documenting your case, and I'll be helping him through the legal hurdles so we can definitively prove that the computer and smart phone do indeed belong to Craig Walker. Please be aware this may take a little time, but once I have the final piece of the puzzle, we'll file your case. In the meantime, it looks like you've brought some other documents with you."

"I did indeed." Rachel opened her satchel and pulled out a thick stack of papers. "As you know, *Sierra Life* is no longer in business, so we unfortunately don't have access to Craig's personnel file. However, I documented as much as I possibly could at the time." She thumbed through her stack, pulling out a sheet of paper and handing it to Debra.

"This is a copy of the email Jennifer Aldrich, Diane Ingalls' niece, sent to the magazine, thanking them for the interview and letting them know she wasn't interested in the art director position."

Debra picked up the paper and gave it a closer look. "I see she referenced the date she interviewed, and the email was sent two days later. Had you accepted the job yet?"

"No. At the time they were still talking to other candidates, and I was one of the last to be interviewed. I was offered the job about ten days after Jennifer turned it down."

"Do you know how many others were interviewed?"

"I'm not sure. There were at least three, not including Jennifer and me."

"Giving them at least four other options, which means there was no guarantee they would have hired Jennifer in the first place, despite Mr. Walker's allegations." She looked at the stack of papers. "So, what else did you want me to look at?"

Rachel pulled a few more sheets of paper from her stack. "This is all of the email correspondence between me and Marie Baldwin, the production manager at Sierra Life, regarding Craig Walker. Marie was my supervisor, and I kept her informed about the more outrageous antics happening outside the office, such as Craig approaching the man I was dating in the men's room at a restaurant. As you can see, her response was always consistent. The magazine wasn't responsible for Craig's actions outside of the office and they weren't going to get involved. He was the best staff writer they had, and they weren't about to rock the boat."

Debra skimmed over the information Rachel had highlighted. "Interesting. She acknowledges him already being reprimanded for harassing you, and as far as she's concerned, the matter is closed. Are you still in contact with her?"

Rachel shook her head. "No. I've not seen or heard from her since our last day at the magazine."

"I see. Now just so you know, we may have to locate her should we need her as a witness."

"I understand." Rachel went through her stack again, this time taking out a large group of papers bound together with a heavy-duty paper clip.

"Here's all the email Craig sent to J. Duncan Advertising, up in Phoenix. I went to work for them as a graphic designer a few months after Sierra Life folded. At the time I started, they had an email directory on their website, which Craig took full advantage of. Not only was he sending me some pretty crass messages, he also sent nasty messages about me to all of the senior staff, including a few to Mr. Duncan himself. He was bound and determined to get me fired. At the time, I thought he'd somehow tracked me through social media. Now I know it was because he'd hacked into my email accounts."

"Wow." Debra raised her eyebrows as she looked the messages over. "He actually emailed the head of the company and accused him of having you as his mistress. Unbelievable."

"Tell me about it. It was so embarrassing when he called me into his office and I had to explain it, but at least he was sympathetic once he realized what was really happening."

"You were lucky. So what did they do about it?"

"They took the directory off the website and replaced it with a contact us form. Unfortunately, it didn't stop him. He made good use of the form. They eventually had to have their IT guy track down his IP address and block it from their email server."

Debra took some notes. "So how long did you stay with J. Duncan?"

"A little over three years. It was a great company to work for and I'd planned on staying until retirement, but they later decided to downsize and outsource, and they eliminated nearly all of the art department staff. I spent the next few months trying to find another position, but came up empty, and my savings was running out. I'm originally from Tucson, and my family still lives here, so my aunt offered to rent me a duplex at cost. So, I came home and start freelancing. I left J. Duncan on very good terms. In fact, they're outsourcing many of their projects to me."

Debra nodded as Rachel reached for another stack of papers.

"These are screen shots of all his attacks on Facebook and Twitter. At least, the ones I'm aware of. He'd set up a phony profile, often times as a woman, find out who my friends were, friend them, and then send me a friendship request. Next thing I knew, he'd start posting his rants. Again, I'm a slut, a whore, and someone who could only land a job if I slept with the boss. He also used his professional Facebook page as a platform for attacking me. I tried putting up a Facebook page for my design business, Matheson Studios. Matheson was my surname before my stepfather adopted me, and it was something Craig never knew, or so I thought. I never had my actual name, or my photo, on that page, and because I didn't know he was hacking into my email, I thought I was safe. He, of course, proved me wrong once he started posting malicious rants on my page. And when he wasn't attacking me on Facebook, he was posting malicious tweets about me all over Twitter and LinkedIn. I finally had to give up and close out all of my social media accounts."

"And because of that you've lost marketing tools for your design business, and a loss of potential clients along with them. It too will all be part of the damages we'll be seeking." Debra glanced at the satchel. "Has he harassed any of your freelance clients?"

"Possibly. A few have mentioned that after contacting me they started getting spam messages, allegedly from other designers, all claiming they could do the job for less money. A few admitted to replying to the emails, but they always bounced."

"Sounds to me like Mr. Walker is hell bent on ruining your business. Do you have any of those emails?"

Rachel shook her head. "No. None of them forwarded anything to me."

"Then we may have to contact them directly to find out more. Is there anything else?"

Rachel reached for the remaining papers. "I have a report from Lamar Northup. He's a private investigator in San Diego who's old friend of Shane, my significant other. Lamar identified the red pickup which keeps driving by my home as Craig Walker's truck. I also have a police report regarding an incident at the La Paloma Hotel last March. I was there for my ten-year high school reunion. In fact, it's where I met Shane, but unknown to me at the time, Craig was a guest at the hotel. As soon as he saw me walk through the door, he called the sheriff's office with some crazy story about me accosting him. Fortunately, we had a witness who was able to debunk his story."

Rachel handed the last bunch of papers to Debra, waiting anxiously as she looked them over.

"You've done an excellent job of documenting your case." She gave Rachel a reassuring smile. "And it certainly makes my job much easier."

Rachel sighed in relief. "Thank you for saying that, and believe me when I tell you there've been times when I thought about dumping it all the trash, because I honestly felt that hanging on to it was a complete waste of time. I'd go to the police. No one would help me. They all told me it was a civil matter, and I couldn't even get a restraining order against him back when I was in Reno."

"Good thing you've brought that up." Debra reached into her folder for some of her own papers. "I have the information about the hearing contesting your injunction against harassment. I'll be representing you, and, if we're able to get everything done in time on my end, we'll have him served for the civil case when he leaves the courtroom. Because these events happened in multiple jurisdictions, and because he violated federal law, we'll be taking it to federal court."

"I see, but what if you're not ready to have him served?"

"It won't be a problem at all. I work with Hank Witherspoon, your process server, all the time. Since Hank's already served him once at the motel, he can drop by a second time."

Rachel finally smiled. "And I can just imagine the look on his face when he sees Hank walk through the door."

Debra gathered up all the papers and stood from her chair. "Please understand this will all take some time, but I think you have a very winnable case, and I have every reason to believe the court will rule in your favor. I'll start working on it this afternoon. In the meantime, Shane fixed your computer and your injunction is still in place, so don't let him get you down."

"At least it's in place for now."

"And with all the documentation you have, the odds of it remaining in place are still in your favor. Meantime, Matt is in his office. Would you like for Terri to buzz his secretary and ask if you can stop by and tell him hello before you leave?"

"Thanks, Debra. I'd like that."

⧽THIRTY-ONE⧼

MATT GREETED RACHEL with a warm handshake and an offer to take her to lunch.

"I appreciate it," she said, "but it's really not necessary."

"Oh c'mon, Rachel. Not only are you a client, you're about to become my sister-in-law, once removed, or something to that effect, so I'm buying you lunch. There's a little soup and sandwich deli down on the ground floor that serves the best chicken salad sandwich in town, and I know Emma would love to say hello to you as well. She's an assistant with another law firm down on the fifth floor, so she can meet us there."

"Well, if you're going to twist my arm…"

He picked up his phone and called his wife, telling her to meet them downstairs. Rachel followed him to the elevators, and once the door opened on the ground floor, he led her to the sandwich shop. Emma arrived as their sandwiches were being delivered.

"Nice to see you again," she said to Rachel as she sat down to join them. "I take it you met with Debra today."

"I did indeed. I've tried my best to avoid this, but the other day I got a letter from the justice court. Craig is contesting the injunction, so I don't I have a choice now."

"No, you really don't," said Matt, "but trust me, you're in very capable hands."

"I agree," said Rachel. "I like Debra. She really made me feel at ease, and she tells me I have a winnable case. Hearing that was such a relief. I've been dealing with this on my own for far too long."

"Then I'm glad I was able to help."

Emma changed the subject. "So, Rachel, how are the wedding plans coming along?"

"So far as I know, they're coming along fine. The invitations have all been mailed, and apparently most of the guests responded right away. The last time I spoke to Alice, she said fifty-seven have confirmed they're coming, with one waiting to see if she can get the night off work. About the only noes we're getting are from extended family out of state."

"Sixty or so would be a nice size," said Emma. "It's about how many came to our wedding. It was just enough for a fun party at the reception, but not so big that it felt like a circus."

"Exactly. We should have just enough people to fill the room. She's booked a DJ, so we'll have dancing. She's also keeping the menu fairly simple, and we'll of course have a wedding cake."

"Good to know, and her bridal shower is this coming Saturday, correct?"

"Yes, it is," said Rachel. "Are you coming?"

"Of course."

"She's registered at Macy's, and I'm afraid I've been such a bad sister. I've been so busy lately I simply haven't had the time to get her a gift, so this afternoon I'll order something online and have them giftwrap it, then I can pick it up on the way to the shower. I looked at her registry the other night and noticed she hadn't picked out any china or crystal. I hear a lot of brides are skipping it these days, so I picked out a set of towels."

"Then I guess you didn't know."

Rachel suddenly looked confused. "Know what?"

"Your grandmother Alice is giving your sister all of her china and crystal, along with all of her sterling flatware."

Rachel was dumbfounded, but she tried to keep her shock to herself. "Really? I just assumed she'd pass all that stuff down to Aunt Laurie, as she's her only daughter."

Emma shook her head. "No. I spoke to Alice the day before yesterday. She said her grandmother told her that with your grandfather being gone now, she won't be doing the big holiday dinners anymore, so she wanted Alice to have all of it."

A server arrived with Emma's soup while Rachel tried to take it all in. She had always had the feeling her grandmother favored Alice over her, but her mother always insisted it was her imagination. She picked up her fork, and as she tasted her salad, she reminisced about the big holiday dinners at her grandmother's house while she was growing up. Grandma Alice had been so proud of her china and crystal, but if Aunt Laurie didn't want it, then why would she give the entire lot to Alice without at least offering part of it to her? It was yet another reminder that she wasn't a full-fledged granddaughter.

"Is everything alright?" said Emma.

Rachel brushed it off. "I'm fine. I was just thinking about my case."

"And you're in the best of hands," said Matt. He then thanked her for referring Pilar, saying he was helping her with the legal paperwork regarding her son and his father.

"She's been a lovely woman to work with," he said

"She's been a good friend to me as well," said Rachel. "I'm glad you were able to help her. It's not easy being a single mother."

The conversation soon steered back to the wedding, but Rachel's heart was no longer in it. She was still in shock over her grandmother's lavish gift to her sister, and her decision to not include her in any part of a family heirloom. Hopefully it was because Grandma Alice simply thought she wouldn't want it. As she finished the last bite of her sandwich she glanced at her watch.

"Hey, guys, it's been fun, and Matt, thank you so much for the lunch, but I really do need to get back to work. I promised my client I'd have his project done by Friday."

* * *

As promised, Shane stopped by on his way home from work. "You seem a little down," he said as he took his seat at the bistro table. "Did everything go okay with the attorney?"

"Actually, the meeting went well. I like Debra. She says I have good chance of winning, and she has a good track record, but I still can't shake this dark, foreboding that nothing good will come from this."

"It's probably just nerves. As we've discussed before, Craig's a bully, and he won't give up without a fight, but I'm in your corner, and so are your folks."

"I know."

Shane's brows furrowed. "But I can see that something else is bothering you. So what is it?"

"Nothing really. Just silly woman stuff." Rachel glanced down at the empty table. "Besides, I'm being a terrible hostess. Here you are, coming in out of the hot sun, and I haven't even offered you anything to drink."

"I'm fine, and I can't stay too long. I have to go walk Lucy, but I'll tell you what. Why don't you stop by my place, in about a half an hour or so? I'll order some pizza, and maybe we can watch a movie."

"I'd like that," said Rachel with a smile, "and while you're out dog walking, I'll make a run to the store and grab some ice cream for dessert. As long as we're wrecking our diets, we may as well go all the way."

Shane wrapped his arm around her waist, giving her middle a pinch. "Funny, I don't feel anything fat. In fact, a few pounds on you would be incredibly sexy."

"Now you're making me blush," she said as she playfully shooed him away. "Go walk your dog. I'll be over with the ice cream in about thirty minutes. Got any chocolate sauce to go with it?"

"I'm not sure, but bring some, just in case." He stopped to give her a passionate kiss. "I can think of a lot of things that go well with chocolate sauce, and oddly enough, none of them are ice cream."

Rachel laughed. "Shane MacLeod. You are such a naughty boy."

"I know." He gave her a smirk as he slipped off his bistro chair and kissed her again. "See you in a bit."

* * *

Rachel arrived at Shane's house thirty minutes later. As he opened the door, Lucy greeted her with a bark and a wagging tail.

"I still say my dog loves you more than she loves me," he said with mock exasperation.

"And as I've already told you, she and I are gal pals." Rachel presented him with her grocery bag. "Here, and I hope you like chocolate."

"My favorite."

He gave her a quick kiss before she put the ice cream in the freezer. Their pizzas arrived a short time later, but over the meal Shane noticed she still seemed a little distant. He reached across the table and patted her hand.

"Are you okay?" he asked. "I noticed you've been kind of quiet."

"I'm fine."

"Worried about your case?"

"A little."

He wanted to reassure her. "It'll be fine. I know you keep saying you have a bad feeling about it, but like I said before, you're just nervous, and who wouldn't be? Honestly, Craig scares me too, but we'll all be with you, and we won't let anything happen to you."

"I know, and I love you all for it."

"Good to know. So, what else is bothering you? You said something before about it being just some silly woman stuff, but I can tell it really is upsetting you. So, what is it?"

Rachel took a deep breath and sighed. "After my meeting with Debra, Matt took me to lunch, and Emma joined us. We talked about Alice's wedding, and during our conversation I found out my grandmother will be giving all her china, crystal, and sterling flatware, to Alice. It's a family heirloom, but no part of it was offered to me, and I can't help but wonder if it's because I'm really not her granddaughter."

"I see." Shane thought it over for a moment. "Have you talked to your grandmother? Maybe she didn't think you'd be interested."

"I thought about calling her to just say hi, and then seeing if she says anything about it, but even if she did, it's still a done deal. And if I were to bring it up, she might think I'm being jealous or resentful, and she may hold it against me."

"I'm sorry, Rachel."

"Yeah, me too. I was three years old when my mother married Bruce, and some of my earliest memories were of me being daddy's little girl." She smiled for a moment. "Al was still around, and for a time I thought I was really lucky, because I didn't have just one dad. I had two." Her smile slowly faded.

"I was five when Alice was born, and it was never the same after that. Don't get me wrong. I love my sister, but kids can sense things. Alice was Bruce's real daughter, and he had a bond with her that he never had with me. It was the same with Grandma Alice. She was never unkind to me, but she was never overly warm or affectionate with me either. But with Alice, her namesake, it was different. Alice always got the bigger slice of cake, and the fancier toy, and the prettier dress." She sighed as her eyes turned misty.

"Maybe she wasn't aware of what she was doing, or if she was, she probably didn't think I'd notice, but I did. So now it continues. Alice gets the entire lot. There was never any family discussion about this, or if there was, I certainly wasn't included. I know I probably sound like I'm whining, but it's really not about the china. It's about the bigger picture. I've never felt like I belonged with the rest of the family. I was the bastard child, and I've always been an outsider. This is why I took the job in Reno when I finished college. I wanted to be someplace where I felt like I belonged, and we all know what happened next."

"I know." Shane reached over and squeezed her hand. "So, what about your other grandparents? On your mother's side of the family."

"They were even worse."

"Really? How so?"

"My mother was born and raised in Indiana, and she came to Tucson to attend the U of A. She was an only child, and both of her parents were extremely strict. They sent her off to college so she could become a teacher, but they also expected her to find a suitable husband while she was there. But when she broke up with the boy they wanted her to marry, had her fling with Al, and ended up with me, they nearly lost their minds."

"I'll bet."

"I can remember us taking a few family trips to Indiana to see my grandparents. They were always cool toward me, but more open and affectionate with Alice. Not much, but enough for me to notice the difference. They came Arizona a few times too, and it was always the same. They never paid much attention to me, but they'd spend some quality time with Alice. My grandmother passed away when I was fifteen, and my grandfather now lives in an assisted living facility in Indianapolis. I haven't spoken to him in years, although he responded to Alice's wedding invitation. He's unable to attend, but sent a gift, and that, as they say, is that."

Shane looked genuinely sad. "I'm sorry, Rachel. I thought you had a good home life. I didn't realize they treated you like a second-class citizen."

"It's not as bad as it sounds. They still love me, and it was never that obvious. In fact, it was so subtle that the only one who really noticed it was me. Then, later on, Alice noticed it too. Sometimes I'm amazed she and I are as close as we are, all things considered. I think it's because she's a caring, compassionate person by nature, and, deep down, I also think she feels a little guilty about it, even though none of it was her fault. Unfortunately, it is what it is, and I guess we've learned to live with it, even though hurts."

⮞THIRTY-TWO⮜

SOMETHING WAS happening at the motel, and it had all of the staff on edge. Room one seventeen, where the shooting had occurred a few weeks before, had been completely renovated. However, Eddie Ravenwood, the motel owner, had given strict orders that under no circumstances was the room to be rented out. Eddie had started wearing more businesslike attire, and he had been seen walking people in business suits around the property a number of times. He and his visitors also spent considerable time in room one seventeen, but so far, he had offered no explanation to his staff. Word amongst the employees was that he would soon be putting the motel up for sale, but so far it was only rumor and speculation. Craig was finishing up a check out when he heard someone walk up behind him. It was his boss, who had a serious look on his face.

"Craig? Would you mind coming into my office for a few minutes? I need to talk to you about something."

Craig's chest tightened. No doubt whatever Eddie had to say wouldn't be good. He gave the other desk clerk a quick glance.

"Don't worry," said Eddie. "Rick can take care of things while we talk."

As they stepped into the office, Eddie closed the door and pointed to the chair in front of his desk. "So, Craig, I understand you're also a writer," he said as he took his seat.

"Yes sir, I am." Craig's breaths grew shorter as he squirmed in his chair.

"And I understand you've been working on an article for a magazine."

"Yes, sir, I have. I'm currently working on a series of articles for a national publication, but I've signed a nondisclosure agreement, so I'm afraid I'm not at liberty to mention the name or discuss any of the other details."

"I understand, and I didn't bring you in here to talk about your other job. My concern is this motel, and I take it you've been working here as a second job."

Craig cleared his throat. "Yes, I have. Unfortunately, in this day and age, it can be difficult for freelance journalists to support themselves entirely on their writing, and—"

"It's okay. You don't need to explain. So, after the shooting we had here a few weeks ago, I realized I needed to make some serious decisions about the future of this property. Did I want to continue being a slumlord, have more drugs and shootings, and risk being shut down by the city? Or did I want to turn the place into a more upscale, family-friendly hotel, and make it a business I'd be proud to pass on to my two daughters someday? Over the past few years the city has been doing a lot downtown revitalization, and we're only minutes away from the heart of it."

Craig felt his body relax. Perhaps he wasn't going to be fired after all.

"Therefore," said Eddie, "after much thought, I've decided to redo the place from top to bottom, and I've been busy getting the project financed. As soon as the funds become available, we'll begin the redoing with the front office." He clicked on his mouse and turned the monitor so Craig could see the architectural renderings.

"We'll remain open for business during the renovation. However, we'll be marketing to an entirely different clientele; tourists, families, convention attendees, and businesspeople. So, as of today, we're cracking down on the hookers and the drugs and all of the problems associated with them. I've already spoken to the Tucson police. They'll be increasing their patrol of the area, and this afternoon I'll send a memo the staff instructing them to call nine-one-one immediately if they see any kind of illegal activity happening on the premises. There will be no more looking the other way, and anyone who does will be terminated."

"I understand," said Craig.

"I'm glad you do, because I'm also making some staff changes. You're a good worker, Craig. In fact, you're one of the best I've had in a long time. Would you be interested in becoming a manager?"

Craig sighed. It wasn't what he expected to hear. "Under other circumstances, Eddie, I would have jumped at the opportunity. However, I only came to Tucson to work on the articles I mentioned before. It was never my intention to relocate here permanently. I'm returning to Sacramento next month, and I've already given notice to my landlady. I'm leaving around September fifteenth, and I planned on giving you my notice at the end of the month."

Eddie frowned with disappointment. "I see. So is there any way I can talk you out of it? If your landlady has already found another tenant, I'd be happy to put you up in a room here until you can find another place."

"I'm flattered, sir, I really am, but I'm a journalist, and there are much better opportunities for me in California. A small publishing company in Sacramento has offered me a position, and I've already accepted the job. I start the first of October."

"I see." A disappointed Eddie stood from his desk and extended his hand. "Well, in that case, I'm sorry to lose you, but I wish you the best of luck with your new job. So, how much longer will you be here?"

"Long enough for you to find my replacement," said Craig.

The two men shook hands, and Craig returned to the front desk. He assured Rick he hadn't been fired but had instead given his notice and would be leaving soon. He smiled to himself as he talked. He had made up the story about the publishing company on the fly, but it sounded convincing, so he repeated it to Rick.

* * *

Craig drummed his fingers on the steering wheel as he waited for the garage door to open. Once it finally rolled up, he parked his truck and walked out to the curb to check the mail. Inside his mailbox was a small, bubble-wrap envelope. It had a Placerville, California postmark, but no return address. Pressing his fingers along the envelope, he felt a small lump, about the size of a flash drive. His long-awaited package had finally arrived. A sense of euphoria swept over him and he hurried inside the house, rushing down the hall to his computer. He tore into the envelope and reached inside for the flash drive, holding it in his fingers and smiling from ear to ear as he waited for his computer to boot up. He was about to put in the port when he remembered he had two deadlines. The second article for *The American Chronicles* was due, along with the article for the British travel magazine.

"It's business before pleasure, my pet," he said out loud as he carefully set the drive down on his desk and opened up a Word file. Two hours later the final revisions were complete and both articles had been emailed to their respective publications. He took a short break to grab a cold beer from the refrigerator. Popping the can open, he prepared his invoices. Five minutes later he hit the send button. Both projects were officially complete.

Taking a deep breath, he slid in the flash drive, and took another sip of beer as the icon appeared on his desktop. He clicked on it and a window opened. The words, "click here to start," appeared underneath a skull and crossbones icon. He chuckled as he clicked on the icon and took a few more swallows of beer. Boris still had his twisted sense of humor.

The screen suddenly went black. He heard a static-like sound, and the screen flickered until an animated skull and cross bones appeared. The jaw moved up and down, and through the static he heard a distorted voice, speaking with a Russian accent.

"I told you, Walker. I'm no longer in this line of work, but you just wouldn't listen, so I guess I'll have to explain it to you another way. Your hard drive is now history, and you really should have hung onto your six hundred dollars, because you need a new computer. Hasta la vista, baby!" The skull laughed a wicked, deep-pitched laugh as the screen flickered a few more times before going black and silent.

A stunned Craig stared at the screen, unable to believe what he had just seen. It had to have been some sort of sick, twisted joke. He tapped on the keyboard and clicked on the mouse, but nothing happened. The screen remained black. He tried to manually reboot the computer, but again, nothing happened. His heart sank and he wondered if his many hours of hard work was gone for good. He grabbed his phone and was relieved to find he still had email and Internet access. He immediately launched his Google app, frantically searching for someone who could reformat his hard drive. A big box electronics store was nearby, and it was open every night until nine. He quickly removed the flash drive and carried his computer out to his truck.

Craig felt calmer once he reached the store. There was a short line at the repair desk, but it moved quickly, and he was soon face-to-face with a young repair technician who looked more like a high school cheerleader than a computer geek.

"This is so embarrassing," he said. "I'm a journalist, and someone sent me an anonymous tip on flash drive, only it was some sort of a computer virus. My screen went blank, and I can't get it to reboot."

"Let me see what I can do." She popped in a flash drive and tried rebooting it off the external drive, but it wasn't working. After several attempts, she gave up.

"Let me take it in back and see what we can do. Do you have a few minutes?"

"Of course." Craig tried to cover the anxiety in the voice. "I can't work without my computer. I'm a journalist. It has all my files."

"I understand. Do you have backup?"

He thought it over for a minute, and the realization dawned on him. "Of course. Yes. I backup my files to an external hard drive, which I would have disconnected before I put in the flash drive." He frowned again. "Only problem is, I haven't done a backup in several days. What about all the updates and revisions I've done since then?"

"Let's not go there yet. We may be able to reinstall your operating system, and with any luck your files will still be intact, but you may want to look into getting offsite backup. It sure comes in handy when stuff like this happens."

She pointed to a nearby row of chairs, telling him she would be back soon. He checked the time as he took his seat. Other customers came and went while he remained in his chair. Ten minutes later his technician came back out, saying that someone else was working on his computer. She turned her attention to the next customer in line and Craig returned to his seat. Time slowed to a standstill, so he walked around the store. Fifteen minutes later he returned to the repair desk. His technician was busy with another customer. Seven more minutes would pass. Once her customer finally stepped away, she excused herself, telling Craig she was checking on his computer. Five minutes later she returned, accompanied by another technician who carried his laptop. He had a sober look on his face when he motioned to Craig to come up to the counter.

"So what happened?" asked Craig.

"I'm told this happened right after you clicked on something off a flash drive, correct?"

"Yes." Craig nodded toward the young female technician. "As I explained to her, I'm a journalist, and someone gave me an anonymous tip for a story I'm working on. I was told the information I needed was on the flash drive."

"I see. Well, I of course have no idea what kind of story you're working on, but somewhere along the line you've must have seriously ticked someone off. That flash drive apparently had a Trojan horse, which has completely obliterated your hard drive. I tried reformatting it, twice, but each time I tested it I found some sort of a glitch I can't get rid of. I've never seen anything like it, so this was obviously the work of a real pro. I could replace your hard drive, but you have an older computer."

"Yes. I've had it for about three years."

"I see, and because of its age, I'd recommend replacing it because the newer hard drives may not be compatible."

"You've got to be kidding me."

"I wish I was. I tried everything I could think of, but I'm afraid there's no easy fix. I'm more than happy to replace the hard drive if that's what you want, but if I have to put in a new processor to make it work, it'll cost you more money, and to be honest, you're better off with a new computer."

"How long would it take to repair? I have a deadline coming up fast."

"I understand, and unfortunately, we're pretty backed up right now. You need to allow at least three to four days for the diagnostic. Once it's ready, you'll know exactly what needs to be done, and how much it'll cost."

Craig clenched his jaw as he seethed in silent anger. He would have to deal with Boris later, but for moment he had to focus on damage control.

"That's way too long. Is there any way that you can put me at the head of the line? As I said, I have a deadline staring me in face, and three days is just too long of a wait."

"I understand. However, we charge extra for emergency services." He picked up a pen and jotted down all the various costs. "This is my best guess so far. As you can see, it all adds up pretty quickly. If it were me, I'd replace it. We have some good sales going on right now, so you're bound to find a good deal on something which will run faster and has a warranty. And if money's a problem, we have financing."

"I take it none of my data can be recovered."

He shook his head. "Unfortunately, it can't. Whatever this was destroyed everything. We can replace the hardware and reinstall the operating system, but unless you have a backup, I'm afraid your data's gone for good."

Craig took a deep breath and let out a long, drawn out sigh. "Well then, I guess that answers my question."

"Sorry I don't have better news for you." He motioned to a nearby sales associate.

"This is Cory. He'll be happy to show you some new computers, and then you can let me know what you decide."

Craig mumbled a thank you, and Cory soon found a similar laptop with a generous mark down. After throwing in a few rebates he was able to close the sale. Craig stopped for a burger on his way home, but by the time he finished setting up his new computer and installing his backup data it had gotten late. He would have to redo his revisions as best he could, but at least the files hadn't been completely lost.

Shutting down the computer, he had one last task to complete. He dropped the flash drive on the kitchen countertop and reached into the utility drawer for a hammer. After two swift blows he swept the broken flash drive into the trash.

~THIRTY-THREE~

THE BACK-TO-SCHOOL shopping season meant the mall was busier than usual for a Saturday morning. Rachel had to wait in line longer than she expected when she picked up her sister's shower gift. When she finally arrived at her mother's house the party was in full swing.

"Sorry I'm late," she said as she handed off her gift to Sara and joined the others in the living room. "I ran into an unexpected delay."

"No problem." Alice pointed toward the kitchen. "We have coffee and pastries, and you need to grab a pencil and paper off the coffee table. We're getting ready to play a trivia game about me and Donny."

Rachel gave her sister a mischievous grin. "Well now, this should be interesting. So how much would you be willing to pay for my silence? I know a lot of things about you that no one else knows."

Rachel glanced around the room. Everyone, with the exception of Grandma Alice, had burst out laughing. Her grandmother, however, remained stoic in her chair as she sipped her coffee and gave her a somewhat disapproving look. Rachel suddenly felt as if she were only a few inches tall. She slunk into the kitchen to get some coffee, along with a cinnamon roll. When she returned, her mother and another guest made room for her on the sofa, but she kept to herself as the others enjoyed the game. A few more games followed before Julie announced it was time for Alice to open her gifts.

Sara picked up her pencil and volunteered to make a list of each gift, and the person giving it. One by one, Alice opened the beautifully wrapped presents while her guests oohed and awed. Finally, Emma handed her one of the larger boxes. Alice opened the card and read it out loud.

The gift was from Grandma Alice. Rachel looked at her grandmother, whose face beamed with pride as she watched Alice tear off the wrapping paper. Lifting up the lid, the box was filled with several items tightly wrapped in tissue paper.

"I already know what's in here," said Alice as she carefully unwrapped a piece of crystal stemware. "My grandmother has generously offered me all of her china and crystal."

"And I wrapped up a few of the pieces so everyone could see it." Her grandmother's face glowed as she spoke.

"I got my own china and crystal when I got married," said Aunt Laurie, "and with all of my kids being boys, Mother and I wanted to pass hers on to you, since you're the only granddaughter. That way it stays in the family, and hopefully, someday, I'll have a granddaughter of my own who I can pass mine on to."

Laurie's words cut into Rachel like a knife. She wondered if her aunt fully understood the implication of what she was saying.

"And I'm truly overwhelmed," said Alice. "I don't know what else to say, other than thank you both, so very much." Alice gave her aunt and her grandmother a big hug, thanking them once again. When she returned to her seat, she unwrapped one of the plates so everyone could see the pattern. As she carefully rewrapped it and placed it back in the box, Aunt Laurie pointed to another package.

"Wait, there's more," she said, proudly. "It's the one with the big, blue bow."

Emma reached for the package, laughing about its heavy weight as she handed it to Alice. Inside was Grandma Alice's sterling chest, filled with all of her flatware. Rachel's heart felt like a ball of lead as her sister gushed once again about their grandmother's generosity. Alice passed a few pieces around the room, and while everyone was busy admiring it, Rachel slipped back into the kitchen.

She poured herself a second cup of coffee and stared at the cinnamon rolls. It was her favorite pastry, but she had completely lost her appetite. She took a few sips of coffee before topping off her cup and returning to the party. To her relief, Alice had set the boxes of china and sterling aside and had moved on to another gift. Rachel's was the last one opened, and while Alice seemed to appreciate the set of towels, Rachel nonetheless felt upstaged by her aunt and grandmother. As the gift was set aside with the others, several of the guests went to the kitchen for more refreshments, while others took a closer look at all of the gifts.

Rachel silently finished her coffee and took her empty cup back to the kitchen. Coming back into the living room, she found her mother and sister ogling over the crystal, and she overheard her mother praising

Grandma Alice's generosity as she reminisced about how her own circumstances had been so different when she married Bruce. Rachel's eyes suddenly welled with tears and she quickly grabbed her purse.

"It's been fun guys, but I gotta run."

"So soon?" asked Julie.

"I've had a hectic week. I need to run to the grocery store, and then I have a mountain of laundry to do."

Her mother gave her a disapproving look and nodded toward Aunt Laurie and Grandma Alice. "I planned on all of us having lunch together."

"Sorry, Mom, but I just can't. You guys go have your fun."

"Your laundry can wait." Her mother's voice was stern. "Today is a big day for your sister, and you should be there to celebrate it with her."

"I know, Mom, and I'm sorry, but I have to be in court next week, and the outfit I plan on wearing is in the wash. Shane and I have plans for tomorrow, so if I don't get it done today it won't get done."

Julie gave her a hard look, but Rachel held her ground. She blinked back the tears and gave them all a quick good-bye. None of them had a clue. They were all too preoccupied with Grandma Alice's gift to her sister. She rushed out the door, but she wasn't quick enough. Tears streamed down her face before she reached her car. Slipping behind the wheel, she turned fired up the engine and turned on the air conditioning, laying her head on top of the steering wheel as she cried. Aunt Laurie's remark about giving it to the only granddaughter so it would stay in the family said it all. Bruce may have adopted her, but she wasn't their flesh and blood, and she would always be an outsider.

She heard two female voices. Looking up, she saw Sara and another of Alice's friends walking toward their car. She reached into her purse for a tissue and quickly wiped her face. She was about to put her car in reverse, but once again, she wasn't fast enough. Sara stepped up to the driver's side window and Rachel quickly rolled it down.

"Are you okay, Rachel?"

"I'm fine. My allergies always kick up this time of year, and something just got to me. I was looking to see if I had any Claritin in my purse, but I came up empty."

"Know the feeling. I sometimes get them myself, but there's also a bug going around. I noticed you seemed kind of quiet, so I hope you're not coming down with it."

"I hope not either, but I'm fine, really. I just need a little antihistamine, and then I'll be good to go."

"You're sure you're okay? Because I can drive you home if you're not feeling up to it. Jessica can follow us in her car."

"Thanks, Sara, but I'm actually feeling a little better. I think I just got a blast of pollen from somewhere, but it feels like it's easing up."

"Well, as long as you're sure. I'll see you at the wedding. Alice has asked me to be the official greeter, so I'll be out front asking people to sign the guestbook."

Rachel gave her a smile. "Well, good for you. I'll see you then, and thank you."

As Sara walked away, Rachel put her car in gear and headed home. Once she arrived, she sent Al an email to him know about her upcoming hearing. After hitting the send button, she called Shane. To her relief, he quickly answered.

"Are you alright? Your voice sounds a little strained."

"Let's just say I would have had a better time having root canal than I did at Alice's shower. Bruce's mother and sister made it crystal clear that I'm really not part of their family." She told him about Aunt Laurie's comments, and her own mother and sister's reactions.

"I'm still in shock. How could she announce to the entire room that Alice was the only granddaughter, when I was sitting there in plain view?"

"Wow." Shane sounded stunned. "How embarrassing for you."

"Tell me about it."

"Didn't your mother or your sister say anything?"

"Nope. They were too caught up in the moment to even notice. In fact, my mother is a little put out with me for not going to lunch with all of them this afternoon."

"I'm so sorry, Rachel. Is there anything I can do?"

"Well, actually, there is."

"What is it?"

Once again, her eyes were misty. She reached for another tissue. "Did you really mean it when you offered me the guest house? Because I'd like to take you up on your offer, but only for the short term. I don't want to live in Aunt Laurie's duplex anymore, so I'm moving out. As soon as possible."

"Whoa! Let's slow down here." Shane's voice was calm, but firm. "I understand you're upset, which is the reason why I don't think you should be making such a big decision right now, especially when you consider she's renting you the place at cost."

"She's also a real estate agent who owns several rental homes around town, and she says she's using this one as a write off."

"All right. So, what do you have in mind?"

"Between Jonathan, Pilar, and my website, business has really picked up, so I can now afford to stay in the same neighborhood. I just need the guest house until I can find another place, and I want to take my time while I look."

"Okay." Shane sounded tentative. "But here's the bigger question. Businesses ebb and flow, so do you have enough in your savings account to cover your living expenses during slow times?"

Once again, her heart sank. Shane stepped in to answer her question.

"It's okay, Rachel. I already know you don't, at least for now, but I also know you'll get there. And I understand how you feel, because, frankly, I'm ticked off too. So, here's my suggestion. We go to court on Wednesday, and I think Debra may have him served for the lawsuit while we're there."

She perked up. "Really? Why do you say that?"

"I was going to tell this you tomorrow, but yesterday afternoon Jonathan positively identified the computer hacking into your email. It, of course, belonged to Craig."

"Of course. No surprise there."

"Agreed. So Jonathan called Debra's secretary to let her know they'll get his official report on Monday. Apparently, the court papers were ready, because she said she'd file them with the court first thing Monday morning, and she'd let the process server know about your hearing because it would be the easiest way to have him served. So, here's what I have in mind. I think you should stay in the guesthouse for a week or two after he's served, just in case he decides to retaliate."

"I agree."

He chuckled. "Good. At least I don't have to argue with you like I did the last time. Then, once the dust settles, we'll sit down and discuss you moving out of your duplex. I'm hoping by then you'll have saved up enough to cover three month's living expenses, and we'll be ready for you to move into the main house with me."

Rachel smiled as she listened to him talk. "Well, I guess we'll have to see about that won't we?"

"I guess so," he said, flirtatiously, "but in the meantime, why don't I bring some Chinese food to your place tonight, and tomorrow we'll take that day trip down to Bisbee just like we planned."

Her phone chimed. "Hang on, Shane. I think Al might have just replied to my email." She quickly checked. Al had indeed sent her a reply.

"Al says he's wishing me luck with my hearing, and he wants me to let him know what the judge says. I'm also to let him know if I need anything." She stopped for a moment. "You know, I wish he were closer. I really do need him right now."

"So, where does he live?"

"Albuquerque."

"Well, I'd like to meet him, so maybe we might think about taking a trip there. Perhaps between Christmas and New Year. It's a slow time of year, so I should be able to get a couple of days off."

A sense of peace came over Rachel. "That's a great idea, Shane. I'll bring it up with him the next time I talk with him and see what he thinks. In the meantime, I'll see you tonight."

❧THIRTY-FOUR❧

EVERYONE IN THE gallery was ordered to rise as the judge entered the courtroom. Rachel took a quick glance around the room as she stood. Craig was seated across the aisle, two rows behind her. The sight of him made her stomach twist into a knot. The judge stepped up to her chair and ordered everyone to be seated. Shane reached over and squeezed Rachel's hand as the clerk called the first case. Once again, it was a routine court matter, as were the next three. The judge then called Rachel's name. Her knees shook as she rose to her feet.

"It'll be okay," whispered Shane.

She gave him a parting smiled and followed her attorney to the plaintiff's table. Debra took a folder from her briefcase and immediately got down to business.

"Your Honor, the defendant has been stalking and harassing my client for the past several years. She thought it was all behind her, but then she started noticing a suspicious truck in her neighborhood. A friend took the license number and contacted a private investigator, who identified the truck's owner as the defendant, Craig Walker."

"I'm just trying to get to and from work," said Craig.

"You'll have your chance in a minute, Mr. Walker." The judge sounded irritated. "Please continue, Ms. Armstrong."

Debra handed copies of Lamar's report to the clerk. The judge took a moment to skim through the pages as the clerk gave a copy to Craig.

"So what do you have to say, Mr. Walker?"

"Your Honor, this nothing but more harassment on her part." Craig nodded toward Rachel as he spoke. "I'm the one who's being harassed here, not her. I'm a respected journalist. I'm in town working on a series of articles for a national publication, and I—"

"Which publication?"

"I'm sorry, Your Honor?"

"I asked you which publication are you doing the articles for?"

"I'm sorry, Your Honor, but I've signed a nondisclosure agreement with the magazine. I can't reveal the name."

The judge was not impressed. "I understand, Mr. Walker. However, this is a court of law, and this information would be relevant to the case. So, what's the name of the publication?"

Craig glanced nervously around the room.

"Tell you what," said the judge. "Why don't you show me a copy of your contract with the magazine?"

"I…um, don't have it with me," he sheepishly said.

"So, you didn't bring the documentation to back up your statement. Is that right?"

"Your Honor, I'm just trying to get to and from work. I have a day job at a motel just off the freeway, and I'm trying to get there the fastest way possible. I have no way of knowing where she lives, and even if I did, I'm certainly not going to stop and knock on her door. She's the one accusing me of harassing her when I've done nothing of the sort. Her lawyer just admitted that she went and hired some private investigator to dig into my personal affairs, yet she can sit here and say that I'm stalking her? Yeah, right."

"Your Honor, if I may." Debra flipped through her folder for more papers. "Mr. Northrup, the private investigator, was also able to obtain Mr. Walker's home address. It's included in his report."

"See, what'd I tell you." Craig sounded defiant.

"That's enough, Mr. Walker." The judge gave him a strong look. "You may speak when I tell you to speak, but until then, you're to remain silent." She turned her attention back to Debra. "Please continue, Ms. Armstrong."

"Thank you, Your Honor. As I was saying, I have Mr. Walker's home address, and I looked it up on Google Maps, along with his work address, and Ms. Bennett's address. I've marked all three on this map. I've circled the location of my client's home with the green marker. Mr. Walker's home, and the motel where he works, are circled in red." She handed the papers to the clerk, who gave a copy to Craig and to the judge.

"As you can see, both my client, and the defendant, live on the east side of town. In fact, they're practically neighbors. I've also highlighted the most direct route from Mr. Walker's home to his workplace. However, there's a problem with his statement. His residence is about a quarter of mile west of my client's home. So, for him to drive past my client's home to go and from work, he would have to drive a fair distance to the east, which would be in the opposite direction of where he needs to go."

"I'm just trying to get to where I can make a left turn across a busy street with a traffic light," said Craig.

"I understand," said the judge. "However, you're still going a good quarter of a mile in the opposite direction, and you're also crossing some other busy roads along the way. But if you were to follow the route Ms. Armstrong has indicated, you would also end up at a traffic light. It would also be a faster and more direct route from you home to your workplace. Sorry, Mr. Walker, but it appears to me that you've been going well out of your way to drive past her home." The judge looked at Debra. "Was there anything else?"

"Yes, Your Honor. I have a copy of a police report regarding an incident this past March at the La Paloma Hotel, where my client had come for her high school reunion."

"Let me see it."

She handed it to the clerk and waited for the judge to look it over.

"I remember this." The judge gave Craig another strong look. "The sheriff's deputy who took the report says you told him the plaintiff approached you at the bar and harassed you, and she allegedly caused quite a scene, yet when he spoke to one of the servers, he was told nothing unusual had happened that day."

"And, as I also explained to the deputy, she's not a stupid woman. She waited until the bartender had stepped away before she approached me, and—"

The judge had heard enough. "But the point is, Mr. Walker, the deputy couldn't find a single witness to back up your story. So, before I hand down my decision, is there anything else you'd like to say?"

"Your Honor, she's the one who's been harassing me the whole time. She's very clever, she's very cunning, and she's a real pro when it comes to playing the victim card, but she's not the victim here, I am. I'm here working on a series of articles for a national publication, and I rented the most affordable house I could find on a six-month lease. I had no idea it was anywhere close to her residence, but because we live in close proximity to one another we would, of course, be driving on the same streets, shopping at the same stores, patronizing the same restaurants, and so forth." He held up his copy of Lamar's report. "I'm not the one who went and hired a private investigator, she did, and this report contains all kinds of other personal information about me and my family background that, frankly, is none of her business. I think that in itself proves that I'm the one being stalked, not her."

"I understand, Mr. Walker. However, this information all came from police reports and other public records. So, do you have any documentation at all to back up your allegations against the plaintiff?"

"No, Your Honor, I do not. If I'd known I would need it, I would, of course, have brought it with me, along with my contract with the magazine, and I apologize to the court for the inconvenience."

"Is that all?"

"Yes, Your Honor, it is."

"Okay, Mr. Walker, you've had your say, and here's what I think. You came into this courtroom, claiming to be working on a story for a national publication, yet you've refused to identify it, nor do you have any documentation to back up your claim. You also claim to have no idea where the plaintiff lives, and you're just taking the easiest route to and from your workplace, yet the map proves otherwise. You have, in fact, been going well out of your way to drive past her home. You've also stated that the plaintiff harassed you and caused a scene at the La Paloma, yet the deputy who responded to the call couldn't find anyone to collaborate your story. The plaintiff, however, has the evidence to back her claim of you harassing her, yet you keep saying it's the other way around, even though you can't show me any proof."

The judge turned her attention back to Debra. "The court rules in favor of the plaintiff. Her injunction against harassment stands. Mr. Walker, I'm going to ask you to please remain in the courtroom for a few minutes to allow Ms. Bennett the opportunity to leave the building."

"Thank you, Your Honor," said Debra. She quickly ushered Rachel back to the gallery. "Hurry up," she whispered. "Hank Witherspoon is here to serve Craig, and I want you out of here."

As they approached the doors, Rachel glanced behind her. Shane was following them. They filed out of the courtroom and Debra rushed them to the elevator.

"As I just told Rachel, the process server is sitting in the gallery. He'll serve Craig as soon as the judge tells him he's free to go, so I want you two to leave as quickly as you can." She rang for the elevator. A door opened a few seconds later and all three hurried inside.

"We're parked in a small lot right across the street," said Shane. As the elevator doors closed he pushed the button for the ground floor.

"Good," said Debra. "I want you to head straight over there as soon as we get off the elevator."

"Don't worry. We weren't planning on sticking around after the hearing."

The doors opened a moment later. All three stepped out and shook hands and Debra told Rachel she'd call her soon. Shane wrapped his arm around Rachel's shoulder and quickly steered her out the door.

* * *

Craig stood from the defendant's table and started to leave.

"Not so fast, Mr. Walker."

"But they just left the room."

"I need a moment to go over something with my clerk. You can leave soon as we're done."

The judge picked up a folder and mumbled something to her clerk. Craig fumed silently as they discussed whatever was in the folder under their breath. After another moment the judge looked up and called her next case, telling Craig he was free to go. He eagerly stepped away as the next party approached the bench. Walking through the gallery, a man seated in the back row stood to help him push the door open and follow him outside. As Craig headed toward the elevators the other man called his name. Annoyed, he stopped and spun around.

"Yeah, what do you want?"

The man looked familiar, but Craig couldn't quite place him. He stood and watched as he reached into the folder he carried and handed him some papers.

"You've been served." He turned and quickly walked away.

Craig looked the paperwork over. What he saw stunned him, and he had to sit down on a nearby bench. He had been presented with a summons to appear in the federal court to answer to a complaint for unauthorized access, cyber stalking, and invasion of privacy. He fumed as he thumbed through the pages. Somehow Rachel had discovered the malware on her computer, and whoever found it must have removed it from her hard drive.

"Shane." His face lit up as he muttered under his breath. "Of course. I forgot you're a computer nerd. You're one crafty son of a bitch, I'll give you that. First you approach me at the La Paloma, with some cock and bull story about being someone named Bill, and then you figured out how I've kept track of her. Well, Billy Boy, you shouldn't have done that, and she shouldn't have filed this lawsuit, because I'm going to see to it that both of you pay the price, so trust me when I tell you this will never see the inside of the courtroom."

ॐTHIRTY-FIVEॐ

THE NEXT TWO WEEKS would be hectic for Craig. He would have to pack up all of his belongings and load them into a cargo trailer. Fortunately, his old apartment complex in Sacramento had another unit available with the same floor plan he had before, and it would be ready by the fifteenth. This would give him enough time to unpack before taking care of what needed to be taken care of. Once the task was complete, he could concentrate fully on his goal of becoming a nationally recognized journalist. The first article in his American Chronicle series on human trafficking would hit the stands in late September. His immediate concern, however, was finding an attorney, as quickly as possible. He only had a short time to file his answer to the court summons. Failing to do so would result in Rachel winning the case by default, which would cause irreparable damage to his reputation and possibly ruin his career.

Craig went straight home after being served, and once he arrived, he went to the bar association website to find an attorney. By the end of the day, he had contacted several prospects, and he eventually chose Leo Hartman, whose office was close to the motel. A meeting was scheduled for the following week.

Leo's office was in an old house which had been converted into an office, and it was filled with rustic, Old West décor. Craig raised his brow as Leo entered the waiting room and extended his hand. He was well into his sixties with thinning white hair and a wrinkled face which had come from spending many years in the sun. He wore blue jeans, cowboy boots, and a plaid western shirt. Upon entering Leo's private office, Craig noticed a black Stetson hanging from a wall hook mounted behind the desk. The hook itself had been made from old horseshoes. As Leo sat down behind his antique oak desk he said most of his career had been spent practicing civil law. He was blunt, cynical, and completely unapologetic. Craig took his seat across the desk and handed over the summons, explaining what had happened, but without admitting any wrongdoing on his part.

"So, Mr. Hartman, can you help me? This woman has been harassing me for years, and she's out to ruin my career."

"Yeah, I can help you," said Leo as he set the papers down. "Think of me as a hired gunslinger. It means you pay me the money, and I take care of the problem for you. That's all there is to it. My fee is two seventy-five an hour, and I need a twenty-seven-hundred-dollar retainer to get started. Take it or leave it."

Craig swallowed hard. Rachel's lawsuit couldn't have come at a worse time. His finances would be tight over the next few weeks due to his moving expenses. He had also put down the security deposit, along with the first six-weeks' rent, on the Sacramento apartment the day before he was served. This left him in a bind. The rent money was nonrefundable, and without it he wouldn't able to pay the retainer. Leo must have sensed the problem.

"And if you don't have the cash, I'm more than happy to take a credit card."

"I see. So, if I win, will I get my court costs and attorney fees back?"

"I can certainly ask the judge, although there's no guarantee he'll agree to it, and even if he does, there's no guarantee she'll pay, but let's not get ahead of ourselves. First of all, I can't guarantee the outcome of your case. She's made some pretty serious allegations, and I've argued a couple of cases against Ms. Armstrong before. Let's just say the woman lives up to her name. She won't take a client unless she's convinced she has a winnable case. However, I can be a pretty tough contender myself."

"Meaning you'll prove there's reasonable doubt?"

"Nope. That's what you do in a criminal case. This is a civil matter, so it's based on something called preponderance of evidence. This means she, Ms. Bennett, has to prove that you did indeed hack into her computer, and the burden of proof is entirely on her. We don't have to prove your innocence. Of course, this doesn't mean I can't question the authenticity, or the reliability, of her evidence, or even question her character in general." He gave Craig a grin. "In fact, I can make this whole thing so downright ugly that she may just decide it isn't worth the fight, and walk away."

Craig reached into his wallet and handed over his credit card. Leo handed him some paperwork to fill out as he processed the credit card through his iPhone.

"The charge will appear on your credit card statement as Leonard G. Hartman, LLC."

"Of course." Craig slipped his card back into his wallet and finished up the paperwork. Once he signed it, he pushed it back to Leo.

"So, I'm curious. You say you've gone up against Debra Armstrong before?"

"Twice." Leo thumbed through the paperwork, checking for any errors.

"So, how'd it all turn out?"

"Fifty-fifty split. Won the first time but lost the second. Guess this one will be the tie breaker."

They shook hands and Craig hurried back to the motel, stopping at a convenience store along the way to grab a soda and a sandwich. He returned to the front desk without a minute to spare.

"Thanks, Tom, for covering for me."

"Not a problem." Tom seemed ill at ease. He looked around to make sure no one was in earshot. "So, did you still want me to do that favor for you?"

"Not anymore. There's been a change of plan, and you're off the hook."

Tom looked visibly relieved. "You mean it?"

"Yep. Things have changed, so I'm taking a whole new approach, starting with the meeting I just had." Craig gave Tom a cold, icy look. "Of course, it goes without saying that you're to never mention anything about what we discussed to anyone, and I mean anyone."

"Consider it forgotten. Besides, it not like I actually went out and did anything."

"Exactly. It was just a hypothetical scenario. Nothing more."

ᴥTHIRTY-SIXᴥ

DEBRA CALLED RACHEL a week later to let her know Craig had an attorney and had filed his answer with the court. "So, what exactly was his response?"

"Nothing I wasn't expecting," said Debra "He denies any wrongdoing on his part, and he's sticking to his story about you being the one harassing him. They're also claiming it's a frivolous lawsuit, and they're threatening to file a countersuit against you."

"Are you kidding me?"

"It's okay, Rachel," said Debra, reassuringly. "It's a typical response. Even with ironclad proof stacked up against them, defendants will still deny any wrongdoing, and sometimes even threaten to go after the plaintiffs. It's just human nature. We're all hard wired to defend ourselves, so, from here on out, you can expect a rough ride. I've been up against Leo Hartman before. He's an old cowboy who lives on a small ranch east of town, and he fancies himself as some sort of Old West outlaw. He even spends his weekends in Tombstone with a gunfight reenactment group."

"Oh brother." Rachel rolled her eyes.

"He's a character alright, and he can be as mean as an Old West gunfighter in the courtroom. However, I've also talked to him at a few bar association events, and he's been a perfect gentleman. I have a hunch that once he reads Jonathan's report he may change his tune, so I'm still hopeful that we may be able to settle the matter out of court."

"But what happens if we can't?"

"Then we take it to the judge, and we put Jonathan on the stand. Don't worry, Jonathan has testified in other cases as an expert witness. He knows what he's doing, and he's pretty unflappable."

"Yes, he told me that as well."

"See? There you go. The law is on our side, Rachel, so chances are pretty good that we'll win this thing. But for now, you need to be patient and not let the other side get to you. It's all part of the game."

"So what happens next?"

"In a nutshell, the case goes to trial, but first we go through a process called discovery, which is when Leo gets to read all those reports. We'll also be taking depositions, which is pretrial testimony. As I've explained before, all of this will take months, possibly years, especially if we end up having to go in front of a jury. Don't worry, you'll get copies of everything, and I'll be keeping you up to date. In the meantime, you go on with your life."

*　*　*

As papers shuffled back and forth with the court, the final preparations were being made for Alice's wedding, and they were happening at a fever pitch. The blue shoes arrived, and they matched Rachel's blue dress perfectly. The dress itself needed a few minor alterations, so she had a fitting at the bridal shop. She would have her hair and nails done the morning of the wedding, and she had scheduled those appointments well ahead of time. The only glitch came at the last minute, when she realized she didn't have an evening bag to go with her dress and shoes. The bridal shop didn't have anything she liked, so she went online, but the few she liked were either of stock, or the shipping costs were ridiculously high. She would have to hit the stores the weekend before the wedding. Luck, however, was on her side. She found the perfect blue clutch purse at a resale boutique. While she was there, she looked for an outfit for her upcoming trip with Shane. They would leave the morning after the wedding, and she looked forward to a few blissful days of much needed peace and quiet. Pilar called her while she was in the fitting room. She hadn't heard from her friend in sometime, and she smiled as she accepted the call.

"Hey stranger. Long time, no hear."

"I know," said Pilar, "things have been hectic, as usual, and you're probably up to your eyeballs with all the last-minute details for your sister's wedding."

"Tell me about it. Everything had been falling into place perfectly, until I realized I didn't have an evening bag, so I'm over at Cactus Couture."

"I love Cactus Couture." Pilar's voice pitched with excitement. "I swear, every time I bring in something to sell on consignment, I end up buying three other things before I leave."

"I hear you, girlfriend. In fact, I'm in the fitting room as we speak, trying on a pair of blue jeans, which just happen to fit perfectly. You know Shane and I are heading up to Sedona next Sunday."

"I know, and how exciting for you." Pilar paused for a moment. "Hey, I know this is last minute, but are you by chance free for lunch?"

"Sure, but right now I'm across town."

"Not a problem. Jacob is with his dad, and Luis lives fairly close to Cactus Couture. There's a really good bakery and sandwich shop called Delilah's at the other end of the strip mall. I can meet you there in about forty-five minutes, and then I can go pick up Jacob when we're done."

Rachel was sitting at quiet table enjoying a glass of iced tea when Pilar came into the small restaurant. She hopped up from her chair and gave her friend a squeeze.

"Good seeing you. How have you been?"

"I'm doing okay." Pilar pulled out her chair and took her seat.

"Just okay, huh?" Rachel looked her up and down. "Well, you look positively radiant to me. So, what's going on?"

A server stopped by their table. Pilar ordered a glass of iced tea for herself, and once the server stepped away, she flipped her menu open. "You know they bake all their bread in house, so it's really fresh. Their tuna melt is awesome, and they have the best chicken club sandwich in town. It's always hard to decide."

"Stop changing the subject, Pilar. What's got you all happy?"

"Okay, okay." Her face lit up as she smiled. "Well, first of all, I want to thank you for referring me to Matt. He's been a pleasure to work with."

"You're welcome, and he said the same about you. I take it you were able to make arrangements for child support and visitation."

"We were, and Luis and Jacob are bonding nicely. In fact, I've been seeing a positive change in Jacob. Children really do need both of their parents."

Her remark, while well meaning, made Rachel feel sad. "Yes, they do. I can certainly attest to that."

"I know, and you've been a great motivator for me to get this done, even though you probably weren't aware of it."

Pilar's iced tea arrived, and she ordered chicken sandwiches for both of them. "My treat," she said.

"Thanks," said Rachel, "but my stomach's been little upset lately, so I'd like to get the chicken and rice soup instead."

Their server made the change and hurried away while a concerned look came over Pilar's face. "Are you feeling okay?"

"Yeah, I'm fine, but between the lawsuit, and all the chaos surrounding the wedding, I've had a nervous stomach over the past few days. But once I'm in Sedona, chilling with Shane, I'll be feeling fine."

"Well, hang in there. You only have another week to go."

Rachel grinned and took a sip of her tea. "Exactly. So, enough about me, let's get back to you and why you look so gosh darn happy."

"Well, okay. Jacob has spent the past few Saturdays with his dad, and Luis has always invited me along. In fact, today is his first time going solo. So, a couple Saturdays ago, he asked me if I could find a sitter for Jacob that night, because he wanted to take me to dinner."

Rachel raised her brow. "Really?"

Pilar nodded. "He sure did. He took me to a nice restaurant, and we had a long talk. He still feels bad about the way he treated me before, and he said if he had it to do over again, he would have taken his time and gotten to know me better before we got seriously involved."

"I see."

"So, to make a long story short, he said he'd thought about me after he went back to his old girlfriend, and it was one of the reasons why things just weren't the same with her. He said he'd like for us to be friends, and this time around we'd take our time. He also says he's not making any promises, but gosh, wouldn't it be something if it worked out? Then Jacob would have his real family."

"Yes, it would be wonderful, but please, take your time. Remember, he dumped you once before."

"I know he did," said Pilar, "and yes, we are taking it slow. Right now, we're just friends, and we've both agreed to really get to know one another before taking it to the next level, assuming it ever goes that far. So, as I'm getting to know him, I'm learning that we have a lot in common. I'm also realizing he really is a good person who's made some bad choices in the past, and now he's trying to make up for those bad choices."

"Well, I hope it works out, Pilar, I really do, because a stepparent just isn't the same as a real parent."

Pilar looked surprised. "Really? Whenever you've talked about Bruce before, you always said he was just like a real father. So why this sudden change?"

Rachel's face turned sad. "It's not Bruce. It's the rest of his family." She told Pilar about her grandmother's decision to give her china and crystal to Alice, and Aunt Laurie's remark at the bridal shower about it going to the only granddaughter.

"Wow," said a shocked Pilar. "You mean she said all that, in front of you, and everyone else?"

"Yep. She said it in front of the entire room. It was as if I didn't exist."

"How awful. So what was she thinking, and did your mother, or your sister, say anything?"

"Not a word. Either they didn't notice, or it didn't bother them."

"You're joking. So did either of them bring it up after the shower?"

"Nope. In fact, my mother was a little put out with me when I backed out of going to lunch with all of them afterwards."

Pilar shook her head. "Wow. I'm so sorry, Rachel. I don't know what else to say."

"It's okay. The point I'm making is that I wish you the best with Luis, and I sincerely hope, for Jacob's sake, as well as yours, that it works out between the two of you. Intentional or not, no one should ever feel like an outsider because they're not a biological child, and it doesn't matter if the child is a toddler or an adult. It still hurts to know that you were never really a part of the family."

❧THIRTY-SEVEN❧

RACHEL GROANED AS The alarm went off. Shane snuggled next to her and wrapped his arm around her waist, pulling her in close. His skin felt soft and warm against hers.

"Rise and shine. Today is your big day."

Rachel groaned again. "No, it's Alice's big day, and right now, I wish I were an only child."

He chuckled and kissed the side of her face as he squeezed her naked breast. "Now, now, you don't need to be so grumpy. I can think of a much better way to wake you up."

"I know you can, but you need to hold that thought for tonight. I have to be at the hair salon in forty-five minutes."

Shane moaned in protest while Lucy scratched at the bedroom door. Rachel got up and let her in. The dog immediately jumped on top of Shane, who let out a loud grunt.

"Tell your daddy to take you out for a walk while I hop in the shower."

Ten minutes later Rachel was showered and dressed. She found Shane in the kitchen. He greeted her with a smile and offered her a cup of coffee.

"I would if I could, but I gotta run."

"You're sure you don't want to ride to the wedding with me?"

She gave him a squeeze. "I really wish I could, but I'll have my dress on a hanger, and I have to be there at least an hour before the ceremony starts, if not sooner."

"I know. So I'll see you there." Shane gave her a goodbye kiss. "Love you."

"Love you too, and I'll see you tonight." Rachel gave him a quick, parting kiss and flew out the door.

She arrived at the salon right on time. Kathy, her stylist, added more highlights, making her blonde hair shimmer even more, and after a quick trim and a blow dry, it was time for a manicure. Rachel thought a bright red polish would make a nice contrast with her royal blue ensemble, and the manicurist agreed. It was past noon when she left the salon. Checking her messages, she found several texts from her mother and her sister, reminding her once again to be at the hotel no later than four o'clock to allow enough time to be ready for the photographer to take their pictures before the ceremony. Rachel stopped at the grocery store on her way home to grab a Caesar salad and a bottle of fruit juice, but when she sat down to eat, her stomach was once again tied in knots. She picked though her salad, and, when she finally finished, it was time to grab her suitcase and start packing. She would stay with Shane that night, and they would drop Lucy off at his parent's house the following morning on their way out of town.

It was a few minutes after three when Rachel lugged her suitcase out to her car and loaded her dress, shoes, and other necessities. The hotel where they were having the wedding was in the nearby town of Oro Valley, and it would take some time to get there. After securing the house, Rachel hopped in her car and headed off.

The late afternoon sun felt warm when she stepped out of her car. She felt the crispness of the early fall in the air, but as she threw her small overnight bag over her shoulder a sudden feeling of uneasiness came over her. She felt as if she were being watched. Scanning the parking lot, she spotted three red pickup trucks among the sea of cars and SUVs.

"C'mon, Rachel," she said to herself as she grabbed her dress. "He's been locked out of your computer for some time now, and Debra said his attorney told her he moved back to Sacramento two weeks ago." Rachel shrugged it off as she threw her dress over her shoulder and made her way to the hotel entrance. Once inside, she was directed to a small meeting room. Her mother was zipping up Alice's gown as she stepped in.

"Wow," said Rachel. "You look fantastic."

Alice's hair had been swept back into a chignon, with loose ringlets framing her face. Her small, pearl headpiece added the perfect, final touch.

"Thanks," said an emotional Alice. "The trick will be getting through the ceremony without my makeup running down my face."

"You'll be fine, although I think I can conceal a Kleenex or two beneath my bouquet."

"That's enough chitchat," said Julie, firmly. "Rachel, you need to get changed, and when you're done, you need to take your bag out to your car. The photographer will be here soon, and we don't need any clutter laying around."

Rachel stepped off to a corner to change her out of her undergarments and put on a pair of pantyhose. Once she was ready, her mother helped her into the blue dress.

"They did a nice job on the alterations," said Julie. "In fact, this reminds me of your high school prom dress."

"Sort of," said Rachel. "That dress was pink, if you recall, although it had a similar style to this one." Rachel stepped into her blue shoes and touched up her hair and makeup. When she was finished, she threw her other clothes in her bag and was heading toward the door when Sara came in.

"I thought you were wearing a red dress," said Alice.

"I was," said Sara, "but when I got it out this morning, I noticed it had a stain in the front, and it's a dry clean only, so I had to make a last-minute run to the mall. This was the best I could do on short notice."

Sara's two-piece ensemble was the same shade of blue as Rachel's dress. Both women were also blonde and wore a similar hairstyle.

"It's not so bad, Alice," said Rachel with a grin. "After all, the best man and the groom are identical twins, so why not have your sister and your best friend look like twins too? Besides, Sara's dress is tea length, where mine is floor length, and instead of lace trim, hers has gold buttons and a little jacket." Rachel gave Sara a reassuring smile. "Besides, I think you look great, so you should just ignore her, because she's being a little bridezilla right now. And if she doesn't want to be your friend anymore then you can hang out with me."

"Thanks, Rachel."

Sara gave her a hug, and Rachel grabbed her bag and raced out to the parking lot, returning just in time for the photographer to arrive. He started with a few shots of Sara and Alice, and when he was done Sara hurried out to the wedding gazebo to greet the guests. He then took photos of Alice, Rachel, and their mother. Bruce soon joined them, and by the time the photographer had finished it was time to go to the gazebo.

"Well, this is it," said Rachel. "Are you ready?"

"As ready as I'll ever be," said Alice, "and if there's one piece of advice I could give you, it's this. Elope."

"I'll second that," said Bruce.

"Don't worry, I've already made the decision myself," said Rachel. "I'm going to Vegas, assuming I ever decide to get married in the first place."

Sara gave them a nod as they approached the gazebo entrance. She took her seat while Julie and Donny's mother were escorted to their seats at the front. A piano version of *Here Comes the Bride*, played over a loudspeaker. It was Rachel's cue to enter. Her face beamed as she slowly walked up the aisle toward Donny and Matt. Shane's face glowed as she walked past him. He gave her a broad smile and mouthed the words, "I love you." She smiled and nodded in return, and as she stepped up to the altar, she turned and watched Alice and Bruce as they came up behind her.

The minister began the ceremony, and Bruce stepped away once Donny took Alice's hand. Rachel had her tissues handy in case her sister needed them, but Alice made it through without becoming weepy. Finally, the minister told Donny to kiss the bride, and he introduced them to their guests as Mr. and Mrs. Donald Wheeler. *The Wedding March* played as the bride and groom, along with Matt and Rachel, walked back down the aisle and formed a receiving line to greet their guests as they headed to the ballroom where the reception would be held. Once the last guest departed, they had to pose for more pictures. Finally, the last photo was shot, and they joined their guests in the ballroom.

Shane greeted Rachel with a kiss as soon as they arrived, but before he could take her to his table other guests came up to congratulate her. They were uncles, aunts and cousins, as well as a number of old family friends. She finally got a break and sat down next to Shane as the toasts were made, and the bride and groom cut the wedding cake. The DJ started the music and invited everyone to dance. Shane took her by the hand and led her to the dance floor, but after a few dances more guests approached Rachel.

"Sorry, Shane," she said as the last one walked away. "I'm the bride's sister, so I guess everyone wants to talk to me, and some of them are relatives who haven't seen me in a very long time."

"It's okay, Rachel. I know how family obligations go."

Matt walked up them, saying Emma had wandered off somewhere.

"She's around here somewhere," said Rachel, "and since it's only a matter of time before someone else decides to come over to talk to me, why don't you and Shane go hang out for a while, and if I can manage it, I'll try to grab some food and come over to join you." She nodded toward a group of men gathered around a table at the back of the room. "Rumor has it one of Donny's firefighter buddies snuck in a tablet, and they're watching a football game."

"You're sure you won't mind?" asked Shane.

"I'm positive. You guys go do some male bonding. I'll be fine."

Another woman walked up to Rachel and started talking to her so Shane and Matt took their leave. A short time later the DJ announced it was time for Alice to throw her bouquet. She tried to toss it to Rachel, but one of Donny's cousins intercepted it. Rachel and the other women stepped away and was time for Donny to toss the bride's garter. This time it landed squarely in Shane's hands. He and Rachel had a laugh as they posed with their prize for the photographer.

"I'm about ready to whisk you out of here," he said.

"I hear you. Donny and Alice should be making their grand exit fairly soon, and once they're gone, we'll head out."

"Aren't they staying here tonight?"

"Are you kidding?" Rachel gave him a grin. "The wedding night location is top secret. They haven't told a soul where they're going, not even Matt, and identical twins supposedly share everything. I know they're taking a cruise to Alaska for their honeymoon, but they both turned their cellphones off before the ceremony. Alice says they won't turn them back on until they return next week."

"Well, good for them," said Shane. "I think we'll do the same after we leave tomorrow."

Once again, someone walked up to Rachel. Shane excused himself and rejoined the other men. A short time later Julie and Emma approached her.

"It's going on eight o'clock," said Julie, "and we only rented the room until nine. Your father and I loaded as many of the wedding gifts as we could in our car. Would you mind loading the rest in yours?"

"Well, I suppose I could, but Shane and I are leaving for Sedona first thing tomorrow morning."

"I know that. You can drop them off at our place on your way home tonight."

Rachel felt relieved. "Thanks, Mom."

"You're welcome. I'm going to try to sneak Alice out of here and help her change out of her gown so she and Donny can leave. Bruce went to the men's room, but Emma says she'll be happy to help you carry the gifts out to your car."

Julie stepped away, and Emma followed Rachel to the table where the remaining wedding gifts sat on display.

"Wow, that's a lot," said Rachel. "We may have to take two trips." Rachel grabbed her car keys and two women gathered up as many of the packages as they could carry. Rachel led Emma out to her car. It was well after dark, and the parking lot was dimly lit. Rachel set the packages down on the hood and popped the trunk open. Emma started handing her some of the gifts.

"Looks like I'm going to have to do a little rearranging," said Rachel.

"Good thing there aren't too many left," said Emma.

"You got that right. Tell you what, why don't you run and get them while I finish loading these up."

"Good idea. I should be able to get the rest of them on one trip."

Rachel shuffled more of the boxes around. "I'll be here when you get back."

Emma hurried back inside as Rachel busied herself with loading the remaining packages. As she worked the last one in, she heard footsteps coming up behind her.

"Perfect timing."

"Thanks. I thought so too."

Her hair stood on end and her body froze in fear. She knew the voice behind her, and it wasn't Emma's. She slowly turned around. His jacket collar was turned up to conceal his face, and he wore a baseball cap. As his cold eyes bore into hers, and her fear turned into anger.

"What the hell are you doing here? You're supposed to be in Sacramento."

"I came back to take care of some unfinished business."

"Get the hell away from me, Craig."

In an instant, Craig had his arm wrapped tightly around her waist, and something sharp poked against her ribs. She looked down. He had a sweater draped over his hand and forearm, which he pulled back with his other hand. To her horror, he was holding a large knife. He reached up and slammed her trunk shut.

"You're coming with me."

She tried to struggle against him, but he held her tight as he pushed the knife harder against her chest. It felt like it would puncture her skin.

"Keep that up, and yes, I will hurt you," he said, "and if you try to scream, you're dead." As Craig pulled her away from her car, Rachel dropped her keys and kicked them underneath the rear bumper.

✎THIRTY-EIGHT✎

EMMA BROUGHT OUT the last load of packages, but when she walked up to Rachel's car, Rachel wasn't there. She looked around, but Rachel was nowhere in sight. She tried the latch and the trunk popped open. Thinking Rachel had gone back inside, she quickly loaded the remaining packages in the trunk. When she returned to the reception she saw a blonde in a royal blue dress across the room. Obviously, another guest had sidetracked Rachel, so she would let her know she had loaded the last of the gifts in her car. As she started toward her Matt called her name.

"Don't go anywhere," he said. "Donny and Alice are getting ready to leave, and we need to go out to see them off."

A few minutes later the DJ made the same announcement, and everyone flocked out to the front entrance, cheering and throwing confetti once Donny and Alice finally made their way outside.

"Thank you, everyone, for coming," said Donny as he and Alice walked up to a waiting golf cart.

"So where's the honeymoon?" shouted one of the guests.

"Alaska, and don't bother calling us. We've turned off our phones. Goodnight everybody." Donny helped Alice into the backseat of the golf cart and climbed in next to her. Both waved goodbye as the cart sped away.

"Have you seen Rachel?" asked Shane.

Matt looked around and pointed out a blonde standing on the other side of the crowd.

"I see her," said Shane. "Looks like she's busy talking to someone."

"Par for the course," said Matt. "So let's go back and watch the rest of the game. There're still nine minutes left to go in the fourth quarter."

The party was still going strong when they went back inside. Emma grabbed a plate and joined her husband and the other men to watch the rest of the game. Shane scanned the room for Rachel, who sat at a table across the room with a group of women. Her back was turned toward them, but he noticed she was eating. At last she was finally getting a meal. He turned his attention back to the game. The party was winding down by the time it was over. Many of the guests had left, and the wait staff had started clearing off the tables. Julie walked up to them with a concerned look on her face.

"Shane, have you seen Rachel? I can't find her anywhere."

He pointed across the room. "She's right over there, with those other women."

"No, that's Sara."

"Sara? Are you sure?"

"Yes, Shane, I'm sure. I was just over there talking to her a couple of minutes ago. She said she hasn't seen Rachel for a while."

Shane stood up and started toward the other table. As he came closer the women rose to their feet and the blonde turned around. She was indeed Sara. She smiled and extended her hand.

"It was nice seeing you again, Shane. We're all heading out, but before we go, I wanted to say goodnight to Rachel."

"Thanks Sara, but at the moment I'm not sure where she is. Have you seen her?"

"No, not lately. Her mother's looking for her too. When you see her, please tell her goodnight for me."

"Will do."

Sara and her friends headed out and Shane scanned the room. Rachel was nowhere in sight, but something else caught his eye, Rachel's clutch purse. It had been left unattended at a table where she had sat earlier that evening. The table was now empty, and a couple of servers were clearing it. As Shane walked up to them one of them pointed to the purse.

"Do you by chance know who this belongs to?"

"Yes, I do."

"Good," she said. "Because it's been sitting here for quite a while now, and we need to finish clearing this table."

Shane was getting a bad feeling. He picked up the purse and looked around for Julie, but now she was nowhere to be found. Emma, however, was still with Matt. Both had concerned looks on their faces as he approached them.

"Is everything okay, Shane?" asked Matt.

"I don't know. Turns out it was Sara, not Rachel, who was at that other table. I found Rachel's purse, and one of the waitresses told me it had been laying there for some time." He looked at Emma. "When exactly did you last see her?"

"When we took some of the wedding gifts out to her car. She had to move some other stuff in her trunk, so she told me to go back and get the rest of the gifts. When I came back, she wasn't there, but the car was unlocked, so I loaded them up and came back in. That's when I saw her talking to someone across the room. I was going to let her know I'd finished loading the gifts, but then Matt called me, so I didn't get the chance."

"Do you remember about what time it was?"

"I'm not exactly sure." She thought it over for a moment. "It was a few minutes after eight. Maybe eight fifteen at the latest."

Shane checked his watch. It was twelve minutes past nine. His heart sank. Julie came up to join them.

"I just checked the ladies' room. She's not in there either."

"Shane found her purse," said Emma.

"It was sitting on one of the tables," he said. "It apparently had been sitting there for some time." The realization hit him. "My god, this is all my fault. All this time I thought she was sitting at that other table, but it wasn't her. It was Sara. They were both wearing blue dresses."

"You didn't do anything wrong, Shane," said Julie. "I'm the one who sent her out to the parking lot with the gifts. Bruce was in the men's room, and I didn't even think to ask you to help her."

"Because I'd already volunteered," said Emma. "This is a five-star hotel, in an upscale neighborhood. There was no need for us to be concerned about going out to the parking lot."

"Stuff happens, even in good neighborhoods." Matt's voice was firm. "You two should have had one of us go with you."

Bruce came back into the room, and he brought another man in a business suit with him. "This is Gilbert," said Bruce. "He's in charge of hotel security."

Shane struggled to remain calm. "We think she's been missing for almost an hour."

"Trust me, we're looking for her," said Gilbert. "We've already talked to the parking valets, but none of them have seen her. Keep in mind they can get pretty busy shuttling cars back and forth, especially when we're having a special event like a wedding, so she could have easily walked by without being noticed. I've got a couple of guys driving around the perimeter in golf carts, and I have a female employee checking out all of the women's restrooms, including an employee restroom. There's another restaurant in a building across the main parking lot. One of my team is over there looking for her as we speak. If she's on the property, we'll find her."

His walkie-talkie went off. "Copy, Robert. Where are you?"

"I'm at The Baja Cantina. No one has seen a blonde woman in a long, blue dress."

"Ten four. Go help John and Julio finish sweeping the parking lots." He turned his attention back to Julie and Bruce. "Well, she hasn't been in the other restaurant."

"Don't you have security footage?" asked Bruce.

"We do, but most of the outside cameras are pointed at the front entrance. We have a couple of cameras that sweep the parking lots, and I've got someone going over the footage as we speak. She'll let us know if she finds anything."

His walkie-talkie went off again. This time it was a female employee, saying she checked out all the women's restrooms, but found no sign of Rachel. Gilbert told her to go check the patio and the wedding gazebo. A minute later another employee came on the radio, saying Rachel wasn't in any of the parking lots, or behind the building. As they talked back and forth Shane asked Emma if she would mind taking him out to Rachel's car.

"Of course," she said, "come with me."

"I was about to ask you that myself," said Gilbert.

"I'm coming with you," said Julie.

"Me too," said Bruce.

Matt tagged along as Emma led them out to Rachel's car. Gilbert became concerned once he saw where she had parked.

"Unfortunately, the cameras only have limited access to this area of the property. They're mounted quite a ways away, so we may or may not have caught something." He pushed the button on his walkie-talkie, letting them know which camera to check. While he was talking Shane opened the trunk. All of the wedding gifts, along with Rachel's luggage, appeared to be undisturbed.

"It's just how I left it," said Emma.

Shane tried the driver's side door. It too was unlocked. His face turned pale as he addressed the others. "Rachel would never leave her car unlocked. Not even for five minutes."

"I know," said Bruce. He circled around the car, and as he passed the back bumper he suddenly stopped and looked down.

"What the hell?"

"What is it?" Julie sounded frantic.

Bruce held up a set of car keys. "I just stepped on these."

"Those are Rachel's keys," said Shane. "Where did you find them?"

"Right here." Bruce pointed to the ground as he spoke. "Just underneath the rear bumper."

Shane's chest suddenly felt tight. It was hard for him to speak. When the words came, they sounded like a monotone.

"Rachel would have never, ever, dropped her keys and just walked off. She's left us a message. She's telling us that someone's taken her." He paused for a moment. "Craig. Craig Walker did this."

Matt shook his head. "That's not possible. Craig Walker left town two weeks ago. He went back to Sacramento."

Julie burst into tears. Bruce tried to console her.

"So what do we do now?" Bruce asked. "Do the call the police?"

Emma pointed to Matt and Shane, who'd stepped away from the others. "Actually, they're already on it."

✞THIRTY-NINE✞

CRAIG KEPT HIS knife pressed against Rachel's ribs as he walked her through the back rows of the parking lot. Her entire world had suddenly become surreal. Her only thought was to do whatever it took to stay alive.

"You're doing fine," he said as they walked up to his pickup truck. "Just don't do anything to attract attention, and you'll be okay. I'm going to open the driver's side door. Then I want you get in and slide over to the passenger seat. Make one false move, and it'll be your last."

Rachel froze once he opened the door. "I have to lift up my dress. Otherwise I can't reach the step."

"Then you'll need to lift it up really slowly, and remember, I'm watching your every move. Try anything stupid and you're dead."

Rachel took a deep breath, reminding herself to stay calm as she slowly lifted her dress to her knees. Hopefully, he would put the knife down once he was inside, and she would try to talk him into letting her go. She hoisted herself into the truck, carefully scooting over to the passenger seat as Craig jumped inside. He slammed the door shut with one hand while he grabbed her arm with the other.

"Lean forward," he said.

"Why?"

"Because I said so," he said with a growl, "and no talking."

Rachel leaned forward, trying to suppress her sobs as he pulled out a piece of rope from underneath the driver's seat. She gasped as he wrapped it tightly around her wrist, pulled her arm behind her back, and then grabbed her other arm. Once her hands were secured behind her back he told her to sit back up. The rope cut into her circulation. She flexed her fingers to try to keep the blood flowing.

"Why are you doing this to me?"

He gave her an evil grin. "Because I can, and now I have to buckle you up, because we're going for a ride."

Rachel held her breath as he pulled down the seatbelt. To her relief, he didn't touch her breasts. He snapped the belt into its buckle and then fastened his own belt, ordering her to look straight ahead as he fired up the engine.

"My knife is right where I can reach it." Craig patted the cup holder as he spoke. "And if I catch you doing anything to attract attention, I'll take out a kidney, without anesthesia. Understood?"

Rachel nodded. She was too frightened to speak. Her eyes stayed glued straight ahead as they left the hotel and turned onto the main road. She checked the clock on the console. It was sixteen minutes after eight. Surely by now Emma would have brought out the last load of gifts to her car and would have noticed she was missing. Then, once her car keys were found, Shane would know something had happened to her, and he would call the police. With any luck she would be found quickly, before Craig had the opportunity to harm her. Craig remained silent as the made their way to the freeway, where he took the eastbound on-ramp. As they sped out of town, Rachel's hopes waned.

"Well, I'm sure by now you must be wondering where we're going," he said.

"Yes, I am." She barely spoke above a whisper.

"You and I are going on an adventure so we can get reacquainted. In fact, we'll be getting to know one another really well."

Rachel shuddered. Whatever he had planned would not be good. She would have to figure out a way to convince him to let her go.

"Look, Craig, everyone knows I'm missing by now, and no doubt they've already called the police. If you'll just pull over at the next exit and let me go, I'll tell them I wasn't harmed. And if they ask if it was you, I'll just say no, it was a total stranger. You'll get away scot-free. I promise."

"Well, Rachel, you at least tried to make it sound convincing, but my answer is no. Like I said, you and I are going to get reacquainted. We were friends once, so maybe we can be friends again."

He had given her an opportunity. She would have to make the best of it. "You're right, Craig. We were friends. Good friends. I even considered you a mentor. Then it all changed. So what happened?"

He gave her a hard look. "What happened? You mean you have to ask? You defied me. You went and got that promotion, behind my back, without consulting me first."

"But it wasn't about you, Craig. It never was. You worked in the editorial division, and I worked for the art department. It was like working for two separate companies under the same banner."

"I know that, but you knew damn well that you were supposed to talk to me about it first. I would have helped you, because I would have told you no. You weren't ready to make such a big step."

"But I was ready. I worked hand in hand with Stacy from my very first day there. She, too, had mentored me, and when she announced that she was leaving, she told Marie she wanted me to take her job."

Craig burst out laughing. "Wow, Rachel. I had no idea you were bisexual. You mean you like to do it with women too? Who knew? So tell me, which do you prefer? Men? Or women?"

Her stomach turned. She hoped she wasn't about to be sick. "I'm not bisexual, Craig, nor was I having sex with any of the other staff. I got that job because of my hard work as a graphic artist. I'm not a whore."

His mood abruptly changed. "All women are whores! Got that? All women. Each and every one of you of lies on your back to get what you want, whether it's to get some guy to feed you and put a roof over your head, or whether it's to climb the corporate ladder. There isn't a one of you who isn't screwing some guy, or gal, so you can get something. At least the streetwalkers are honest. They only do it for cash."

Rachel struggled to keep her wits about her. "So what do you want from me? I'm truly sorry if I upset you, or if my actions made you feel slighted in some way. That was never my intention. Stacy was leaving. She thought I'd be the best person to fill her job. That's all there was to it. It had nothing to do with you, nor would it have had any effect on your position as a staff writer. I was never in competition with you. There, I've apologized. So please, just let me go."

"No can do, sweetheart, but I do accept your apology, and I must say, it's been long overdue. However, I meant it when I said you and I are going on a little adventure. You can beg me all night long, but I'm not letting you go."

Both went silent. As they drove through the small towns of Benson and Wilcox, she prayed he would make a stop, but they kept going. She knew the further they went, the less her chances of being rescued. They were near the New Mexico state line when he finally spoke again.

"You know, you really shouldn't have taken that spyware off your computer. It only made things harder for you."

Rachel remained silent.

"Cat got your tongue?" Craig chuckled for a moment. "You know, that's pretty funny when you stop and think about it. I keep seeing this image in my mind of my tongue getting caught in your, well, you know."

Rachel kept her eyes focused on the road, still flexing her fingers. Her arms and back ached. The rope burned into her wrists.

"Well, at least I thought it was funny," Craig finally said. "So, lucky for you, or maybe unlucky for you, just before you blocked me out of your email, I printed out the message your sister sent you with all the details about her wedding. And if it means anything to you, my original plan wasn't to abduct you from the wedding. It was something much simpler. So, would you like to know what it was?"

Rachel didn't answer.

"Okay, I'll take that as a yes. First, I was going to have a little fun with you, and then I was going to completely destroy your career. You see, I was working a day job at a motel. Oh, wait. You already know that. Your nosy boyfriend, Bill, or Shane, or whatever the hell he calls himself, got that private investigator's report on me, and yeah, I've read it. So, I was going to have Tom, my coworker, contact you about creating a website, and he was going to meet you for coffee, you know, so you could discuss the project. Then, while he distracted you with some sketches of the ideas he was working on, he was going to slip a little something in your coffee. As soon as it kicked in, he was going to take you back to the motel and put you in a room I'd reserved in your name. Then he and I were going to have a little fun with you."

Rachel felt the bile in her stomach. She swallowed hard to keep it down.

"You may recall that I'm also a photographer," said Craig. "So I was going take lots of photos, and maybe even make a little x-rated video of Tom and me having a ménage à trois with you. We would, of course, be disguised with hats and wigs and sunglasses in case you tried to call the cops on us later on, but not you. In fact, I was going to get plenty of close ups of your face so everyone would know it was you. Then, when we were done, I was going to put a wad of bills in your hand and shoot some photos of you lying naked with the all that cash. Then I was going to have Tom send Shane an anonymous email with a link so he could see it all online. At that point he would have dumped you, and your design career would have been over too."

"Stop it!"

"What's the matter, Rachel? Didn't you like my idea? I thought it was rather clever myself. I especially liked the idea of you coming to later on, finding yourself completely naked in a strange motel room, and wondering what the hell happened, but it's okay. You can relax now. I won't be slipping you any drugs, nor will I be posting any revenge porn of you on the Internet. Everything changed once you filed that lawsuit against me, and trust me when I tell you that by the time I'm through with you, you'll wish to hell I'd gone through with my original plan."

"Craig, please, I'm begging you. Just let me go. We're still in Arizona, so you haven't committed a federal crime. Please, just turn the truck around, take me to the nearest town, and let me go. You've had your fun. You've spent the past few hours terrorizing me. I'll even agree to drop the lawsuit. But please, please, please, just let me go."

"Not a chance." He pointed out a road sign. "Besides, we've just crossed the state line. Welcome to New Mexico."

Craig went silent once again while Rachel worried about his next move. She would have to keep her wits about her and wait for the right opportunity to escape. In the meantime, her back and shoulders were throbbing, her wrists were burning, and her hands felt numb and swollen. A sign about a gas station ahead soon appeared. It might be her last chance to save herself.

"Craig, I have to go to the bathroom. Really, really bad."

"Do you now? Well, I guess we'll have to see about that, won't we?"

"There's a gas station up ahead. If I ever was your friend, and if you have any decency left in you, then please, at least let me have a bathroom break."

"Well, Rachel, it's all very touching, so, okay. Not because I'm being kind, but because we're running low on fuel. But I'm warning you, one wrong move, and you'll be begging me to kill you to put an end to your pain and suffering."

They pulled into the gas station a short time later. It was open twenty-four hours, but for the moment there were no other customers. Craig parked next to one of the pumps and filled the tank. Once he finished, he moved the truck to a far corner of the parking lot and untied her hands. Rachel was horrified when she examined her red, raw wrists. Craig noticed them too. He picked up the sweater he had carried earlier and threw it in her face.

"Put this on," he said. "It'll cover your wrists, and don't even think of showing them to anyone."

Rachel put on the sweater and climbed out of the truck. Craig took her by the arm and walked her into the minimart. A clerk sat behind a panel of bulletproof glass. Craig asked him where the restroom was and he pointed to a small hallway in the far back corner of the store. Craig thanked him and walked her to the ladies' room door.

"I'll be waiting right here," he said, "and if you try to pull anything, you'll regret it."

Rachel hurried inside. The tears started as soon as she entered a stall, and she cried uncontrollably for several minutes. Once she pulled herself together, she looked around for something she could use to leave a clue behind. Rummaging through a trashcan, she found an old tube of lipstick. She removed the top. It was hot pink and used up, but it would do. She walked up to the mirror and started writing the word, "help," but before she could finish the door opened, and another woman came inside. Her heart leapt with joy. It was a young female state trooper.

"Oh thank God," she said. "You have to help me. I've been kidnapped and—"

"I know all about it, Rachel. Your brother is waiting for you outside. He's very worried about you. He told me you stopped taking your medication, so he's taking you home. Come with me."

"No! Wait! You don't understand. I really have been kidnapped." She pulled back her sleeves, exposing her raw wrists.

"Yes, I know. Your brother told me you've been injuring yourself so he's taking you home. You need to get back on your medication, so please, come with me. It'll be okay."

She wrapped her arm around Rachel's shoulder and walked her to the door.

"No! You don't understand. No!"

The trooper opened the door and handed her over to Craig.

"I'm so sorry about this," he said. "I had no idea she'd gotten this bad, although her insisting on wearing this dress today should have been my first clue. She thinks she's back in high school and she was waiting for her date to take her to the prom. When he didn't show up, she wandered off and injured her wrists. Thank goodness a friend found her, and as soon as we get home she's going back on her medication. She'll be good as new in a few days."

"You know, she really should be in a hospital. Are you sure you don't want me to call the paramedics?"

"I'm positive, but thank you, ma'am. I've already alerted her doctor. This isn't the first time this has happened, so I know the drill. And even though she can get a little loud at times, she's not violent or aggressive, nor is she suicidal. She only injures herself to get attention."

"Well, as long as you're sure, but call us if you need any help, and I hope she feels better soon."

Rachel's heart sank into the pit of her stomach as the trooper walked away. Once she was gone, Craig squeezed her arm so tight she yelped in pain, but he held his grip as he walked her back to his truck. He opened the driver's side door and told her to remove the sweater. She slowly handed it back and reluctantly stepped inside as he unleashed his anger.

"I warned you, bitch, not to try anything, but you wouldn't listen, so from here on out, it's no more Mr. Nice Guy."

He hoped inside and slammed the door shut. She yelped in pain as he wrapped the rope around her wrist and tied her hands back together.

Once he finished, he removed her shoes and stuffed them underneath the driver's seat.

"You know Rachel, there is one thing I've always wondered about you. I've always wondered if you're a natural blonde, so now I'm going to find out, once and for all."

He opened the glove box and took out a flashlight. Rachel's heart skipped a beat and her blood turned to ice.

"No Craig! Don't! Please don't!"

He reached down and grabbed her ankles, yanking them up to his lap so forcefully that she nearly toppled onto the floorboard. Surrendering would be her last hope of staying alive.

"Look, Craig, I know you're going to rape me." Her voice trembled as she spoke. "But please, please, please, when you're through with me, just let me go, okay? If you promise me that you'll let me go, then I'll promise not to fight you."

Craig wasn't listening. He slipped his hand underneath her buttocks to lift up her hips as he pulled her dress up past her waist.

"Dammit. You're wearing panty hose, and they're such a pain in the ass to take off."

Rachel clamped her knees together. Craig brandished his knife.

"Didn't I just hear you promise you weren't going to fight me? I'd keep my word if I were you."

She wept softly as he rolled her on her side, turning her face toward the seat back. She felt the cold air as he rolled the waistband down her backside. Once it cleared her bottom he stopped. She cringed as he stroked her bare cheeks.

"Nice. Very nice. I'll have some fun with this."

He turned her on her back and pulled her dress up over her face. Rachel felt the upholstery on her bare bottom as he swooped in and yanked her pantyhose off. It brushed her arm as he tossed it aside. A small beam of light pierced through the dress fabric. She braced herself for the worst, praying that once he finished, he would let her go. To her relief, he switched off the flashlight without touching her.

"Son of a bitch! What is this? A damn donut shop? What is it with this place and cops?"

Rachel's prayers had been answered. She screamed at the top of her lungs. Craig pulled her dress off her face. He grabbed her pantyhose and wadded up a small piece. She screamed again and he stuffed the wad into her open mouth, pushing it in as far as he could. She chocked and gagged as he quickly wrapped the rest of it around her mouth. Grabbing the back of her dress with his free hand, he pulled her back up in her seat, securing the pantyhose into a tight knot behind her head. Bound and gagged, he quickly strapped her in her seatbelt as she made muffled noises. She still felt the truck upholstery on her bare bottom and looked down. The front of her skirt draped over her knees, keeping her covered. Craig fired up the engine and drove out of the parking lot.

"So you're a natural blonde. You know, that really does surprise me. I didn't think you were."

Rachel kept making muffled sounds until she realized panicking would get her nowhere. As they got back on the Interstate, she took a few deep breaths through her nose and resumed flexing her fingers. She felt the back of her dress bunched up behind her. It covered her hands. As long as she stayed calm, she might be able to work it to her advantage. She stretched out her fingers, feeling along the knot until she found the right spot. She pulled at it. It wouldn't budge. She tried again. After the third attempt, a tiny bit pulled loose.

They soon reached the town of Lordsburg and he exited the Interstate. Rachel's chest tightened as they drove past several motels, but Craig continued on, making his way through the town and turning onto the highway to Silver City. After driving a few more miles, he finally spoke up.

"A few weeks ago I wrote an article about New Mexico ghost towns for a travel magazine, and while I was here I spent a few days in the backcountry. There's an area about twenty miles or so up the road that's both scenic and remote, and it's where you and I are going. I have a tent in the back of the truck, and once we arrive, I'll leave you in here while I pitch it. Then, when I come back for you, I'll give you your shoes back so you can walk to the tent. Once we go inside, you'll see a blanket spread out the ground. You're to lie down on top of that blanket, and I'll have a stake in the ground at each corner. Better get used to being bound and gagged, because I'm leaving that gag in your mouth and tying your hands and feet to those stakes. That way you can't run away or draw attention to yourself if anyone else should happen by. Then we can focus on getting reacquainted with one another, and we'll be getting up close and very, very personal." He ran his hand up and down her thigh. Her skin crawled once again.

"Don't worry, I'll cover you up with another blanket at night so you won't catch cold. And I'll take you out for a few times each day for a bathroom break. However, I'm afraid I have some bad news for you." He lifted up the front of her dress, bunching up the fabric in his hand. Once again, she braced herself.

"First, I'll have to cut this pretty dress off of you and shred it. I know you probably like it, but you won't be needing it anymore." He dropped the dress and put his hand back on the wheel. Rachel sighed in relief.

"We'll also to be here for at least a week, maybe longer, but I only brought enough food and water for one. And since I'll be the only one up walking around, you'll have to miss out on mealtime."

She made more muffled sounds.

"What was that? You said you're hungry? And you want something to eat?"

Rachel shook her head and made more noises.

"Well, now that you've brought it up, there is one thing that you can eat, and don't worry, you'll be eating plenty of it. Would you like to know what it is?"

She knew where he was going. She shook her head back and forth and made louder noises. He responded with a laugh as he reached down and unzipped his fly.

"I know it's kind of dark in here, so I'll turn the flashlight on so you can see it better. And just so you know, I'm only doing this to be fair. I got to see yours, so now you get to see mine." Craig reached into his fly. Rachel clamped her eyes shut. He laughed at her again.

"Aw, what's the matter? Don't you want to see it? Well, that's okay. I'll leave it out until we get to where we're going. That way you can still see it if you change your mind."

Craig went silent for moment. When he spoke again, his voice had a sober tone. "As I said before, we'll be here for about a week to ten days. Then, once the food runs out, I'll have to finish you off. If I don't, someone could find you. You would, of course, tell them what I did, and I can't allow that happen. I'll also bury you before I leave. I have to be sure you're never found, but if it means anything to you, I'll try to find you a real pretty spot."

Rachel's blood turned to ice and her body broke out in a cold sweat. Craig must have smelled her fear.

"So why am I doing this? It's because I wanted you from the first day I met you, but you never gave me a chance, and then you spurned me when you went and got that promotion behind my back." His tone turned angry. "No woman ever snubs me and gets away with it. I may not be the first man to have you, but I'm sure as hell going to be your last." His tone then lightened. "But let's not worry about that just yet, because the next few days are going to be fun, fun, fun."

He began describing the graphic details of the various things he intended to do to her once he had her pinned to the ground inside the tent. The bile built up in her stomach, but she kept her eyes closed and concentrated on loosening the knot. Failure to free herself in time meant her fate would be sealed. After several anxious minutes, Rachel finally pulled the knot out. Seconds later her hands were free, but the rope was still tied around one of her wrists. Perhaps she could use it to her advantage. She slowly opened her eyes. Craig was staring straight ahead. He had a full erection, but he was too immersed in the lurid details of his sexual plans for her to notice as she pulled off the gag and carefully unfastened her seatbelt.

"You are one sick bastard."

Before he could react, Rachel had the rope around his neck, crossing her hands and snapping it tight with every ounce of strength she had. Craig made loud choking sounds as he slammed on the brakes. The truck swerved and skidded. Rachel realized they might crash, but it would be far better to die in a car crash than to be repeatedly raped and killed. He jabbed her ribs with his elbow, but she held her grip. He gave her one final blow to her chest, so hard it knocked the wind out of her. He quickly regained control of the truck and punched the accelerator. Rachel slipped the rope around his neck once again, yanking it with all her might. Craig hit the brake and slammed her against the passenger door, once again knocking the wind out of her. Before she could catch her breath, he hit the gas, opened the passenger door and shoved her out of the moving truck. She had never before experienced the searing pain she felt as her body crashed and tumbled onto the terrain below.

* * *

Craig stomped on the brakes and pulled over. His throat throbbed with a sharp, stabbing pain. Something blocked his airway, making it difficult for him to breathe. He tried to swallow, but it too was difficult. Rachel had done some damage. Hopefully, it wasn't serious. Going to a hospital wasn't an option, and at the moment he had more pressing business to attend to. He turned his truck around and grabbed his flashlight, slowly driving in the opposite direction and quickly finding what he was looking for. A motionless Rachel lay in a heap about five yards off the side of the road. She looked like a broken doll. He would have to bury her before someone found her.

He pulled over and parked, but by the time he reached her body, he was racked with a coughing spell. Foamy blood splashed down on the ground near her head. When it finally stopped, a pair of headlights appeared in the distance. He crawled behind a piece of brush and turned off the flashlight. A car drove past about a minute later. To his relief, they were out of range of its headlights. Once it was safely away, he turned the flashlight on and walked back to the truck. His breathing labored as he climbed up a slight incline. More blood came up and he fought to catch his breath. As soon as it settled down, he opened the tailgate, hopped into the truck bed, gasping for air as he unlocked the large cargo box. He reached inside for his shovel and slowly made his way back to Rachel's body.

The ground was harder than he expected. Digging into it would take an extra effort. Pounding the shovel labored his breathing and he soon coughed up more blood. He had to stop and rest. Burying her would be a long, difficult process. He caught his breath and turned a few more shovelfuls of earth. Resuming the digging, the shovel made a loud, clanging sound. He had hit a large rock. He cleared the dirt around it and tried to lift it out, but it wouldn't budge. After a few feeble attempts, he nearly collapsed from exhaustion. Dropping to his knees, he heard a sound in the distance. Two more headlights were approaching. Once again, he dove under the brush and switched off the flashlight. This time it wasn't a car, but a pair of motorcycles. They slowed as they passed his truck. He held his breath. Bikers were the last thing he needed to deal with. To his relief, they zoomed away.

He switched the flashlight back on and checked his watch. It had taken him more than thirty minutes to dig a single, small, shallow hole. He would have to start over, but with his injured windpipe it would take hours for him to dig anything deep enough to conceal her remains, and dawn would surely come before his task was complete.

He looked down at her. Her dress was tattered, and her face was bloodied. She had no identification, and he had driven her across state lines. She would be a Jane Doe. He would have to smash her skull and leave her face unrecognizable. He raised his shovel up high over his head, and once again, hacking coughs racked his body. More blood came up as he slowly lowered the shovel. He gave her one final kick to her ribs and stomped away.

❧FORTY❧

THE NINE-ONE-ONE dispatcher told Shane to meet the officer at the front entrance. The first cruiser arrived within minutes of his call. As the officer stepped out of his car, everyone began talking at once.

"Wait a minute," he said. "One at a time here. Who made the call?"

"I did," said Shane. "My girlfriend is missing. We think she's been kidnapped."

Gilbert stepped forward, stating that he was with hotel security. His walkie-talkie went off as he talked.

"Yeah, what is it, Greta?"

"I think I may have found something on one of the cameras. You'd better come take a look."

"Ten four. On my way." He turned to the others. "I can only take one of you with me."

Julie stepped forward. "I'm her mother."

"Okay then, come with me. Someone will be here shortly to take the rest of you some place private."

Julie stepped away with Gilbert and the officer, and a concierge soon arrived to take the rest of the group to a small meeting room.

"Is there anything I can get you?" she asked. "Coffee? Bottled water?"

"I need to get my purse," said Emma. "It's still in the ballroom. So is Julie's." Emma stepped away, returning a few minutes later with the purses.

"Everyone's left," she said, "but I don't think any of them knew about Rachel."

"Probably best that we keep it quiet, at least for now," said Bruce. "Hopefully whatever is on the security tape will lead us to whoever took her, and we'll have her back within the next few hours."

"I hope you're right, Bruce," said Matt. "The sooner they can figure out what happened, the better the chances of finding her safe. Let's keep our fingers crossed and hope we get lucky."

"My gut still tells me it's Craig," said Shane. "I know you said he moved back to Sacramento, but it was two weeks ago, and who's to say he's not back in town?" He looked down at Rachel's purse, resting in his lap. "Wait a minute." He reached for his phone and placed a call. It went to voicemail.

"Lamar, it's Shane. Call me as soon as you get this message. Rachel's been kidnapped. Word is Craig Walker moved back to Sacramento two weeks ago. I need you to verify it and I'll need his address."

Julie and the police officer stepped into the room as Shane disconnected the call.

"A detective is on her way," said the officer. "She'll be here shorty, and we need you all to stay here until she arrives. She'll want to get statements from all of you."

"Trust me, we're not going anywhere," said Shane.

"So what was on the footage?" asked Bruce.

"The first shot is of her and Emma," said Julie. "They're leaving through the front entrance, and they're both carrying wedding gifts. The other was shot a few minutes later. It's kind of fuzzy, and it only lasts for a few seconds, but you can see Rachel walking past the corner of the screen. There's a man walking next to her, but we can't identify him. He's wearing a baseball cap, and his face is turned away from the camera. I recognized Rachel's dress, so we know for certain it's her."

"I know what Craig looks like," said Shane. "I talked to him that night at the La Paloma, and I was at Rachel's court hearing a few weeks ago. He was there too."

"Come with me," said the officer.

Shane followed him down a hallway leading to the business offices. The officer took him through an open door, where a security officer sat at her desk. The police officer asked her to play the footage for Shane. She clicked on her mouse and rows of parked cars filled her monitor. Two small figures walked into the background. The woman was definitely Rachel, but he couldn't be certain about the man.

"Can you make it any larger?"

"We already tried," said Gilbert, "and when we did, it got too pixelated. Unfortunately, we can't make out the man's face."

"Which way are they headed?"

"Away from the hotel, toward the back of the parking lot."

"And there's no other footage?"

"Nothing other than her and the other lady walking out the front entrance. That's all we were able to get."

"Damn." Shane asked them to play it back again. "He looks like he's about the same height as Craig Walker, and he has the same build. I know it's him. He's been stalking her for years. Who else would do something like this?"

The police officer's radio went off. The detective had arrived. He quickly escorted Shane back to the meeting room.

"What did you find out?" asked an anxious Bruce.

"He's appears to be the same height and build as Craig Walker. I'm convinced it's him."

The detective was a middle-aged African American woman named Lanelle Norman. She had a gentle smile and a warm, comforting aura about her. She quickly got down to business, taking each witness aside for an interview, starting with Julie. When she got to Shane, he told her he felt particularly upset about mistaking Sara for Rachel.

"I can't believe I was so stupid," he said. "What the hell was I thinking? Why didn't I walk up to her and say something as soon as I saw her? I would have known right then and there that she wasn't Rachel, and we would have started looking for her much sooner."

"I understand," said Lanelle, "but as I just told her mother, getting upset and blaming yourself isn't going to help Rachel. I'm told both women are about the same height, with similar hairstyles, and they both were wearing the same color dress. With all the confusion going on, anyone could have easily mistaken one for the other. Now, you said you're sure that a man named Craig Walker is the person who abducted her. Can you tell me more about Mr. Walker?"

"Of course. He's an ex-coworker of Rachel's. They had a falling out when she got a promotion he felt she didn't deserve." He told the detective all that he knew.

"What was the most chilling was that night at the La Paloma," he said. "Rachel had already left, so I went up to the bar and talked to him. To say the man is sexually obsessed with her would be an understatement. He even bragged about having his way with her, whether she wanted it or not." His heart skipped a beat and he paused for a moment. "Oh my god. He's going to rape her. That's why he's kidnapped her."

"We don't know that yet, nor have we even determined if he's the person who abducted her. Trust me, we're trying to find her as quickly as we can, hopefully before any real harm comes to her. I'll be contacting the Tucson police shortly to bring them onboard. I'm an Oro Valley officer, so his residence and former workplace are out of my jurisdiction."

"How long do you think it will take to find her?"

Lanelle looked Shane in the eye. "I'm going to be honest with you. Right now, we don't have much to go on, and her abductor had a good one-hour start before anyone realized she was missing. She could be anywhere by now, so we're going to follow up on all of the leads as quickly as we can, and, hopefully, we'll soon know if it was indeed Craig Walker who took her."

Before leaving, Lanelle asked if any of them had any other information. Emma raised her hand.

"I just wanted to say I'm sorry I didn't see her keys underneath the car. I should have known something was wrong when I went back out and she wasn't there. But then I came back inside and saw the other girl, Sara, and thought she was Rachel." Emma burst into tears. "I'm so sorry. This is all my fault."

Matt wrapped his arms around his wife. "This isn't your fault any more than it's anyone else's fault. We all messed up, and like the lady just told us, it's not going to help us find her."

Julie looked at Bruce. "So, what about Alice? Do we try to find out where she and Donny are staying tonight so we can let them know?"

"I've been wondering that myself," said Matt. "They were both very firm. They were shutting down their phones, and they didn't want to be disturbed. Period. I'm his twin, and he wouldn't even tell me where they're staying tonight."

"Let's hold off, for now," said Bruce. "Detective Norman just went to call the Tucson police, and, hopefully, they'll find her soon. If Craig has her, he could have easily taken her back to the motel where he used to work and hidden her in one of the rooms."

"No doubt the cops will serve a search warrant," said Matt, "but if she's not found within the next twenty-four hours we'll have figure out a way to let Donny and Alice know. I know they're going on an Alaska cruise, but I don't have a copy of their itinerary, and neither do our folks."

"Nor do we," said Bruce.

"In that case, I'll go online to see which cruise ships are leaving tomorrow for Alaska, and I'll start making some phone calls. I hate the thought of interrupting their honeymoon, but Alice needs to know about her sister."

Detective Norman came back in and handed Shane a slip of paper. "Rachel's case has been assigned to Detectives Martin Cruz and Duane Anderson of the Tucson Police Department. Here is Detective Cruz's phone number. He would like to talk to you, as soon as possible, regarding the private investigator's report you have on Craig Walker."

"Thanks." Shane looked around the room. "Are we done here?"

"Yes, you're all free to go. As soon as we know anything, we'll let you know. And if any of you think of anything later on please call me. You each have my card. Something that may seem small or insignificant to you could make a difference."

Bruce spoke up as the detective stepped away. "It's late, and I'm afraid we're all in for a long night. Please, any of you, if you hear anything, please let the rest of us know. I don't care if it's three o'clock in the morning, call us, please."

"Same for Emma and me. I'll check out those cruise lines and I call you as soon as I can figure out what ship they're on."

"Thanks, Matt."

After a long, emotional goodnight the others left. Shane stayed behind to place a call. Moments later Detective Cruz was on the line.

"I need more information about Craig Walker. What can you tell me about him?"

"Plenty." Once again, Shane told him everything he knew.

"I see. I'll contact the Sacramento police, and as soon as I know something, I'll let you know."

* * *

Large sheets of plastic hung from the ceiling to the floor, blocking off half of the front office. A sign reading, "Pardon our dust. We're remodeling" was taped on one of the sheets. Detective Cruz stepped around the construction mess, presenting his badge to the young man at the front desk. The clerk suddenly appeared nervous.

"What can I do for you, officer?"

"I'm looking for Craig Walker. I'm told he works here."

"He did, but not anymore. He left about two weeks ago."

"I see. So why did he leave?"

"He said he was moving to Sacramento."

Cruz took a small notepad from his shirt pocket. "Did he leave a forwarding address?"

"I guess."

"Well, can you find out?"

"I don't have access to the personnel files."

"Is there anyone here who does?"

"Let me call my boss." The desk clerk picked up the phone and placed a call, saying a police detective needed Craig's forwarding address. As he was speaking he picked up a pen and jotted something down, disconnecting the call a few minutes later.

"My boss just gave me the okay," he said. "If you'll wait a couple of minutes, I'll have his forwarding address."

He entered something into the computer, and a short time later he handed the detective a slip of paper with the address for an apartment in Sacramento. Cruz stuffed it into his pocket. The young man still looked anxious.

"Before you go, sir, I need to tell you something."

"What is it?" asked Cruz.

The young man looked even more nervous. "A few weeks ago, Craig wanted me to help him play a practical joke on somebody, only I didn't think it was very funny"

"What kind of practical joke?"

"It was on some girl named Rachel."

Cruz got his notepad back out. "Do you know who this Rachel was?"

The young man shook his head. "No. According to Craig, she was someone he once worked with, and he must have really had some sort of a grudge against her. Whatever it was, he was sure upset about it, and he wanted to get even with her."

"So, what was he planning on doing to her?"

"Apparently, she designs websites, and he wanted me to contact her about building a website. I was to meet her for coffee. Then I was supposed to slip a mickey in her drink, bring her back here, and put her in one of the rooms. Craig said he'd be there with his camera set up, and he was going to film to an x-rated video of him and me having sex with her. I said no way would do I anything like that, but then he told me if I refused, he'd turn me in."

Tom took a deep breath and sighed. "My parents came here illegally from Mexico when I was six months old. I've lived here my entire life and consider myself an American, but I've never had a green card. So, it was either be a party to drugging someone and shooting a porn video, or risk being kicked out of the country. I have a wife and a little daughter, and I didn't want to be taken away from my family. I really had no choice, so I finally agreed."

"I see. So, you agreed to rape someone."

"No!"

Cruz was firm. "When you drug someone and then have sex with them, without their consent, it's considered rape."

He shook his head back and forth. "No. It never actually happened. Later on, Craig told me it was just a hypothetical scenario."

"Did he say anything else?"

"No. He just said I was off the hook, and then he said never intended to go through with any of it. Apparently, the joke was on me, but like I said, I didn't think it was very funny."

"So, when was this?"

"About a week before he left."

The detective asked a few more questions. Once he returned to the station, he called the Sacramento police.

❧FORTY-ONE❧

TAYLOR KAUFMAN LOVED the great outdoors. She and her classmate, Hannah West, left their college dorm rooms in the predawn hours on Sunday morning for an all-day backcountry excursion for their photography class. There were only a few cars on the road in Las Cruses, and traffic on the Interstate was light as they headed west to Lordsburg. Exiting the freeway, they went through a fast-food drive-thru for coffee and breakfast sandwiches, eating in Taylor's truck as they took the highway north toward Silver City. Dawn was breaking. As Taylor drove, Hannah scoured the roadside, searching for an interesting place to take photos when something unexpected caught her eye.

"Look over there." She nudged Taylor and pointed to something up the road. "Did someone lose a mannequin off of a truck?"

"What the hell?" Taylor slammed on the brakes and hastily pulled the truck over. "That's not a mannequin. That's a body. Call nine-one-one."

Taylor dove out of her truck ran over to take a closer look. The woman wore a torn blue dress, and she appeared to be seriously injured. Taylor bent down to feel for a pulse and shouted back to Hannah.

"She's alive! Tell them she's still alive!"

Taylor raced back to her truck. Hannah was on the phone with a dispatcher, and it was obvious that they were asking her too many questions. She grabbed the phone away from Hannah.

"We're heading north on Highway Ninety, and we're about twenty miles south of Silver City. There's a woman lying unconscious on the side of the road. We don't know who she is, or how she got here. All I can tell you is she's still alive, but if you don't get off your lazy asses and send some help, she'll die."

Taylor tossed the phone aside and raced back to the woman, taking off her jacket and covering her up as best she could. She knelt down next to her and reached for her hand, giving it a squeeze. What she saw next would horrify her. A piece of rope was tied around the woman's wrist.

"I don't know who did this to you, but whoever they are, they're long gone and we're getting you some help. The paramedics are on their way, so just hang in there, okay?" Taylor held tight to her hand and kept talking to her, but it seemed like an eternity before she finally heard an approaching siren. A state trooper pulled over and jumped out of his cruiser.

"What happened?"

"I don't know. My friend and I saw her, so we pulled over and called for help. No one else was around."

He took a closer look, noting the bloodstains on some of the rocks and a small, freshly dug hole a few feet away. He radioed for a helicopter and cordoned off the area. Minutes later the first paramedics arrived. Taylor and the trooper stepped aside and as the paramedics checked her vitals and hooked her up to an IV line. Two more highway patrol cruisers and an ambulance soon arrived. The road would have to be blocked off to make room for the helicopter to land. Taylor and Hannah gave their statements to the officers as the paramedics worked. Before long, they heard the helicopter. It landed on a level section of highway a few hundred feet away. The paramedics had her on a backboard. They carefully loaded her into the back of the ambulance and transferred her to the helicopter. Once it lifted off, one of the paramedics returned Taylor's jacket.

"Will she be okay?" Taylor asked.

"Hopefully. She's on her way to a trauma center in Albuquerque."

* * *

Sunday afternoon Bruce called Matt and Shane to tell them there had been a breakthrough in the case, and one of the detectives would be coming over within the hour. Everyone looked haggard as they gathered around the dining table. Julie offered to brew a fresh pot of coffee, but they all declined.

"Were you able to find out what ship Donny and Alice are on?" asked Bruce.

"Yes, I was," said Matt. "I contacted the cruise line and found out the ship leaves port in Seattle at four o'clock this afternoon. Someone from the cruise line will talk to them as soon as they check in. I have my phone turned on, and I expect to hear from them within the next hour or so."

"I still can't believe this happened," said Shane. "It's been a couple of months since I blocked him out of her computer, and we changed all of her passwords. So this morning I took her laptop to the office, and I've spent most of the day running diagnostics and doing forensics, but so far I've not found any evidence of him hacking back into her email accounts. So how did he know where to find her?"

"Alice has been sending out emails about the wedding for some time," said Julie. "He could have intercepted one before he was locked out of her account. We'll have to ask the detective about it as soon as he gets here."

"And we still don't know for certain if it was Craig who abducted her," said Bruce. "It could have been one of those random things, and Rachel just happened to be at the wrong place at the wrong time."

"Did he tell you what the breakthrough was?" asked Matt.

"No," said Bruce. "He just said they had news, and he wanted to meet with the family. I'm hoping it means they've found Rachel, and they're getting ready to make an arrest, if they haven't made one already."

The doorbell rang. Bruce went to answer, returning a moment later with a balding man in a wrinkled gray suit. He introduced him to the others as Detective Duane Anderson. He too declined the coffee as he took his seat at the table and opened a folder.

"We now know who kidnapped your daughter. The suspect is forty-two-year-old Craig Thomas Walker."

"I knew it," said Shane.

"Please, just tell us what happened," said Bruce.

"Last night Detective Cruz stopped by the motel where Mr. Walker used to work. He was told that the suspect no longer worked there and had moved back to Sacramento. Detective Cruz was able to get his forwarding address and he contacted the Sacramento police. Early this morning they went to the apartment complex to serve a search warrant. Mr. Walker wasn't there, and according to a neighbor, he hasn't been seen in the past few days. They searched the apartment and found his laptop and smartphone. They took both items into evidence, and they found something on his laptop."

Bruce's patience was wearing thin. "What was it?"

Anderson sighed. "I'm afraid there's no easy way to tell you this, so I'm going to be as straightforward as I can. We've learned that Mr. Walker is a photographer as well as a journalist. In fact, many of his photos were related to the articles he's written. Unfortunately, his interest in photography goes well beyond photojournalism. They found a number of photos of nude women. He's also been recording videos of himself having sex with different women, and he's into bondage. All of the women in the photos and the videos were tied down on the bed, with either ropes or chains, and most of them were gagged as well."

Julie burst into tears while a badly shaken Shane covered his face with his hands. The detective went on.

"While Detective Cruz was at the motel last night he interviewed one of Craig Walker's former co-workers who admitted that Walker had wanted him to contact Rachel about designing a website. He was to meet her for coffee, slip a drug into her drink, and then bring her back to the motel, where Walker planned to shoot a video of the two of them having sex with her."

"Dear god," said Bruce. "So, when was this?"

"A few weeks ago."

"And this creep was willing to help him rape her?" The anger resonated in Shane's voice.

"Not exactly." Anderson's tone was firm. "The young man admitted he'd been brought into the United States illegally as a young child, and Walker had threatened to turn him over to the authorities if he didn't cooperate. He also said that later on Walker told him he'd changed his mind and had never intended to go through with any of it."

"So when was this?" asked Shane.

"Just before he went back to Sacramento."

"But it doesn't prove that he took Rachel," said Matt.

"I'm getting to that," said Anderson. "The Sacramento police have also learned that Craig Walker withdrew five hundred dollars from an ATM late Thursday night, and there's been no further activity on his bank account. In the meantime, Detective Cruz went back to the motel a few hours later. By then someone else was at the front desk, and this man became extremely nervous as soon as Detective Cruz presented his badge and started asking questions. He admitted that Craig Walker had shown up at the motel late Friday night, and he'd let him stay in a room that had been closed for remodeling. He also said Walker paid him fifty dollars under the table."

"I knew it." Shane's fist pounded on the table. "I knew he was back to town."

"He certainly was, and he's gone to great lengths to cover his tracks," said Anderson. "He left his cellphone behind so he couldn't be tracked. He paid cash for his food and gasoline, and he secretly stayed at his former workplace the night before Rachel disappeared. The desk clerk also admitted seeing Craig leave early yesterday morning. We searched the room, but he didn't leave any evidence behind. Earlier today Detective Norman went back to the La Corona to question some of the employees, and a bartender recognized Walker from a photo. He said Walker came up to the bar around six o'clock yesterday evening. He ordered a burger and fries with a beer and he paid cash. No one has seen him since."

Bruce appeared to be in shock. "Which was about same time the wedding started, and he was right there."

"Yes, sir, he unfortunately was," said Anderson. "We know Craig Walker has a long history of harassing your daughter. We know he made a secret trip back to Tucson, and he was last seen at the same hotel where your daughter was kidnapped, two hours before she disappeared."

"Do you have any idea where may have taken her?" asked Bruce.

"At the moment I'm afraid we don't. We've learned that he recently re-registered his truck, and we have the license number for his new California plates. We've also alerted the media. Hopefully someone with information will come forward soon."

Julie was desperate. "Could she be at the motel? If he hid in a closed room, then who's to say he didn't bring her back there?"

"We've already served a search warrant," said Anderson. "We've checked every room, including the ones they're remodeling. Unfortunately, she wasn't there, but we've staked it out just in case he shows up later on. In the meantime, we've put out an APB on his truck, and we've alerted every law enforcement agency in the state, as well as in California. The Sacramento police have also staked out his apartment in case he tries to bring her back there. He can't hide forever. He'll surface sooner or later, which is why we're asking for the public's help. Someone somewhere has seen them, and the sooner that person comes forward, the better the chances of finding Rachel unharmed."

After assuring everyone that he or his partner would let them know as soon they had any news, Detective Anderson saw himself out. The others sat around the table in stunned disbelief. Shane finally stood up. His face was chalky.

"I need to use your bathroom."

"It's down the hall, on your left," said Julie. Shane stepped out and Matt's phone rang.

"That's Donny." He accepted the call and put the phone on speaker. His brother sounded angry.

"What the hell is going on? We've just been told to call you because there's some sort of family emergency, but they wouldn't tell us what it was. This had better be damn good, or so help me, your ass is getting kicked."

"Donny, Rachel's been kidnapped."

It took a moment for it to sink in. "What?"

Bruce spoke up. "Donny, it's me, Bruce. Your brother is telling you the truth. Rachel's been kidnapped. She's missing, and we don't know where she is. Right now, all we know is that Craig Walker abducted her from the hotel parking lot sometime around eight o'clock last night, and she hasn't been seen since. Can you put Alice on the line?"

"Hold on a second."

"No problem, son, we can wait."

They heard voices in the background. Moments later Alice was on the line. Her voice was shaking.

"Dad? What's going on? Donny just said Rachel's been kidnapped."

"It's true," said Julie. "Craig Walker showed up last night and he took her from the hotel parking lot."

Julie burst into tears. As Matt tried to comfort her, Bruce filled his daughter in on what had happened. Shane returned while he was speaking. His face looked ashen. As Bruce finished, Alice started crying, and Donny came back on the line.

"I told the lady from the cruise line what happened, and she's going see about getting us a flight home. I'll call you back in a few minutes."

Matt disconnected the call. Once again Julie offered to brew a fresh pot of coffee, but the others declined. Matt's phone rang a short time later. Donny was calling back, and he put the call on speaker.

"Okay," said Donny, "we were able to get a flight out of Seattle which leaves in about four hours, but it's to Phoenix, not Tucson."

"Not a problem," said Matt. "I'll drive up there and pick you up at the airport. What time does it arrive?"

As Matt and Donny finished up their business Julie grabbed a tissue and dabbed her eyes. Returning to her seat, she looked at Shane.

"Can we fix you anything to eat?"

"I'm fine. Thanks."

"Have you had any sleep?"

"Nope."

Julie looked concerned. "You need to get some rest, Shane. You won't do her any good if you make yourself sick."

"I know."

"Have you told your folks about this?"

"No." He ran his hands through his hair and let out a sigh. "We were supposed to drop my dog off at their place this morning on the way out of town, so I sent my mom a text to let her know something had come up and we were running late. She's called a couple of times, but I let it go to voicemail. I just can't talk about this right now."

"It's okay, Shane. I can call her." Julie looked at Bruce. "Would you mind taking him home when I'm done? He shouldn't be driving right now."

"I can do it," said Matt. "Donny and Alice are supposed to land in Phoenix at eight forty-five. I need to go home and try to take a nap."

Shane punched up his mother's number and handed his phone to Julie. She stepped away and returned his phone a few minutes later.

"She and your father are on their way. They'll take you home."

"Thanks."

Shane put his phone away and stared into space. Matt took his leave, and Kelly and Colin arrived a short time later. Bruce led them into the dining room, where they introduced themselves to each other, regretting that they had to meet under such tragic circumstances. Shane remained in his chair. He appeared to be in shock.

"I should have been there," he said. "If I'd been there, I would have been able to protect her."

"You don't know that." Bruce's voice was firm. "I know my daughter, and she's always been a fighter. Trust me, she would have never gone with him willingly. He had to have had a weapon on him, so what would have stopped him from killing you?"

Bruce's phone rang. He checked the caller ID. "This might be Detective Norman." He took the call, and as they spoke his face turned pale. He gave them a sober look once they disconnected.

"It was Detective Norman. She said they've removed the crime scene tape from Rachel's car, and we can go pick it up at the hotel. Gilbert, from security, has the keys. She also said they recovered three sets of fingerprints from the trunk. The first two they couldn't identify, so they think they're Rachel's and Emma's. The third set belonged to Craig Walker. So we now have our smoking gun." He turned to his wife. "We need to go get her car."

Colin spoke up. "Don't worry about it. Kelly and I will pick it up and we'll get Shane's car when we drop it off. You guys need to get some rest."

"Thanks."

Shane's parents helped him from his chair, and Bruce walked them to the door.

ɷFORTY-TWOɷ

CRAIG WOKE UP WITH another coughing fit. This time, the sun was up. Nearly thirty-six hours had passed since Rachel's attempt to strangle him. He still had a partially blocked airway, and he had coughed up more blood.

He looked at his watch. It was seven-thirty on Monday morning. Craig had planned on laying low for at least a week to allow enough time for the authorities to call off their search for Rachel, but now things had changed. He would either have to get medical attention, or risk dying in the wilderness. Unable to eat, he opened another boxed fruit drink, slowly sipping its contents as he figured out his next move. The route he intended to take home would take him north through Colorado to Wyoming, and then Interstate 80 to Sacramento. Now he would have to come up with a faster way to get to California. He opened the glove box and took out his road maps. If he went through eastern Arizona to Interstate 40, he would be in California by day's end, and he would look for a hospital in Needles. Along the way he would have to come up with a good cover story about camping alone, slipping on a rock, and somehow landing on his throat.

He stuffed the road maps back into the glove box and took down his tent. His labored breathing made even the simplest of tasks long and painful. An hour later, he locked up the cargo box and fired up his truck. The drive through the New Mexico backcountry was uneventful, but his senses went on high alert once he crossed into Arizona. He stopped for gas in the town of Pinetop, but he had difficulty speaking when he tried to tell the cashier he would be paying cash.

"Sounds like you have a really bad case of laryngitis," said the woman behind the register.

Craig gave her a smile and nodded his head.

"I'm so sorry. Why don't you give me a couple of twenties and I'll turn on the pump. If it's gonna be more than that, you can come back in and we'll figure the rest of it out. Otherwise, I'll give you your change and you'll be on your way."

Craig smiled again and mouthed the words, "Thank you." Ten minutes later he was back on the road, being extra careful to not go over the speed limit or do anything else to attract attention. His body relaxed once he reached the town of Holbrook and got on the eastbound Interstate. A few more hours and he would be in Needles.

The traffic grew heavier as he drove into Flagstaff. He stayed in the right lane, trying to blend in as he made his way through town. Checking his rearview mirror, his heart skipped a beat. A highway patrol cruiser was on his tail. He reminded himself to stay calm. Plenty of cars and trucks were passing him in the left lane. Sooner or later some speeder would come along for him to chase. He kept his eyes focused straight ahead, but the cruiser never passed. He looked back in the rearview mirror. It was still on his tail, only now its lights were flashing. Beads of sweat popped out on his forehead and he checked his speedometer. He wasn't speeding. Moments later he heard a siren.

His mind raced as he cursed under his breath and fought the urge to panic. He had come up with the perfect plan, but then Rachel somehow got loose and tried to strangle him. No doubt her body had been found by now. Somehow, they must have identified her and linked him to her disappearance.

He had two options. Pull over and surrender, and end up serving life in prison, or worse, or simply run. If he could ditch the cops and find a place to hide, he might, with any luck, make his way into Mexico, especially if he traveled at night. It would be risky, but he had no other choice. He punched the accelerator and wove his way through the traffic. The cruiser stayed on his tail. Three more soon joined the chase. Craig was doing well over ninety miles per hour as he drove out of Flagstaff, weaving in and out of traffic and nearly colliding with a minivan and a tractor-trailer rig. As he tried to outrun the cops, the ending scene from the old movie, *Butch Cassidy and the Sundance Kid*, played through his mind. Butch and Sundance fought until the very end, choosing to go out in a blaze of glory instead of being captured. He would do the same, and even if he didn't make it, he would at least have the satisfaction of knowing he had taken his revenge on Rachel Bennett by making sure she had proceeded him in death. With any luck, he would get to spend an eternity in Hell tormenting her.

Craig whipped around a gray Jeep, nearly knocking it off the road. He was now well past the city limits, and, for the moment, there were no other cars immediately ahead of him. He clamped down on the accelerator. The truck was now going over one hundred miles an hour. He looked back in the rearview mirror. Five cruisers were in pursuit. He turned his sights back to the road ahead. Traffic had suddenly bunched up in both lanes. Seconds later he realized it had stopped, and he was coming up too fast on a tanker truck. He slammed on the brakes with both feet, but it was too late. He heard the loud boom as his airbag deployed, along with the sound of metal crunching into metal as he was engulfed in a fireball. He screamed in agony as the flesh burned off his body. Several excruciating seconds would pass before his world finally went black.

* * *

It was a few minutes past nine o'clock on Monday night when Bruce called Matt and Shane for another meeting. Detective Anderson had new information for the family. Donny and Alice were already there when Matt and Emma arrived. Shane rang the doorbell a few minutes later. As he came into the dining room, Alice stood from her chair and greeted him with a hug.

"How are you holding up?" she asked.

"As well as can be expected. How about you?"

"The same."

She pointed to the empty chair on her right. The doorbell rang again as Shane took his seat between Alice and Emma. Both detectives had somber expressions on their faces as they came in and took their seats.

"So, I take it you have news for us," said Bruce.

"Yes, we do." Cruz looked at his partner. "Earlier today a state trooper in Flagstaff spotted a red Dodge Ram truck with California plates on westbound Interstate Forty. He ran the plates, and they matched Craig Walker's truck."

"Thank God," said Julie. "Our prayers have been answered. So, where's my daughter?"

"I'm afraid we still don't know where Rachel is," said Anderson.

"What do you mean you don't know?" Shane was clearly angry. "Didn't you question him once you got him into custody?"

"I'm afraid it's not that simple. They tried to pull him over, but it quickly escalated into a high-speed chase."

"Wait a minute!" exclaimed Matt. "I saw the story on the six o'clock news tonight. Is this the same red pickup truck that crashed into a tanker truck and burst into flames? They said they couldn't release any of the names until they notified the next of kin."

"I'm afraid so," said Cruz. "They set up a roadblock a few miles west of Flagstaff. Unfortunately, Craig Walker's truck crashed into a tanker truck carrying gasoline. The tank ignited and the pickup truck caught fire. Fortunately, the truck driver escaped injury and no one else was hurt. However, the driver of the pickup truck was killed."

The color drained from Julie's face. Her voice sounded mechanical. "Was my daughter in the pickup?"

"No ma'am, she was not," said Cruz. "They only recovered one body. It was a male, burned beyond recognition. The body has been taken to the coroner's office in Flagstaff. They'll have to use dental records to make a positive ID, but we have every reason to believe he's Craig Thomas Walker."

Everyone sat in stunned silence.

"They recovered something from the wreckage we think may have belonged to Rachel." Cruz opened his folder and removed a photo. "This was found inside the truck cab. It's part of a woman's shoe. Do you recognize it?"

He handed Julie the photo. All that remained of the shoe was the heel. A section of the leather hadn't burned and was still blue. As she studied it, her eyes filled with tears.

"It's from one of her blue shoes. The ones she wore at her sister's wedding." She dropped the photo and started sobbing. Alice picked it up and also started crying.

"So what happened to my sister?"

Donny squeezed her hand. "No, Alice, don't."

Alice was undaunted. "So why aren't you out looking for my sister? She wasn't in the truck, which means she's still out there somewhere, and you need to go find her."

"No, Alice," said Donny.

"Ma'am, I know you want us to find your sister," said Cruz, "and I wish, more than anything, that we'd been able to get to her in time, but I'm afraid it didn't work out that way. Based on the evidence found in the suspect's home, and by some of the witness statements, we believe that Craig Thomas Walker kidnapped your sister with the intention of raping her."

Alice cried harder. Donny tried to console her.

"They also found a shovel locked in a steel cargo box in the back of the pickup truck. It was undamaged by the fire, and there was fresh dirt on the blade, indicating that it had been recently used."

Julie and Bruce fell into each other's arms. Both were crying.

"No!" shouted Shane. "She's not dead, and you'll never convince me that she's dead. I'm going to find her. If I have to look under every rock, tree, and bush between here and Flagstaff, I'm going to find her."

Alice wrapped her arms around him. Emma grabbed him from the other side and both women tried to console him. Julie turned to Bruce.

"I have to call Al. He needs to know." She started sobbing again.

"I really wish we could have had a better outcome for this," said Anderson. "However, based on the evidence, we believe Rachel was killed sometime between Saturday night and this morning, and, as well all know, there's a lot of open wilderness in northern Arizona, especially up on the Navajo reservation. I'm afraid the chances of her body being found are slim at best. My partner and I are both very sorry for your loss." He placed a few of his business cards on the table. "The case is officially closed, but please, don't hesitate to call us if you have any further questions. We can see ourselves out."

❧FORTY-THREE❧

RACHEL WAS SOMEHOW trapped inside a deep dark tunnel with sounds and voices fading in and out. A young woman shouted that she was alive. She felt her squeeze her hand as she talked to her, but she couldn't understand the words. Other voices faded in and out, but she couldn't understand what they were saying either. People were touching her and moving her. She heard sirens and loud noise that sounded like a helicopter. People were lifting her, moving her, grabbing her. She wanted to respond. She wanted them to know she was in a lot of pain. Each touch and each movement felt agonizing, but she couldn't speak. Darkness followed, and she felt her body being moved again. More voices faded in and out. Fingers probed inside her mouth. Someone said she had some broken teeth. Something hard and cold was pushed up between her legs, and she felt a cramping pain. As they poked around inside her, a different voice announced that looked like she hadn't been raped, but she had another problem they would need to take care of. The cramps became more severe, but so far as she knew, she wasn't having her period. Finally, the voices went silent, and she started dreaming. One minute she was a child, safe in her mother's arms. Another minute she was trapped in Craig's truck. Other times she heard soft voices, asking her how she was feeling.

At long last, her eyes fluttered open. Florescent lights shined through translucent Plexiglas ceiling panels. The inside of her mouth felt sore. She moved her tongue around. Three of her teeth were broken, all on the right side of her mouth. Her right hip and shoulder hurt, and she felt a dull ache in her right wrist. She looked down. Her blue dress was gone. She now wore a hospital gown. Her right arm was in a sling, and her wrist was in a splint. An IV line was hooked up to her left arm. The rope around her left wrist was gone, and it was covered with bandages. She turned her head to her right. There was a picture window next to her bed. It was nighttime, and the room appeared to be several stories above the ground. She saw city lights. Had she somehow made it back to Tucson?

She turned her head and faced the other way. The door was open. Outside was a brightly lit hallway. A young man, wearing dark blue scrubs, came into her room. He approached her bed and gave her a big smile.

"Well, I see you're finally awake. How are you feeling?"

"I'm not sure." Her throat felt dry. Her voice sounded raspy. "Where am I?"

"You're in Robert H. Goddard Memorial Hospital."

"Robert H. Goddard? There's no such hospital in Tucson."

"Tucson? You're in Albuquerque."

She had to still be dreaming, but decided to play along. "Okay, I'll bite. So, what day is it?"

"It's Tuesday. No, wait. I take it back. It's Wednesday morning. It's a few minutes after midnight."

He injected something into her IV line and asked her more questions, but she felt too sleepy to answer. She closed her eyes and drifted off.

* * *

Kelly MacLeod arrived at Bruce and Julie's home early Wednesday morning. Rachel's car remained parked in the driveway, and a few news trucks had parked in the street. Several reporters and cameramen stood on the sidewalk in front of the house. Kelly grabbed her casserole dish and pushed her way past, refusing to answer any of their questions as she rang the doorbell. Alice finally answered. Her face looked pale and her eyes were red and swollen.

"You must be a friend of my parents," she said, eyeing the casserole dish.

"Actually, I'm Shane's mother."

"Pleased to meet you. I'm Alice, Rachel's sister. Please, come in." Alice led her to the kitchen and opened the refrigerator door, pointing out a spot for Kelly to slide her dish in.

"So, how are you doing, Alice?"

"As well as can be expected, I suppose. I keep thinking that I'm supposed to be on my honeymoon, and why can't I wake up from this awful nightmare?"

"I understand. I feel the same."

"I'm an emergency room nurse. I see tragedies like this every day, but never imagined it happening to my own family. We don't even know when she died, or how it happened." Her voice broke. "All I know is we weren't there, and she died in fear."

Kelly wrapped her arms around her and held her until she was able to compose herself. "Is there anything I can do for you?" Kelly asked.

Alice reached for a tissue and shook her head. "No, there isn't, but Donny, my husband, and my folks, are all out on the patio. I'm sure they'd appreciate it if you came out and said hello."

"Of course."

Alice took Kelly outside, and after the greetings were exchanged, Julie invited Kelly to take a seat on one of the empty chairs.

"We thought we'd come out here to get away from all the reporters," said Julie. "Hopefully they'll all leave soon. We don't need them around here."

"No, you certainly don't," said Kelly.

"So, how's Shane doing?"

"Not well, I'm afraid. He called us as soon as he got home Monday night, and when he told us what happened, my husband and I rushed right over. He was still in denial that she was gone, and he got so agitated that Colin finally made him take a sleeping pill. I stopped by and checked on him on my way here. He seems to be a little calmer, and he now understands that she's gone, but he's totally exhausted. He was going back to bed, but he said to tell you all hello and he'll call you soon."

"He needs his rest," said Julie. "I know he's hardly slept in days. None of us have."

"We've been trying to figure out what to do for a memorial service," said Bruce, "but so far we haven't had much luck. The only thing we can seem to agree on is that we should have it next Thursday, on what would have been her twenty-ninth birthday. Maybe he can help us decide the rest."

"Yes. I think he'd like that. Thank you for including him."

"I called Rachel's father, her biological father, yesterday morning," said Julie.

"It's okay," said Kelly. "Shane already told me the story. So, how'd he take it?"

"Not well. Apparently, he and Rachel have been in contact with one another. She was keeping him up to date about the Craig situation. Anyway, he's pretty upset with the rest of us. He thinks we should have done a better job of protecting her."

"Please, don't go blaming yourselves." Kelly's voice was firm. "I'm already going through this with my son. All of you thought he'd gone back to California, so no one would have seen this coming. I keep telling Shane this isn't his fault, but he still feels a lot of guilt, which isn't helping."

"No, it's not," said Bruce, "but it doesn't mean it's easy for us to let it go either. Rachel had been gone for nearly an hour before any of us realized she was missing. Yes, there was a wedding reception going on, so yes, there was plenty of confusion, and yes, we all mistook Sara for Rachel. Sara hadn't planned on wearing a blue dress that night, but apparently something happened to her other one. It's not any one person's fault, yet we're all to blame, in one way or another, and now Rachel's gone because of it. I wish I knew what the answer is, but I don't."

"I don't either, Bruce," said Kelly. "It's all so senseless, but if it means anything to you, Rachel truly was the love of Shane's life, and there'll never be another one like her. He told us he'd planned on marrying her. He even showed us the ring he'd recently bought for her. He was trying to decide whether he should give it to her on her birthday or wait until Christmas. And, for what it's worth, I really wanted her for my daughter-in-law."

Julie stood up and wrapped her arms around Kelly. Both women quietly wept. Once they calmed down it was time for Kelly to leave.

"You know, Shane really did think of himself as a part of your family. As time goes on, I hope you'll consider including him in holiday celebrations and other family get-togethers. It would mean the world to him."

❧FORTY-FOUR❧

RACHEL OPENED HER eyes and realized it hadn't been a dream. She really was in a hospital. She looked out the window. The sun was up and she saw mountains, but they didn't look right.

"Well, good morning. How are you feeling?"

A young nurse stood next to her bed. She reminded her of Alice.

"I'm not sure," said Rachel. "It's kind of hard to move, especially with this sling, and I'm sore all over. So what happened?"

"You were in an accident. The doctor will be here soon, and he can tell you more."

"So how long have I been here?"

"They brought you in on Sunday."

"Sunday?" Rachel tried to put the pieces together. Craig kidnapped her on Saturday night. She remembered the rope, and how she tried to strangle him, but she didn't know what happened afterwards, or how she ended up in the hospital.

"What time on Sunday?" she asked.

"I'm not really sure. I was off on Sunday. The doctor will fill you in, but for now, I need to take your temperature and check your blood pressure."

Rachel wanted to know where Craig was. "Was anyone with me when I was brought in? Have I had any visitors?"

"You were brought here by a medevac helicopter, so the only people with you would have been the nurse and a paramedic, and so far as I know, you've not had any visitors. Now, if you'll please be still, I need to check your vitals."

Rachel held her tongue as the nurse did her job. Once she finished, she made some notes on her tablet.

"We have you down as a Jane Doe. Do you remember your name?"

"It's Rachel. Rachel Bennett."

The nurse gave her a smile. "Well, it's nice to meet you, Rachel. Is there anyone we can call for you?"

"Last night sometime told me we're in Albuquerque. Is that right?"

"Yes, that's right. We're in Albuquerque."

"Then I need you to call my father. His name is Al. Alfred Matheson. He has a custom paint shop for motorcycles. I'd give you the number, but it's on my phone, and I don't seem to have my phone with me."

"Not a problem, Rachel. We can look him up."

The nurse stepped away. A few minutes later a man wearing a white coat entered. He greeted her with a warm smile and extended his hand.

"So, Rachel, we finally get to meet in person. I'm Harold Collins. I'm an orthopedic surgeon, and I'm in charge of your case."

Rachel extended her left hand. It felt awkward. "Nice meeting you. So, what happened, and how did I end up in Albuquerque?"

"Well, you ended up here after you were flown in by helicopter, and you were brought here because we have a trauma center. And you, young lady, are our miracle patient."

"Really? How so?"

He pulled a stool up next to her bed and took his seat. "You were found by the side of the road early Sunday morning by a couple of college students. It was about twenty miles south of Silver City, and you either fell out, or you were pushed out, of a moving vehicle and were apparently left for dead."

"Was there a red Dodge Ram pickup anywhere around? I don't remember how I got out of it."

"Not that I'm aware of. You'll have to talk to the police about that."

"The police?"

"Yes. They're investigating your case, and, now that you're awake, I'm sure someone will be here soon to talk to you."

Rachel remembered the state trooper who handed her back to Craig. "I'm not sure I want to talk to them."

"Why not?"

"I have my reasons. My father is on his way. I'll talk to him, and then he can talk to the police. So, what happened to me?"

"You were brought into the trauma center. You were wearing a blue dress. There was a rope tied around your left wrist, you were barefoot, and your undergarments were missing. They examined you, and, thankfully, they've determined that you hadn't been raped."

"No, I hadn't. He started to, but then he got interrupted, and after that I apparently escaped. I just need to make sure he won't find me here."

"Don't worry. Hospital security is keeping a close watch on you. Other than your father, no other visitors will have access to you, other than the police, without your approval."

Rachel felt relieved. She was finally out of danger. A tear rolled down her cheek. "So, what happened to me? I'm hurting all over."

"I'm not surprised. You landed on your right side when you fell, and you have several broken bones. Your wrist and shoulder are both fractured, but we've set both. They'll heal on their own over the next few months, and you'll be doing a lot of physical therapy, starting soon."

"I will?"

He patted her good shoulder. "Don't worry, they won't give you anything you can't handle. You also have three broken teeth."

"Yes, I know."

"I'm not a dentist, and if you don't have one here we'll be happy to refer you to one. You'll probably need some crowns. You also have a few cracked ribs, and hairline fractures on your cheek and upper pelvis. You have a lot of cuts and bruises too, and you may have noticed that your right cheek is bandaged."

She reached over and felt a large bandage. "So, what happened?"

"You had some lacerations on your cheek. We've closed them up with butterfly bandages."

"Will my face be scarred?"

"Hopefully not. Once we remove the bandages, we'll give you some ointment to help prevent scarring. You also have a black eye. It looks worse than it really is, and it'll heal in time. We will, however, be running some tests to see if it's affected your vision. You also have some pretty big contusions on your chest and arms. They may look scary, but they too will heal on their own over the next few weeks. Now, would you like to know why you're our miracle patient?"

"Sure. Why not?"

"You're our miracle patient because in spite of everything, you have no sign of brain swelling or any other internal injuries, other than a bruised kidney. You were lucky indeed."

"I guess so," said Rachel. "So, am I going to be okay?"

"I think so. You should be pretty much back to normal in about four to six months. However, there is one other thing you need to know about."

Rachel's chest tightened. "What is it?"

"I'm sorry to have to tell you this, but you've had a miscarriage. They discovered it while they were doing the rape exam. You were about four weeks along. They removed the fetal tissue, and, once you're back on your feet, you should be able to have other children without any complications."

Rachel was in shock. "Are you sure I didn't just start my period? I wasn't pregnant."

He patted her hand. "No, Rachel, you were pregnant. The blood work proves it." He pulled up her chart on his tablet. "You were only in your fourth week of pregnancy, so you might not have experienced enough symptoms to notice. My wife never suspected a thing with any of her pregnancies until she was about ten weeks along. I'm very sorry for your loss, but don't worry, you can still have other children."

Rachel thought it over and wondered if it could have been the reason why her stomach had been so upset lately. She thought it had been all the stress from the wedding.

"I'm sorry," she said, "but I'm having a hard time wrapping my brain around this."

He squeezed her good shoulder. "It's okay. You've been through quite an ordeal, but now it's over. Whoever did this to you isn't here, and we're going to get you well again."

"Before you go, can I ask you one other question?"

"Of course."

"Was I in a coma? I don't remember much of anything between Saturday night and early this morning."

"No, you were never in a medically induced coma. As I said, you had no brain swelling. However, you were in surgery for much of the day on Sunday, and we had you on some pretty potent pain medication for a couple of days, so you may not remember when you were awake, but we've now changed your medication. You'll be awake more often, but you'll still tire easily, and you'll be taking a lot of naps. Your body has had a major shock. You'll need to rest so you can heal."

The doctor stepped out. Rachel tried to make herself comfortable, and she soon drifted off. She woke up about an hour later, wondering what had happened to Al. The nurse came back to once again check her vitals. As she was leaving another man stepped in. He wore blue jeans and a leather vest, and his long, white hair was pulled back in a ponytail. He froze in his tracks as soon as he saw her.

"Oh my god! It really is you."

"Al?"

He wrapped his arms around her, being careful not to disturb her injured shoulder. She felt his body shaking as she cried along with him. His voice choked with emotion when he finally spoke.

"They told us you were dead. We thought we'd lost you."

"I escaped, but I don't know how. I can't remember anything between late Saturday night and early this morning. I kept trying to wake up, but I couldn't."

Al stepped back to take a closer look. "My god. What did he do to you?"

"Apparently I fell out of his truck. I don't know if he pushed me, or I fell out. I don't remember." Rachel looked him up and down and smiled. "I haven't looked at myself in a mirror, and I'm not sure I want to. I probably look like hell right now, but look at you. You look just like I remember, except your hair is white instead of blond, and I don't recall the wire glasses."

"They're new, and I'm not here to discuss my looks. I want to know what the hell happened."

"Craig Walker. It was Craig Walker. They need to hunt the son of a bitch down and put him out of his misery once and for all. Problem is, I can't trust the cops either."

Al squeezed her hand and looked her in the eye. "You don't have to worry about him anymore. Craig Walker is dead. He'll never hurt you again."

Rachel thought it over for a moment and shook her head. "No. It's a trick. It has to be. I couldn't possibly be that lucky."

"Hey, I'm your father, and I'm not going to lie to you. I never have, and I never will. Craig Walker was killed the day before yesterday. The cops caught up with him in Flagstaff. They tried to pull him over, but he gave chase, so they set up a roadblock outside of town. He ended up crashing into the back of a tanker truck. It exploded, and he burned to death. They found what was left of your blue shoes, along with a large knife. There was also a shovel in the back of his truck, with dirt on the blade. It's why we thought you were dead."

"Wow." Rachel stopped to take it all in. Fresh tears ran down her cheeks. "He said he was going to kill me, and I knew he meant it. And he had a knife all right. He pulled it on me in the hotel parking lot, and when he stuck it against my ribs I knew he meant business. I thought if I went along with him, I could somehow convince him to let me go. Instead, he drove me into New Mexico. No, he didn't rape me, but he made it pretty clear that was his intention, and he said he'd kill me once he was through with me. I want to see the autopsy report, a copy of the death certificate, and a photo of his dead corpse. I need proof that he really is dead."

"Not a problem." A middle-aged woman in a business suit stepped into the room. "I'll be happy to bring it all to you as soon as I can."

Rachel tensed up. "So who are you?"

"It's okay, Rachel," said Al. "Her name is Leona Trent. She's with the Albuquerque police and she drove all the way out to my home to bring me here. Sherry and I live north of Albuquerque. It's why it took so long for me to get here." He turned his attention to the detective.

"I need to call my wife. I think she may have Rachel's mother's phone number. I don't have it with me."

"It's okay. I just got off the phone with Detective Anderson with the Tucson police. They've reopened the case, and he said he would set up a meeting with her family within the hour."

"Good to know, but I'm still going to step out for a few minutes to call my wife." Al looked at Rachel. "I'll just be around the corner. If you need anything have someone come get me." He kissed her forehead and hurried outside.

❧FORTY-FIVE❨

JULIE WAS FRANTIC when she returned to the living room. "Shane's still not answering his phone, and I've left him three messages now. Has anyone seen that piece of paper with his mother's phone number on it? I can't seem to find it anywhere."

"Mom, relax." Alice's voice was firm. "Let's wait for the detective to get here and find out what he has to say. Hopefully, they've found her body. Then we'll finally know what happened to her and she can have a proper burial. I'll go over to Shane's house as soon as we're done and talk to him in person. Trust me, it'll be better that way."

Detective Anderson arrived a short time later. Once again, they gathered around the dining room table.

"I take it you have some news for us," said Bruce.

"I do indeed," he said with a smile. "Earlier today I got a call from a police detective in Albuquerque investigating a Jane Doe, who arrived by helicopter at a local hospital early Sunday morning. The patient had no identification, but she was blonde, approximately thirty years of age, and she was wearing a long, blue formal dress."

"Are you saying they've found my daughter?" Julie's hand went up to her mouth. Tears rolled down her face as Alice hugged her. "So what happened to her?"

"According to the Albuquerque detective, she was found unconscious along the side of the road near Silver City. Apparently, she's been under sedation for the past few days, but she's now awake and responding. She said her name was Rachel Bennett, and once she understood she was in Albuquerque she asked them to call Al Matheson. She said he was her father."

"He is. My husband is her adopted father. So, why hasn't he called me?"

"I'm told he lives a few miles outside the city, and apparently only got to the hospital a short time ago. However, he's positively identified her as his daughter. I also wanted you to know we've reopened her case, and we'll be working with the New Mexico authorities so we can determine exactly what happened."

"What's her condition?" asked Bruce.

"I'm afraid I don't know the extent of her injuries. I was simply told they were non-life threatening, and she's expected to make a full recovery. I was also told that they plan on releasing her from the hospital within the next couple of days."

Julie looked at Bruce. "Let's get the car loaded. I'm bringing her home with me."

"Not so fast, Mom," said Alice. "We don't know the extent of her injuries, so it may be some time before she's well enough to travel. I'll call the hospital as soon as we're done. I'm a nurse. It's probably best that I be the one who talks to them."

"Which hospital?" asked Donny.

Anderson checked his notes. "Robert H. Goddard."

Donny pulled out his phone. "I'll look it up."

As Donny punched buttons on his phone Bruce asked more questions. "Do you have any other new information on her case?"

"Yes. The coroner in Flagstaff has positively identified Craig Walker through his dental records, which we, of course, expected. We're expecting the preliminary autopsy report later today, but it's a foregone conclusion that he died of extensive burns in the crash."

Bruce looked relieved. "Then our prayers have finally been answered. He's dead, and Rachel is still with us, and she never has to worry about him hurting her again."

Donny handed his phone to Alice. "I'm on hold, waiting for a real person to come on the line."

"Thanks." Alice stepped away to take the call while Bruce walked the detective to the door. Alice returned ten minutes later.

"Okay, here's what I was able to find out. She was either pushed out, or she fell out of a moving vehicle and was left for dead."

"Which sounds exactly like something Craig Walker would have done," said Julie. "But I have to know. Did he rape her?"

"No," said Alice. "Her undergarments had been removed, but the rape tests came out negative."

"Thank goodness, but I still want to dig up his corpse and mutilate his body."

"I know, Mom, and frankly, I'd love to help you. Since her undergarments were missing, it means he still sexually assaulted her, but we don't know the details."

"What about her other injuries?" asked Bruce.

"She took a hard fall alright. She has a broken shoulder, a broken wrist, a cracked pelvis, a few cracked ribs, some broken teeth, and a cracked cheekbone, along with some cuts and bruises. She also apparently has one hell of a black eye, but she's awake, she's talking, and she seems to be good spirits, all things considered. They expect her to make a full recovery, at least physically. Emotionally, however, may be another story. It sounds like it hasn't fully hit her yet. I'll know more once I see her."

"Okay, then. I need to get all of us on the next flight to Albuquerque. I'll try to get the five of us together, but I can't guarantee it."

"Don't worry, I'll stay here," said Donny. "Someone needs to hold down the fort, and now that we know she's going to be okay, I want to get back to work so I can take time off later on. As soon as she's back on her feet, Alice and I are going on our honeymoon."

* * *

Shane heard pounding off in the distance. Lucy kept barking, and whoever it was kept pounding. Opening his eyes, he heard a woman calling his name. He grabbed his glasses from the nightstand and stumbled to the front door. Alice stood on the other side.

"Sorry, Alice. I was asleep. C'mon in."

Lucy greeted her with friendly sniffs and a wag of her tail as she came inside. Shane led her to the kitchen, offering her a seat at the kitchen table before he took Lucy to the side door and put her out in the yard.

"Sorry the place is such a mess. I guess I haven't been myself lately. Can I get you anything?"

"I'm fine, Shane, but you need to sit down."

He looked her up and down before taking his seat. "You know, you do look joyfully happy for some strange reason. So, what's up?"

Her face beamed. "They found Rachel. She's alive."

He felt a jolt. "What?"

She reached across the table and squeezed his hand. "She's alive. You need to pack your bags. My mom just booked us on a flight to Albuquerque and it leaves in a little over three hours. Your mom will be here soon to pick up your dog."

"Albuquerque? Wait a minute. Slow down. What happened?"

"Craig took her to New Mexico, but she somehow managed to escape. Someone found her by the side of the road early Sunday morning. She has several broken bones and she's still in the hospital, but she—"

Alice's phone rang. She stopped to check the caller ID. It was an out of state number. "Wait, this could be Al."

Alice took the call. Al was on the other end of the line. After a quick introduction she put him on speaker.

"Can you hear me?" he asked.

"We hear you just fine, Al. Is Rachel there?"

"Yeah, I'm right here." Her voice sounded tired, but relieved. "Aren't you supposed to be on your honeymoon, sissy?"

Shane's eyes grew misty and a tear rolled down Alice's face. He wanted to say something but was unable to speak.

"Are you still there, Alice?" asked Rachel.

"Yeah, I'm still here." Her voice choked with emotion.

"Well, go get yourself a tissue and a glass of water. I'll wait. I'm not going anywhere."

Shane hopped up and her got a glass of water. Alice took a sip as Shane raced to the bathroom for a box of tissues. He returned a few seconds later and set it on the table. Alice pulled one from the box and dabbed her eyes while he grabbed one for himself.

"Okay, we've got the tissues, but I'm fine, really. Matt called the cruise line Sunday morning to tell us you were missing, and we caught the next flight home, but not to worry. Donny and I will be booking another cruise, very soon. So how are you feeling?"

"Well, if you really want to know, I feel like hell. I've been completely out of it for the past three days, and I'm still on a lot of pain meds. I can't stay awake for very long, and the slightest thing seems to wear me out."

"Par for the course, but it's okay. It'll get better."

"So they tell me. How's Shane? Is he okay? I really need to talk to him, because I know he's probably blaming himself for this, but so far I—"

"I'm right here, Rachel."

His voice shook with emotion and she went silent. They heard her weeping through the phone, along with voices in the background. Al was telling someone to leave and come back later.

"Rachel, it's okay," said Shane. "He's dead. He can't hurt you ever again."

"I know. They told me he's dead, but I've asked them to bring me proof."

"Which is perfectly understandable. Would you like for me to call Lamar?

"I might," said Rachel, "but first I need to explain something to you. Shane, none of this is your fault. Mom asked me to take the wedding gifts out to my car, and she said Emma would help me. I figured we'd have it all done in about ten minutes or so. Then, once we got to my car, I had to do a little rearranging, so Emma went back to get the rest of the gifts. A couple minutes later someone came up behind me. I thought it was Emma, but it wasn't. It was Craig, and he had a knife. So I dropped my keys and kicked them underneath the car when he wasn't looking. I knew that once you found them, you'd know something had happened, and you'd call the police."

"Which is exactly what I did."

"Let's finish this later," said Al. "She's getting tired and she needs her rest. That lady detective was just here. I sent her away, but she'll be back in another couple of hours."

"Al, would you mind closing the door? Before she comes back, I have to tell you all something."

"What's up, Rachel?" Shane's voice was still strained.

"I need a lawyer. I'm not talking to the cops again until I have a lawyer."

"Rachel, it's okay," said Alice. "He's gone. He can't hurt you."

"That's not it." Rachel let out a loud sigh. "Earlier today, while my father stepped out to make a phone call, the policewoman told me they'd found blood on the ground, right next to where they found me. She said it was human blood, but it wasn't my blood. I told her I was tired and didn't want to talk anymore."

"So do you know whose blood it is, Rachel?" asked Al.

"It's probably Craig's, and what I'm about to tell you stays between the four of us. Got it?"

"Of course," said Al. "So, what happened?"

Rachel's voice sounded oddly calm. "Craig had me in his truck, and we were out on some dark, deserted road, who knows where. He'd tied up my hands with a rope, but I'd managed to work the knot loose. He was describing all the gory details about what he planned on doing to me once we got to wherever we were going, and trust me, none of it was going to be good. So, it was either take him out before we got there, or spend the next few days being repeatedly raped and then killed, because he made it crystal clear that he wasn't going to let me live once he was finally through with me. That's when I slipped the rope around his neck and pulled it as hard as I could. Naturally, the bastard fought back, which is probably how I got the cracked ribs. About the third time he hit me, I lost my grip, but he was still conscious, so while he was busy trying to regain control of his truck I went after him a second time. That's when I felt something pop in his neck, but I don't remember anything after that. He must have pushed me out of the truck, because I would have never jumped out. So, Alice, I need you to call Matt and have him find me a lawyer, because there's no way in hell I'm going to prison for attempted murder. There. I've said it. I'm done. And I don't want to talk about it anymore."

Alice and Shane sat in stunned silence.

"That was a fight to the death," said Al. "I'm a Marine, and you were just like a soldier in hand-to-hand combat."

"You absolutely did the right thing," said Shane. "You did what you had to do to keep him from killing you, and Hell will freeze over before I allow anyone to arrest you, much less put you on trial."

"I seriously doubt they would ever charge her," said Al, "but stranger things have happened."

"It sounds like she may have fractured his larynx," said Alice. "If so, it'll show up on the autopsy, and because it's an unusual injury, they may question her about it."

"And if they do, they can phrase their questions in such a way as to make her look guilty. We could have a problem," said Al. "I have a good friend who's an attorney. I'll call him as soon as we're done here. I think under the circumstances, she should have legal representation until this thing is all wrapped up. Meantime, she's pretty agitated and her monitor just started beeping, so I expect someone will be here any minute to sedate her."

"I'm sure they will," said Alice. "Please tell her we're on our way. We'll be there tonight."

"That's fine, but don't make it too late. She's already had enough excitement for one day."

Al disconnected the call and Shane looked at Alice. Her eyes were red and puffy. He gave her hand a quick squeeze.

"Are you alright?" he asked.

Alice nodded as she reached for a tissue and dabbed her eyes. "I've just spent the past few days thinking my sister was dead, when she's not." She started sobbing again. "She's going to be okay."

He got up and hugged her. His voice shook with anger as he spoke. "That son of a bitch is damn lucky he's in the morgue right now. Otherwise, I'd hunt him down finish him off myself. Burning to death was too good for him."

"I know, Shane. I feel the same, but at the same time, I'm so incredibly proud of her. She didn't panic. She kept her head, she fought back, and she won. Had it been me instead of her, I wouldn't have been able to handle it."

"You'd be amazed at what you can do when you really have to."

"I know, but Rachel has always had an inner strength few people seem to have. All I can tell you is I'm damn proud of her."

Shane gave her another hug. "Me too, and I can't wait to get her home where she belongs."

Alice's mood abruptly changed. "There's something else I need to tell you, and I didn't want to mention it in front of Al. Shane, you need to sit back down."

"Why? What is it? Is it serious?"

"Yes, it's serious." Alice waited for him to return to his seat, and once he did, she looked him in the eye. "When Rachel arrived at the hospital, she was still wearing her blue dress, but her undergarments were missing."

"But she just told us how she fought him off." He suddenly felt nauseous and his blood ran cold. His head shook as he spoke. "No. Please don't tell me he raped her."

"The tests came back negative, but please understand he still sexually assaulted her. We don't know the details, because she hasn't talked about it yet. What I'm trying to tell you is that even if he didn't actually rape her, she's still been traumatized in a very personal way, and it may have an effect on her relationship with you."

He felt his stomach twist as he seethed in anger. "I understand, and I'm certainly not going to force myself on her or do anything she's not ready to do."

"That's good, but you just heard her. She's been through a major ordeal, so you may need to give her some space and let her heal."

"I understand."

"I hope you do. Now, there is one other thing."

"What is it?"

"Shane, did you know that Rachel was pregnant?"

His heart skipped a beat. "What? No. Are you sure?"

"Yes. They've determined that she was pregnant, but she was only four weeks along. She may not have even known herself."

Shane felt a flood of emotions. Not only was Rachel alive, they were about to have a family. "So what happened? Is the baby okay?"

"No, I'm afraid not. She lost the baby. She had a miscarriage while she was in the emergency room. There was nothing they could do. I'm so sorry, Shane. The doctors took care of it, and she didn't have any complications, so once she's completely well, you guys can try again."

Shane felt as if he'd been stabbed in the heart. He covered his face with his hands as the doorbell rang. "Alice, would you mind seeing who's there?"

"Of course."

She stepped away, returning a minute later with his mother. Kelly too was blinking the tears away as she wrapped her arms around her son.

"I just got off the phone with Julie. I'm so incredibly relieved, and so happy for all of us. Not only is she alive, she should make a full recovery. Are you alright, Shane?"

"Yeah, Mom, I think so. I'm just a little shell-shocked. I was finally coming to terms with her being gone, and now I just spoke to her on the phone." Shane stopped for a moment as he finally realized a huge weight had just been lifted off of him. His face lit up and he smiled for the first time in days. "Wow. She's alive. She really is alive. And we're on our way to see her? Right?"

Alice smiled and nodded. "Yes, we are. You need to go pack, because we'll be picking you up in about an hour, although we may end up staying at different hotels. Something about a big balloon race happening in town. I need to go home and pack myself. See you in an hour."

✥FORTY-SIX✥

RACHEL OPENED HER eyes and saw a woman seated in Al's chair. She too wore blue jeans, and her dark hair was cut in a bob. A broad smile broke out across her face as they made eye contact.

"Well, I see you're finally awake. How are you feeling?"

"Fine, I guess." Rachel's eyes swept the room. "So where's Al?"

"He went downstairs to get some dinner."

"Really? So, what time is it anyway?"

The woman glanced at a clock mounted on the wall. "It's going on seven."

"Then I guess time really does fly when you're having fun." Rachel looked at her visitor again. "You know, you look familiar to me for some reason."

She nodded and smiled. "We've met, but it was a long time ago, and you're all grown up now."

"Okay, let me think for a minute." Rachel placed her left hand over her brow. "Didn't you once have really long hair? Almost down to your waist?"

"I sure did, but that was some twenty years and forty pounds ago."

"So you would be Sherry, right?" A bright smile broke out across her face as she remembered. "Is it really you?"

Sherry smiled in return as she walked up to the bed and hugged her, being careful not to disturb the sling. "Yes, Honey Bun. It's really me."

"Wow. And you remembered my nickname too." Rachel squeezed Sherry's hand and smiled again. "Now, let's see how well I can connect the dots together. You were Al's girlfriend."

"That's right."

"And you really loved kids. Anywhere we went, if someone had a baby, you went nuts, and you always treated me as if I were your own."

Sherry's face beamed. "Guilty on all counts."

"But then Al moved to New Mexico. Later on, my mother told me he'd gotten married, but she never said to whom, so I'm glad it was you." Rachel suddenly felt sad as the memory played back in her mind. "All she said was he'd gotten married, and I wouldn't be seeing much of him anymore."

"Your dad moved here because he got a job offer he simply couldn't refuse. As you know, he's an artist who loves motorcycles, and when he got the chance to work for a shop doing custom paint and graphics for motorcycles, he jumped on it. A few years later, his boss decided to sell the business. Your dad ended up buying it, and he's done really well with it, which is how he was able to help you with your college expenses."

"For which I will always be grateful. I'd just wish we'd been able to see each other more often while I was growing up."

"I know. We would have liked that as well, but we were told you'd bonded with Bruce, and even though your mother never came out and said it directly, we knew she wanted us to stay in the background. Apparently, she was having issues with some of the family."

Once again, Aunt Laurie's comments played back in Rachel's mind. She tried to brush it away. "You know what I wish? I wish we could all go back in time and do things differently. There were times when I was growing up when I truly felt that my father had abandoned me. But then, when I started college, and Mom told me he was the one paying for most of my tuition, I started realizing it wasn't the case. You may recall it was when I started reconnecting with him."

"I remember. Your dad missed you as well, and he was much more at peace once you two started talking again."

"I'm glad." Rachel's eyes suddenly turned misty. "You know, I'd hoped to land a job in Albuquerque when I graduated, but I ended up taking that job in Reno instead." She looked down at her arm, covered by the sling. "It's a mistake I'll pay for, for the rest of my life."

"None of this is your fault, Rachel." There was a no-nonsense tone in Sherry's voice. "Apparently one of his articles is in the current issue of *The American Chronicles*, and all of the talking heads on Fox and CNN are speculating about how such a well-respected journalist could have had such a dark side."

"Aw, jeez." Rachel shook her head in disgust. "So he finally has the fame and recognition he's coveted for all these years, and he got it at my expense. The man tried to rape me, and he nearly killed me, and now it's being plastered all over the national media, which means once again, Craig Walker wins. Even in death, Craig Walker always wins."

"I wouldn't call it a victory. Not by a long shot. For one thing, he's dead, so he's hardly able to enjoy the fame, or should I say, the notoriety, he's earned. Nor has the media been kind to him. They've labeled him as the sexual predator he was, and some of his former girlfriends have come forward with their own horror stories about him. And earlier today *The American Chronicles* announced that they've pulled his article from their website, and they won't be publishing any of the other articles he wrote for them. So don't go getting yourself all worked up. They're all trying to distance themselves from him, while you're going to make a full recovery and enjoy the rest of your life."

A young nurse entered the room, greeting her a smile as she made some notes in her tablet. Another nurse came in to join her. She carried a small tray loaded with supplies and a freshly folded hospital gown.

"My name is Beth," said one of the nurses, "and I'll be changing your bandages while Stephanie removes your catheter. We'll only be a few minutes, and I promise none of it will hurt."

"Do you want me to leave?"

"No, Sherry, you're good," said Rachel. "I just hope the damage on my face isn't too horrific." She laid still as the nurses went to work.

"Your face is actually healing nicely," Beth finally said.

"Will I be scarred?"

"Hopefully not. As soon as I get the rest of these bandages off, I'll put some antibiotic ointment on it and cover it with a fresh bandage. You'll need to keep it bandaged for about a week after you get home."

Rachel remained still as the nurse finished bandaging her face. "Are we done?" she finally asked.

"Almost," said Beth with a smile. "As soon as we take care of your wrists."

Rachel watched closely as Beth unwrapped her left wrist. Once the bandages were gone, she gasped in horror.

"It's okay," said Beth. "It's healing quite nicely as well, and it'll fade over time. It doesn't need to be bandaged anymore and we'll put a little Vaseline on it to keep it moist. I'll leave the tube here so you can apply more later on." She gently removed the bandages on Rachel's other wrist. It too was red, but not as much as her other wrist.

"This one's healing as well. They'll put a cast on your wrist in the morning, before you go home."

"I'm leaving tomorrow?"

"It's what we're hoping. Now comes the fun part. Stephanie and I are going to help you out of bed, and you're going to do a little walking. Are you ready?"

"I don't know. What about the back of my gown?"

"Not to worry, we'll cover your back with this other gown."

"And I have something for you as well." Sherry picked up a large shopping bag resting by her feet. "Your dad and I thought you might feel better if you had something nicer to wear, so I've brought you some pajamas."

"Gosh, Sherry, I don't know what to say, other than thank you."

"Enough talking, young lady," said Stephanie. "Up you go."

"Wait." Sherry reached inside the shopping bag. "Don't forget her slippers. I hope medium fits."

Rachel nodded as Sherry handed the slippers to Beth, and the nurses helped Rachel sit up. She groaned as they got her on her feet. She felt unsteady, but they stood on either side of her, grabbing her IV pole and helping her walk back and forth between the bathroom and her bed. Al stepped back in, handing Sherry a sandwich and a soda as the nurses got her back in her bed.

"You know what I'd really like?" said Rachel. "I'd really like to take a shower. I feel pretty grungy, and my hair feels like it's still full of dirt from the fall. The rest of my family is on their way from Tucson, and I'd like to look presentable when they get here."

"I'll see what I can do," said Beth. The two nurses stepped out as Al made himself at home in the other chair.

"So," he said, "I take you and Sherry have been getting reacquainted."

"Yes, we have," said Rachel.

"And she remembers me." Sherry set her sandwich aside and took the pajamas from the shopping bag. "I took a guess and got you the medium size."

"That'll work."

"Both pairs are cotton, so they should be comfortable. Do you prefer the pink with the kittens? Or the white with the pink roses?"

"I think I'll go with the white," said Rachel.

Sherry nodded. "I like those better myself." She reached back in the bag. "I also got you a few toiletries. A toothbrush, a comb, a little bottle of shampoo—"

"Oh, thank goodness," said a relieved Rachel. "I just want to feel clean again."

A female aide arrived a short time later. Her name was Candace, and she brought a plastic cover for Rachel's sling. "I heard you want to take a shower," she said, "so I'm here to help you."

Rachel smiled with delight as Candace helped her from her bed. "You know, it's really not so bad the second time."

Rachel grabbed her IV pole as Sherry handed the bag off to Candace. Closing the bathroom door, Rachel caught her reflection in the mirror. It shocked her to her core. Her hair was stringy. A large bandage covered her bruised and swollen right cheek. Her eyelid was also swollen, and she had a huge black eye. She shook her head stunned in disbelief.

"This can't be me. I look like a monster."

Candace wrapped her arm around her shoulder. "It's okay. You've had a very serious fall, but it will all go away, I promise. Now, let me help you out of your gown, and we'll cover your sling."

Rachel gazed in horror at her naked body in the refection. Her arms and chest were covered with big, dark bruises, and Craig's fingermarks were still visible on her forearm. Once again Candace tried to comfort her.

"I'm so sorry, but it really will heal, I promise. In the meantime, a nice, warm shower will help you feel a lot better." She led Rachel into the shower stall, sitting her down on the ledge and turning on the water. Ten minutes later she wrapped her up in a clean towel as someone knocked at the door. Another aide was dropping off a hair dryer.

"Perfect timing," said Candace as she began combing out Rachel's hair. "You've got some beautiful highlights."

"Thanks. I had them done the day of my…accident. It was my sister's wedding day. I was her maid of honor, and I was wearing this beautiful blue dress. I wonder what became of it." She looked closely at her hands. "Well, I'll be damned. I got my nails done the same day and look. After everything I've been through, none of the polish has chipped off. Too bad the rest of me didn't fare so well." She remained silent as Candace turned on the blow dryer.

"I'm afraid I'm not much of a stylist, but at least your hair will be clean. Maybe your mom can take you to the hairdresser once you feel up to it. A day of pampering would do you some good."

"Maybe." Rachel thought it over for a minute. "She's actually my stepmother."

"Really? I would have never known. She's a lovely woman."

"She is indeed." Rachel kept to herself as Candace finished drying her hair and helped her into the pajamas.

"These look pretty on you," said Candace. "The pink flowers go nicely with your complexion."

"Thanks, but somehow I doubt I'll ever be pretty again."

Candace put her hand on Rachel's shoulder. "The swelling in your face will go down. All the bruises will fade, and your broken bones will all heal. Now, let's get you back to bed."

Al and Sherry looked up and smiled as Rachel emerged from the bathroom. Candace helped her back to her bed and stepped away.

"So, how are you feeling?" asked Sherry.

"I don't know. I just saw my reflection in the mirror."

"You're alive," said Al. "Trust me, just seeing you here is the most beautiful thing I think I've ever seen in my entire life." He introduced another visitor who had arrived while Rachel was in the shower.

"This is Les Sorenson. He's one of my biker buddies and he's also an attorney. The police detective will be back within the hour, and Les will be here while she talks to you."

Les extended his hand. "Your father filled me in about what happened with you and Mr. Walker before you were pushed out of the truck. He kidnapped you at knifepoint, and the marks on your wrists speak for themselves. And while I highly doubt they would ever charge you, I also have to agree with your father when he says stranger things have happened. So, before she gets here, I want to go over what you should, and should not, say to her."

❧FORTY-SEVEN❧

DETECTIVE TRENT GREETED Rachel with a smile as she came into the room and handed her a large manila envelope. "You asked for proof that Craig Walker is really dead, so I've brought it to you. This is a copy of the preliminary autopsy report, as well as a photo, but I have to warn you that he burned to death, so the photo of his body is extremely graphic."

"It's okay," said Rachel as she set the envelope on the tray next to her bed. "However, I won't feel safe until I'm completely satisfied that he's dead and can never come after me again."

"I understand how you feel, and before I close out your file, I have a few questions for you."

"All right, but I would like for my family, and my attorney, to be present."

"Of course." She looked around for a chair. Al offered her his as he stood next to Sherry. Taking her seat, she quickly got down to business.

"First of all, I've talked to the detectives in Tucson, Oro Valley, Flagstaff, and Sacramento, along with the New Mexico State Police, so I have a pretty good idea of what happened. This past Saturday you were kidnapped at knifepoint in a hotel parking lot in Oro Valley, correct?"

"Yes. My sister's wedding was being held there, and my mother asked me and another woman, Emma, to put her wedding gifts in my car. Emma went back to get the rest of the gifts, and while she was away, Craig Walker snuck up behind me and stuck a big knife against my ribs. He told me if screamed or tried to run he would kill me, and I knew if I didn't cooperate, I'd be dead. Please understand, I was going with him against my will, and I was hoping I could reason with him and talk him into letting me go." She held up her left hand. "As soon as he got me in his truck, he tied up my hands. This is how I got the rope burns on both of my wrists."

"I know he tied your hands. The rope was still tied to your wrist when you were found."

As the detective took notes, Rachel noticed a water pitcher on her tray and asked if someone could help her pour a glass of water. Sherry hopped up and filled her glass. As she returned to her seat, the detective asked another question.

"So what happened after he got you into his truck?"

"He set his knife down in the cup holder and told me if I did anything to attract attention he would, in his own words, take out one of my kidneys without anesthesia."

"So I take it you didn't try to escape."

"No ma'am, I did not. What I did instead was try to reason with him. I kept telling him that if he would just let me go, I wouldn't say anything, but he wasn't listening, and once we drove out of Tucson, I knew I was in big trouble. Even so, I tried to stay calm. Each time we drove through a town I'd ask him to let me go, but it was obvious that he wouldn't. So, after we crossed into New Mexico, I told him I needed a bathroom break, and we stopped at a gas station out in the boonies."

"Do you know where it was?"

"It was off the Interstate, somewhere between the state line and Lordsburg. I'm sorry, but I can't recall the name of it."

The detective took more notes. "It's okay, Rachel. You're doing fine. So what happened next?"

"He gave me a sweater and told me to put it on. Not out of compassion, but so the sleeves would cover the rope burns on my wrists. He said he would kill me if I tried to show them to anybody. We went inside and he walked me to the ladies' room. He said he'd wait for me to come out. So I went inside, and while I was there I found a tube of lipstick in the trash. I was going to use it to write a note on the mirror saying that I'd been kidnapped, with a description of his truck, but I got interrupted before I could finish it."

"So what happened?"

Rachel's voice shook as she answered. "A policewoman came in. I thought I was about to be rescued. I told her who I was, and that I just been kidnapped, but she wouldn't believe me." Her eyes welled with tears and she reached for a tissue. "Craig had somehow convinced her that he was my brother, and I was a mental patient. She kept telling me I was going to be okay; my brother was taking me home and I'd be taken care of."

"What the hell?" Al was livid.

"Please, Mr. Matheson," said Detective Trent. "I understand you're upset, but I need to find out exactly what happened. Please go on, Ms. Bennett."

Rachel took a deep breath. "I showed her my wrists, and I kept telling her I'd been kidnapped, but she still wouldn't believe me. She said my brother told her I'd been injuring myself. Then she dragged me outside and handed me over to Craig. After that, she left." Rachel started sobbing.

"You're telling me that a police officer turned you over to the man who kidnapped you?" The anger resonated in her attorney's voice.

"That's it. We're filing a lawsuit." Al's voice sounded equally angry. "If that woman had done her job, my daughter would have gotten away from that monster unscathed."

"I agree." Detective Trent was also clearly upset. "And trust me, I'm going to get to the bottom of this. Do you know who the policewoman was?"

"Her name badge said Hopkins or Harkins. I'm not sure."

"And this was somewhere outside of Lordsburg? Correct?"

"Yes." Rachel nodded as she grabbed another tissue.

"So it would be the New Mexico State Police," said the detective. "Don't worry. I'll be giving them a call as soon as we're done here. So what happened after that?"

"He was furious, and he told me no more Mr. Nice Guy. He grabbed me, really hard, and he forced me back into his truck." She pointed out the finger mark bruises on her forearm. "That's how I got these."

"Did he tie your hands again?"

Rachel nodded.

"Then what happened? Did you leave after that?"

Rachel shook her head and kept crying. Al's patience was wearing thin.

"She's really getting agitated. I think it's time for you to leave."

"It's okay, Dad. I want to get this over with."

"Are you sure?"

Rachel nodded and dabbed her eyes. "Yeah, I'm sure."

The detective phrased her question a different way. "Is this when he tried to rape you?"

"Yes, but he was interrupted. He suddenly stopped and started yelling something about the cops. Apparently, another highway patrol car must have pulled into the parking lot, but I was down on the passenger seat so I couldn't see out the windows. I just started screaming as loudly as I could. That's when he gagged me with my pantyhose and yanked me back up in my seat. I was pretty panicky by then. I remember him driving out of the parking lot and getting back on the Interstate, but I was still pretty freaked out. Then a voice in the back of my head told me to calm down and try to find another way to escape. So I took a deep breath and started feeling along the rope. Once I found the knot, I started pulling on it. It moved just a little, so I decided just to concentrate on pulling out the knot."

"Did you pull it loose?"

Rachel's heart skipped a beat. She glanced at her attorney, who gave her a slight nod of his head.

"I'm not sure. It all gets kind of fuzzy after that."

The detective laid her hand on the manila envelope. "As you know, Rachel, when they found you, the rope was still tied to your left wrist, but your right hand was free. They also found fresh blood on the ground around you, but they've determined it wasn't your blood. There was also a freshly dug hole a few feet away from your body. Someone was trying to bury you alive, but whoever it was, was also injured in some way, so they were either interrupted, or they gave up. We believe that person was Craig Walker. I've also read the preliminary autopsy report. Craig Walker had a fractured larynx, and it appeared to be a recent injury."

Sorenson spoke up. "I believe she's just told you that she doesn't remember what happened after they left the gas station. What we do know for a fact is that she was kidnapped at knifepoint, held against her will for several hours, taken across state lines, and nearly raped. Then she was somehow ejected from Mr. Walker's truck while it was still in motion and left on the side of the highway for dead. She's answered all the questions she needs to answer, detective, and she has nothing further to say."

"Look, counselor, please allow me to put your mind at ease. She's not been charged, nor would charges ever be filed against her. If she did indeed attempt to strangle Mr. Walker, as we believe she did, then she did so in order to save her own life. I've read all of the reports. Had I been in her shoes, I would have done the same thing."

Rachel wept silently as the detective placed one her cards on the tray and softened her tone.

"I think I'm pretty much done, Rachel, but I'll leave you my card in case you have any questions later on. We're officially closing the file on Craig Walker. However, as I mentioned before, I'm going to let the state police know what happened at the gas station, so you can expect to hear from their internal affairs department. Do you have number where they can contact you?"

Rachel shook her head. "No, I'm afraid I don't. My phone is somewhere in Tucson, but I have no idea with whom."

"You can reach her on my phone." Al handed her one of his cards. "She'll be staying with us until she's well enough to travel."

The detective took the card, thanking Al before turning her attention back to Rachel and extending her hand. "What you did was very courageous. Far too many women in your situation would have panicked and ended up becoming a statistic. If I can be of any further assistance, please let me know, and I wish you a speedy recovery." She gave the others a quick nod as she hurried out of the room.

❧FORTY-EIGHT❧

LES GRABBED HIS briefcase and reminded Al to call his office to set up a meeting as soon as Rachel felt up to it. This time she didn't argue about not wanting to file a lawsuit. Her dinner arrived a short time later.

"I don't know whether to laugh or cry," she said. "I'm sure this chicken noodle soup is delicious, but I've got one arm in a sling, and the other is hooked up to an IV line."

"Well, I'm sure we'd be happy to feed you," said Al.

"Dad, please," she said. "It was bad enough having a total stranger helping me shower."

Beth stepped back into the room and gave her a sheepish grin. "I'm so sorry. We were supposed to take out your IV before your dinner arrived."

"Not a problem." Rachel extended her arm and lay back in her bed as Beth disconnected the line.

"So does this mean I'm going home tomorrow?"

"It appears that way. You'll be starting your physical therapy soon, and you'll need to get your teeth fixed."

"We're already on it," said Sherry. "I've made appointments for both."

Rachel ran her tongue along her three broken teeth. She had been blessed with nearly perfect teeth for her entire life. Craig Walker had left her with yet another scar.

"There we go." Beth put a small bandage on her arm. "All done and enjoy your dinner. I'll be back later to check on you." She grabbed the IV pole and pushed it out the door as Rachel sat back up and gave Al and Sherry a grin.

"Okay. Let's see how well I do eating with my left hand." Rachel placed her napkin in her lap and picked up her spoon. It felt awkward in her left hand. She carefully dipped it in her bowl, spilling a couple of drops as she brought it up to her mouth. The soup tasted slightly bland, but it felt warm and soothing as she swallowed it down.

"Doing okay?" asked Sherry.

"I'm fine," she said with a nod. "I think the last time I ate was Saturday afternoon. I grabbed a salad on my way home from the hairdresser. I tried to eat it, but my stomach was doing flip-flops. I thought it was just nerves but—"

She stopped short of completing her sentence, realizing she may have said too much. Al immediately jumped in.

"Rachel, we know you just lost a baby. The doctor filled me in on your injuries."

Her face turned red, and she looked down at her lap. "I see. Well, I'm okay, and it's really not that big of a deal. At the time I thought it was just nerves. Alice was getting married, so naturally everything was pretty chaotic and stressful. I had no idea what was really going on, but since I didn't know about it before it's not like I feel any great loss."

"Uh huh." Al gave his wife a look as Rachel changed the subject.

"So," she said, "tell me more about Michael. I remember when I was a kid, I used to send him presents for his birthday and for Christmas, and he'd write me these cute little thank you notes. Mom told me he was Sherry's son from a prior marriage, and that you adopted him, just like Bruce adopted me."

Once again, Al and Sherry exchanged surprised looks.

"Rachel," Al's voice sounded strange, "I'm not exactly sure why your mother would have said that, but Michael was never adopted. He's our son. Sherry's and mine. We'd been married for a little over two years when he was born. He's your half-brother."

This time it was Rachel who was surprised. "Really? So why would Mother have told me he was adopted?"

"That's a really good question, and it's something you'll have to ask her about, because I'm just as surprised as you are. But to answer your question, he's fine. He just turned twenty-one this past August, and he's going to school at New Mexico State, down in Las Cruces."

As Rachel finished her meal, Al and Sherry told her more about her brother. He had played football in high school and had always been popular with the girls, but so far he hadn't settled on a steady girlfriend. Unlike his parents, he wasn't big on motorcycles, but he loved the idea of running a business and he looked forward to taking over his father's shop someday.

"He's not artistic himself," said Al, "but he has a good eye for design, and I'm sure, when the time comes, he'll find the right creative people. Of course, that day is still a long way off. Somehow, I can't see myself as ever retiring, at least not as an artist."

"I hear you." Rachel looked down at her injured wrist. "Although my own business is a little uncertain right now. I had a few projects I hadn't yet completed, and if the Tucson media reported that I died...well, hopefully, someone will bring me my phone, so I can at least check my email."

"I have it right here."

Rachel looked up and her heart skipped a beat. Shane walked up to her bed with her phone in his hand. She pulled up her blanket, trying to cover herself, placing her hand over her injured face as she turned the other way.

"Thanks. Just put it on the tray." She nodded toward it as her parents and her sister surrounded her. Shane sat down on the bed, holding her gently in his arms as he kissed the top of her head, but she kept her hand over her injured cheek, gazing down at her bed as the rest of her family took turns embracing her.

"Sorry, guys. I didn't want you seeing me like this." Tears streamed down her face as she spoke.

Al stood from his chair. "Sherry and I are going to take a short break. She's had a long day, so don't get her overly excited."

"Thanks, Dad."

Julie sat down on the other side of bed, cradling her in her arms as she cried. "This is all my fault. I'm the one who sent you out to the parking lot. I should have gone with you or waited until your dad returned and sent him with you instead of Emma."

"It's not your fault, Mom."

"You can discuss it later, Julie." Bruce's voice was firm.

Alice handed them both a tissue, asking Rachel how she was feeling, and if she knew when she would be released from the hospital.

"I guess I'm doing as well as can be expected." Rachel dabbed her eyes but kept her hand over her face as she talked. "They're supposed to release me sometime tomorrow, but I don't know exactly when. We'll have to wait and see."

"In that case, we'll be taking you home," said Julie, firmly.

"I already told you, Mom," said Alice. "She's not well enough to travel."

"Thanks, Alice." Rachel looked at her mother. "She's right. It'll be sometime before I'm able to travel, and in the meantime it's all been arranged. I'll be with Al and Sherry for the next few weeks. I have to start my physical therapy. I also have to see a dentist. I've got three broken teeth. Hopefully, they can fix them."

She reached for the manila envelope. "The detective, here in Albuquerque, dropped this off for me a little while ago. It's the preliminary autopsy report on Craig Walker which I requested. Now that you're here, Alice, maybe you can help me go over it, you know, in case I have any questions about the medical terminology."

"Sure. I'd be happy to."

Rachel handed the envelope to her sister, asking her to open it. "It's kind of hard for me to do things right now. I only have one hand."

"Of course," said Alice as she opened the envelope. The report was on the top, and she began reading through it.

"Well, there's no need to go over every little detail. The cause of death was extensive burn injuries, and his body was identified through his dental records. No surprise there." Her eyebrows raised as she read the next part. "Wow. You really did fracture his larynx. In fact, it was a pretty significant injury. He was in serious need of medical attention."

"Yeah, the detective asked me about that. Fortunately, Al called his lawyer buddy, and he was here when she asked. I just said I didn't remember anything, like he told me to, and then he gave her a good talking to. She said not to worry. They're closing the file, and I won't be facing any charges."

Alice skimmed through the rest of the report. "I didn't think you would, and that pretty much sums the autopsy report. He's dead and gone, and he won't be coming back." She turned to the next page. What she saw caught her off guard.

"Whoa! There's a photo."

"I know. I asked for it."

"You did?"

"Yes, I did," said Rachel. "I want to see his dead corpse. Then I'll know for certain it's really him, and he's really dead."

The others exchanged concerned looks.

"Are you sure you want to see this?" asked Alice. "It's pretty graphic."

"Yes, Alice, I'm sure." Rachel gave the others a stern look. "After everything he's put me through, I think I've earned the right to see his dead corpse, and if the rest of you can't handle it, then please feel free to step outside. I'll only be a few minutes."

Julie's face turned pale and Bruce looked troubled. Shane spoke up.

"Let her see it. She needs closure."

"Thanks, Shane," said Rachel.

Alice hesitated before she handed it over. "Okay, but be forewarned."

Rachel stared at the photo. Craig looked more like a bizarre piece of sculpture than a human being. Pieces of charred, black skin clung to his red, exposed flesh. His hair, mustache and eyebrows had burned away. His eyes were closed and the remains of his nose, ears and fingers looked distorted. His mouth was open, and what remained of his lips were curled and twisted. He had most certainly died a painful, agonizing death. She looked at the photo for another minute before placing the report back on top of it and handing it back to Alice.

"Please, put it back in the envelope, and I'll have someone throw it away."

"Of course." Alice gave her a concerned look. "Are you okay?"

"I'm fine, Alice. I had to see for myself that he's really dead, and now it's done. And while I don't mean to sound like I'm gloating, he certainly paid the price for everything he's done to me and I think justice has been served. So now that he's gone, I'm going to try to move forward, if I possibly can."

She took a sip of water. "Thank you, Shane, for bringing my phone."

"You're welcome." He gave her a smile and reached into his bag. "And here's your purse."

"Thank you." She took it from him and set in on her lap. "So, I guess this is all that remains of my maid of honor outfit. I have no idea where my dress went. No doubt it was ruined in the fall, and I don't know what became of my shoes either."

"They found what was left of one of your shoes in Craig's truck," said Bruce. "The detectives showed us a photo so we could identify it. They also found a shovel, with fresh dirt on it, so they came to the conclusion that he had killed you and buried you somewhere in the desert."

"Which is exactly what would have happened if I hadn't freed myself and fought back, but I don't want to talk about it." She looked at Shane. "Did you bring my laptop?"

"Sorry, I forgot."

"Don't worry. I'm sure I can borrow a computer until someone can send me my laptop. I need to get back to work. I also need to send a rent payment to Aunt Laurie."

A strange look came over Bruce's face, and he looked at Julie.

"What's going on, guys?" asked Rachel. "Just because I'm going to be laid up for a while doesn't mean I won't be paying my rent."

Bruce sighed and put his hand over hers. "This is kind of awkward, so I'll try to get to the point as quickly as I can. We were told you were, gone, on Monday afternoon. As soon as the detectives left, I called your aunt and your grandmother."

"I understand, Bruce. I didn't have any ID on me when they found me, and I was too drugged up on Monday and Tuesday to talk to anyone, so you had no way of knowing I was here. So, what happened?"

He gave her an embarrassed look. "As I said, I called Laurie on Monday afternoon. She called on Tuesday, just to see how we were doing, but she didn't stay on the phone long. Then, late this afternoon, I called her from the airport, while we were waiting to board our flight, to let her know you'd been found alive, and we were on our way to get you. She was happy, of course, but then she told me."

"Told you what?"

"Apparently, she thought she was doing us a favor. She said she'd brought in a crew to pack up your belongings and take them to a storage room she rented. She said it would save your mother and me the trouble, and then later on, when we were ready to deal with it, we could decide what we wanted to do."

"Well, you told her to stop, didn't you?"

"I tried, but it was too late. She said they were loading up the last few boxes in the truck."

Rachel bristled. "So, where's my laptop?"

"I don't know, Rachel. It's packed up in a box somewhere, but I'm sure we can find it. She said she'd—"

"Actually, Rachel, I still have it." Shane gave her hand a squeeze.

"You do?" she asked.

"Yes I do, but I was in such a rush to get to the airport I didn't even think to pack it."

"It's okay, Shane. At least I know where it is, and you can send it to me later." She turned her attention back to Bruce. "So, what about the rest of my stuff?"

Bruce remained ill at ease. "Your aunt told me she planned on dropping off the keys to the storage unit on her way home this evening, so I told her to hang onto them, as I'll have to get them later. I'm sorry this happened, but not to worry. Everything's locked up safe, and believe me, she had no idea you were still alive."

Rachel seethed in anger. "So she wasn't willing to wait until I was cold in the ground, assuming I'd actually died. Wow. First, she announces to everyone at Alice's bridal shower that I'm the bastard child. And now this."

Julie took a defensive tone. "What are you talking about?"

Rachel started to reply, but Alice intervened. "C'mon, Mom. Don't tell me you didn't hear Aunt Laurie going on and on about Grandma giving me all her china and crystal because I was the only granddaughter and they wanted to keep it in the family. It had to have bothered Rachel, and it put me in an awkward position as well. I didn't say anything in front of the other guests because I didn't want to cause a scene, so I played along. I planned on taking Rachel off to the side at lunch to talk to her about it, but she made other plans, so I was going to wait until after the honeymoon." She looked her sister in the eye.

"I was never overly fond of Grandma's blue willow china, and I knew you always liked it, so I set it aside for you and picked out some other dishware. So now you all know what to get Donny and me for Christmas."

A man's voice chimed in. "Thank you, Alice, for including her. I'm just sorry that others have made her feel like she's an outsider."

Al and Sherry had returned. Neither one looked happy. "My daughter will be staying in our home for as long as it takes her to recover from her injuries," said Al. "As soon as she feels well enough, I'll put her to work designing bike graphics. That way she'll still have an income. Then, when she feels she's ready, she can decide where she wants to go next. In the meantime, I think she's had more than enough excitement for one day."

Bruce pointed out a suitcase and small travel bag, set off to the side. "We found those in the trunk of your car."

A bittersweet feeling came over Rachel. "Yes, I know. Shane and I had planned on taking a trip up to the mountains this week. We were supposed to leave on Sunday morning."

"It's okay." Shane once again squeezed her hand as he spoke. "I'll take you there, real soon."

"And in the meantime, you'll have something to wear until Mom and Dad can get to the storage locker and send you more of your clothes," said Alice.

Beth came back in to check Rachel's vitals and bring her some pills. As she swallowed them down, Bruce announced it was time for them to leave.

"Al's right. She's had a busy day, and we can come back tomorrow."

"I'm staying here tonight." Julie's voice was firm. "I'm her mother, and she needs me."

"The recliner leans all the way back," said Beth, "and we can certainly provide you with a blanket and a pillow."

"No." Rachel's head shook as she spoke. "I appreciate the offer, Mom, but no. I need to be alone for a while."

"But you've—"

"No, Mom, I mean it. I'm fine. You need to go with Bruce. And Al, you and Sherry need to go home as well. You've both put in a long day today, so go get some rest. I'll be fine, and I'll see you all in the morning." Rachel settled back in her bed telling each of them good night before they stepped away.

"Shane, would you mind staying for a couple of minutes? I need to talk to you in private." She looked at her mother and Bruce. "Would you mind waiting outside? We won't long."

"Of course." Julie gave her a final hug and kiss and stepped out with the others. Once they were gone, Shane tried to hug her, but she quickly pointed to a chair and told him to take a seat.

"So why do I get the feeling this is something serious?" he asked.

"Because it is." Rachel sighed. "Shane, I've been through a hell of a shock, and I'm not the person you knew before."

"It's okay, Rachel. I know you've been traumatized, and you may even need some counseling, but you'll get over it in time."

"He tried to rape me."

"I know he tried, but he didn't succeed."

"Only because a cop pulled into the parking lot before he had a chance to do more damage. Later on, I managed to free myself, and you know the rest of the story."

"Yes, I do," he said, "and I'm damn proud of you for taking him on."

"Then please understand, I need some time and space to heal. It's not that I don't love you, because I do. But right now, I don't know if I'll ever be the way I was before, much less be able to be able meet your needs."

"Rachel, please. Having sex is the last thing on my mind right now. I just went through my own kind of hell. I was there, at your folks' house, when the detectives came and told us you were dead."

"I understand." Her voice was firm. "What I'm saying is I need a time out so I can sort out not only what happened to me this past weekend, but everything I went through for the past few years. This man was like the devil, and he truly made my life a living hell."

"I know he did." He too took a more somber tone. "But Rachel, I'm also partly to blame for this."

"No, you're not."

"Yes, I am. While you were busy at the reception I went and hung out with the guys watching the ballgame. Then, when Emma came to join us, I looked around for you and thought you were sitting at another table with a group of women, only it wasn't you. It was Sara. If I had taken the time to walk over to her, I would have known it wasn't you, and we would have started looking for you much sooner. But I didn't, and because I didn't, an hour went by before we realized you were missing."

"It's not your fault. He loaded me up in his truck and whisked me out of town. Even if you'd called the police sooner, they still wouldn't have known where to look for me." She paused for a moment, searching for the right words.

"I'm not saying it's over, Shane. I'm just saying I need a time out, and besides, you just heard Bruce. Thanks to Aunt Laurie, I'm also homeless."

"No, you're not. As soon as you're well enough to travel, we'll take you home and I'll put you up in the guesthouse until you can find another place."

"To be honest, I'm not sure if I even want to go back to Tucson. I've always been an outsider to Bruce's family, and now I have an opportunity to spend some time with Al and Sherry and learn about the rest of my family. I just found out Michael wasn't adopted. He really is my half-brother, but for some reason my mother kept it from me."

Shane looked stunned. "You're kidding."

"No, I'm not, and trust me, I'm going to have a serious talk with her before she leaves." Once again, she stopped for a moment.

"And then there's something else you need to know."

His eyes met hers. "I know about the baby, Rachel."

She suddenly felt defensive. "I didn't know I was pregnant, nor did I want to be. I ran out of pills, so I was using sponges until I could get a new prescription, and there was one time when I forgot to put one in."

"Rachel, it's okay. We would have managed, but I have to ask you something, and I want you to be completely honest with me."

"Of course. What is it?"

Shane's eyes locked onto hers. "Once you realized you were pregnant, would you have had an abortion?"

"No. Even if I'd wanted to, I don't think I could have gone through with it." Her tone turned softer. "My mother could have easily aborted me, and frankly, her life would have been a lot easier if she had, but she chose not to, and it's a decision for which I will always be grateful. That said, maybe it's for the best that this happened. I'm not ready to be a mother, and I'm not sure I ever will be."

Shane touched her forearm. "It's getting late, and I can tell you're getting tired. Why don't we both get a good night's rest and we'll take this up in the morning."

"No." Rachel shook her head. "Tomorrow morning, I want you to go back to Tucson, and let me deal with what I have to deal with. It's like I said before. It's not over between us. I just I need a time out. But in the meantime, if someone else catches your fancy, then you should take her out. You have your life too, and it's certainly not fair for me to keep you on hold for weeks, maybe months."

"Rachel, you're talking nonsense. I happen to love you, and trust me, I'm not interested in seeing anyone else."

Rachel closed her eyes. "I'm sorry, Shane, but right now I can't be what you need."

"Rachel, please, I—"

"Shane, please. Just go. I want you to go home and get on with your life and not worry about me. I'll be fine, and hopefully we can pick up where we left off, but it may be some time from now, and I'm not making any promises."

He tried to say something, but she cut him off.

"Goodnight, Shane. You're right. I really am tired right now." Her eyes remained closed as she turned her face toward the window. Moments later she heard his footsteps as he walked out of the room.

❧FORTY-NINE❧

SHANE'S HEART FELT like lead as he walked out of Rachel's room. In less than a week, he had lost her twice. Beth looked up and greeted him with a smile as he approached the nurse's station.

"If you're looking for the rest of your party, they're down the hall in a small waiting room. It'll be on your left, across from the elevators."

He muttered a thank you and shuffled down the hall. Entering the room, he found the others involved in a heated conversation, which abruptly went silent.

"Are you okay, Shane?" asked Julie.

"No, I'm not."

Alice wrapped her arms around him. "It's okay, Shane. It's like I mentioned to you earlier. She needs time and space to heal."

"Rachel's known to push people away when she's hurting," said Julie. "She didn't tell you it was over, did she?"

"No."

"I didn't think so. I can usually tell what she's thinking, and I can guarantee you that within the next few days she'll start realizing she's made a mistake. And while she may not contact you right away, trust me when I say you two will be back together within the next few weeks. If not by Thanksgiving, then most certainly by Christmas. And, for what it's worth, I expect to hear a similar speech from her tomorrow."

Shane nodded. "It's coming. She's not too happy with you for telling her Michael was adopted."

"I know. We were just discussing it when you came in. As I was explaining to Al, at the time Michael was born, Rachel was asking a lot of questions about where her real father was. She was worried that he'd abandoned her, and Bruce and I were both concerned that if we told her she had a new half-brother, she might think she'd been replaced. So we told her that her father had gotten married and had adopted his wife's little boy, just like Bruce had adopted her. And, much to our relief, she took it well. In fact, she felt a special kinship with him. Then later on, when she said she wanted to write him letters and send him presents, we decided to go along with it. We planned on telling her the truth once she got older, but as the years went by we simply forgot about it. I'll explain it all to her tomorrow. Hopefully, she'll understand."

"Hopefully," said Shane.

Julie changed the subject. "Since she's not well enough to travel, I went ahead and booked a flight home for you and Bruce for tomorrow morning. Both of you need to get back to work. Alice and I will stay with her at Al and Sherry's house to help them look after her. I'll leave on Saturday as I too need to get back to work, and Alice leaves on Sunday. Alice and I will keep you in the loop Shane, and you're still part of the family. I'm also expecting you at our place for dinner on Sunday."

"And don't even think of trying to wiggle your way out of it," said Alice.

Julie gave her daughter a look and turned her attention back to Shane. "I'll bring you up to date on her condition, but you'll still have to be patient, and let her come to you."

"Thank you for thinking of me, but I—"

"You've had a rough ride yourself, Shane," said Alice. "You need to get some rest and focus on taking care of yourself for a while. You'll need to be strong for her once she's ready to come back."

"Alice is right," said Julie.

"Let's call it a night," said Al. "Sherry and I will see you two ladies in the morning." He shook hands with Bruce and Shane and gave Julie a lingering hug before he and Sherry stepped out. Once they were gone, Alice wrapped her arm around Shane's shoulder.

"I don't know about you, but I'm dead on my feet, and since none of us have eaten in hours, we've decided to stop for a burger on the way back to the hotel."

* * *

Rachel was on the phone when Al and Sherry and the rest of her family arrived the following morning. She greeted them with a smile, pointing to the chairs as she ended the call.

"That was Debra Armstrong, my attorney," said Rachel as she set the phone down on her tray. "She's filed a motion for dismissal of my lawsuit against Craig, and she called Leo Hartman, Craig's attorney.

She's going to file a claim against Craig's estate for my medical expenses. Leo told her Craig didn't have much in the way of assets, but he's agreed to do whatever he can to help. So, I guess that'll be my next big battle. I have a high deductible and copays, and I have no idea how I'm going to pay for it all. She also mentioned something about Donny setting up a crowd-funding account for me."

"He did," said Alice, "and as of this morning it's up to almost four thousand dollars. You were on the ten o'clock news in Tucson last night and on the early news in Albuquerque this morning. The story is also in the paper and on all the local news websites, so people are pitching in to help you."

"Wow," said Rachel. "So guess there really is something to the kindness of strangers."

"Indeed there is."

A nurse came in to check her blood pressure. "So," she said, "you'll be leaving us later today."

"I sure am," said Rachel, "and it's not that I haven't appreciated your hospitality, but I'm anxious to get out of here."

"I understand," she said with a smile. "Your doctor will be in soon to talk to you, and once he signs off, we can start your paperwork." She made a few notes in her tablet and stepped away.

"It looks like the swelling in your face has gone down," said Julie.

Rachel reached up to touch her face. "It has?"

Sherry nodded. "Yes, it has. You really do look a lot better this morning, and are you putting the Vaseline on your wrists?"

"Yes, and it looks like the swelling on my right wrist has gone down as well. They're supposed to put it in a cast before I leave. In the meantime, would one of you mind opening my suitcase? My regular purse is in there, and I need to change back into it. I also need my phone charger. It should be in the side pocket."

Rachel's breakfast arrived while her mother rummaged through the suitcase. Her appetite had improved and eating with her left hand felt less awkward. Her doctor came in as she finished her meal. Once the introductions were made, he examined her and went over her chart.

"You're looking much better today, young lady." He too was smiling. "In fact, I'm booting you out of here."

Rachel nodded toward her luggage. "My bags are all packed."

"I see, but first we'll have to put your wrist in a cast. Someone will be here shortly to take care of it, and then I want you to get started with your physical therapy. You also need to schedule a follow-up appointment at my office."

Rachel nodded toward Sherry. "Not to worry. It's all been arranged."

Dr. Collins stepped out and a technician soon arrived to put the cast on Rachel's wrist. Once it was finished, she showed it off.

"Well, it certainly is pink," said Julie.

"Yep. I'll have to live with it for the next few weeks, so I figured I may as well get a color I like. Anything but royal blue. I don't ever want to wear royal blue again." Rachel picked up her now empty blue clutch purse. "Would any of you like to have this? I don't want it anymore."

"The hospital has a thrift shop," said Sherry. "It's at the end of the block. In fact, I was planning on going over there to see if I could find something comfortable for you to wear while you're recuperating, so I'll take it with me and donate it for you. Alice, would you like to come with me?"

Alice sprang from her chair. "Good idea. We'll be back soon, sissy, so don't go anywhere without us."

"I wasn't planning on it," said Rachel with a wink.

Alice and Sherry stepped out while Rachel looked closely at Al and Julie.

"You know, I can't quite recall the last time I was with both of my biological parents at the same time."

"Your mother and I have decided that the three of us need to sit down and have a little family conference," said Al.

"Uh-oh," said Rachel. "I hope I'm not about to be taken out to the woodshed."

"Actually, that would be me," said Julie. "So, I guess we'll begin by talking about your brother. At the time he was born, your father—I mean, your stepfather and I, were concerned that you might think your dad had left you and replaced you with another child. This is why we told you he adopted Michael. We honestly meant to explain it to you once you were older, but we simply forgot about it. It was our oversight, and we're both truly sorry."

"It's okay, Mom. I thought about it last night, after you all left, and I figured it must have been something like that. I would, however, like to reconnect with him, if it's at all possible."

"Of course it's possible," said Al. "I spoke to him on the phone several times yesterday. He said he'd recently friended you on Facebook, but then you closed out your account a short time later."

"I did," said Rachel. "I'd gotten tired of Craig harassing me on Facebook, so I finally gave up closed out all my social media accounts. Maybe now I can reopen them." She looked at Al. "Perhaps you can give me his email address. I can at least let him know what happened."

"Of course, but we did fill him in about most things." Al and Julie looked at one another. "I also want to discuss a few other things with you, starting with my decision to allow Bruce to adopt you."

"Go ahead, Dad."

"First of all, I honestly like Bruce. He's a good man, and he did a damn good job of raising you in my absence, but if I had it to do over again, I would have never allowed it. At the time, I was living paycheck to paycheck, barely making my rent, and living on beans and rice so I could make my child support payments. Then your mother got engaged to Bruce. I knew she really loved him, and I was genuinely happy for her. I also knew she'd gotten a lot of grief from her family because you were born out of wedlock. She said that by allowing Bruce to adopt you, her parents would be more accepting of you, and I'd no longer have to worry about paying child support." He took a deep breath as his expression turned sad.

"So, the circumstances being what they were, I reluctantly agreed, but it didn't mean I would ever give up being your father. I still came to see you whenever I could, and I still sent you whatever I could from every paycheck. Then, after your mom and Bruce set up your college fund, we all agreed that I would take it over. By then I was in a much better place financially, and it gave them more of an opportunity to save money for Alice."

"Mom told me, a long time ago, that you took care of my college expenses, and I always be grateful."

"You're welcome," said Al with a smile. "One of the reasons why I took the job here in Albuquerque was because the pay was much better than what I was making in Tucson. Sherry and I were able to get married, and we've been able to put both of you kids through college, but there was a price to pay. I wasn't able to see you anymore, because once I bought the business, I was putting in a good sixty hours a week, and I had no time for a vacation. In fact, Sherry and Michael didn't see much of me either me during those first few years. By then I'd been told that you'd bonded with Bruce, and your sister, so I kept my distance, but it's something I'll always regret. Someday, I hope to make up for it with my grandkids."

Rachel winced at his words and looked down at her lap.

"I know about the baby, Rachel," said Julie.

"Seems like the whole world knows about it." Rachel immediately regretted her words and looked her mother in the eye. "Sorry, Mom. I don't know what came over me."

"It's okay. Your dad and I have both been lucky. Neither of us have ever lost a child, so we probably don't understand the pain you're in, but we're both grieving the loss of what would have been our first grandchild."

"It's okay, Mom. As I already told Al, I didn't know I was pregnant, so I don't really feel a loss."

"Right now, you're dealing with other issues, but trust me, it'll come. Shane, however, is taking it pretty hard."

"I know he is. He really wants to have kids, but I was never sure myself. It's one of the reasons why he's better off without me."

"No, Rachel, he isn't," she said, firmly. "He's totally devoted to you. He was with us at the house when the police came and told us you were gone, and as soon as he heard it he went into shock. It was like a part of him died right then and there."

Rachel's heart sank. "I understand, but I really don't want to talk about Shane right now."

Al and Julie exchanged knowing looks as someone tapped on the door. A man in a business suit presented a badge.

"I'm Felipe Ortega. I'm with the internal affairs division of the New Mexico State Police. Ms. Bennett, if I could have a few minutes of your time?"

"Of course." Rachel glanced at the others. "However, I'd like for both of my parents to be present."

"Not a problem." He took his seat and quickly got down to business.

"I understand you were kidnapped in a hotel parking lot near Tucson last Saturday night, and Craig Walker, the man who abducted you, crossed state lines and brought you to New Mexico. Is that correct?"

"Yes, sir. It is."

"And I also understand there was an incident, involving a New Mexico state trooper, while Mr. Walker was holding you captive."

"Yes, there was." Rachel took a deep breath and sighed. "I was being held at knifepoint, and after we crossed into New Mexico, I saw a sign about a gas station ahead, so I told him I needed to take a bathroom break. He agreed, and I was going to try to escape. I found a tube of lipstick in the trash and was going to leave a note on the mirror. That's when the trooper came in. I tried to tell her who I was, and that I'd been kidnapped, but I didn't have any ID on me, and Craig had somehow convinced her that he was my brother, and I was a mental patient. He'd tied up my hands when he abducted me, so I showed her the rope burns on my wrists, but even that didn't convince her. She said my brother told her I'd injured myself so I could get attention."

"Did she try to contact the authorities in Arizona to validate your story?"

"No, sir, she did not."

"Did she contact the paramedics or try to take you to a hospital?"

"No, sir, she did not. She all but dragged me out of the restroom and handed me over to Craig. I think she may have said something about wanting to call the paramedics, but I'm not sure. I was pretty shook up by then. Craig kept telling her he had everything under control and was taking me home."

"Do you know who the trooper was?"

"No. I don't recall her giving me her name. She was about the same height as me, and I'm five foot six. She was slender, with dark hair. I think it may have been pulled back into a bun, but I'm not sure. She had brown eyes, and a medium complexion. And she looked young. I would say early twenties. The name on her badge was either Hopkins or Harkins."

"Her name is Bobbie Sue Hopkins," said the detective, "and in case you're wondering, she's been placed on administrative leave."

"Will she be fired?" asked Al.

"It has yet to be determined," said Ortega. "So, Ms. Bennett, I understand that at the time you went into the ladies' room, you hadn't been seriously harmed. Is that correct?"

"Yes, that's correct. Other than the rope burns, which weren't as severe as they are now, I was fine. At least physically. Emotionally however, it was a different story. At that point, Craig hadn't actually touched me, but he'd made some lewd comments about me, and he'd also made it pretty clear that he had no intention of letting me go, so it was obvious that whatever he was up to wouldn't be good. So yes, by the time I got to the ladies' room, I was in genuine fear for my life, and I knew it would be my last chance to escape."

"So what happened after the trooper handed you over to Mr. Walker?"

"She left." Rachel blinked several times to fight the tears as the scene played back in her mind. "Then, once she was gone, Craig grabbed me, really hard. It's how I got these bruises on my arm."

Rachel pushed up her sleeve. The fingermark bruises were still visible. Julie let out a gasp and muttered something under her breath as Rachel went on with her story.

"He took me back to his truck, and that's when he tried to rape me. Fortunately for me, he was interrupted. He started yelling something about the cops, so I'm guessing another trooper must have come along, but I was unable to see out the window. We left right after that, and then later on I managed to free myself and fight back. Somehow, during the struggle, I was pushed out of the truck, but I really don't remember. I just remember working the knot loose and getting my hands free. Then yesterday morning I woke up and found myself here. As you can see, I ended up with some pretty serious injuries."

"I know you did," said Ortega, "and I'm very sorry it happened. Had the trooper called for backup, we also may have been able to apprehend Mr. Walker alive."

His words jolted Rachel as a scene of what could have happened played through her mind. No doubt Craig would have told the arresting officers she had come with him of her own free will, and he tied her hands at her request because she had a fetish. Then, once the case went to trail, his defense attorney would have done everything possible to destroy her reputation. She shuddered at the thought.

"Are you all right?" asked Julie.

"I'm fine, Mom." She turned her attention back to the detective. "Are we about done here?"

"I think so." Ortega handed her one of his cards. "We'll let you know if we need any additional information. In the meantime, I wish you a speedy recovery."

Ortega stepped out and Julie looked at Al. "You're doing the right thing by having her meet with your attorney. Please let us know if you need help with the costs."

"Thanks, Julie, but he's working on contingency." Al turned his attention to Rachel, who still looked shaken. "Are you okay?"

"I'm fine, Dad. I was just thinking about what would have happened if Craig had been taken alive. He would have gotten out of prison eventually, and then he would have come after me again. I hope I don't sound too harsh when I say that how it ended really was for the best, because now I don't ever have to worry about him hurting me again."

"He made his choice." said Al. "As far as I'm concerned, he committed suicide by cop. Now we need to focus our energy on you getting well so you can get back to your life."

Sherry and Alice returned a short time later and presented Rachel with several shopping bags.

"We did good," said Alice. "We found you a couple of pairs of sweatpants, one of which still has the original store tags, and we found you some nice, button down blouses which look like they've never been worn. You won't be able to wear any pullover tops until your shoulder heals, and, best of all, nothing is royal blue."

Sherry handed her the receipt for her clutch purse. Rachel thanked them both and carefully eased herself out of her bed.

"What are you doing?" asked Julie.

"I'm going to pick out some fresh clothes, and then I'm getting dressed. I can't wait to get out of this place."

❧FIFTY❧

RACHEL FELT ANXIOUS as the hospital aide pushed her wheelchair out the main entrance. A late-model white Chevy Suburban waited at the curb. Al hopped out of the driver's seat and stowed her bag with the other luggage while Julie and Alice helped her from her chair. Sherry opened the back door and Julie stepped inside to help Alice guide Rachel into the back seat. Once she settled between her mother and her sister. Al and Sherry hopped into the front. Julie reached over and tried to buckle Rachel's seatbelt.

"No!" she screamed.

A badly started Julie let go of the seatbelt as everyone looked at Rachel. Her heart pounded and she could feel her body shaking.

"I'm so sorry," she said, apologetically. "I didn't mean to frighten anyone. It's just that when you started pulling down my seatbelt, I suddenly saw myself back in Craig's truck, but I'm okay now."

"Did he fasten your seatbelt for you?" asked Alice.

"Yes. My hands were tied, so he had to strap me in. He didn't grope me, or anything like that, but I was still trapped."

"It's okay." Julie gave her daughter a reassuring pat on the arm. "He's gone and he's never coming back." Once again, she reached for the seatbelt, but this time she moved her hands slowly. "I'll pull it down just enough to hand it off to you, and then you can fasten yourself in."

"Thanks, Mom."

Julie waited anxiously as Rachel carefully strapped herself in. Once secure, she gave the others an embarrassed smile.

"See? I did it. I'm okay now. Again, I'm so sorry."

"I think we may want to look into a crime victim's support group," said Alice. "You could be suffering from Post-Traumatic Stress Disorder."

"Oh, come on. That's what happens to soldiers who've been out on the battlefield."

Alice's voice was firm. "No, it doesn't just happen to soldiers. It can happen to anyone who's experienced a traumatic event, which you most certainly have."

"I'm not crazy." Rachel's voice was equally firm. "And I won't allow anyone to push psychotic drugs down my throat."

"No one says you're crazy," said Alice, "but I'm a nurse. I've taken care of people who've been victims of violent crimes, and a support group can help you heal. It's a chance for you to talk it out, with other crime victims, who understand what you're going through, because they've been through it themselves."

"Your sister's right," said Sherry. "So I'll look into it."

"Thanks, guys, but really, I'm okay. It was just a fluke. He's dead and buried, and I'm moving on."

"No, you're not," said Al. "You're going to need some counseling. You may not have served in the military, but what you've experienced isn't that different from what a soldier experiences on the battlefield, and it won't go away by itself. If you don't deal with it now, it will continue to haunt you, and I don't want you ending up with a drug or alcohol problem because of it."

"Thanks, Al," said Julie.

"You're welcome." Al put the truck in gear and headed toward the exit. As they turned onto the main road a TV news truck turned into the hospital entrance. "Looks like we left just in time."

Rachel perked up. "Are they there because of me?"

"They very well might be," he said. "They were here yesterday as well, but security wouldn't let them in the building. Someone may have tipped them off that you were leaving, but even if they did, it's too late now."

Rachel chucked. "And the only forwarding address I left was my place in Tucson, which, thanks to Aunt Laurie, I no longer live in." Her smiled faded. "Guess I'll have to rent a mailbox somewhere, since I don't know where I'll be going next."

Julie reached up and stroked her hair. "It's okay, Rachel. You dad—I mean your stepdad, and I can pick up your mail and forward it to you. Then, when you're well enough to come home, you can move back in with us until you find another place.

"Thanks, Mom, but at the moment my future looks kind of uncertain, and I'm not ready to make any big decisions." She looked out the window and took in her surroundings.

"Nice town. Sort of reminds me of Tucson."

"It's similar," said Al. "It too is kind of laid back. It's also home to a state university, just like Tucson, and it's in the desert, but we're at a higher altitude, so it's about ten degrees cooler."

"We even get a little snow in the winter," said Sherry. "It doesn't really accumulate in town, but it stays on the mountains. Then the big balloon fiesta starts this weekend. It's a huge event, and for the next ten days or so you'll be seeing a lot of hot air balloons from the backyard."

Rachel leaned back in her seat and closed her eyes. She still tired easily, and she looked forward to a long nap once they arrived at Al and Sherry's house. She began drifting off, but a beeping phone soon jarred her awake.

"I just got a text message from Bruce," said Julie. "He and Shane are about to board their flight. It was forty-five minutes late because of bad weather in the Midwest. He says Shane's been unusually quiet. He didn't want any breakfast, and he's hardly talking."

"He'll be fine, Mom," said Rachel. "I didn't tell him it was over. I just told him I needed a time out."

"For how long?"

"For as long as it takes," said Rachel. "C'mon, look at me. I'm damaged goods. I've got broken bones, broken teeth, my face is bruised and scarred, and I don't know if the scars will be permanent or not. He deserves someone who's whole."

Julie started to say something, but Rachel leaned back into her seat and once again closed her eyes. The others kept quiet so as not to disturb her.

Al and Sherry lived in a spacious two-story Santa Fe style home in the neighboring town of Rio Rancho. As they turned into the driveway, Al pushed the remote, and the center door of the three-car garage opened. Inside, a red sedan was parked on the right, with a pair of motorcycles on the left. Sherry and Alice unloaded the bags while Julie tried to help Rachel out of the truck.

"I've got her." Al swooped in and gently lifted her out. "I'll bet you thought I couldn't pick you up anymore."

"Thanks, Dad." She gave him a warm smile as he set her down, holding her firmly until she got her balance.

"Don't worry. You'll be going to all your appointments in Sherry's car. We had to take the Suburban today because we had to pick up your mother and sister at the hotel, since Bruce and Shane took the rental car to the airport."

Sherry opened the side door and a pair of German Shepherds bounded into the garage. "Meet Sampson and Delilah," she said. "They may look tough, but they think they're lapdogs.

As the two dogs wagged their tails and greeted everyone with a friendly sniff, Sherry motioned to them to go through the door. A large kitchen with granite countertops and a big center island waited on the other side. Sherry took the dogs to the living room and opened a sliding door to the backyard. The two dogs rushed outside and she returned to the kitchen.

"Rachel, you'll be staying in the downstairs guestroom. It's right across the hall from the master suite, and if you'll follow me, I can show you where it is."

She took her down a hallway, opening a door on her left. Inside was a pleasant room with a corner group and an oak dresser. A sliding glass door opened to the backyard. Alice and Julie followed with Rachel's bags.

"Very nice," said Alice.

"I agree," said Julie, "and I'd be happy to stay in the other bed."

Rachel smiled and shook her head. "I'm fine Mom, and it's not that I don't love you, but I don't need you hovering over me."

"I'm not hovering. You only have one arm."

Rachel held her ground. "I know, but I've got to start using my other one, even if it's just a little. Besides, I start physical therapy tomorrow, and they'll probably torture me."

"They may at that," said Alice with a smug grin. "So, do you need help unpacking?"

"I'm fine. If you wouldn't mind putting my suitcase on one of the beds, I think I can manage on my own. Then I'd like to take a nap. It's been a busy morning, and I worn out."

"Of course."

Alice put the suitcase on the bed and before they left Sherry told her where the bathroom was. A sense of sadness came over Rachel as she unfolded her clothes and hung them in the closet. They were the outfits she planned on wearing in Sedona with Shane.

* * *

Sherry led Alice and Julie upstairs and down another hallway, opening one of the doors.

"This is Michael's room. He's going to college in Las Cruces, so I doubt he'll mind you using it." Inside was a full-sized bed with a sports-themed comforter set. The light-blue walls were covered with football and baseball posters.

"I think I can handle this one," said Alice with a smile. "I always wondered what it would have been like to have a little brother, so this sort of gives me a sense of it."

As Alice took her bags inside, Sherry led Julie to the room at the end of the hall. A sewing machine and small worktable took up one wall, with a love seat on the opposite side.

"It's a sleeper sofa," said Sherry. "My niece stays here whenever my sister comes to visit, and she says it's quite comfortable."

"It'll be fine." Julie noticed a partially finished project on the worktable. "Do you make quilts?" she asked.

"When I have the time," said Sherry. "I'm an income tax preparer, so from mid-January through mid-April, I put in some incredibly long days. The rest of the year, however, I only have to work one or two days a week, so it gives me something to do. It also means that taking Rachel to all of her medical appointments won't be a problem for me."

"You have no idea how grateful I am to hear it."

"Hey, I'm mom too, and I always loved Rachel. She even remembered me from before."

"She did?"

"Yes, she did. She also remembered how long my hair used to be." Sherry smiled at the memory. "I cut it short when Michael was a baby. He kept pulling at it."

"Kids do that."

"They sure do. The girl Al dated before me never liked kids. In fact, I don't think Al ever introduced her to Rachel."

"No, he didn't. You're the only one."

"That's what I thought." Sherry smiled again. "Al broke up with her because she didn't like kids, so when we started dating, he told me upfront it would be a package deal, and if I couldn't handle his daughter, he'd be happy to show me the door."

"Al and I both had baggage once Rachel was born. Before Bruce came along, I had friends who'd offer to introduce me to people, but then nothing ever happened. Later on, I'd ask them about it, and it was always the same. They were so sorry, but he wasn't interested in someone with kids. That really hurt, you know, but I wouldn't have traded my daughter for the world. Then one day I met a fellow teacher named Bruce."

"Al wouldn't have traded her either, and he was still fond of you, you know."

"And I was fond of him as well. I wouldn't have gotten involved with him if I didn't think that underneath that rough exterior he was a decent guy. However, at the time we met, I was on the rebound from someone else, and I certainly had no intention of getting pregnant. It really was an accident, but I also knew he wasn't the right guy for me, so I wasn't going to tie him down. I'm glad he found you."

"Me too, although it took me awhile to get used to you being in the picture. I knew you were married to Bruce, but for a time I still felt a little jealous. You and Al share a bond, and you always will, but once I got to know you better I realized you were okay. And I adore Rachel. I always have. She gave Al a sense of purpose, and as strange as this may sound, I can't help but wonder if maybe Craig bringing her to New Mexico happened for a reason, because now that she's here, she has a chance to spend some time with her father. Al has really missed her over the years. He never told her that because he wanted her to live her own life and not feel guilty about it, but believe me when I tell you he couldn't be happier to have her here. She's welcome to stay with us for as long as she wants."

"Well, that's good to know," said Julie. "Looking back, it was a mistake to not have her spend more time with her father, but Bruce and I are both teachers. We just didn't have the means to cover her travel expenses, and I didn't like the idea of her traveling alone."

"And Al was putting in such long hours back then. Michael hardly saw him either."

Alice entered the room and walked up to her mother. "I'm all unpacked and I just went downstairs to check on Rachel. She's out like a light, so I found a quilt and covered her up. The best thing to do is to let her rest."

Sherry checked her watch. "Wow. I didn't realize what time it was. I need to run downstairs and take care of lunch."

"Can we help you with anything?" asked Julie.

"Nah," said Sherry. "I went to the grocery store this morning and picked up a couple of extra-long sub sandwiches."

❧FIFTY-ONE❧

RACHEL CAME INTO the kitchen as the others were finishing their lunch.

"I thought you were taking a nap," said Julie.

"I was, but then my phone rang and woke me up. It was Pilar, wanting to know how I was doing and if there was anything she could do to help."

Sherry got her something to drink and offered to fix her a plate, but Rachel politely refused, saying she could do it herself. She sliced off a piece of one of the sandwiches and joined the others at the table.

"I no sooner got off the phone with Pilar when Grandpa called. Can you believe that? He was relieved that I'm still alive, and he wanted to know if I was all right."

"He's your grandfather," said Julie, firmly. "Of course he'd be happy you're still with us, and he would want to know if you were okay."

"I know, Mom, but we were never that close. So I thanked him for calling and we chatted for a few minutes. He said he'd call you later."

As Rachel bit into her sandwich, the dogs began barking. Al rose from his seat and headed to the front door. It opened before he could reach it, and a young, dark-haired man entered.

"What are you doing here?" asked Al.

"I live here," he said.

"Not anymore. You moved out."

"Jeez, Dad. I'm only home for a visit. The Balloon Fiesta is in town."

Al grumbled as he headed into the kitchen. Sherry rose from the table, greeting her son with a warm hug before introducing him to the others. She started with Julie, and after they shook hands, she introduced him to Alice.

"So, you're either my sister once removed, or my sister-in-law, or perhaps my step-sister? I'm not sure how this all works."

"Neither do I," said Alice with a grin. "So I'll just say I'm your sister from different parents, since we share a half-sister."

"Works for me." He gave her a quick hug and stepped up to Rachel, who stood from her chair.

"Finally." He wrapped his arms around her, being careful not to disturb her sling. "After all the years of letters, emails, Facebook, and of course, all the presents, we finally get to meet in person." Once the embrace was over, he stepped back and studied her for a moment at arm's length.

"So, are you okay?"

"I'm fine," said Rachel, "all things considered."

"You look like female version of our dad."

"Really?"

Michael nodded.

"Funny," said Rachel, "I was about to say the same about you. You've got his face, but with your mother's dark hair. Of course, it's shorter than his, but still, you look just like him."

"Okay you two," said Al. "That's enough of trying to butter up the old man."

Sherry made a place for Michael at the table and offered him some lunch. As she fixed his plate, Al announced he was heading back to the office. They said their goodbyes and once he left, Michael turned his attention back to Rachel.

"Craig sent me a friendship request on Facebook just before you closed out your account. I thought it would be a good opportunity to monitor him, so I accepted the friendship."

"So what all did he post?" asked Rachel.

"Most of the time it was about the research he did for his articles, or an announcement that an article had just been published, and he'd include a link. He also posted links to his blog, which were mostly about the business of freelance writing. However, from time to time, he'd post a rant, either on the blog, or on Facebook, about his critics who were out to ruin his reputation and undermine his credibility as a writer, but he, of course, was a man of integrity, and the only reason they were after him was because they were all hacks who felt threatened by him. Then he'd occasionally go off about an ex-co-worker, who he tried to mentor, but she stabbed him in the back, and while his career was on the rise, hers was faltering, because she was a would-be if she could-be who didn't know what the hell she was doing."

"Of course," said Rachel. "He hounded me on social media for years, even though I never once made any reference to him in any of my posts or tweets. No doubt my ignoring him just made him angrier."

"It didn't matter. He was a bully. His last post appeared on Facebook about a week ago. He said his first article for *The American Chronicles* had just been published, and he posted the link. He said he finally had the recognition he felt he deserved, and he would celebrate by going camping in the Sierras. He also said his critics would soon be silenced, once and for all."

Rachel felt a shiver go down her spine. "Did he say anything more specific?"

Michael shook his head. "No. He kept it pretty vague, but I called the Tucson police and told them he'd posted a cryptic message on Facebook."

"They went through his Facebook and Twitter accounts," said Julie, "which is one of the reasons why they alerted the authorities in California, but not New Mexico"

"I know, Mom," said Rachel, "and I'm not angry with anyone, other than Craig. You all did the best you could. Luckily, I had a guardian angel looking out for me, which is why those two college girls found me. I just need to find out who they were, so I can thank them in person."

Before leaving the table, Alice offered to stay in another room, but Michael turned her down, saying he would make do on the couch. The following morning the family enjoyed coffee on patio as hot air balloons filled the sky. Once breakfast was over it was time for Sherry to take Rachel to her first session of physical therapy. Julie tagged along, and after they left Michael took Alice to the balloon festival. He talked about growing up as an only child, but knowing he had a half-sister, and he was happy she'd made the effort to connect with him. He also told Alice he considered her his other sister.

Julie left late Saturday afternoon, and after a tearful goodbye Al and Sherry drove her to the airport. Once they left Michael and Alice announced they would be taking Rachel out for dinner that night.

"But I look like hell," she said. "My face is still bandaged."

"Not for much longer," said Alice. "It's ready to come off."

"But my face is still bruised."

Alice held her ground. "And once I take your bandage off you can put on a little makeup. Rachel, we're not going to let you become a recluse. You need to start going out in public again."

Rachel started to say something, but Michael cut her off. "We're not going any place fancy. It's just a steakhouse a couple of miles down the road. Don't worry, Alice and I will be with you, and it'll be an opportunity for the three of us to hang out together and bond, since Alice and I are both leaving tomorrow."

"But I—"

"No buts." Alice's voice was firm. "So let's go pick out something nice for you to wear. Then you can shower, and I'll help you with your hair."

Rachel looked more like herself once the bandage was removed and she had some makeup on, but she still felt ill at ease once they arrived at the restaurant.

"You okay?" asked Alice as they settled in their booth.

"It depends. Can I have a glass of wine?"

"I think we can arrange it, but only one." She turned to Michael. "Hey, bro. Don't just sit there. She wants a glass of wine, and you can order one for me as well."

* * *

The following morning Michael volunteered to drop Alice off at the airport on his way back to Las Cruces. When the time came for them to leave, Rachel gave each of her siblings a hug, but she held tighter to Alice.

"Well, kiddo, this is it. It's all going to be different now. You're a married woman, and it's time for you to go home to your husband."

"But we'll still see each other."

"Of course we will. It just won't be as often as it was before." Rachel reached up and brushed a wisp of hair away from Alice's face. "As of today, Donny comes first. So go take that honeymoon you had to postpone, and go live your lives. We'll always be sisters, but now you're someone's wife, and someday you'll be someone's mom too. In the meantime, our new little brother can watch over me. I'll be fine."

They hugged one last time, and then Rachel told her it was time to go. Al and Sherry joined her as they walked out to Michael's car. After a last goodbye, Alice got into the passenger seat and rolled down the window. She promised to send Rachel a text when she arrived home. The two sisters waved goodbye one last time as Michael backed his car into the street. Once they were away, Alice reached into her purse for a tissue.

"You okay?" asked Michael.

"Yeah, I'm all right. I just have a funny feeling that it'll be a long time before I see her again."

"Well, it's like she said. You just got married, so your lives will be different."

"That's not it. Rachel never really felt like she was a part of the family. My dad treated the two of us like equals, but the rest of his family has always kept her at arm's length. And now that my aunt has packed up all of her belongings and put them into storage, I have a feeling that once she's recovered, she'll decide that she doesn't want to go back to Tucson."

"What about Shane?"

"I'm afraid the jury is out on Shane," said Alice with a shrug. "He's an amazing guy, and I know she really loves him, but you saw it. She sees herself as damaged goods and she feels she's no longer worthy of him. Hopefully, she'll get over it soon. It would be a real shame if he moved on and found someone else."

✦FIFTY-TWO✦

SHANE STILL FELT numb when he arrived to work Friday morning. Once he got past Marissa, he headed into his office and started going through his email. Jonathan soon tapped on his door.

"You okay?" he asked.

"I've been better."

"So how's Rachel?"

"She took quite a tumble. Lots of cuts and bruises and a few broken bones, but, fortunately, no life-threatening injuries." He thought about the baby they lost. It was too painful to talk about. "She said he tried to rape her, but, luckily, he was interrupted before he could do too much damage."

"Thank goodness, and it sounds like she should make a full recovery. So, why are you here?"

"Good question." Shane stopped for a moment. "Sorry, Jonathan. I didn't mean sound sarcastic."

"Hey, I understand. You've been through a lot. You may recall a similar thing happened to my daughter."

"Yes, I remember you telling me about it. However, Rachel tells me she needs some time and space to heal."

"She's been through a major trauma, Shane. You'll have to be patient with her."

"But your daughter went through her own ordeal. Did she push people away?"

"No, she didn't, but we're all unique individuals, and we all have different ways of coping. Give Rachel some time. It's what she needs, and while she's recovering, there's plenty for you to do around here. I swear, the hackers always seem to stay a step ahead of us."

Shane felt a sneeze coming on and chill ran through his body. He quickly grabbed a tissue and covered face.

"You okay?" asked Jonathan once Shane sneezed loudly into the tissue.

"Yeah. I woke up with a sore throat this morning, so I took a cold pill. I'll grab another box of Kleenex from the supply room, and I think Marissa has some herbal tea, so I'll brew myself a cup. I'll be fine."

"You're sure?"

"I'm fine, Jonathan. You know how it is in the desert in October. Hot one day, cool the next, and there's all kinds of dead grasses and pollens in the air. It's probably just allergies."

"Hopefully, you're right."

Jonathan excused himself and Shane went back to work, but it was difficult for him to concentrate. He kept seeing Rachel's bruised face and her voice kept echoing through his mind. He sighed as he worked. He managed to get over Fiona, and if he had to, he could get over Rachel too, although getting over her would be more difficult.

By the time Shane arrived at Bruce and Julie's home on Sunday night a cold had set in. He assured them he was feeling better, but it was obvious by the way Julie talked that she was deeply concerned about Rachel's state of mind. As she described the seat belt incident, his heart sank even lower. Rachel's mental and emotional state was worse than he had thought. He left soon after the meal was over, thanking Julie for the update, but saying he needed to get some rest. Both Bruce and Julie told him to get well soon, and they would let him know if there were any changes.

Shane's cold lingered for another week, and he developed a hacking cough which remained once the cold finally subsided. Two more weeks passed, and his cough grew worse. His chest felt tight, and he was experiencing some shortness of breath. He shrugged it off as changing weather, compounded with high levels of stress. Nearly a month had passed without word from Rachel or her parents. Depression set in. Shane wasn't eating. He was having a hard time sleeping, and each day he dragged himself to work. Sitting at his desk one morning, he started having chills. He put his sweater back on, but he still couldn't get warm. Once again, he was coughing hard when Jonathan stepped in.

"You look like hell," said Jonathan.

"Halloween is only a few days away, so this year I thought I'd be a real-life zombie."

"Very funny. However, I think you should go home and get some rest."

"I'm fine, Jonathan."

"No, you're not. Your face is pale and drawn, and you've got circles underneath the circles under your eyes. Go home and get some rest."

"Wouldn't do me any good. I hardly sleep anymore."

Jonathan gave him a concerned look. "When was the last time you saw a doctor?"

"I'm fine, Jonathan. It's just a lingering cough."

"That's been going for weeks now."

"It'll get better. I've been taking some over the counter stuff."

"No." Jonathan's voice was firm. "You're going home, and you're not coming back until you're feeling better."

It was pointless to argue. Shane took a deep breath, and as he rose from his chair, he was once again racked by another coughing spell. His chest hurt and he fought to catch his breath, but knees buckled, and he collapsed into a heap on the floor.

"Shane!"

"I'll be all right." Shane spoke in a hoarse whisper as he tried to reassure Jonathan. He grabbed onto his chair and tried to stand as Jonathan came to his aid.

"Whoa! You're burning up. I'm calling nine-one-one. We need to get you to a hospital."

"Fine. Just help me get back into my chair."

Marissa rushed into the room as Jonathan sat Shane back into his chair. "What l happened? I could hear the commotion all the way up front."

"You need to call the paramedics," said Jonathan. "Shane's very sick and he's running a really high fever. He needs to get to a hospital."

Marissa hurried out of the room. Shane sat with his face in his hands until she returned with the paramedics. She stood by with Jonathan as they checked his vitals and started an IV. As expected, they were taking Shane to the hospital by ambulance. They loaded him onto a stretcher, and Jonathan asked if there was anyone he should call.

"My mother," said Shane. He gave them the phone number as they wheeled him outside.

"Which hospital?" asked Jonathan.

"Catalina Community," said one of the paramedics as they loaded him into the ambulance.

The ambulance doors slammed shut and Shane closed his eyes while the attending medic went over his medical history.

"I've been going through some stuff," said Shane. "My girlfriend was kidnapped from her sister's wedding. It happened a few weeks ago."

"Wait a minute. Are you talking about Donny Wheeler's sister-in-law?"

"Yeah."

"So you're that Shane. I thought you looked familiar. I was there that night. I remember you all were looking for her at the time we left, but you thought she was in the ladies' room or something. We didn't know she'd been kidnapped until we heard about it on the news the next morning. I'm Bart. I'm the one who snuck the iPad into the reception. So, how's she doing?"

"I'm not sure. She ended up in Albuquerque. She was able to fight him off before he had a chance to rape her, but then he pushed her out of his truck while it was still moving, and she ended up with several broken bones. Anyway, she decided she wanted to end it, so I don't know how she is now."

"Sorry to hear it."

"Yeah, me too. So I went back to work and promptly came down with a bad cold. It lasted almost two weeks, but the cough lingered on. I thought it would go away, but it just kept getting worse."

"It sure did, and it looks like it's turned into pneumonia."

"Well, no wonder I feel like hell."

"I'll bet you do, but no worries. The doctors will get you fixed up in no time."

Shane remained silent for the rest of the ride. Once they arrived at the hospital he was wheeled into a cubicle where a nurse drew some blood. A doctor soon arrived to examine him, and he was sent to x-ray. Once he was returned to his cubicle, the nurse came back and as she made notes in his chart Shane's curiosity got the better of him.

"Is Alice Bennett, or Wheeler, here today?"

She smiled. "You know Alice?"

"I'm a friend of the family, but I haven't spoken to her in a while."

"I see. Alice isn't here today. She and Donny were leaving this morning to go on their honeymoon. They had to postpone it, you know."

"Yeah, I know. Any word on her sister?"

"From what I hear, she's still in Albuquerque, and is apparently doing better." She made more notes on his chart and stepped away. Shane's mother arrived a few minutes later. A shocked look came over her face as soon as she saw him.

"What happened?"

"I woke up feeling like hell this morning, and after I got to the office I collapsed. They think I've got pneumonia."

"What? You told me you were feeling better. So how long has this been going on?"

"Well, I was feeling better, sort of. The cold cleared up, but I kept coughing. I figured it would go away on its own."

"Which it obviously didn't," said Kelly.

"I know, Mom. I'm exhausted, and I'm probably run down. I haven't had a decent night's sleep since the night Rachel disappeared."

"I know you haven't, and I know you haven't been eating right either, but once you realized it wasn't getting better you should have seen a doctor and gotten treatment. Pneumonia can be very serious."

"I know. I've probably had walking pneumonia for the past week or so and didn't know it." He started coughing again. Kelly handed him a tissue, and as it subsided the doctor came in.

"Well, Mr. MacLeod, I've gone over your x-ray, as well as your blood work, and I'm afraid you have bacterial pneumonia."

"Damn," said Kelly.

"She's my mom," said Shane.

"I also used to be a nurse."

"Then you know the drill." He turned his attention back to his patient. "I'm prescribing a round of antibiotics, along with a cough suppressant, something for the chest pain, and a mild sedative in case you're still having trouble sleeping. You need to go on strict bed rest for the next couple of weeks, and you'll also need to see your regular doctor for a follow up."

Kelly reached for her phone and called Colin, asking him to pick up the prescriptions on his way home. Once the paperwork was signed, Shane was released.

"You can take me back to the office," he said. "My car is there, and I'll drive straight home. I promise."

"Not a chance." Kelly's voice was stern. "Shane, this is serious. People die from this."

"I'm not a frail, old man."

"No, you're not, but you're still very sick, and I don't want you having complications which could put you in the hospital. We're going back to your place so you can get Lucy and pack a bag, then I'm taking you home with me. You'll be staying with your dad and me until you're back on your feet."

"But Mom—"

"Don't 'but Mom,' me. I meant what I said. Your father and I will pick up your car later, but right now you're not well enough to be on your own. You can call your boss from the car, and then you're leaving your phone and your laptop at your place. The rest of the world can wait. You're too sick to worry about work or anything else right now."

❧FIFTY-THREE❧

RACHEL SPENT A QUIET birthday with her father and stepmother. Over the next few weeks her cuts and bruises disappeared and the rope burns faded away. To her relief, her face would not be permanently scarred, nor would her three broken teeth have to be extracted. They were covered with dental crowns, and once the procedure was complete, she looked as she did before. Her physical therapy sessions continued, and, while painful at times, her wrist and shoulder were healing nicely, as were her broken ribs. Physically, she was on the mend. Emotionally, however, was another matter. Craig Walker may have been dead and buried, but he continued to haunt her from the grave.

Rachel often had trouble sleeping, and she occasionally had nightmares about being trapped inside his truck. She no longer wished to be totally blonde, so she had brown streaks put in her hair. But even with her new look, she wondered if she could ever be intimate with a man again. She felt apprehensive every time she walked through a parking lot, and the thought of going anywhere alone chilled her to the bone.

Decisions would soon have to be made about where she would go next. Her kidnapping made the Tucson headlines, and as a result, her design business evaporated. She had no income, and her medical bills piled up. She was neither well enough to return to work, nor did she have a home to return to. Curious, she looked up her old address on a real estate website. Sure enough, Aunt Laurie had her old duplex up for sale. She, of course, was the realtor, but what shocked Rachel was the number of days it had been on the market. Aunt Laurie had listed it within a week of her kidnapping. Her blood boiled.

"Packing up my stuff to help out my mother and Bruce my ass. You just couldn't wait to get me out of there, could you? You cold-hearted bitch."

"What?"

"Sorry, Sherry. I didn't hear you come in. I was just finishing reconciling my checking account." Rachel was seated at the kitchen table. She glanced at the stove clock. "Whoops. I didn't realize it was getting late. Did you want me to help you with dinner?"

Sherry looked troubled. "Dinner can wait. What's got you all riled up?"

"My aunt, if you want to call her that. She's actually Bruce's sister. I rented a duplex from her when I moved back to Tucson, which she was renting to me at cost. At the time, I thought she was doing it because I was family. Turns out it wasn't the reason at all. She owed Bruce a favor for something."

"Would this be the same aunt who announced to everyone that Alice was the only granddaughter, and that's why she was getting all the china and crystal?"

"The same." Rachel frowned as she shut down her laptop and slipped it back into its case.

"So, what's she done now?"

"You knew she packed up all my belongings right after I disappeared and put them in a storage locker."

"Of course," said Sherry, "but I'm told it was before she knew you'd been found alive. Your mother said she thought she was helping them out."

"So she said, but I've just discovered that she put the duplex up for sale the same day I was released from the hospital. She never bothered asking me if I wanted to move back in, much less ask how I was doing."

"I'm sorry, Rachel."

"Thanks, Sherry. I appreciate it. You know, my mother really tried her best. I think Bruce did as well, but the truth of the matter is, his family has always considered me an outsider."

Al entered through the side door as Rachel was talking.

"What was that?" he asked.

"Rachel's aunt put the duplex she was renting up for sale," said Sherry.

"Which means I officially have no home to return to," said Rachel, "not that I would have had the means of paying the rent once I got there. Sometimes I wonder if my surviving was even worth it."

"Get that thought out of your head right now." Al was genuinely angry. "I don't ever want to hear you talking like that again."

"So where am I supposed to go, Dad? My design business tanked. I'm homeless, and I'm depending on the kindness of strangers to help pay my medical bills. If Donny hadn't set up that crowd-funding account for me, I'd probably be filing bankruptcy right about now. Craig told me that night his intention all along was to destroy my career, and by golly, he succeeded." She picked up her laptop case. "I'll go put this away, and then I'll come back and help you, Sherry."

"Take your time."

Al was still in the kitchen when Rachel returned. He asked her, and Sherry, to take a seat at the table. Once they were settled in their chairs, he looked Rachel in the eye.

"We'd planned on discussing this with you later, when you were fully recovered, but under the circumstances, I think maybe we should talk about it now."

Rachel's body tensed up. "Dad, I'm sorry if my remark about surviving upset you, but right now my future is pretty uncertain, and I'm under a lot of stress."

"I understand, and it's what we wanted to talk to you about." His tone turned serious. "As you know, I plan to pass my business onto your brother someday."

"Yes, I know."

"Michael has a good head for business, and when the time comes, I know he'll do well. However, he's not an artist."

"Yes, I remember you telling me this before."

"Before your accident, Sherry and I were in the process of restructuring the business as a family partnership so we could bring Michael onboard, and, now that you're here, we would like to bring you onboard as well. I've been following your career ever since you were with the magazine in Reno. You have an impressive resume, as well as genuine creative talent which would be a real asset to the company. However, we also know you were in a serious relationship with Shane. So, were you two were planning on making a long-term commitment? And if so, would he be willing to relocate?"

Rachel was stunned. "Wow, Dad. I'm totally overwhelmed here."

"You don't need to give us an answer right this second. We're simply asking you to think it over, and if you decide you want to go back to Tucson it's okay. Someone like Shane doesn't come along every day, and if he's established there, then the last thing we'd ever want is for you to sacrifice your chance to get married and have a family of your own. We simply wanted you to know you have this option, and we want you to discuss it with Shane before you make any decision."

Rachel still felt overwhelmed. "I honestly don't know where I stand with Shane right now. I haven't spoken to him since the night he saw me at the hospital."

"Really?" Al sounded concerned. "Then it's been about a month now, and he's probably worried sick. You need to give him a call."

She took a deep breath and let out a long, drawn out sigh. "I know I do, but for some reason I can't make myself do it."

"Why?"

"Because I'm damaged goods."

"Because Craig tried to rape you?" asked Sherry.

Rachel stared at the floor and nodded her head. "He tried to rape me in his truck, while we were still at the gas station. At that point, I figured my best chance for surviving would be to tell him that if he'd agree to let me go when he was finished, I wouldn't fight him, so that's what I did. He didn't respond, so I started to struggle. That's when he shoved the knife in my face and told me I'd better keep my end of the bargain or else. So, I didn't move. Thankfully, he got interrupted a couple of minutes later, but even then, it was nearly too late. He only needed another minute or so to get the job done. Maybe less."

Tears streamed down her face. Sherry stepped into the kitchen to retrieve a box of tissues. Al walked over and hugged her.

"This isn't your fault, Rachel," he said. "You didn't do anything wrong."

"It doesn't matter. I was still unfaithful to Shane."

"No you weren't."

"That's what everyone keeps saying, but it's not how I feel. I should have fought him off."

"And you did," Al reminded her. "Maybe you weren't able to defend yourself in that moment. You said it yourself. He was armed. You were doing what you had to do to stay alive, and if you'd tried to fight him, he very well may have cut your throat. But afterwards you kept your wits about you, and you managed to turn the tables on him. Big time. Alice read the autopsy report, and later on she told us that had you been able to hold your grip just a little longer, you would have strangled him to death. That's light years away from willfully cheating on Shane, and if he were to think you cheated on him, it would most certainly prove he's not the man you thought he was. However, my gut tells me he's damn grateful you're still alive, and even if Craig had raped you, he would have still wanted you."

Sherry returned to the table, offering Rachel a tissue. "Did you ever follow up on finding a support group?" she asked.

"Yes, I did. Detective Trent gave me a couple of websites to refer to, and I found an online forum. I prefer talking about it online so I can keep my anonymity. Yes, I know, it could have been a whole lot worse, and some of the other women have had some truly horrifying stories to tell. And, interestingly enough, more often than not, they were raped by someone they knew and trusted, but I still feel like I cheated on Shane. I know it probably doesn't make any sense, but it's how I feel."

"Then I think you need to have this conversation with Shane," said Sherry.

"I don't think I can."

"Yes, you can." Al's voice was firm, but kind. "He already knows what Craig did, and you told him about fighting him off that day when you had all of us on the speakerphone. Trust me, he's not going to reject you. As a matter of fact, he thinks you're the one rejecting him."

"I don't know, Dad, but what if he won't talk to me?"

"Tell you what," said Sherry. "Halloween is a few days away, so why don't you email him a Halloween card? It'd be a good way to break the ice. Then you two can have a long talk and decide where you want to go from here."

Rachel smiled as she thought it over. "You know, that's a good idea. I used to email thank you cards to my clients." She stepped away to get her phone. Ten minutes later she found the perfect Halloween card.

"Well, here goes nothing," she said as she hit the send button. Her phone beeped an instant later. Rachel checked her email. Inside her inbox was the standard confirmation that her card had been sent.

"And now we wait." She looked at Sherry and smiled. "So, let's go start dinner."

"About time," said Al as he headed into the living room.

Rachel's phone beeped a short time later. She anxiously went into her inbox, but what she found made her heart sink.

"Did he reply?" asked Sherry.

"No. The email bounced."

"Maybe his server thought it was spam."

"No." Rachel shook her head. "The emails are always sent with my email address identifying me as the sender."

"Well, sometimes weird things happen in cyberspace. Why don't you try sending it again?"

Rachel felt a little embarrassed. "I hadn't thought of that. Good idea." She resent the card. Minutes later it bounced again. She bit her lip as she looked it over.

"I never could understand all the technical gobbledygook that comes with the failure notice, but if there's one thing Shane is meticulous about, it's keeping his inbox clean." Once again tears streamed down her face. "This can only mean one thing. It's over. He's blocked my email address."

She burst into tears as Sherry wrapped her arms around her and tried to comfort her.

"It doesn't matter what I do, or how hard I try, Craig Walker always wins. Even from the grave, Craig Walker always wins."

* * *

Shane spent two weeks bedridden in his old room at his parents' home. Halloween came and went, but he was hardly aware of the holiday. By the time he felt well enough to return home, his voice mailbox was full, and his email inbox was overflowing. Playing back his voicemail, he heard a message from his sister, asking him how he was doing, and letting him know she'd tried to email him a get-well card, but it had bounced. He made a mental note to reconfigure his spam settings before he called her back.

✑FIFTY-FOUR✑

AT LONG LAST, Rachel had the sense of belonging and acceptance she had sought her entire life. She graciously accepted Al's offer to join the family business, and she started the following week. Her new job was similar to the ones she had before. She would meet with the customers to find out what they were looking for, and she would create a design they liked. Once approved, it would be sent to the painters, who would airbrush the art. She also soon discovered the business wasn't limited to motorcycles. They created custom graphics for all kinds of vehicles, including hot rods, boats, horse trailers, food trucks, and tractor-trailer rigs.

As the weeks passed, she continued to recover. The cast came off her wrist, and she was out of the sling. By all outward appearances, she seemed to be her old self, and the time had come for her to be back on her own. One of Sherry's clients was a property manager who helped her find a small bungalow close to Al and Sherry's home that was ready for move in. As she signed the lease, she fully realized she would not be returning to Tucson, or to Shane. Julie was disappointed, but accepting, just as she had been when Rachel took the job offer in Reno.

"Are you completely sure that this is what you want?" she asked.

Rachel knew her mother was referring to Shane. "I think it's best for all concerned, Mom. I know I made a big mistake when I sent Shane away, but he's moved on, and there's nothing I can do about it."

"Have you thought about calling him? Maybe if the two of you talked it person you could work things out."

"He's blocked me out of his email account, so there's really nothing for us to say, nor do I want to be like Craig Walker. I have to respect his wishes and let him go. But while we're on the subject, you've got my new phone number, right?"

"Of course. So does Bruce, and your sister."

"Good. Now I just need to make arrangements to get my stuff moved up here."

"You dad and I can help you. Thanksgiving is next week, and so far the weather forecast looks good, so we'd be happy to rent a truck and bring it to you."

"It's a long drive, Mom."

"It's not a problem. I'll call Laurie and see if she can arrange for someone to load the truck."

"I'm sure she'd be more than happy to do that." Somehow Rachel managed to mask her anger as she spoke.

"No, I don't think she'd mind at all. Then, if we leave really early Thursday morning, we should arrive in time for dinner. We'll help you unload on Friday, and we'll fly back to Tucson on Saturday. That way we can at least have a little quality time together while avoiding the heavy holiday traffic."

Rachel felt relieved. "Thanks, Mom. You know I really am going to miss you."

"And we'll miss you too, but your father has given you a once-in-a-lifetime opportunity, and you're doing the right thing by taking it. Bruce and I are both very proud of you. I just wish Shane could have somehow been included with the package."

"Me too, but apparently we weren't meant to be after all, and life goes on."

Rachel's stomach twisted into a knot as she imagined Shane with another woman. After ending the call she tried to go back to work, but the image stayed in her mind.

* * *

Bruce and Julie arrived Thanksgiving night in the rental truck with Rachel's car in tow. As they gathered around the dinner table, they brought her up to date on Alice and Donny. Bruce started to say something about Aunt Laurie, but Rachel quickly changed the subject.

"I know it's a long shot, but I was wondering if by chance you've heard anything from Shane?"

"Not a word, I'm sorry to say," said Julie. "It's like I said before. We had him over for dinner the Sunday after I returned home, but he wasn't feeling well."

"I know. You said he'd come down with a bad cold."

"He had, and like I also said before, he emailed me a few times afterwards to ask about you, but the last one came about a week or so before Halloween, and I haven't heard from him since."

"And then I tried to email him a Halloween card, but it bounced. So, he's given up on me, or he's met someone else. Either way, it's over, and I've made the right decision." Rachel pushed her dessert plate away. "Would you all mind if I excused myself? I'm suddenly feeling tired."

"Of course," said Sherry. "You have a big day ahead of you tomorrow."

Rachel said her goodnights and stepped away. Once she was gone, Julie looked at Sherry.

"She's putting up a good front, but she still misses Shane terribly."

"I was with her when the email bounced," said Sherry. "She was absolutely devastated."

"So was Shane, after we left the hospital that night. And with all they've been though, I'm really surprised he moved on so quickly."

"It happens," said Al. "First, she sends him home, then she doesn't contact him for weeks afterward. I'm not saying she didn't have issues to work through, because she did. However, he was still left in the dark, and rightly or wrongly, he assumed she didn't want him back. Had I been in his shoes, I would have thought the same."

"I have to agree with Dad," said Michael. "I would have moved on as well, and I told her to be careful, but I guess she just wasn't ready to deal with it."

"We all know she's hurting," said Al, "but hopefully, once she settles into her new job, her luck will change. We get a fair amount of single men walking through our doors, and many of them are doctors, lawyers, architects and what have you. Give her time. She'll find someone else, and this time around she won't have to worry about Craig Walker."

"Yeah, but none of them are Shane," said Julie. "They were a perfect match. He was that one in a million man for her."

* * *

Rachel felt apprehensive as she stepped behind her parked car the following morning.

"Are you all right?" asked Julie. "You seem far away all of a sudden, and your face is pale."

Rachel didn't respond. Al walked up to Julie and whispered in her ear. "Give her a moment." He softly said her name. "Rachel?" He waited a moment. "Rachel? Are you okay?"

"I'm fine, Dad."

He walked up next to her. "It's okay. He's not here."

"I know. I just had a moment." Rachel looked at the others. "I was standing here, right behind the car. I was rearranging the wedding gifts in the trunk when he came up behind me. I heard the footsteps, but I thought it was Emma, so I didn't turn around. But if I had—"

"He had a knife," said Julie. "If you'd tried to fight him, he may have killed you on the spot, and if you'd tried to run, he would have chased you down."

"I know."

"But you still did the right thing," said Julie. "You tossed your keys underneath the bumper, and your stepdad found them."

"And then Shane spoke up," said Bruce. "He knew it meant you were in trouble, so he called nine-one-one, right then and there."

"We had your car detailed," said Julie, "and we've driven it a few times. We also took it in for an oil change, so you're good to go. Would you like for me to drive?"

Finally, Rachel gave her mother a reassuring smile. "No, thanks. I've got it."

"Why don't you ride with her?" asked Bruce.

Julie hopped into the passenger seat as Rachel slipped behind the wheel.

"This is the first time I've driven a car since that night, so here goes nothing." Rachel took a deep breath and fired up the engine.

"I can still drive, if you don't feel up to it," said Julie.

"I'm okay, Mom. Sometimes I have flashbacks. It's all part of it, but it really is getting better."

She put the car in gear and drove off. Once the truck was unloaded and the furniture was set up, the men left while Julie and Sherry stayed behind to help unpack the dishes and make up the bed. The house was bigger than her old duplex, so one bedroom remained unused.

"I'll use it as a storage room for now," said Rachel. "Then later on, when I get the rest of my medical bills paid off, I'll invest in some furniture and turn it into a guest room. That way you and Bruce will have a place to stay when you come and visit." She went on to say she had signed a year's lease, and once it was up she would see about making her landlord an offer to buy the place.

"I fell in love with it the first time I saw it," she said. "It's got a nice sized kitchen, which will come in handy now that Sherry's been teaching me how to cook, and I love the view of the mountains."

All three women were exhausted by the time the sun sent down. Sherry offered to let Rachel stay with her and Al that night, but she declined.

"I appreciate the offer," she said, "but I have to get used to being on my own again."

"I know you do. Would you like for me to run home and get Sampson? He's really bonded with you, and trust me, no one will harm you as long as he's around."

"I'm fine, Sherry, but give the big guy a hug for me when you get home. I'm fine. In fact, I really would enjoy some alone time."

"Well, let's at least get you some dinner before we leave," said Julie.

"Good idea, Mom." Rachel's face lit up as she spoke. "I think we've earned ourselves a girl's night out. I'll drive."

Rachel slept better than she expected that night. The following morning she picked up her mother and Bruce at their hotel. After a leisurely breakfast, it was time to take them to the airport, where they had an emotional goodbye as she dropped them off at the curb. Afterwards, she returned home and did more unpacking. The weather was changing, and she was happy to finally have all of her winter clothing. Hanging up the last sweater in her closet, she tore into the next box, and what she found took her breath away. It was the framed photo of Shane that she kept on her work desk in her old duplex. For the moment she was unsure what to do. Her logical mind told her to throw it away, but she couldn't bring herself to do it. After several minutes of arguing with herself, she put it back on her desk.

❧FIFTY-FIVE❧

IT HAD BEEN AN exhausting Thanksgiving weekend for Julie and Bruce, and the next two weeks would be hectic as they prepared for the upcoming Christmas holiday break. Fortunately, the time passed quickly, and after the last day of school they both looked forward to two weeks of down time. The Sunday afternoon before Christmas Julie went to the supermarket. The store was busier than usual, and as she pushed her cart around a corner she nearly collided with another shopper.

"Whoops. Sorry about that." Julie gave the other woman a closer look. "Well, hello, Kelly. How have you been?"

Kelly smiled in return, but she seemed a little ill at ease. "I'm fine, Julie. How's Rachel?"

"She's doing a lot better. She's pretty much recovered from her injuries. Emotionally, however, she's still a little shaky, but she's so much better than she was before. So, how's Shane."

"We've been going through our own ordeal with him."

"Really? So, what happened?"

"He came down with a bad cold right after he got back from Albuquerque."

"I remember him not feeling well the night he came over to our place for dinner. So what happened?"

"He somehow ended up with pneumonia. He collapsed one morning at work. His boss called the paramedics, and they took him to the hospital by ambulance."

Julie was stunned. "Oh my god. So is he okay?"

"He is now, but for a while he was pretty sick."

"I'll bet."

"After we left the emergency room, I took him back to our place, and we kept him there for two weeks. Then he spent another week recuperating at his place before he was well enough to go back to work, and then it was only part time."

"Wow. He really must have been pretty sick."

"He was. Colin wanted to put him in the hospital, but he refused to go."

"I'm so sorry, Kelly. It's awful when your kids are hurting."

"Tell me about it."

Julie thought it over for a moment. "Kelly, when did this happen?"

"He collapsed just before Halloween."

"Was he by chance checking his email?"

"Are you kidding? He was so sick he hardly even knew his own name, and I told him to leave his phone and his laptop at home. Why do you ask?"

"Because that's when Rachel tried to contact him, but her email bounced. She thought he'd moved on and found someone else."

Kelly shook her head. "No, Julie. There's no one else. In fact, he thought Rachel had ended it."

"No, she actually hadn't. She'd been through a terrible shock, and she had the additional trauma of Craig trying to rape her, but I told Shane that night at the hospital not to worry, she'd be back."

"And she apparently did try to come back," said Kelly, "but he was ill at the time, and didn't know. So, where is she?"

"She decided to stay in Albuquerque. Her father offered her a job, and she took it, thinking Shane had moved on." Julie reached into her purse and pulled out her phone.

"She has a new phone number. Please, have Shane call her, as soon as he can. They need to try to work things out, for both their sakes."

Kelly reached for her phone and entered the new number into her notepad.

* * *

Julie had barely finished putting the groceries away when her phone rang. Not recognizing the number, she thought about letting the call go to voicemail, but something told her to take it. Hearing the voice on the other end, she was glad she followed her hunch.

"Mrs. Bennett, it's me, Shane. I just got off the phone with my mother. So, how's Rachel?"

"She's nearly recovered. How are you?"

"Nearly recovered as well. Apparently, my mother told you what happened."

"She did. Are you okay?"

"Pretty much. I still don't have my stamina completely back, so I get tired easily, but other than that, I'm okay. So what's this about Rachel staying in Albuquerque?"

"Her father not only offered her a job, he made her a partner in the family business, which means she and her brother will be running the place someday. She simply couldn't turn it down."

"No, she couldn't, and I would have done the same. So, I need you to do a little favor for me, if you wouldn't mind?"

"What is it?" asked Julie.

"I just booked a flight to Albuquerque that leaves at eleven o'clock tomorrow morning, but I don't want my folks to know I'm going."

"Look, Shane, if you're not well enough to travel, then you should wait."

"I'll be fine. I just wanted to know if you and your husband would mind looking after Lucy, my dog."

"Of course. We'd be happy to. Do you need a ride to the airport?"

"I can take Uber."

"Don't be silly. Bruce and I are off for the next two weeks. We'll pick you up tomorrow morning and take you to the airport. How long are you planning on staying?"

"For as long as it takes to convince her to take me back."

Julie's face lit up as she smiled. "You don't know how happy I am to hear you say that."

"Good to know. And can you do me one more favor?"

"Sure. What is it?

"Don't tell her I'm coming. I want it to be a surprise."

"Oh, she'll be surprised all right, and don't worry. I just got home a little while ago and haven't had a chance to call her yet."

* * *

Shane's flight touched down in Albuquerque right on time. Once he got his bag, he hurried out of the terminal and launched his Uber app. He tried to relax during the drive, but his heart was in his mouth. Before long, they pulled up to a warehouse in an industrial part of town.

"Here you go," said the driver. "Matheson Custom Graphics."

"Thanks." As the car drove away, he took a deep breath and stepped inside the building. No one was at the front desk. He waited for a moment, and as he reached for his phone an older woman entered from a side door.

"Sorry 'bout that," she said as she took her seat behind the desk. "I didn't hear you come in. Can I help you?"

"Yes. Is Rachel in?"

"Sorry, but you just missed her."

"When will she be back?"

"Tomorrow morning. Is there someone else who can help you?"

Shane's heart sank. He wondered if the surprise would be on him. "Is her father in by chance in?"

"He is. And you are?"

"Shane. Shane MacLeod."

She paged Al and offered him some coffee while he waited.

"I'm fine. Thanks."

Al entered a moment later, obviously surprised to see Shane. "Can I help you?" he asked.

"Yes. I came to see Rachel, but I'm told she isn't here."

"Come with me. You can leave your bag out here." Al took him past the reception area and down a hallway.

"Rachel has left for the day. This afternoon is her very last day of physical therapy, and afterwards she planned on doing some Christmas shopping." Al opened the door to his office, telling Shane to take a seat. "She tried to contact you, about six weeks ago, but the email bounced, so she's under the distinct impression that you've moved on."

"I know, and I'm sorry it happened. I was down with pneumonia at the time, and I was too sick to bother with my email or my voicemail. Later on, my sister told me one of her emails had bounced as well, and I've since corrected the problem."

Al looked both surprised and concerned. "I thought you looked a lot thinner. Are you alright?"

"I'm pretty much over it, but I've never been so sick in my life."

"I'll bet. So I take it there's no other woman."

"I don't know. Does my mother count?"

Al chuckled. "No, I suppose not, and you certainly wouldn't have come all this way if your intentions weren't sincere." He stood from his desk. "Come with me. I want to show you something."

They walked down the hallway to another door. Al opened it and flicked on the lights.

"This is Rachel's office."

As Shane stepped inside something immediately caught his eye. Hanging on the wall was a framed enlargement of a photo of him and Rachel at her sister's wedding. Both of their faces were beaming as he held a garter in his hand. He went up to take a closer look.

"Wow. This is the last photo taken of the two of us together. I'd just caught the garter, and I told her it meant we would be next. Right after it was taken someone came up and started talking to her, so I sat down with some of Donny's friends. A few minutes later her mother asked her and Emma to go take the gifts out to her car."

"She told me the story about the photo as well, which is why she has it. She was devastated when that email bounced. She honestly thought you'd moved on and found someone else."

Shane shook his head. "Nope. Not even close."

They stepped out and Al took him into a large garage where a woman was hard at work airbrushing a motorcycle. He pointed out the small RV parked next to her. Several large paw prints had been painted down the sides.

"This is Rachel's first project." Al's face beamed with pride as he spoke. "It's for a mobile dog groomer, and she created a whole package. The logo, business cards, a website, and the RV. It'll be finished tomorrow afternoon."

"Rachel has a talent alright," said Shane. "She was doing logo and website design back in Tucson and had built up good a following before Craig kidnapped her."

"She's a real asset here as well, but you need to know she isn't just another employee. I've made her a partner. She and her brother will be taking over the business someday."

"That's what I'm told, and believe me, I'm not going to try to take her away from it. We'll have to work out the details later."

Al led him back into his office, once again offering him a seat. "I noticed the tag on your luggage. Did you rent a car at the airport?"

Shane shook his head. "No. Rachel's mother gave me the address, and I took Uber from the airport, thinking, of course, she'd be here. I thought about sending flowers ahead of time, with a note saying a surprise was coming, but when I thought it over a second time, I decided not to. With everything she's been through with Craig, it may have frightened her."

"And it certainly could have. Rachel is doing much better, but she's still a victim of a violent crime, and she'll never be like she was before. Fortunately, she's not overly paranoid, but she's keenly aware of her surroundings, and she tends to keep people at arm's length."

"I can't say I blame her."

"None of us can. However, I can't be certain of how she'll react to you. She thinks you've moved on, so it may take her awhile to warm up to you again. And while she's never told anyone the exact details of what happened, you need to understand that Craig tried to rape her that night."

"Yes, I ready knew that, but she also said he was interrupted before he got too far."

"Well, yes and no. He was interrupted, but it was barely in the nick of time."

Shane felt a wave of nausea. "I'm just grateful he got interrupted, for all our sakes, and I'm damn proud of her for fighting back. If she hadn't, she wouldn't be with us today."

"I'm proud of her too, and I think justice has been served. I'm also grateful she won't ever have to worry about the stress, and the humiliation, of being put on the witness stand."

"No, she won't," said Shane, "nor does she have to worry about Craig getting out of prison some day and coming after her again."

Al checked his watch. "I have to make a few phone calls, and then I can probably sneak out of here early. We're planning on taking Rachel out to dinner tonight to celebrate the end of her physical therapy, and somehow I don't think she'd mind if you came along. While you're waiting, we have sodas and snacks in the break room if you'd like. I shouldn't be too long."

❧FIFTY-SIX☙

RACHEL HASTILY PARKED her car and quickly snatched the two grocery bags from her trunk. She ran up to the front door and rang the bell, taking a deep breath while she desperately tried to pull herself together. As door opened, she forced herself to smile.

"I think I remembered everything on your list," she said as she followed Sherry into the kitchen and set the bags on the countertop. Sherry quickly rummaged through them.

"It looks like you did." Sherry started putting perishables in the refrigerator. "Your dad called a little while ago. He said he was leaving the office early, so he should be here soon. Would you like some iced tea or a soda while we're waiting?"

"I'm fine, Sherry."

Sherry gave her a closer look. "You don't look so fine to me. Was there a problem at physical therapy?"

Rachel shook her head. "No. Everything went well. It's finally over and done with."

"I see. So how come you look like you just lost your best friend?"

She shook her head as she fought back the tears. "It's nothing. It's just something silly."

"No, it isn't. Let's go sit down in the living room so we can talk." Sherry took a few steps out of the kitchen, but Rachel remained next to the sink, with her back to the side door.

"I'm fine, Sherry. Really. It's nothing."

Sherry came back into the kitchen. "No. Something has obviously upset you. So what happened?"

Rachel finally gave in. "I was waiting in the checkout line, and the woman in front of me had a baby in the front of her cart." As she was speaking the side door started opening. Sherry shot Al a quick look. He stopped in his tracks as Rachel kept talking.

"It was a baby girl. She looked like she was only a few weeks old. The mother was busy unloading her cart, so I'm standing there, watching the baby, and thinking she's really cute, and somehow I made eye contact with her, so she started watching me too. We looked at each other, and then, all of a sudden, my mom gene switched on." She choked back a few sobs. "The baby I lost would been a girl too." She took a deep, shaky breath. "I'm sorry if I sound like a blathering idiot. I'm not sure you even understand."

A familiar voice spoke up. "I understand, Rachel. More than you know."

Her eyes popped open wide and she froze in disbelief. Shane quickly stepped into the room. Hearing his footsteps, she slowly turned and looked him up and down. Tears streamed down her face and her hand came up to her mouth. He wrapped his arms around her, kissing the top of her head as she wept in his arms. Al motioned to Sherry to join him in the garage. Sherry quietly closed the door behind her, giving them some privacy. Shane held her tight, but his body was also shaking. Finally, Rachel started calming down.

"Are you okay?" he asked.

"I don't know." Rachel stepped up to the sink and splashed some cold water on her face. Shane handed her a paper towel, and as she patted her face dry, she looked at him more closely. Part of her felt elated to see him, but another part was angry.

"You look like you've lost weight," she said.

"About twenty pounds."

She was shocked. "That's a lot."

"Tell me about it."

"So what happened, and why are you here?"

"I'm here to set things straight between us." He wrapped his arm around her shoulder and gently guided her to the kitchen table, helping her out of her coat and pulling out a chair for her before he took the seat next to hers.

"First of all, I had no idea that you'd tried to contact me, or that your email had bounced. Trust me, you were never blocked, nor was there ever another woman."

"All right. So, what happened?"

"I had my own issues to deal with. I wasn't eating and I wasn't sleeping, and I came down with a bad cold right after I got back to Tucson. A few weeks later I ended up with pneumonia, and I was completely out of it for a couple of weeks. Unfortunately, that was when you tried to send the email."

"I'm so sorry. I had no idea." She looked more closely at his face. It was still a little pale. His cheeks looked hollow, and he had faint circles under his eyes.

"I can see you haven't been well. Are you okay now?"

"I'm fine, Rachel. I'm more concerned about you."

Finally, she smiled. "Well, as you can see, I'm doing much better. The bruises are gone, the rope burns are gone, the broken bones have pretty much healed, and I got my teeth fixed. In fact, today was my last day of physical therapy. I've officially graduated."

"So I'm told. You father already filled me in." He picked up a lock of her hair, smiling as he held it in his hand. "And I like the new look."

"Thanks. I've decided I don't want to be completely blonde anymore." She prayed he wouldn't ask her why. Instead, he smiled again.

"Either way, you still look fantastic to me, and I'm glad you're doing better." He took a more serious tone.

"My world turned upside down the night you disappeared. It didn't take long to figure out who'd taken you, and we spent the next three days in hell, not knowing if you were dead or alive. Your family was great, by the way. They really kept me in the loop, and they made sure I was there every time the detectives brought us up to date. Then they showed us a photo of what remained of your blue shoe. That's when they told us you were gone. Afterwards I went home, but I still have no idea of how I got there. I didn't eat and I hardly slept, but I don't remember much else. I must have been on autopilot. Then Alice showed up a few days later, and when she told me you'd been found alive I felt as if I'd been reborn. But then she told me you were pregnant and had lost the baby."

"Shane, I had no idea I was pregnant, but believe me, had I known, I would have fought him a lot sooner, and a lot harder."

He wrapped his arms around her and pulled her in close. "Actually Rachel, you managed quite well. You're still with us." He gave her another squeeze and she leaned her head on his shoulder.

"The doctor told me there was nothing genetically wrong with the baby. I was in my fourth week, and the miscarriage was the result of the shock from the all other injuries. She also told me it was a girl, and I shouldn't have any problem conceiving or going full term the next time."

Her phone beeped. She excused herself and grabbed her purse, laughing as she read the message. "Al and Sherry are out driving around the block. They want to know if it's okay to come home now."

"In a minute," he said, "but first I want to make sure you understand that I never, ever, gave up on you. In fact, I thought you'd given up on me."

She shook her head. "No, I never gave up on you, but you have to understand that he tried to rape me. I felt dirty. I felt ashamed. And I felt as if I'd been unfaithful to you."

"Rape isn't cheating." His voice was firm. "And even if he had raped you, I would have still wanted you. He's the one who did the wrong, not you."

"I know, or at least I know it in my head, but the rest of me still feels like I failed you. When he first showed up in the parking lot that night, why didn't I try to run? Why didn't I try to kick him? Or bite him? Or—"

"Because he had a knife. They recovered it from his truck. What do you think would have happened if he'd used it on you? You handled yourself extremely well. You didn't panic. You tried to reason with him, and when that failed, you not only managed to get yourself free, you damn near strangled him to death. None of this was ever your fault. You thought he'd gone back to Sacramento. We all did, and we all let our guards down, but now it's over and done with. He's never coming back, and it's time to exorcise his ghost, once and for all. So tell your dad to come back, because we're taking you to dinner."

"You're coming with us?" she asked.

"Well of course I'm coming with you."

"And where are you staying?"

"I'm not sure. I didn't book a hotel."

She chuckled as she picked up her phone and started texting. "Rather presumptuous, aren't you, Mr. MacLeod?"

"Actually, I prefer to think of myself as an optimist. So, are you feeling better now?"

"About you, yes. About the baby, no," she said as she hit the send button.

He hugged her again. "I'm afraid it'll always be this way for us. Even if we have other children, we'll always feel the loss, and we'll always wonder about what could have been."

"You want us to have more children?"

"Of course I want us to have more children, and I just heard you say your mom gene has kicked in, so don't even think of trying to argue with me. I said I'm here to set things straight between us, and I meant it. We'll discuss the rest later, but right now I'm starving."

Rachel stepped away to repair her makeup. Al and Sherry were back when she returned, and she and Shane followed them to the restaurant in her car. To her relief, no one questioned them about their future plans. Al and Sherry were more interested in getting to know Shane better, and once the meal was over, they asked if she or Shane wanted coffee or dessert, but Rachel declined.

"I hate to be the wet blanket," she said, "but I can tell that our friend here is getting tired."

"So let's get his bag out of the Suburban and put it in your car," said Sherry.

Al flagged down their waiter and asked for their check, but once it arrived, he and Shane argued over who should pick it up.

"You missed several weeks of work," he told Shane firmly, "but don't worry, you can pick it up next time."

Once Shane's luggage was transferred to Rachel's car they drove back to her place. "Al seems awfully sure of things," she said once she exited the parking lot.

"Your father and I had a long talk. He's quite a guy. He really loves you, and he truly regrets his not being there when you were growing up, so he's trying to make up for it now."

"I know he is, and I wish he'd been around when I was younger too, but for whatever reason, it was meant to be this way. You know he's made me a partner in his business."

"Yes, I know. He already told me about it. It's the opportunity of a lifetime for you, Rachel, and I would have been disappointed if you'd turned it down. Not only will you have a job for life, you'll have something you can pass on to your own children someday."

"But what about you? You're established in Tucson with a good job and you own a house. I can't expect you to give that up."

"Business is booming alright. As Jonathan keeps saying, the hackers somehow manage to stay one step ahead of us."

Her heart sank. "Yes, they do, and I know Jonathan needs you."

"Yes, he does, but circumstances have changed. I was unable to work for weeks, and then I was only well enough to go back part time. In the meantime, Jonathan had more work than he could handle, so he had to hire someone else."

"You're joking. You mean you lost your job?"

"Not exactly. I'm now working with him as an independent consultant, and we've both been happy with the arrangement. He sends me the job, I work on it outside the office, and then I send him a bill. I like having a more flexible schedule, and I'm making about the same money as before. He also says he likes New Mexico, and, if business keeps growing, he says he may consider opening a branch office here. But even if he doesn't, I can still work independently. In fact, your dad was saying he might want me to go over his website while I'm here."

Shane leaned back in his seat and yawned. "You know, I really have had a long day."

"I know you have, and as happy as I am to see you, I don't want you having a relapse."

"I'll be fine. I'm over the bug. My stamina just isn't quite back yet."

"So tell me, how did you know about the email?"

"Yesterday afternoon my mother ran into your mother at the supermarket, and they started comparing notes. My mom called me as soon as she got home, and I booked a flight as soon as I got off the phone."

"So why didn't my mother tell me this?"

"Because she was sworn to secrecy. I told her I wanted to surprise you, so she and Bruce took me to the airport and they're taking care of Lucy."

"I've missed her."

"And she's missed you too. In fact, I still think my dogs loves you more than she loves me." He yawned again, relaxing in his seat and looking out the window as she drove.

"It's not much further," said Rachel, "and it's a big step up from the place I had in Tucson." She filled him in about everything her aunt had done.

"This is why I would have stayed in Albuquerque, even if Al hadn't offered me a job. My mother and Bruce did they best they could, but the rest of his family never accepted me, and they never will, but it's different with Al and Sherry. As far as they're concerned, I'm their daughter, and anyone who thinks otherwise will have to answer to them. It's why I feel like I finally have a place where I belong. Mom and Bruce were either in denial, or they never wanted to rock the boat."

"I suspect it's probably a little of both." Shane's phone beeped. "Uh-oh. I just got a text from my mother."

Rachel braced herself. "So, what does she have to say?"

Shane laughed. "She says, 'Your dad and I will miss you, but you need to stay in Albuquerque.' So there you have it."

Rachel turned into her driveway a short time later as Shane yawned again. Rachel offered to get his bag, but he shook his head.

"I can get it."

"You're sure?"

He gave her a look. Rachel laughed as the garage door rolled up. "Okay, okay," she said. "I believe you."

"Nice place," he said once they stepped inside.

"I really like it. It's nice and roomy, and it has a big backyard with a nice view of the mountains."

Rachel pointed out the master bedroom, and Shane excused himself while she checked her email and made sure the house was secure. Stepping into her bedroom, she found him curled up in her bed, sleeping soundly. A broad smile broke out across her face as she watched him sleep. Craig had turned Shane's life upside down as well, but now it was finally over for both of them. She kissed him on the cheek and went into the bathroom. When she returned, she undressed and curled up next to him. His skin felt warm and soothing next to hers as he moaned happily in his sleep. She too fell into a blissful sleep, and when she woke up the following morning, he was still sleeping soundly. He stumbled into the kitchen as she finished her coffee.

"You okay?" she asked.

"I'm fine." He yawned as poured himself to a cup. "You know, this is the first time I've really slept since the night you disappeared."

"You do look a lot better this morning. The color is returning to your face."

"It's because I finally feel like myself again." He took a sip of his coffee and checked the time, reminding her that he would spend the day working on his next project for Jonathan. When she returned that evening, she found something unexpected waiting for her in the living room.

"What's this?" she asked.

"It's Christmastime. I found your box of ornaments, but you needed a tree, so Sherry and I went out and got you one. Do you like it?"

"Of course I like it, but you didn't have to do this."

"Yes, I did. We finally have our lives back, Rachel, and we need to start living them again." He pointed out the stocking hanging on the mantle. "Santa came early this year, and there's something he wants you to open now."

Rachel reached into the stocking and pulled out a small, black velvet box. Her heart skipped a beat.

"Oh my god."

"Before you open it, I want you to know that I bought it for you just before your sister's wedding, and I was trying to decide if I should give it to you for your birthday, or wait until Christmas, but after all we've been through, I want you to have it now."

Her heart pounded and her hands trembled as she opened the box. Inside was a diamond solitaire ring.

"Shane, I don't know what to say."

He wrapped his arms around her and kissed her passionately. "This is supposed to be the part where I ask you to marry me. So, will you marry me?"

Rachel laughed. "Yes, Shane. Of course, I'll marry you."

He slipped the ring on her finger. It fit perfectly. As she admired it, he picked her up and carried her back to the bedroom.

"Not so fast," she said. "I'm not on the pill anymore, and I don't have any protection."

He gave her a sly grin as he laid her across her bed. "You know, under the circumstances, I really don't think we need to worry about it."

She giggled as she watched him unbutton his shirt. "No, I suppose we don't."

❧Epilogue☙

SHANE AND RACHEL'S families were elated to hear the news of their engagement. Shane flew back to Tucson the day after Christmas to pack up his essentials and put his house on the market. The agent seemed to think it would sell quickly. Once the paperwork signed, he put his furniture and household items in storage. The following morning he loaded up his car, and he and Lucy were back in Albuquerque in on New Year's Eve. While he was away, Rachel bought a cream-colored cocktail dress and booked a resort in Sedona for their wedding. Both wanted a small ceremony with only their immediate family present, along with Luis and Pilar. Their wedding took place the week after New Year's, and after the ceremony they had a big family dinner before leaving for their honeymoon.

Shane's house sold a few weeks later, and after the sale closed, they bought a house near the home Rachel had rented. It too had a good view of the mountains, but it was also a bigger house with a better floor plan. They spent the spring and summer sprucing it up. Rooms were repainted, the kitchen cabinets were refinished, granite countertops were installed, and the carpeting was replaced with ceramic tile. Summer was nearly over when all the renovations were complete, and it was time to return to Tucson for a short visit. Donny and Alice were celebrating their first wedding anniversary. They too had recently purchased a new home, and both Shane and Rachel wanted to visit their families. Rachel presented her sister with a bottle of wine as she opened the door.

"For you and Donny," said Rachel. "It's a local New Mexico wine for you all to enjoy, even though I can't have any."

Alice's eyes bulged as Shane and Rachel stepped inside. "Look at you. You're huge."

"Gee, thanks sissy, and it's good to see you too. However, I'm in my seventh month now, so what did you expect?"

"I know you're in your seventh month, but that's still a big baby."

Julie came into the living room to greet them. "Good lord, you've gotten big."

"Thanks, Mom."

"Are you sure you're not carrying twins?"

"We're sure, Mom," said Shane, "but he is going to be a big boy. Al says he weighed a little over ten pounds when he was born, and I weighed almost nine pounds myself."

"You poor thing," said Alice. "You're going to have fun with labor and delivery."

"Maybe, maybe not," said Julie. "With both of you girls it seemed like I had about three contractions and then I was fully dilated. Both of you just popped right out, and you each weighed a little over eight pounds. Somehow I think you'll do just fine when the time comes."

"Thanks, Mom. That's good to know."

Rachel followed her mother and sister to the kitchen. Shane helped her into a chair at the kitchen table before going out to the backyard to join the other men.

"It's hard to believe it's been a year since I was last in Tucson," said Rachel.

"And not much has changed," said Alice. "Donny's still a paramedic, I still work at the hospital, and Mom and Dad are still teaching."

"Well, it's good to know some things have stayed the same."

Julie brought her a glass of lemonade and sat down next to her. "So, how's your case against the state police going?"

"The trooper who handed me over to Craig was reprimanded, but never fired. However, it appears that they're going to settle out of court. Of course, they're not admitting any wrongdoing."

"They never do," said Julie, "but the fact of the matter is they're still at fault, even if they won't admit it. Had she done her job properly, you would have gotten away from him unscathed, and you wouldn't have lost your other baby."

"I know, Mom, but then I wouldn't have the one I'm carrying now, as he was conceived well before what would have been her due date. I'll always regret losing her, but for whatever reason, this is the baby who was meant to be." She suddenly stopped and put her hand on her belly. "And here we go again. I swear this kid is playing soccer in there."

"May I?" asked Julie.

"Go ahead."

Julie placed her hands on Rachel's belly, smiling with delight as the baby moved. "That's my grandson," she said proudly.

"Have you decided on a name?" asked Alice.

"Benjamin Alfred," said Rachel. "Benjamin, for Shane's grandfather, and Alfred, for Al."

"It's funny how life goes," said Julie. "Seems like it wasn't so long ago when my friends all but dragged me to a disco one night, and while I was there I just happened to meet an auto shop worker who'd gotten out of the Marine Corps the year before. He was everything my parents would have disapproved of, and I was on the rebound, looking for a little fun. And we all know what happened next." She squeezed Rachel's hand. "I know you didn't have the easiest of childhoods. I know not everyone has accepted you, and I know that over the years you had your doubts about marriage and family because I decided not to marry your father. But Rachel, you're married to a man who absolutely adores you, and you're going to be a terrific mother. That I know for certain, and your son won't have to deal with the hardships you had to face. But do you want to know something?"

"What's that, Mom?"

"If I had it to do all over again, knowing everything that I know now, I wouldn't have changed a thing."

THE END

Rachel's Italian Style Pork Roast
with Mushroom Gravy

1 to 3 lb pork roast
2 packages fresh, sliced mushrooms, rinsed and drained
1 medium onion, chopped
3 cloves minced garlic
2 tablespoons butter
2 tablespoons cooking oil
3 tablespoons flour
2 cups chicken broth
1 teaspoon salt, (if desired)
1 teaspoon Italian seasoning
1 tablespoon basil
$^1/_4$ teaspoon black pepper

Preheat oven to 350 F. Generously season pork roast with salt, pepper, and Italian seasoning. Bake at 20 minutes per pound. Begin preparing gravy during the last 30 minutes of cooking time.

Place butter and cooking oil in a large skillet or saute pan. Once butter is completely melted add onion, garlic and mushrooms. Stir frequently until onions and mushrooms are thoroughly cooked. Add flour and stir until all the flour is moistened. Pour in chicken broth and bring to a boil, stirring frequently. Once gravy is boiling reduce heat to a simmer and add seasonings and salt, (if desired.) Spoon over sliced pork and serve with pasta, rice, or mashed potatoes.

ABOUT THE AUTHOR

Like Gillian Matthews, the heroine in her debut novel, *The Reunion*, Marina Martindale began her career as a graphic designer and artist. After successfully submitting articles to trade publications, she discovered that writing was her true calling. Her life experiences, and those of the people around her, are the inspiration for her novels.

Marina Martindale is currently working on her sixth novel, *The Letter.* She resides in Tucson, Arizona, and in her spare time she enjoys music, traveling, photography, and cooking.

For more information about Marina please visit her website at marinamartindale.com.

Also from Marina Martindale

The Reunion

Gillian Matthews is becoming famous in the art world. All her hard work has finally paid off and her paintings are being sold in several prestigious galleries. She expected her opening night at a Denver gallery to go flawlessly, but her perfect evening was disrupted when a man from her past suddenly appeared. Her long lost true love. The one man she never forgot, never got over, and never expected to ever see again.

The Deception

A string of misfortunes has left photographer Carrie Daniels penniless and desperate. When her former mentor, Louise Dickenson, steps forward to offer her a job as an art model for a private commission, Carrie has no choice but to accept. Things seem to be looking up when she meets Scott Andrews, however her friends soon realize Scott isn't who he appears to be, and Carrie's luck goes from bad to worse when Louise's photos of her fall into the wrong hands.

The Journey

Cassie Palmer's world is shattered when a car crash leaves her hospitalized and fighting for her life. Her husband, Jeremy, begins his own frightening journey when he meets Denise, one of Cassie's nurses. Denise seems familiar, but while he may no longer remember her, she has neither forgiven nor forgotten how he jilted her, years before. Denise seeks revenge and Jeremy soon vanishes under mysterious circumstances, leaving his grieving wife behind. As Cassie struggles to recover her life will take another strange turn, when an unexpected visitor reveals that things are not as they appear.

The Betrayal

Emily St. Claire's life turns upside down when she discovers that her husband, Jesse, has been unfaithful to her. Determined to rebuild her life, she returns home to her father and pursues her life-long dream of becoming a concert pianist. As Jesse fights to win Emily back, her life will be shattered once again when an unforeseen tragedy forces him into an alliance with a corrupt police detective to frame her for a crime she didn't commit. While another detective, Kyle Madden, puts his career on the line to prove Emily's innocence, the plot against her turns deadly, and it may be too late to save her.

For more information about Marina's novels please visit her website at marinamartindale.com.

A sample chapter from

The Betrayal
by Marina Martindale

ꙮ ONE ꙮ

EMILY ST. CLAIRE reached for another tissue to dab the sweat off her forehead and grab her water bottle, but the once-cold liquid had turned lukewarm. She took a few swallows and glanced at the clock on the waiting room wall. It was only eleven-fifteen. The air conditioning had stopped working at nine forty-five. Ninety minutes of down time and the office was sweltering. She heard Dr. Lerner's voice coming from the hallway. He was performing a root canal and having to apologize to his patient for the added discomfort of the heat.

The front door opened as she gulped down the last of her water. Andrea, who worked a few doors down, stepped inside. Her makeup was beaded and creased, and wisps of her red hair had stuck to the sweat on the side of her face. "It feels even hotter in here than it does in our office," she said as she walked up to the counter in front of Emily's desk.

"Must be one of Murphy's Laws," said Emily. "The air conditioning will always conk out on the hottest day of the summer."

"Any word on when they'll get it fixed?"

Emily shrugged her shoulders. "Your guess is as good as mine. I tried calling the property manager again about twenty minutes ago, but I'm still getting a busy signal. I'm sure by now they're aware of the problem."

"Yeah, I kept getting busy signals too, which means they must really know. Meantime Dr. Hapner had me reschedule all our afternoon patients. Turns out two of them are really sick, so they're on their way right now. Then, once we're done, we're closing up shop and calling it a day. I love the idea of having an afternoon off, but why does it have to be on a day when it's over a hundred and ten degrees outside?"

Emily gave her another shrug. "It's the price we pay for living in Phoenix. At least we don't get snowed in during the winter."

"Yeah, but a good, old-fashioned ice storm would sure feel nice right about now, and I'll bet you're glad now that you got your new haircut."

Emily ran her fingers through her short, blonde hair. It felt strange to no longer have her long locks. "It's lower maintenance all right, but Jesse wasn't too thrilled with it."

"That figures. So have you told him yet?"

"No, not yet."

"Well, keep me posted. I'm anxious to hear how he reacts. Meantime, I have to get back to work. I just wanted to stick my head in the door to see how you're doing. Hopefully, we'll all be back to normal by tomorrow morning."

"I'm sure we will be."

"Are we still on for lunch Friday?"

"You bet. See you, Andrea."

Andrea took her leave while Emily called the property manager once again. This time her call went through. After punching a few buttons, she got a live person on the line. A repairman was on the way, but the air conditioning would not be back online until much later in the day. She heard footsteps as she hung up. Dr. Lerner had finished with his patient. His normally crisp, white shirt was wrinkled and soaked with sweat.

"Any word on the air conditioning?" he asked.

"I'm afraid it won't be back on until the end of the day. Meantime your eleven-thirty has already rescheduled for next Tuesday. Your next patient is due right after lunch."

Dr. Lerner frowned. "And if it's this hot now, it'll be unbearable by this afternoon. Go ahead and take care of Mrs. Baxter. After that, I want you to call everyone who was supposed to come in this afternoon and have them reschedule. We're taking the rest of the day off. Hopefully, we'll all be back to normal by tomorrow morning."

"I'm sure we will be. Thanks, doctor."

He nodded and walked away. Fifteen minutes later Emily stepped out into the blazing midday sun and smiled to herself as she walked across the parking lot. She wanted to stop at the grocery store on the way home so she could prepare a surprise dinner for Jesse. Hopping into her car, she fired up the engine, and turned the air conditioning on high. After a few hot moments, the air began to feel deliciously cool. A smile broke out across her face as she drove off. Tonight's dinner would be the perfect opportunity for her to tell Jesse the time had come for him to keep his end of their bargain.

She soon turned into the grocery store entrance and hunted for a parking space. Once inside the store she grabbed a cart headed down the aisles. Tonight, she would prepare her famous chicken divan. It was Jesse's favorite dish. She picked out her ingredients and tossed in a bouquet of fresh flowers before heading to the checkout lane.

Ten minutes later she pulled into her driveway and frowned. Annette's white Civic was parked in front of the house. Jesse's assistant usually didn't come on Wednesdays, so something unexpected must have come up. Emily sighed as she pressed the button to open the garage door. Shutting down the engine, she quickly grabbed the grocery bags and hurried out of the hot garage. The air conditioning felt heavenly as she stepped inside the house and went straight to the kitchen.

"Hi guys. I'm home."

There was no response. The house seemed unusually quiet. Emily set the bags on the counter and went down the hallway. Jesse had converted one of the downstairs bedrooms into his office. She tapped on the door and smiled as she slowly pushed it open.

"Hey guys. The air conditioning went out and I'm—"

Her smiled faded. The room was empty. The lights were out, and Jesse's computer was shutdown. She was getting a funny feeling, but quickly brushed it off. Perhaps Jesse and Annette were out by the pool. She went to the living room and opened the sliding glass door.

"Jesse! Annette!"

Again, there was no answer. The backyard was eerily quiet, and no one was by the pool. Emily closed the door and headed toward the staircase. The upper floor contained the master suite and a rarely used guest bedroom. Jesse would be leaving for Houston on Friday to facilitate a seminar. Perhaps he and Annette had gone upstairs to decide what he should pack. Emily took a deep breath and started up the stairs. Upon reaching landing, she heard muffled voices behind the bedroom door. Jesse must have had the TV on. She hurried up the remaining flight and stepped inside.